Shadow of Ra

Stephen Jensen

AVALON BOOKS, LLC

SALT LAKE CITY

Printed in the United States of America by Avalon Books, LLC

The AVALON CLOCK colophon is a trademark of Avalon Books, LLC. Registration pending

Hardback ISBN 978-1-960860-06-4

Paperback ISBN 978-1-960860-07-1

Ebook ISBN978-1-960860-08-8

avalonseriesbooks.com

First Edition

Cover by Stephen Jensen and Lincoln Writes

Author Photo by Stephen Jensen

Book Design by Lincoln Writes and Stephen Jensen

Maps created by Stephen Jensen

Interior Art by Stephen Jensen

In Memory of
Chessa

ANCIENT EGYPT

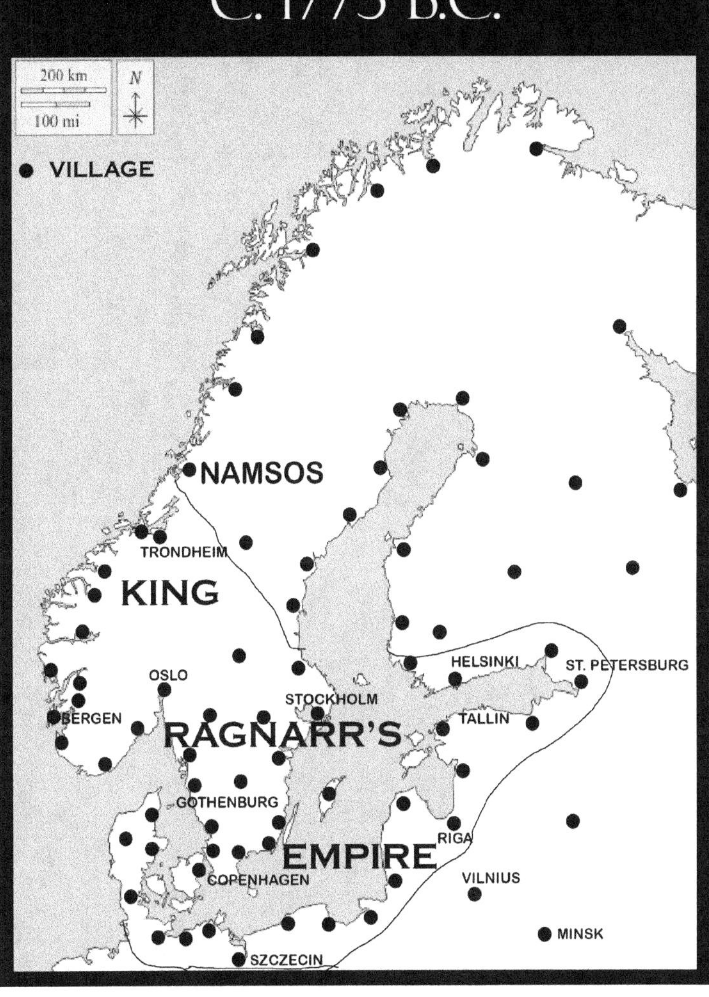

ANCIENT SCANDINAVIA
C. 1775 B.C.
200 km
100 mi
N
VILLAGE
NAMSOS
TRONDHEIM
KING
OSLO
BERGEN
RAGNARR'S
STOCKHOLM
HELSINKI
ST. PETERSBURG
TALLIN
GOTHENBURG
EMPIRE
RIGA
COPENHAGEN
VILNIUS
MINSK
SZCZECIN

Contents

RAGNAROK

O DILIA HAD GONE TO the river to draw water. Rain was falling, cold as ice. The leaves had begun to turn. Summer was rapidly changing to winter. She followed the path to the cliffs overlooking the fjord. It was one of her favorite places. Whenever it rained, the walls of the sound were decorated with a thousand waterfalls, manifesting as if by magic.

The rain became a torrent. She began making her way back to the village as quickly as possible. The path became rather slippery, and the many waterfalls began to multiply even faster.

There was a sudden flash in the sky, brighter than the sun. Lightning strikes began tearing across the sky, awe-inspiring ribbons of light – accompanied by the terrifying roar of thunder.

Odilia realized these flashes were all emanating from a single point. It was ...? Was it a man? He was flying through the sky like a bird. The sparks of light were coming out of a hammer that he held in his hand.

He floated towards her, and though she longed to run, fear held her captive. As he neared, a deluge of water cascaded down upon her, sweeping her down the steep slope.

She tumbled in a chaotic frenzy, and then she fell. She braced for death. All she could think was that 18 years of life wasn't enough. She shut her eyes as hard as possible, but the ground never came.

The torrent of water abated. When she opened her eyes, she

found herself in a man's arms. His flowing blonde hair whipped in the wind, and his piercing green eyes fixated on hers. It was the man with the hammer. She felt a mix of fear and wonder.

As they landed on a cliff ledge, he said, "My name is Thor. What is your name?" He spoke in her language, except how he pronounced everything was strange.

"Odilia" was all she could say.

"You're quite beautiful, Odilia, and a name to match." She didn't know how to respond to the stranger's compliment.

She considered that he could fly and summon lightning; he must be a god!

He moved to kiss her, and she was helpless against him. He took her right then and there as the rain fell around them.

When her wits returned to her, she was stunned to discover the rain was not touching them.

"Are you a god?" She was mesmerized.

"I am."

"Why are you here?"

He turned his gaze from her as if examining the far side of the fjord.

"Ragnarok." He almost whispered.

"The fate of the gods." Odilia knew what that meant.

"Surtr attacked Asgard. I had to fight the great Jormungandr, who was intent on flooding the world. Asgard was destroyed. Fenrir was eating the whole of the universe. Vidarr killed Fenrir. But Freyr couldn't stop Surtr from bringing flames to all of Mid-guard. My father, Odin, fell to Fenrir. The rest of the gods as well." Thor paused, seemingly lost in thought. "I stopped Jormungandr, but not before he partially flooded Mid-guard. I fell down, as if dead. By the time I came to, The Bifrost had been destroyed. I am stranded here. But all is not lost; you are proof of that."

Thor rose from their bed of grass. Odilia rose to meet him. He traced the curves of her body.

"Are you here to rule over the world?"

"I will be watching."

Thor kissed her deeply and then raised his hammer to the sky. A bolt of lightning tore down to meet it. Just as it arrived, he flew up as if following its trail, quickly disappearing into the clouds.

Odilia stood naked in the cold rain, in awe of her divine encounter. Should she tell anyone what Thor told her? About Ragnarok? Would anyone believe her if she did?

PART I: THE PARILS OF TIME

CHAPTER 1: SQUARE ONE

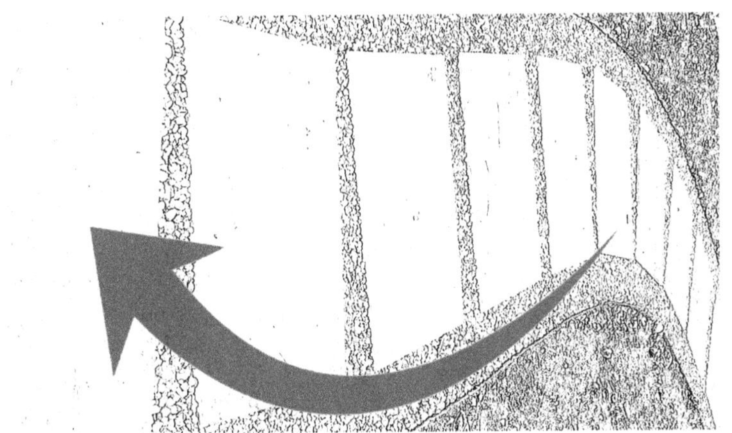

Cold Awakening

J ULIE'S MIND BEGAN TO clear, and as consciousness returned, she realized her head was aching. She squeezed her eyes, trying to quell it. This was always the worst part of the act of time travel.

She attempted to move, but then she realized she couldn't. Her hands were tied behind her back. Her legs were bound at the ankles. She opened her eyes and saw that she was in a small thatch-roofed wooden hut. Her vision kept fluctuating between blurry and clear. As it cleared entirely, she could tell the hut was being guarded, which meant that perhaps she wasn't alone; maybe Micheal was here somewhere.

"Jules?" Micheal spoke as if on cue. "You're finally awake?"

"How long have you been awake?"

"Maybe five or 10 minutes."

"Do you know where we are?"

"Somewhere in Norway, I think." He said in a dry tone.

"Very funny!" She shook her head.

"We must have been found just after our arrival."

"Do you know by whom?"

"Not entirely sure, but they sound Germanic. And we were landing in Norway, so I assume they were Norse. I have been trying to listen to them speak, but I'm miles from being able to talk to them."

He was interrupted by the entry of several bulky men who shouted something at them she couldn't understand. All she could do was indicate a lack of understanding.

The attempted interrogation went on for hours. As time went on, the interrogators became more and more frustrated. Eventually, they boiled over and occasionally hit or kicked them. Which mostly didn't hurt because of one of their advanced technology items. They were still wearing their tri-poly clothes.

"How are you holding up?" Julie asked Micheal, who she had heard was receiving the lion's share of the abuse.

"I've been better," he said facetiously. "Any luck with the bindings?"

"No... They really know how to tie a knot." She gave up trying. Her hands had gone numb. "Do you have any ideas?"

"It appears for the time being that a physical means of escape is not going to happen. I think we need to try to befriend them."

"Oh sure, they seem exceptionally friendly." She tried not to laugh.

The men returned for another round. One of them got tired of yelling and was about to backhand her when someone grabbed his wrist. She looked up in surprise to see a woman arguing with them. She then slapped them a few times, and they exited the hut.

The woman looked too young, maybe late teens. She had stark red hair and soft, deep blue eyes. She was decently tall, perhaps five-foot-eight or maybe nine. She had high cheekbones. She was absolutely gorgeous. If they were in modern times, she could easily be a supermodel.

She spoke softly and kindly, offering Julie some water, which she drank thankfully. The woman spoke again. Julie gestured that she did not understand anything.

The woman kneeled beside her, wiping her face with a wet cloth. When she finished, she offered Julie more water.

The woman rose and smiled at her momentarily and then went to tend to Micheal.

Julie was exhausted from the day and dozed off. She was startled awake by the howl of a wolf. It sounded close, too close.

Language Barrier

As twilight came, which this far north was like nightfall, Micheal thought this wasn't the best start in the 18th century BC. The tri-poly clothing he was wearing had protected him from most of the beatings. But unfortunately, it couldn't save his face, which was likely black and blue by now.

He was bracing for another beating when they called off the dogs. It sounded like a woman. She must be treating Julie. He took the respite from punishment gratefully and then passed out.

He was awakened from his doze by a woman's voice. He opened his eyes to see a doe-eyed beauty kneeling next to him.

After she tended to him, she seemed about to leave when he spoke. "I'm Micheal."

She stopped and turned back.

"Micheal." He repeated.

She appeared to be considering something. "Ee em Odilia." She touched her chest. She held out her hand, indicating him. "My-kel."

He nodded. "Micheal." He repeated.

He had been listening since he woke up. There were trace sounds of Old Norse, but it was clearly an ancestor of Norse. Likely the speculative Proto-Scandinavian.

He proceeded to attempt communication with the Old Norse that he did have. He had done a bit of research on the subject out of curiosity. His father's side of the family descended from Scandinavia.

His attempts seemed like a miss at first, but after a couple of tries Odilia's face lit up. She went and grabbed different items and had him try to identify them. Then, she would say what term they used for the same thing.

This really did help him to begin building a linguistic matrix for the protolanguage. After a little while she indicated it was late and that she would return again.

The next day, Odilia returned, and with a couple of warriors as escorts, she arranged for them to be released from the post. They were still bound, but he and Julie could see each other for the first time since the jump.

Micheal was angered by Julie's bruises on her face and arms. She gave him a look to settle him down to the task at hand.

Odilia continued the exercise from the previous day, and the larger his vocabulary became, the more differences between Old Norse and Proto-Scandic became apparent.

This process continued for a few more days, and Micheal began to understand what was being said by the people around him.

He also spent a good deal of time trying to help Julie understand as well.

Following their most recent lesson, Micheal didn't sleep much. He spent most of the night meditating. He organized everything he had heard and learned into a clear, orderly system in his head. By the next morning he felt he could try full communication. He knew it would take a bit more time to become fluent, but he was confident he was at least now passable.

When Odilia arrived for their lesson, he attempted a greeting in Proto-Scandic. "Good morning, Odilia. How are you?"

Her eyes lit up. "You can understand me now?"

"Mostly."

"And Jew-lee?" She looked at Julie.

"Not quite. I have a way with words." He answered her question before she asked it.

Odilia seemed to consider something. "I need to ask... Who are you? And why are you here?" She looked directly at him.

He looked at Julie for a moment and then explained. "We are travelers from a distant land. In a storm, we crashed on your shores."

Odilia considered that for a moment. "There is someone who desires to speak with you." She said, and then she left the hut.

<u>The Chief</u>

Odilia was gone for a while, so Julie took the opportunity to discuss things with Micheal.

"So when are we going to try to escape?"

"I don't think we can."

"Of course we can. We've escaped worse than this before."

"Have you heard the howling at night?" He caught her off guard.

"How could I not?" Some of her recent nightmares flashed through her mind. The howling at night had only enhanced them.

"I think we need to help this village first," Micheal said with certainty. "From what I've deduced by listening to the villagers. There's a demon pack of wolves that has been hunting them—dozens have been killed so far."

"And you want to play hero? Not every crisis is our responsibility."

"No... But who else can?"

Julie shook her head. "Let me guess. Now you're going to quote Spider-Man?" She closed her eyes.

"Well, do you think the sentiment is wrong?"

"I try to do what's right. However, it's difficult for me to forget what they've done to us." She was still angry about the beatings.

"You know I can't forget that. But I can't punish the innocent for the actions of a few." He reasoned. "This pack is killing women and children."

Julie sighed deeply. "Fine. Just promise me one thing..." She paused.

"Okay?" he asked cautiously.

"... We will get payback against those who delivered the beatings."

He considered for a second. "I promise."

Odilia reappeared with the escorts. "Right this way." She said something Julie kind of understood.

As they walked through the village, everyone was staring at them. And Micheal considered Julie's attitude. They had experienced many horrors and did many questionable things during their five years in the post-apocalyptic wasteland. After the bombs fell and Atlantis sank into the sea.

Julie's guilt over the apocalypse and the terrible times that followed had hardened her quite a bit. Micheal had his share of hardening but his whole life had been about compartmentalization. Whereas Julie typically wore her emotions on her sleeve.

It had been a tough five years, and Micheal worried Julie might have lost herself. He had tried to be her shield. To protect her from her own critical judgment. She always said she wanted to take care of herself. But Micheal knew she needed some respite from all the terrible things she had had to continuously deal with over the past 50 years in the temporal ether.

It was his seemingly futile effort to maintain the carefree innocence she had once enjoyed. While he still did believe there was a soft kindness behind the walls she had built around her heart. He worried it was becoming her own Fort Knox.

They arrived at a large wooden hut. They were escorted inside to a modestly large room. It was around 20 x 20 feet.

"Remain here," Odilia instructed.

Several men entered a few minutes later and sat on the benches, flanking three central chairs. Subsequently, a young man dressed in finer attire followed them. Next came an older woman dressed similarly. Micheal deduced that this was most likely the Prince and the Queen.

A minute later, an older man who looked to be the young man's father entered the room. So Micheal assumed he must be the chief.

The man spoke. "Lady Odilia informs me you now understand our words."

"I do... Mostly." Micheal qualified.

"And the lady?"

"A bit."

"Very well... Who are you?"

"I am Micheal from Avalon, and this is my wife Julie." He introduced them. He decided they had to be from somewhere.

"Micheal and Julie of Avalon? Where is Avalon?"

"A great distance across the sea." He replied vaguely.

"Why have you come?"

"We were on a great journey of exploration when our ship was caught in a storm. We ran ashore, and when we awoke, we were guests of your generous hospitality."

"They are a bad omen." One advisor interjected.

"Fenrir's attacks are escalating. And now they come, bringing doom with them!" Another advisor snarled.

"How do we know they're not here to deliver us from Fenrir?" Odilia countered.

The chief raised his hands to quiet the room. "What do you know about Fenrir?"

"We are not familiar with this being."

"Fenrir is a wolf demon; it leads a ferocious pack that has been hunting our people," Odilia explained.

"They are agents of Fenrir. We cannot trust them!" The first advisor put in again.

"They were sent by the gods!" Odilia countered.

"The gods? The gods abandoned us many years ago." The second advisor said in irritation.

"They have returned!" Odilia said with certainty.

"How could you possibly believe that? It's been centuries..." The advisor was saying.

"Because I met one..." Odilia said bluntly. Everyone stopped."... It was Thor!" The room sat in stunned silence.

"The God of Thunder?" The chief raised a brow.

"Yes, he was very tall, even taller than him." She indicated Micheal. "He had long blonde hair and green eyes. He wielded a hammer that shot lightning, and he can fly!" She was rather animated in the telling.

"We must discuss this further." The chief ended the debate. "Micheal and Julie of Avalon, we will see about you." Then, the chief walked out of the room.

<u>Square One</u>

Micheal and Julie proceeded to a new hunt under escort. They were still bound and under guard. Then Odilia spoke.

"I will be right next door. And I will return in a little while to work with you some more."

Julie only understood part of what she said. It was frustrating. They were shown inside their new home. While small, it was twice the size of the previous cell.

Once alone, Micheal filled her in on the discussions with the chief.

"... Thor?" Julie questioned skeptically.

"All I can tell you is she believes it. Now, is this the actual God of Thunder? I don't know. But would that be the strangest thing we've seen in the timeline?"

"Maybe..." She thought. "... They could be someone like us."

"Or maybe they could be an alien. Didn't you ever see The History Channel show Ancient Aliens?" He seemed to be only half joking.

At that moment, Odilia entered. Micheal would need more information.

"I apologize; they won't let me untie you yet." Odilia seemed frustrated.

"What happened between you and Thor?" He asked bluntly. "Forgive my imposition."

"It's no trouble... Well, it was seven months ago..." She began. "... Caught in a storm, I was walking back to the village when I saw him. He was flying, hammer in hand, shooting lightning into the heavens. In my distraction, I was washed off a cliff. He caught me. Flew me to safety. Then we..." She sputtered to a halt. "... Well, anyway. He then told me about Ragnarok."

Odilia's awkward pause made Micheal think something must've happened between them, but he didn't want to press her.

"Ragnarok?" He asked. He, of course, knew about Norse mythology.

"The gods fought to save the world from the monsters. Thor alone survived. But the world has been reborn." Odilia was pretty animated.

"Why did you tell them we were sent by the gods?"

"You arrive on our shores so mysteriously. And I know the gods have been reborn out of the ashes of Ragnarok. But I have not told anyone else of my encounter with Thor.

"Odilia, we were not sent by the gods."

"Maybe you are, and you just don't know it yet. The gods place us where we're supposed to be." She said with great conviction.

"You don't even know us. How do you know we aren't here for evil purposes like the chief's advisor suspects?" He played devil's advocate.

"You're wrong. I have come to know you these past few days. You are good, kind people..." Odilia paused. "... And you haven't tried to escape." She looked at him directly.

He looked at her with consideration.

"I know you hear the howling. And with how quickly you learned our words. I know you've heard the fear in the village. I know you're here to help." She finished firmly. He decided not to refute her.

Odilia seemed to wait to see if he would reply. When he didn't, she changed the topic. "You are from... Avalon? What is it like?"

Micheal thought about the mythical Avalon. "It's an island. The forest is full of fruit trees. Deer and rabbit run through the meadows of gold as they sway in the sea breeze that blows in over the white shores." He poetically painted a picture.

"That sounds amazing." Odilia seemed caught up in her imagination.

"It is beautiful."

"You will tell me more tomorrow?" Odilia asked hopefully.

"I promise." He smiled and bowed. Then Odilia left.

"How's it going?" Julie raised a brow. She was a little jealous of how friendly Micheal and Odilia were becoming.

"I believe I am almost fluent." Micheal smiled.

"That's great!" She feigned excitement. "So what plan do we have to escape and find our things?" She was frustrated.

"Our things are gone. Odilia said our ship's wreckage was strewn along the coastline after our arrival. And that that storm the other day washed most of it away."

"And, of course, you believe her!" Julie couldn't stop her irritation from showing.

"She has no reason to lie. And you have nothing to be jealous of."

"Fine... So we lost everything. So now what?"

"I'm not saying we don't still try to find what we can. But we should be prepared for a square one reset."

"A square one reset?" Julie hated the idea. After five years of struggle, this was supposed to be a fresh start.

"I know it's been tough for you these past few years, but this is a chance to start over. These people need us. And I think we need them." Micheal tried to convince her.

Julie closed her eyes. She didn't need anyone except him. But she knew how stubborn he could be. "So what's your plan?" She surrendered.

"We help this village against the wolves. We gain their trust. Then, they can help us get back what we lost. And I don't mean the things we brought with us."

"I don't think that's possible. Those hurts run too deep."

"I hope not. I still believe that softhearted woman is still in there somewhere. And I want her back. I want my wife back." Micheal countered bluntly.

Julie hid the tear that that jab evoked. She didn't want him to see the weakness she still evidently possessed.

CHAPTER 2: TERROR IN THE DARK

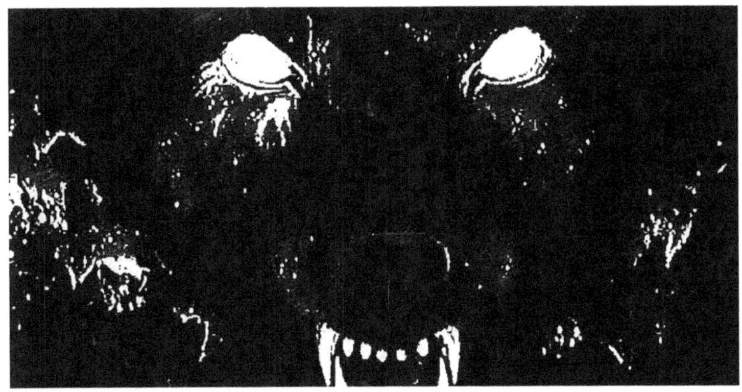

<u>The Hunt</u>

"Get up!" One of their guards shouted, kicking Micheal awake. He roused Julie, and they got to their feet.

"Where are we going?" He inquired.

"The hunt," Odilia answered for the man.

Micheal gave a confused look.

"The hunt can be delayed no longer. Our food stores are running empty. And every able-bodied man must go. So must the two of you. Not to be left unguarded." Odilia explained.

They just droned along with the hunting party.

"This is our chance," Julie whispered as they stood near the edge of a ravine.

"For what?" Micheal asked suspiciously.

"To escape!" She was still intent on leaving together.

"No!" He decided firmly. "But this hunt is our chance to do

something else." He added cryptically.

"What?" Julie said in irritation.

"To get our guards back." He nodded in both of their directions.

Their portion of the hunting party came upon a small herd of caribou. Everyone crouched down as they all drew their spears and arrows. Then, in a coordinated attack, they launched everything. Four large male caribou took the brunt of the volley. The rest of the herd stampeded away.

As the kill were being prepared for transport back to the village, Micheal turned to Julie and asked. "Have you worked your hands free yet?"

She revealed herself free. "Piece of cake."

Micheal heard a snarling sound from the surrounding thicket. Just then, several wolves pounced on a couple of members of the party.

"Let's move!" He dropped his bindings to the ground. "Follow my lead!"

Julie watched as Micheal ran full speed past one of the men who had beaten them. He laid a vicious jab with his elbow to the side of the man's face. He, then proceeded to attack one of the wolves.

She duplicated the process. She rolled into a cartwheel kick that connected with force to another man's face. She carried her momentum from the rotation, springing off her feet and tackling another wolf. She wrapped her arms around the wolf's neck and used her momentum to whip its body. She heard a sharp crack, and the wolf fell dead.

After assuring it was dead, Julie repeated the process. She gave a power elbow to another of her tormentor's ribs. Then lunged at another wolf. It attempted to elude her, but she grabbed its hind legs and flipped it over, smashing its head against some rocks.

With the second wolf dead, she quickly made her way across the scene. She made another pass, laying several bruising shots on the other two guards. Before she could engage another wolf there was movement to her left.

She met the wolf's fangs with her left forearm. She immediately gouged its eyes. It yelped, releasing her arm. She punched the wolf in the middle of its neck. It seemed stunned and writhed around on the ground, gagging.

She rose over the wolf, then proceeded to stomp its head several times until it stopped moving. At that moment, the remainder of the pack ran away.

Julie assessed the aftermath. In all, six wolves lay dead. And she and Micheal had put a beat down on their tormentors.

She inspected the last wolf she had killed. It was huge, all of them were. They were probably 150 to 200 pounds each. They must be dire wolves, she thought.

She felt some satisfaction at their small measure of justice.

Micheal surveyed the damage. Along with the six dead wolves, there were numerous injured members of the hunting party. Then he heard the sound of distant screaming and wolves snarling.

"Let's go!" He yelled to Julie.

They quickly found the next battlefield and dove straight into the fight. After he and Julie had each eliminated several wolves, he noticed a large wolf on top of the prince.

Micheal tackled the wolf, then sent it flying into a rock wall.

As he rose to his feet, he realized this wolf must be the alpha. It was huge, perhaps 250 pounds of black and gray fur.

It snarled at him, preparing to attack. He caged his leg, and as the alpha attacked, he kicked it straight in the mouth. It rolled to its feet and immediately came back at him. He dropped to his back, and the beast slid over him. He caught it by the tail, and, as he sat up, he whipped it over his head, slamming it hard into the ground. Then quickly whipped back words, slamming it again.

Micheal got to his feet. As the alpha was writhing on the ground, he stomped hard on its neck, and it stopped moving. The rest of the pack scattered.

As he and Julie found each other, and he was inspecting her arm. He noticed that all of the hunting party were staring at them with stunned looks on their faces.

The prince approached them and said. "You really were sent by the gods." And he slapped them on the shoulders.

While there had been some injuries, most were relatively minor. The men were in a celebratory mood as they were dragging back the haul from the hunt. But Micheal was concerned. He had noticed that the alpha was female. That meant there was a chance that she wasn't the alpha.

Terror in the dark

Julie felt better, having paid the men back. She and Micheal were celebrated the whole way back to the village.

"This isn't over," Micheal whispered as they came through the gates.

"What do you mean?"

"The alpha wolf was actually a beta. We haven't seen the actual alpha yet. We'll have to do something about that arm," he said of her left forearm.

As he wrapped her arm, Odilia came to the hut.

"You [stopped] them! You [killed] Fenrir!" Odilia seemed amazed.

"We killed wolves. Not Fenrir." Micheal shook his head. "The [black] wolf is a [beta]. The [alpha] is still out there."

Odilia looked at them skeptically. "The chief [wants] to [honor] you at dinner tonight. "Julie understood an invitation to dinner.

The whole situation was frustrating to Julie. Having to understand Proto-scandic was an unexpected annoyance. They were supposed to wake up, put together their small boat, and sail to Egypt. She already spoke ancient Egyptian, so there would be no language barrier.

At dinner, Micheal ensured that she understood what was said. The villagers thought they had vanquished Fenrir and that the attacks would stop. Most of the men who had tormented them came and apologized.

Odilia expressed amazement at Julie's actions. She didn't like Odilia. She could see the way she looked at Micheal. Julie had seen it all before. In Atlantis, when they were the gods, every woman seemed smitten by Micheal. Odilia had claimed a divine encounter and believed the gods sent them. Which probably amounted to the same thing. Micheal held the aspect of a hero or god, and Julie was concerned about how friendly he was toward Odilia.

Despite Micheal's belief that the alpha was still out there, the attacks had stopped for a while at least. It had been a month since they arrived in the 18th century BC, and Julie finally grasped Proto-scandic.

"Time to go," Micheal informed her.

"Do you think we will find anything?" Julie asked, pulling on her wolf-skin cloak.

Odilia says no, but I'm holding out hope," he said with uncertainty. They had been added to the hunting parties for the past few weeks. Finally, Chief Hildebrand allowed them to go in search of their missing items. Odilia and three men accompanied them.

"This is where we found you," Odilia said of a beach beside the ocean. It was nestled between a couple of rock outcroppings. When they went around one of the outcroppings, there were tiny fragments of one of their capsules. It had clearly broken up in the numerous storms that had passed through in the last month. After thoroughly searching the area they came up empty for the second capsule.

"It must be in the water," Micheal said, removing most of his clothes. Julie followed suit, and they dove into the frigid sea, diving as deep as possible.

When they were in Atlantis, they had spent some time learning how to free dive so they could go very deep. Julie went down, probably 500 feet, about as deep as she could see, but there was no sign of the capsule. When she returned to the surface, Micheal asked, "Did you see anything?"

"No. You?"

"No, the water goes down too deep too quickly. If it's down there, it's too deep to reach," he concluded.

She sighed in frustration. They spent the rest of the day scouring the coastline and only found a few items before returning to the village.

Julie awoke in the middle of the night to the howling of a wolf. She walked out of their hut, and the gates of the village swung open.

"What happened?" she asked the guards.

"Fenrir has returned. And he's angry," one of them said, with fear all over his face.

They awoke the chief with the man's body. Julie had also awoken Micheal.

"I tried to warn you that she was a beta," Micheal said matter-of-factly.

"What are we going to do now?" Chief Hildebrand asked urgently.

"We must pray that the gods come to our rescue," Priest Oddvarr said.

"Clearly, the gods have abandoned us to the demon Fenrir," the war chief said angrily.

"My Lord and Lady of Avalon, what say you?" the chief asked.

"We need to set a trap," Julie suggested.

"And how do we do that?" the war chief snapped.

"Where have all the attacks occurred since all the attacks began." Micheal raised a brow.

"They have been about the same in all directions until Fenrir attacked just now. Never had he attacked the village," Prince Eadrich said with worry.

A scream and subsequent howling abruptly ended the meeting. Rushing to the south gate, they discovered yet another guard mauled.

"It appears Fenrir has been hunting us. I say we turn the tables. We hunt the wolf agents of Fenrir until he's forced to come out into the open. Then... we kill him," Julie said with a menacing tone.

Dire Wolves

When morning broke, Micheal and Julie led the hunting part south from the village, where the tracks came from.

"What do you think is really going on here?" Julie asked Micheal.

"I don't know, but it's obvious there's some level of intelligence behind this."

Micheal had been trying to make sense of the pattern. Clearly, this wasn't some demon, but the attacks at the village felt like retaliation. Were the wolves really that smart? He didn't think so, but they had encountered many so-called supernatural things in the past fifty years, so who knows, he reasoned, as they approached a rock outcrop that might be a wolf den. Micheal led two other men inside to investigate.

The place was empty. Then, there was a howl; it sounded very close. He came out and realized that a few dozen wolves had surrounded them. The pack of wolves was led by a giant black wolf similar to the one he killed a few weeks earlier. The wolf stared at him and then howled again. At that, the pack attacked.

Micheal fought multiple wolves at a time. He had blades in each hand and rapidly cut his way through several waves, attempting to reach the alpha. Before he could get there, he saw Julie break through. The wolf pounced at her in response. Julie evaded the attack and cut open the wolf's side in the process. Julie went on the offensive, preventing the alpha from escaping. Many other wolves attempted to go to the alpha's aid, but Micheal fought them off long enough for Julie to finish off the alpha. With their leader dead, the rest of the pack retreated. Micheal assessed the damage. There were about a dozen dead wolves, including the alpha. The alpha was perhaps 200 pounds and was once again female. Five of their party were injured, three seriously. Micheal had a couple of bites, but nothing he considered an injury.

The next day, they led a party east. The weather turned bad as a cold June rain began to fall. The forest began to thicken. After a while, they came to a clearing. There was a sudden rush of noise coming from the woods around them. Then, a mass of wolves, maybe four dozen, attacked from all sides. Micheal and Julie began coordinating with each other to cut their way through a dozen wolves until they reached the alpha or perhaps yet another beta. The wolf had just finished tearing out the throat of another man. Micheal slid in, slashing with his blade. The wolf dodged, then came back around, biting into his ankle. Micheal lost his balance and went to the ground. The wolf pounced, and Micheal deflected its jaws away from his neck. He got a hold of its two front legs and flipped him and the wolf head over heels, landing on top of it. He retrieved one of the blades he had dropped and plunged it into the wolf's side several times. It yelped and writhed on the ground. Another wolf growled, then howled, and the rest of the wolves continued the attack. The new lead wolf charged at Micheal, but Julie intercepted. She and the wolf rolled around until Julie was on top, both of her blades stuck into its sides. And at that, the rest of the pack fled. Twenty more wolves lay dead, along with two of their party with them. Several more were injured.

"Another beta." Julie shook her head. "Where is the alpha?"

"We'll see him soon." Micheal was sure of it.

The Alpha

"I've developed a theory," Julie began when they returned to the village.

"And what is that?" Micheal looked at her.

"What if the alpha has taken control of all the dire wolves in the region? It's far too many to control, so it has generally delegated subpacks to its betas. That's why we haven't seen him yet. He's lording over all of them."

Julie had been trying to understand why there were so many beta packs, and they just kept coming.

"If that's true, we'll see the alpha very soon," Micheal predicted.

A sudden alarm was raised in the village while they were eating dinner in the great hall. Everyone ran to see what was going on. They came to find that the village wall was on fire. Everyone went quickly into action, forming fire lines. Micheal and Julie sprinted with their blades to break the wall's connections, attempting to make a mini firebreak. Then, they assisted in putting out the flames. The battle ran deep into the night. As dawn broke over the smoldering ruins, a third of the village wall and several other structures had burned. They went to ask the guards what happened.

"A couple of wolves tried to attack me. I swung my torch to fend them off. One of them bit into the torch. We wrestled for a moment, then the torch flew out of my hand and landed on the haystack."

"What happened with the wolves?" Julie inquired.

"When Njall and Aghi came to my aid, they ran away," Eyvindr replied.

"Okay, you may leave," Chief Hildebrand dismissed him.

"So what do we do now?" the chief asked.

"Our defenses are down; we are vulnerable," war chief Ælfric pointed out.

"Place as many men as possible on defense. We need another team felling trees to repair the wall," Chief Hildebrand ordered. Then turned to them, "Lord and Lady Avalon, what about Fenrir?"

"We must put together a full war party and hunt this alpha... Fenrir, down. Until we kill him, this won't end," Julie said definitively.

"My Lord?" the chief prodded Micheal.

"I agree. We kill Fenrir, and the rest of his drones will abandon the hunting area."

Julie and Micheal retired momentarily to their hut.

Micheal sighed deeply, "We need to end this now." He shook his head.

"It's crazy how aggressively these wolves have been attacking." She could see how these people would attribute supernatural elements to this situation.

"How are you holding up?"

"I'm tired. After all those years of chaos, I was hoping for a break." He pulled her into him, and she closed her eyes.

The howl of a wolf nearby woke her. They grabbed their weapons and hurried to find hundreds of wolves flooding through the breach. Most of the villagers were running for their lives. At that moment, there was a loud howl. Julie looked up. On top of the wall, there was the largest wolf she had ever seen. It was more than twice the size of the already giant dire wolves. It was clearly the alpha. It was black as night, with glowing yellow eyes in the twilight. It had to weigh between three and four hundred pounds. It was flanked by two betas similar in size to others they had already killed. All of the wolves had paused at the howl.

The alpha, Fenrir, who she could almost imagine was a wolf demon, stared straight at her like he knew they were the ones that had been killing his betas. Fenrir howled, and the betas echoed him. This was the signal to attack. Julie made a be-line toward them; Micheal was on her heels. A couple of dozen wolves moved into a protective position. There were screams mixed with growls from all over the village.

She and Micheal coordinated to move through the mass of fur and fangs. She knew they would be overwhelmed if they got stalled out in such a mess. It was chaotic, but all the years of training and real-world battles had made her reaction speed like lightning. One wolf suffered a blade in its eye, while another's belly was split open. She jabbed the back of a wolf's neck, biting Micheal's leg. When another bit her arm, she swiftly sliced its mouth open, extending the cut down the side of its neck. They finished off the last few that were protecting Fenrir. At that, Fenrir and his betas jumped off the wall and charged at them. Fenrir was huge, over four feet tall. Julie stabbed him in the side as they collided, grabbing his front leg with her left hand, and they rolled over a few times. She came to her feet. Fenrir easily doubled her body weight. She was suddenly hit from one side by one of the betas, taking her legs out from under her. Then, in a flash, Micheal ripped the beta away.

Once again, it was her against Fenrir. He was on top of her, trying to bite her neck. She stabbed him in the stomach; he snapped at her hand as she pulled the blade out for another go, causing her to drop it. But she was able to get the leverage to roll him off of her. As she rose to her feet again, Fenrir turned back at her and pounced. She dodged to the side, taking a partial impact as he went by, knocking her to the ground. She rolled back to her feet, and he pounced right at her, hitting her full-on. They rolled a few times until Fenrir was on top of her, and she was barely too slow to defend her neck. His vice jaws latched onto the front of her neck, crushing her windpipe. She began to strangle as he tried to rip her throat out. She grabbed a stick from beside her and plowed it into his eye. He released her throat for a second; then she realized Micheal was on top of Fenrir, and he had stabbed his blades into the sides of Fenrir's neck. Fenrir and Micheal rolled off her. As she gained her feet, Fenrir was standing there. He growled viciously, then charged her but was slowed by his wounds.

"Julie!" Micheal yelled.

She turned just in time to catch the blade he tossed her. She caught it, and just as Fenrir collided with her, she stabbed him in his chest right between his front legs. She aimed for his heart, and the responding squeal confirmed her accuracy. She threw him off from on top of her. He slowly got to his feet, took a couple of steps, then fell over dead. Several wolves howled in reaction, and the remaining wolves in the village made a hasty retreat.

As Julie tried to assess the fallout, she was beginning to feel lightheaded. She grabbed her neck, which was bleeding profusely. She heard Micheal yell her name, and then it all faded to black.

CHAPTER 3: FALLOUT

M ICHEAL HAD TO PERFORM minor surgery on Julie's neck. He debated using one of the Nectars of Life but decided against it. If he could keep her wounds clean, she would fully recover. She was in a deep sleep, so he went to help deal with the fallout of the battle.

The sun had risen on a scene of destruction. Half the village had burned down, including more of the wall. Over 100 wolves had been killed, including Fenrir, who weighed nearly 400 pounds. But the village casualties were numerous as well. Perhaps two dozen dead, dozens more injured. The biggest loss was Prince Eadric.

A rainstorm dowsed the remaining embers, but it turned everything into mud. As he looked at the pain and misery around him, Julie's sentiments came to mind:

Even here in the 18th century B.C., they were supposed to get some kind of break from the horrors of the post-nuclear holocaust. But at least so far, it wasn't to be. And to make matters worse, the chief didn't take his son's loss very well. He was despondent. The war chief and priest were also severely injured.

"What are we going to do now?" Odilia asked him.

"You're asking me? I'm an outsider," he balked.

"There is no one else, My Lord."

He sighed. Even after all these years, he had trouble under-standing why everyone wanted to put him in charge of everything. Fifty years ago, he was just the neighborhood mailman. He had to grin at a thought that crossed his mind: he wasn't even the Utah Jazz Mailman. He had to digress. He may be the distant descendant of King Arthur, but that doesn't mean he is a leader. But once again, into that breach.

"Bring everyone before the front of the Great Hall."

While Odilia rounded everyone up, he went to check on Julie again. After that, he decided to talk to the chief one more time.

"Eminence... Eminence!" He got no response from Chief Hilde-brand. "The people need to hear from you, your Eminence." He still got no answer. Queen Asdis had been seriously injured, so it would be up to Micheal.

Micheal came out of the Hall to the entire village. He made sure to scan the crowd and make eye contact with as many people as possible.

"Good people! I just spoke with the chief. He wanted me to address you all. Now, I know I am a stranger to this village. I am not one of you. But I have come to think of you as my family. I know we have all suffered much pain and sorrow due to the demon Fenrir! But we have vanquished this terror! The sacrifices of the heroes shall not be forgotten! We will honor them, and then... we will rebuild this village stronger than ever. Are you with me!" Micheal finished, and everyone cheered in agreement. They did seem to have more spirit about them. And now he had to organize the honoring of the heroes.

They spent the rest of the day building a massive funeral pyre. That night, they lit the flame of the heroes, and Micheal did his best to console Odilia, who had lost a couple of her closest friends. Julie was still in a deep sleep, and Micheal invited her to stay with them until her hut could be rebuilt. Half the village had burned down, so he had asked everyone to double up.

"How's she doing?" Odilia asked after Julie.

"She's healing up nicely. She might be awake in a day or so," Micheal explained, taking Julie's hand. "Get well, my love," he said in English.

He went and sat by Odilia.

"I've been meaning to ask you," Odilia said.

"Yes?" he raised a brow.

"Before you, I had never met anyone who spoke differently than us. And you indicated that you were on a voyage. Have you ever met other people who spoke differently than us?"

"Yes, many," Micheal seemed to surprise her.

"How many?"

"Oh, I can speak the words of many people. More than fifty."

"That doesn't seem possible."

So he proceeded to demonstrate the same sentence in every language he knew.

"How is it possible for someone of your age to know so much?"

He considered for a moment and then said, "We are not as young as we seem."

"What does that mean?" She seemed to be examining him.

"I've lived for 78 years... Julie has lived for 81." Micheal looked her in the eyes, trying to decide if she believed him.

Odilia looked away, then said, "You are of the gods." She looked back.

Micheal looked away. "We are not. We are just people."

"Yes, you are—the things you can do. I saw you both against Fenrir and his betas. And I heard the tales of your battles with the wolves. You have to be of the gods."

"I think it's time for supper," he changed the subject. He then went and kissed Julie on the forehead.

After Chief Hildebrand refused to host supper, Micheal supposed he would have to. Everyone was patiently waiting when he and Odilia entered the Hall. The mood was somber. Micheal stood and addressed the room. "We have lost much. We have suffered tremendous grief at the heroes' sacrifice. But this is not the time for tears. We do not dwell on how those loved ones died, but we celebrate how they lived. I encourage you to share your favorite stories of those who have transitioned to Valhalla."

He sat down, and everyone silently looked around, wondering who would be the first to go. After a moment, Odilia stood and told a light-hearted story about her friend Roza, and that encouraged others. As the night went on, the mood elevated. It had been a long couple of days, so Micheal decided to retire. Odilia had already returned to the hut first. When he entered, she was crying on the floor. He went and touched her on the shoulder. She grabbed his hand and looked up at him, then she threw her arms around him and began to cry on his shoulder. As he held her, exhaustion took them, and they fell asleep.

__Recovery__

Julie finally brought herself to full consciousness. She probed her neck, and it was healing well. She wasn't sure how long it had been. She found a pot of soup and a cup of water next to the bed. She quickly consumed both.

She rose to her feet and pulled her cloak around her. She exited the hut to find the village in ruins, and no one could be seen. There had been some cleanup, and everyone must be around here somewhere.

She made her way down toward the sea. All of the villagers were in a large semi-circle along the shoreline. As she approached, the people seemed surprised to see her and opened up a path. She realized this was some kind of funeral. She scanned the crowd and realized that the chief's son, Eadric, was not amongst them.

Micheal seemed to be directing the proceedings. He glanced up and saw her and made his way to her.

"How do you feel?"

"I've had worse," she said in a scratchy voice. "Eadric?" she tried to confirm.

"Yes. And I have to get back to it. I'm kind of in charge until the chief gets past his grief." Micheal changed to English.

"Of course you are," she replied in kind.

She knew his clear, decisive confidence caused people to gravitate to him. She just wished he didn't always think he had to accept the role. She knew he had a bit of a hero complex, and he always felt he had to help people if he could.

Prince Eadric was launched into the fjord, and the sail of the boat caught the wind, blowing it out toward the sea. Priest Oddvarr was speaking blessings to the gods as the ship went further adrift. As the prayers ended, Micheal raised a bow, lit the arrow, drew it back, and let it fly. A few seconds later, it found its mark, and the boat ignited.

Julie stepped up and took Micheal's arm. Everyone watched in silence as the boat became a bonfire. She watched the dichotomy of fire and water and thought of the different funeral traditions in different cultures.

Burial was most common in modern times, but burning was most common in ancient times. Most of the traditions had to do with the locations of the people or some other belief about what comes after. She had already died a couple of times and was certain that where she met Jessica was only a halfway point. But she was also convinced there was no River Sticks, no nirvana, no Elysium, and no Valhalla either.

Sometimes, she wanted to break people out of their delusions, but then, who was she to shatter whatever belief people had about the great beyond?

The fire finally succumbed to the great sea as the boat sank below the sea. All the villagers walked a slow procession, paying respects to Chief Hildebrand. Eventually, it was just them and the chief.

"Thank you, My Lord, for acting in my stead. My Lady... for your sacrifice..." He broke down in tears.

"... you are but strangers amongst us, and yet you fight so bravely to protect us."

Julie didn't know how to respond. While she felt sympathy for him, she was angry that she had to put herself in harm's way on their behalf. She was also mad at Micheal. Their involvement in this whole situation was his fault. They were better off on their own. Some hard lessons in the post-apocalyptic wasteland had taught her that.

"It wasn't enough to save Eadric," she said finally. Her voice was raspy; it almost didn't sound like her.

"You saved the village. That's more than we ever could have asked for. Now that it's over... are you going to leave," the chief enquired.

"Well..." Julie began.

"We will stay until the village is back on its feet," Micheal interrupted.

"... then we must continue on our journey," Julie finished.

Over the next few days, they rebuilt the wall. Micheal remained in charge because the chief continued in his sorrow.

They entered their hut, and Odilia was sitting on the floor.

"Odilia, may we have some privacy," Julie asked sharply. Odilia left quickly without a word. "We need to talk," Julie switched to English.

"Okay..." Micheal seemed nervous.

"What is she doing in our hut?" She was irritated.

"Half the village burned down. I told everybody to double up.""I get that, but why is she staying with us?" she was trying to fight the anger inside her.

"I thought you would prefer someone we already knew well." He seemed confused.

"I saw you!" she accused.

"What do you mean?" he played dumb.

"I guess you thought I was still out of it, but I saw you snuggled up with her!" She was losing control.

"I was..." he began to argue.

"You're attracted to her! Don't try to deny it! You think I don't know you after fifty years!" she exploded.

"You're right, I am! I won't deny it! She's certainly looking better right now!" Micheal left in a huff.

Julie considered following him, but the argument had taken most of her energy. She sat down on the bed, feeling lightheaded. She lay down on the bed, trying to quell it, but drifted off to sleep.

When Julie came to, the village was quiet, and Micheal was still gone. She exited the hut to find it was the summer twilight. It was late June, and here in Norway, just south of the Arctic Circle, there were 21 hours of daylight and three hours of twilight.

She went and mounted a horse. There were no saddles, so she had to mount bareback. She went to search the fjords for Micheal. After a couple of hours, she gave up. She sat on an overlook, waiting for the sun to rise. A wave of pain passed through her neck. She began to think about everything. Her disappointment at the square one reset, the sacrifices she had made on behalf of this village, and she thought deeply for the first time about how the previous five years had hardened her. She swallowed, and the accompanying pain refocused her pain toward Micheal. This was his fault. She felt he chose to stoke his hero ego over her. Right now, however, all she wanted was to talk to him.

She turned her head a little bit, and the pain in her neck shot up into her head, throbbing in her temples. At the same time, the emotions flooded in, and she bowed her head into her hands as tears came to her eyes.

She had a small start when hands grasped her shoulders until she realized it was Micheal.

"I am so sorry," he said softly, massaging her shoulders. "This is all my fault."

She could tell he was crying.

"My hubris has once again brought you pain, and then I go and say such horrible things. Can you ever forgive me?" His massage was easing the tension in her neck, and her headache began to subside. "If I had known you would have to suffer in this way... We should have just left. We can leave now,"

She grabbed his wrists and turned to look at him. "Shh... No..." she said gently. "I don't want you to harden like I have... Your instinct to help people is born out of your caring heart. There's nothing to forgive. I have been being selfish." She had his face cupped in her hands. "We will stay for a while."

Julie pressed her lips against his to stop any rebuff. She dropped her cloak and placed his warm hands over her rock-hard nipples in the cool twilight air. She unhooked his cloak, and his rippling, rugged body glistened slightly in the mellow light. She pressed him on his back and mounted him. As she began riding her way to ecstasy, all the pains in her body drained away. His strong, rough hands were stroking up and down her whole body, adding even more heat. She arched back as she increased the pace. As they exploded together, it was punctuated by the first rays of dawn breaking the twilight, and she collapsed on his chest.

"I still don't know why you're with me," he said as he ran his fingers through her hair.

"Micheal!"

He put his fingers to her lips. He studied her face, tracing the curve of her cheek. "You are impossibly beautiful, and every day I ask that same question."

She looked away.

He turned her back to look at him. "Every day, I pray to God you won't come to your senses and leave me. You are part of me now, and if I ever lost you, I would lose myself." Julie knew he was still apologizing.

"I know you're not perfect, but that's one of the things I love about you. You've been a god to people. Your imperfections show you're still human. I need a man, not a god. And you are the best man a woman could ask for."

Then they went for round two.

As they basked in the morning sun, Micheal said, "I'll tell Odilia she needs to move out.""That's ok, but we need a new house."

<u>Bronze-Age Tech</u>

Over the next two months, Micheal remained in charge. Queen Asdis had been seriously wounded in the battle against Fenrir so Chief Hildebrand had remained at her side. Under normal circumstances, the queen might never have recovered, but Julie had decided to use her medical expertise to nurse her back to health, along with many other villagers.

Finally, Micheal had been able to locate precisely where they were in Norway. They were about 100 miles north of Trondheim, in a place that would become known as Namsos. This close to the Arctic Circle, Micheal would take advantage of the long summer days, upwards of 20 hours, to quickly rebuild the village. He also located some important resource deposits in the area. His memory of a map of the resources in Norway included iron, copper, nickel, and cobalt. After locating deposits of all four, he had put some men in charge of mining some of each so he could use the metal to make pipes, weapons, and many other things out of the different alloys he knew how to make.

He summoned all the villagers to the new Great Hall. It had been built in the center of the village. The main hall was 100 feet long and 80 feet wide, with living quarters on either side.

"I would first like to say how proud I am of all of you. Through hard work these past couple of months, we have rebuilt stronger than before. I know how much you have all lost, but your efforts honor those who have already moved on. It has been my particular honor to guide you through this difficult time, but the time has now come to pass the torch back to your most worthy of leaders, Chief Hildebrand and Queen Asdis." He reintroduced them. The chief and his queen had been out of sight since the battle. Then Micheal went and took his place on the pedestal next to Julie.

"Does this mean we're leaving?" she asked skeptically.

"Well, as you know, I have been pushing the output of the mines, and we almost have enough surplus to construct a new ship. So I thought we would stay for a few months and have these people help us construct it. Then we will sail for Egypt," he promised.

"Are you sure you're not looking for reasons to stay here?" She raised a brow.

"Either we have to build a ship by ourselves, or we can have help. It will likely take the same amount of time. The only difference is how big we can build it."

"All right, we stay. But the longer we stay here, the harder it will be to leave. And who knows what else we get roped into." Julie looked out over the Great Hall.

Micheal knew that was true, so it was a risk, but he felt it was worth it.

After dinner, they went to their new home.

"I know I've harped on you about this over the years, but do we really need to build so big?" Julie asked as they entered their new home.

"Well, why not? And this isn't even that big. It's less than a thousand square feet."

"It's the second biggest building in this village."

"Only if you combine it with the forge."

"And that's another thing... aren't you worried about bringing Iron Age tech to the Bronze Age? Aren't we 500 to 1000 years too early for that? And it's not like we have a tachyon scanner to see how this impacts the timeline." She seemed worried.

"I did consider that. Most of this stuff will be coming with us. And besides, with some of the other things we've done, I think we can trust the timeline to correct itself."

They finally put the finishing touches on their new house. They had saved it for last, and Michale ensured it had all the modern comforts. The forge had come in handy in the fabrication of many useful things. They had engineered small machines to make food processing and preparation more effortless and several other tools for many different uses. Micheal had also put some men to work building the dry dock before the ground froze. And he even made time to craft a guitar for Julie's anniversary gift.

As Micheal walked into the loft, she was tuning it.

"So, what are you going to play?" He smiled at her.

She finished tuning it and said, "I was thinking of one of the best guitar solos of all time. She began strumming the melody to *Fields of Gold* by Sting, then began to sing.

He loved to listen to her angelic voice.

When she finished. "Can you believe that if we were still in the 21st century, that song would be over 80 years old?" she asked rhetorically. "You know, sometimes when I look at you, I try to envision what you would look like if we were still in the 21st century... But then I think I can. It's your eyes... I look into your eyes, and they betray that beautiful, youthful face." She set the guitar down and traced the curve of his face with her hand. "What lives we have lived. We've grown old together and yet have so much further to go."

He looked into her unimaginable eyes and said, "I've loved

growing old with you, and I can't wait to spend eternity together." He proved his words with his body.

<u>Home Sweet Home</u>

- November 12, 1778 B.C.

Three months ago, I was angry. The years of hell we spent in the wasteland had made me distrustful of people. I lost faith in humanity and lost touch with my own. After our mistreatment at the hands of these people, I wanted to hate them. I tried to hold a grudge, but Micheal's optimistic view of people in general has pressed me to remember the good in them. I spent weeks nursing these people back to health. And Micheal was right, as usual. I did need these people. Their gratitude for my tender care and the sacrifices I made on their behalf helped me remember the person I used to be.

Most of our new ship's superstructure was completed before the first snow, and we have spent most of the rest of the time engineering the interior. And I have spent a bit of that time turning our new house into a home. After six months in the 18th century B.C. I am finally able to begin Volume 8 of the Book of Avalon.

Now to Micheal... He has been doing his best to hide it, but he has clearly developed feelings for Odilia. They have obvious chemistry. I have held my jealousy in check, and now I have come up with a new strategy to deal with the situation.

P.S. Today is my 81st birthday.

Julie put down the journal and wrapped herself in her cloak as she walked onto the balcony. The sun was about to set. It was about 2:30 in the afternoon. There were only about 6 hours of daylight at this time of year.

"My Lady!" Micheal gave an elaborate bow from below.

She smiled, shook her head, and returned, "My Lord."

He climbed the front of their house to the balcony. "I take thee at thy word. Call me but love, and I'll be new baptized. Henceforth, I never will be Micheal," he quoted Shakespeare.

"What man art though, that thus bescreen'd in night so stumblest upon my council."

"By a name... your love eternal," he kissed her deeply. "Have you had a great birthday so far?" he brushed the hair out of her face, tucking it behind her ear.

"I enjoyed sleeping in... After you kept me up all night." She gave him a sly smile.

"The nights are particularly long, and I don't expect we'll get much sleep tonight," he kissed the back of her hand. "But first... there are some other people that want to wish you a happy birthday," he indicated the Great Hall.

As they entered the Great Hall, Julie saw Odilia. "Odilia, how nice to see you. Why don't you come sit with us." Julie pulled her by the arm after her.

"I am impressed by how much effort Micheal put into this feast in your honor," Odilia stumbled along behind her.

"Isn't he great?" Julie indicated Micheal.

"You're very lucky," Odilia's envy was plain to see.

"Odilia?" Julie said as they sat on the pedestal. "Why are you without a man?" she feigned confusion.

"Well, I was orphaned when I was young, so I learned to be independent. I had to be more like a man in some ways."

"You *had* been? What changed?" Julie thought she already knew.

"Well... I finally became a true woman... with..." Odilia was stammering.

"... Thor?" Julie finished for her.

"Yes... I looked at men differently after that."

"A god could do that to you," Julie couldn't hide the smile on her face.

"Yes," Odilia seemed embarrassed.

"Any man in particular?" Julie indicated the room.

"Ivarr and Aki," Odilia shyly indicated.

"So what are you doing about it?"

"Ladies, how are we doing this evening," Micheal arrived.

"Lovely!" Odilia perked up at his question. "I can't believe you went to all this trouble," Odilia fawned over him.

"No trouble at all. I would do anything for my love," he gave Julie a peck.

"Oh, the love of a good man," Julie rubbed it in Odilia's face.

The night progressed, and Julie got more and more into the music. It was surprisingly diverse, with the "band" playing a lute, a lyre, some pipes, and drums.

"Would the birthday girl like to dance?" Micheal gave an elaborate bow.

Julie gave him her hand, and he led her to the center of the Great Hall. They found the rhythm and started to get into it. The entire village was soon watching their strange form of dancing, a mix of classical and contemporary styles. After they had been dancing for a good while, Julie noticed Odilia on the edge of the dance floor. She quickly went over and grabbed her hands, pulling her onto the floor with them. Odilia was hesitant at first, but as they put her between them, she seemed to begin to enjoy herself. Julie had truly missed dancing like this.

Later that night, during a lull in their all-night lovefest... "I have something for you," Micheal said, pulling out a large seashell. He had carved an image onto it. It was of him and her kissing, encircled by a heart and bordered by calla lilies. There was an inscription that said,

"I love thee in this life and all the rest yet to come."

"We have already loved a lifetime together," she understood.

"We have indeed." He moved to take her one more time.

CHAPTER 4: VILLAGE LIFE

__Whaling__

MOST OF THE VILLAGE hunters departed for the shore well before sun-up. Micheal was among them. It was late November, and there would only be five hours of sunlight, but the village counselors claimed this was the best time to hunt whales to fill the stocks for the long winter ahead.

The hunters were delighted with the new spears Micheal had forged from the metals they had been mining. Previously, they had primarily used obsidian spear points on sticks. Micheal had brought his new recurve bow with him.

As the first light of dawn broke over the horizon, they launched into the sea. Twelve boats in all, they set off three at a time. Micheal's group were the last to launch. A couple of hours later, they reached the open waters of the Norwegian Sea, and each group took a different course.

A short time later, they spotted their first blow on the horizon. They hurried to catch up. There were three whales. As they were nearing the small pod, he recognized the species.

"No!" he yelled to call them off. "These are far too large to bring back," he explained. It was two adult blue whales, as well as an adolescent calf. Their vessels were only 30 feet long compared with the 100-foot giants. They pulled up right next to the head of one of the adults. It popped its head above the surface and was looking at them. Micheal slowly reached out and touched it on its lip. It looked at him briefly, then dipped below the waves. The water was relatively clear, and as the whales pulled away, he could see the shadow, and it was enormous.

They changed course, and soon, there was blow on the horizon. As they approached, Micheal recognized it as a bowhead whale. It was, by itself, and it was around 40 or 50 feet long. Two of the boats flanked it on either side, and the boat Micheal was on tracked above it. In coordination, they slowed it down. It popped its head out, and the hunters simultaneously launched their spears. Most of them connected, and the whale reacted instantly by diving back under the water. The spears had ropes attached and they had to move quickly to keep up with the whale. It eventually came back up for air, and the hunters that had missed the first time sent another volley. All found their mark, and the whale began thrashing around. At one point, it whipped its tail, knocking one of the boats in the process and sending several men overboard. As Micheal prepared to dive in after them, the whale's tail lifted out of the water. As it smacked down on the opposite end of the boat, Micheal used the jolt to propel himself into the air. He flipped head over heels, landing on the rebound on the other end of the boat. He pulled his bow from his back, drew an arrow, and jumped on the back of the whale. Then he ran to the head, and before it could react, he fired two arrows into its blowhole. It thrashed violently in response, throwing him into the freezing water. When he surfaced, the whale rolled over and was no longer moving.

He helped gather the other men from the water, and they headed for home, towing the whale behind them. They reached the shore as the sun was setting. They were the last to arrive, and all four hunting parties had been successful.

<u>Courtship</u>

While Micheal and the hunters went whaling, Julie decided to push her pupil to the next level.

"How are things coming with Ivarr?" Julie asked.

"Well... he's not..." Odilia was searching for the right word.

"... big enough?" Julie tried, raising an eyebrow.

"... No!" Odilia protested.

"... strong enough?" Julie tried again.

"No," Odilia said more calmly.

"... smart enough?" Julie tried one last time.

"Well..." Odilia fumbled.

"That's it, isn't it?" Julie thought she must be close.

"I mean, that's not the most important thing, is it?" Odilia tried to reason.

"I honestly wouldn't know. I've never had that problem," Julie shrugged.

At that moment, Aiden came to mind. He wasn't on Micheal's level but was definitely above average. It had been years since she thought of Aiden. Her time with him was now a distant memory. It almost seemed like a dream; it was so long ago now. It was as if it was a whole different lifetime.

A moment of guilt came over her. How could she go so long without a thought of the man she was once in love with? It wasn't his fault she vanished on him. She wondered what his life was like now. Had he moved on? Did he have the children he had so much wanted? She certainly hoped so.

That dream she shared with him 45 years ago felt like him letting go. She hoped he had. He most definitely deserved happiness.

These thoughts of the past also reminded Julie of the fact that she couldn't have children. At least not as long as they were trapped in the timeline. She certainly wouldn't want to bring a child into this chaotic life they had to live. But that also meant the chances of having a child of her own were very small.

"Come with me," Julie instructed. She and Odilia crossed the village, where they found Aki, the other man Odilia had shown interest in. He was with another young man, Sveinn, the medicine man, Josteinn's younger son.

"Gentlemen, are you occupied at this moment?" They both

clearly perked up at their intercession. Aki was 16 and Sveinn was 15. She knew they would appreciate a little female attention.

"No!" Aki quickly replied for both of them.

"Because I was trying to find a strong warrior to teach Lady Odilia how to shoot," Julie said, touching Aki on the arm.

"Where do you want to go?" Sveinn asked, trying to hide his excitement.

They made their way to a clearing in the woods overlooking a fjord.

"Aki, why don't you show us how it's done." She handed him her bow. It was a metal alloy recurve bow. The draw was only about 30 pounds, but the reflex of the bow made it shoot like a 100-pound draw.

Julie had become a regular Robin Hood during their time in the wasteland. There had been no guns after the first year or so, so a bow and arrow had become the primary hunting weapon.

Aki took the bow. "How magnificent." He admired the beautiful craftsmanship.

Julie had forged itself at the smith out of low-grade tri-poly. It was low-grade because they were limited in various elements.

"You Avalonians seem so superior in your knowledge," Aki commented. He knocked an arrow, raised and fired at the target they had set up. He hit the target but not the bullseye. "Lady Odilia, want to try?" Aki offered.

She looked at Julie, and Julie nodded. Aki reached behind Odilia to position her correctly. She loosed the arrow to pitiful effect.

"Let's try that again," Aki had a smile on his face. Then, he continued teaching Odilia.

"Lady Julie, you are an archer?" Sveinn enquired with interest.

"Oh, I know my way around a bow," she demurred. "But you, My Lord, I'm sure are a veritable expert. Maybe you can teach me a thing or two," she said flirtatiously. Sveinn seemed flattered by her attention.

"My father said I will be going on the whale hunt next year. I'll be a senior warrior by then. I pretty much am already," he boasted.

He knocked an arrow and demonstrated his skill with a bow,

which was pretty impressive.

"Wait, you killed Fenrir... What could I possibly teach you?" He seemed to remember her great feat.

She took the bow and fired an arrow at the target, intentionally low. "That was pretty good, wasn't it?" she pretended to be impressed with the effort.

"Try another one. Raise it a little bit higher."

She did as he directed but loosened her grip on the bow, firing high and right. Here..." he said, grabbing her left arm. "... Like this," he reached around to assist her draw.

The shot hit just down and left of the bullseye.

"Much better. Try it yourself now, My Lady." Sveinn stepped back a little.

She let loose, hitting the bullseye. "Sveinn, you're quite the teacher." Julie drew again and decided to attempt the Robin Hood legend shot, splitting the previous arrow in two. She had to adjust for the crude bow and arrow. She let it fly, and it moved oddly in the air before returning and plowing right into the end of the other arrow. Sveinn seemed shocked at the result. At that moment, they heard Odilia yelling, and Julie turned in time to see her slap Aki in the face. Sveinn ran immediately to defend her against any potential retaliation. Aki stood glaring for a moment and then ran off. After ensuring Odilia was okay, Julie demonstrated her true skill.

"Let us forget this unpleasantness. Now let us see if I've learned anything."

Julie took her bow and quiver of a dozen arrows. She drew one, and it found the bullseye. She ran across the meadow, firing shots the entire way. She turned back, running across a slight outcropping. She paused and fired off three shots in rapid succession. Then she ran full-speed, letting loose as she dove off the 20-foot high embankment. She landed in a roll, firing as she reached one knee. She sprinted back toward Odilia and Sveinn, firing all along the way. She finished before them, letting the last two arrows fly, landing on both bullseyes.

"How was that?" Julie raised a brow to both of their mouths agape.

<u>Giving Thanks</u>

"What day is today?" Julie asked as Micheal rose from the bed.

"Thursday. Why?" He didn't know where she was going with this.

"It's Thanksgiving," she said with a smile.

"Actually, I think the first Thanksgiving is in about 3400 years," he joked.

"Yeah, whatever," she rolled her eyes. "So what are we going to do?"

"I know we usually go all out for this feast, but it seems the village has decided for us. There's a bonfire celebration of a successful hunt. So whale will be on the menu."

"I feel bad about the whales." She looked away.

"So do I, but this is one of their principal food sources."

He never imagined he would kill a whale, but it was literally them or the whale... so it was an easy choice. And he knew how much the villagers respected the whales. Nothing would be wasted.

"Let's get ready. The sun is almost up."

After a day of smoking and salting, the food stores for winter were more than full, thanks to the best hunt the village had ever seen, according to the villagers. They also had plenty of elk, moose, and caribou, likely because they had run off the wolf pack.

As the sun was setting, multiple bonfires were lit.

"Praise to the gods!" Josteinn spoke loudly. "They delivered us from Fenrir! They brought us great bounty! Thanks, we give, for such good fortune! Praise the gods!" He opened the ceremony to the gods.

There were many ritual dances, and everyone praised the gods for all the many positive things in their lives.

"My Lord, Micheal, praise the gods for sending you to us. Eadric would agree that the gods have given us many blessings," Eadric's widow, Runa, said.

"I'm sorry you lost him. If only..."

"No! This is a time for thanks."

"Is she all right?" Odilia asked as Runa walked away.

Micheal was surprised and temporarily caught off guard by Odilia. She had become his first true friend in quite some time. He had never made friends very easily. That never bothered him, but on rare occasions, he would hit it off with someone.

Now, in this case, the fact that she was the type of beauty he preferred complicated matters. He didn't think he could ever cheat on Julie, but he found his attraction was more than physical. He would need to tread carefully. He knew his willpower would keep him in check.

And speaking of Julie, for the first five months they were in the village, she seemed to hate Odilia, but they seemed to become friends in the last couple of months. He wasn't sure what changed.

"She was thanking the gods that we came, although I feel she is still grieving Eadric," Micheal replied.

A tear came to Odilia's eye at the statement.

"I'm sorry, Odilia, I should been more delicate." He touched her shoulder.

"It's okay. This is a festive occasion. Let's talk of happier things... So what thanks do you have of the gods?" she asked, wiping her eyes.

"Your friendship. The gods allowed me to meet you and, as such, become friends," he admitted as he studied her face. "You're so beautiful..." he added, without thinking. "...I'm sorry, I shouldn't have said that," he turned to leave.

"Stay."

He considered a moment. "Okay."

"I'm glad you said that. I've desired you from the start. Even more than Thor."

He hadn't had urges like this in such a long time. He needed out of the situation. "I'm sorry, Odilia, I have to go," he said, heading for the nearest bonfire, leaving Odilia behind the woodpile.

"Micheal?" Julie came over.

"Enjoying Thanksgiving?" Micheal asked casually.

"Are you all right?"

"Just giving thanks to the gods," he joked.

"Of course, I know how much you owe to the gods," she replied in kind. "You wouldn't happen to know where Odilia is, would you?" Her question sounded like an accusation.

"No."

"Hmm. Runa said she was with you." She raised a brow.

"Oh, that was a while ago. I haven't seen... Wait, there she is," he said, pointing behind Julie.

"Well then, continue giving thanks to the gods." She winked and walked off toward Odilia.

The festivities continued into the night. By midnight, most had turned in. Micheal lay behind the wood pile, watching the curtains of the northern lights. Ribbons of purple, green, and pink, dancing across the sky. It was his favorite aspect of the high latitudes.

"Am I interrupting?" Odilia asked, approaching.

"It's ok. Join me."

She laid down next to him and they stared up at the sky.

"I need to apologize. I put our friendship at risk by saying too much."

"You said what was in your heart."

"I'm married. I love Julie... beyond reason."

"You care for me, do you not?"

"Of course I do. In the nearly 80 years of my life, I have only called five people 'friend' and you are one of them. I don't want to lose that, but these other feelings complicate things. And even if I somehow felt inclined to act on them. Julie and I will be leaving in the near future."

"You still plan to leave? I had hoped you would change your mind." She sounded like she was about to cry.

"There are so many things I wish I could tell you, but I can't. We must continue on our journey. You wouldn't understand even if I told you." He wasn't sure what to say.

She sniffled and sighed. "Ok... We never really told each other what we are thankful for," she tacked away from their quandary.

"Honestly, sometimes in my life, I felt the gods had abandoned me, but if I can remind myself to focus on the positives, I can remember how many blessings the gods have bestowed upon me. The most valuable is the wealth of knowledge I possess. And what about you? What blessings of the gods?"

"They blessed me with great beauty, good health, and a vast curiosity. To which I wonder, of these beautiful emanations in the sky," she referenced the Aurora above them. "You clearly have superior knowledge from the gods. Do you understand what these lights are?"

"Heimdall, Bringer of Light, is working to rebuild the Bifrost. I know Asgard was destroyed in Ragnarök, but Thor survived. Heimdall resurrected. They are rebuilding Asgard," Micheal explained through mythology.

"Thor said I was hope for rebirth," Odilia said in total belief.

"Am I interrupting?" Julie said as she approached.

"Join us. The gods are blessings our festival with color and magic." Micheal took Julie's hand, helping her lie down next to him. "It truly is beautiful, isn't it?"

After a long while, Julie turned to him and said, "All this magic in the air has me wanting something else." She sat up, grabbing his hand. "Come with me."

"Odilia, will you join us?" she added, turning back.

"Um, okay," Odilia got up, and the three of them made their way through the quiet village to their home.

As they came into the multipurpose room of the house, Micheal asked, "So what are you wanting?"

"Upstairs," Julie climbed to the top. Odilia followed.

Micheal was a little confused by this game of mystery, but he made his way up after them. As he reached the loft, he saw Julie removing Odilia's cloak. She then kissed the side of Odilia's neck. "Join us," Julie said as she slid her hands up inside Odilia's blouse, apparently caressing her breasts.

Micheal didn't know what to think. "Jules, what's going on?" he asked in English.

"What? Don't you find Odilia beautiful," she asked in English as she kissed the other side of Odilia's neck.

Micheal was tempted, but he knew Julie better than that. He suspected she was testing him, and now that he thought about it, she might have recognized his attraction to Odilia.

Julie pushed Odilia forward until she was right in front of him. "Feel how soft her skin is." Julie took Micheal's hands and placed them on Odilia's sides, moving them slowly up her body. "Look at those big, beautiful eyes."

He locked eyes with Odilia, who seemed just as confused as he was. As his hands slid over Odilia's breasts, her erect nipples tickled his palms. He knew he needed to stop this. He looked at Julie and shook his head.

"We can't do this," Micheal said firmly, removing his hands from Odilia's breasts. He looked back at Odilia. "Odilia, it's late. I think we will call it a night," he switched to back Proto-scandic.

"Good night, Micheal. Good night, Julie." Odilia grabbed her cloak and headed down the stairs.

Once he was sure they were alone, "What was that about?"

"I think you know what that was about," she said in accusation.

He sighed deeply. "You think I'm attracted to Odilia..."

"Aren't you? Hell, after feeling those firm tits, I was tempted to go through with it," she interrupted with a smile.

"You determined I was attracted to Odilia, so you tested me?" he said, mildly exasperated. "What if I had called your bluff?" he chuckled a little.

"I knew you wouldn't."

"I can't believe you took it that far." He shook his head.

"I wasn't originally planning to, but, come on... those were some perfect tits. And I wanted you to experience them," Julie said, removing her blouse.

She grabbed her breasts with her hands, and he was drawn to her enormous, erect nipples. She began gently massaging them between her fingers. "Like I said... I nearly convinced myself to go through with it. Now those amazing tits got me all hot and bothered. What are you going to do about it?" she asked as she slipped her right hand between her legs.

Micheal strode over to Julie. He slid her skirt to the floor and replaced her hand with his, slipping two fingers inside her and using his thumb for extra stimulation. He probed her body with his left hand, finally finding her long, delicate neck. He walked her backwards into the wall, and as she was approaching climax, he lifted her off the ground by her neck. About two minutes later, she tightened in spasms on his fingers, signaling the arrival at the precipice. He spun around, carrying her by the throat to the bed. As he dropped her to the mattress, she sucked in her first breath in a few minutes. As she tried to catch her breath, he began exploring her with his mouth, eventually finding the sweet spot between her legs. Over the next half hour, he worked magic with his tongue, taking her to the pinnacle over and over again. Then she took over.

She pressed him on his back and took several rides on his joystick.

They retired to the balcony. "It truly is color and magic," Julie said of the curtains of light flowing through the clear night sky.

"Indeed it is," Micheal agreed.

Ship of the Gods

The day had finally come, and Julie couldn't wait to hit the open sea. Their new ship, The Valkyrie, was ready for test runs. The entire village was there for the launch ceremony.

"Today, we honor the great warriors of the gods, Lord Micheal and Lady Julie of Avalon. Sent by the gods to deliver us from Fenrir, the wolf demon," Chief Hildebrand announced. "Many days of sacrifice we happily gave to help restore My Lord and Lady's great ship. The amazing ship of the gods!" he finished with great luster.

Advarr began chanting blessings on the Valkyrie as Micheal prepared to release the dry dock. With one fell swoop, the dam collapsed, and the water flowed quickly in, filling the dock and raising the Valkyrie.

"Jules," Micheal indicated for her to board. The chief and queen followed her. Then, the medicine man and his wife boarded, followed by Odilia and Sveinn. Micheal boarded last, retracting the draw plank behind him.

"Take her to sea, Captain Hall. Let's stretch her legs," he instructed her. The system was completely manual but very well-engineered. Julie dropped the sails, adjusting them to the wind, and the Valkyrie began to move into the inlet. She implemented the turbine repulse system when the forward speed reached three knots. It was designed to magnify the force of the water flowing through the turbine to spin a set of propellers at the stern. It was a perpetual motion drive system.

The Valkyrie began accelerating. Soon, they were flying over the surface of the sea, approaching 30 knots. That's when the governor would kick in. They rounded the bend five minutes later, hitting the open Norwegian Sea.

"Truly the ship of the gods," Odilia marveled at the speed they were making.

"Do all Avalonians usually possess such magnificence?" Sveinn inquired.

"Not quite. We are of the noble class. This type of vessel is usually reserved for the elite," Julie said simply.

"Surely the gods have blessed you with wisdom to craft such an amazing ship," Josteinn ventured.

"We have been truly blessed by the gods," Julie agreed. "Micheal, can you take over?"

"Of course." He took the wheel.

"Odilia, can we talk?" Julie indicated for her to follow as she made her way to the bow. "You've been awfully quiet this past week,."

"Well... That whole situation at the Festival of Thanks made me unsure how to interact with you and Micheal." Odilia averted her eyes.

"I'm sorry if you felt that way. You are most beautiful, and I got carried away. But I don't regret it," Julie admitted honestly.

"It's okay; I've been a little occupied of late," Odilia said shyly.

"Who's the lucky man?" Julie deduced.

"Sveinn." Odelia looked past her.

"Aw, the hero of a couple of weeks ago." Julie couldn't help but smile.

"He's a strong warrior; his father is well respected. He's really nice, and... he's quite cute," Odilia blushed.

"I'm happy for you." Julie's plan worked. And Odilia was actually becoming a friend.

"Julie?" Odilia seemed nervous again.

"Yes?" Julie raised a brow.

"I... uh," Odilia stammered.

"Odilia... What is it?" Julie was becoming impatient.

"I was curious, you... well, you felt my... my breasts, and I was curious about yours." Odilia averted her eyes.

Julie tried not to laugh. "Okay. You face the back of the ship." Julie positioned herself so she shielded Odilia. "Now, just reach up under my blouse."

Odilia's cold hands on her breasts made her nipples rock hard.

"They're firm, yet soft... I have a question," Odilia asked, still caressing her breast, seemingly entranced.

"Yes?" Julie touched Odilia's cheek to make Odilia look at her.

"Are you really 81 years old?" Odilia was searching her face.

Julie grabbed Odilia's wrist, stopping her. Clearly, Micheal had told Odilia their ages. "I just turned 82."

Odilia dropped her hands. "How is that possible?"

"We found a fountain of youth. It made us young again," Julie explained, only half lying.

"Of course, the gods blessed you with youth so that you could serve their purpose," Odilia reasoned.

"The gods didn't send us."

"Those chosen rarely understand their calling."

Julie sighed, deciding not to argue Odilia's point. But she hated the idea that she was *chosen* for anything.

Over the next few hours, they put the Valkyrie through its paces, testing all of its systems.

"That looks ominous," Julie said of a storm to the west.

"I think it's time to go," Micheal agreed.

Halfway back, the winds picked up, and so did the waves.

"I guess we get to test how it does in rough weather," Micheal said as the rain overtook the Valkyrie.

Everyone took cover in the cabins. Julie was laser-focused, steering the ship through the rising waves. It was also a race against the sun, as it would likely sink below the horizon within the hour.

The winds gusted over 80 miles an hour as they neared the inlet. And despite rolling the sails up, they had clearly taken a beating, but the ship had performed rather impressively in rough seas.

Now, in the protection of the fjord, the wind was far more calm, and they were able to dock at the pier, which they had adapted out of the dry dock. They had made good time. A small break in the storm had allowed Julie to see they had about half an hour before sundown.

During the fifteen-minute trek back to the village, everyone was discussing the Valkyrie and the storm; Julie realized something wasn't right.

"Everyone stop! Be quiet!" Julie exclaimed.

Micheal stepped up next to her, assessing the situation. "Stay here. We will go see what is going on."

Julie and Micheal stealthed their way next to the wall, then Julie accelerated quickly. She locked arms with Micheal, who tossed her atop the village wall. Upon landing, her new view showed her that they had been invaded.

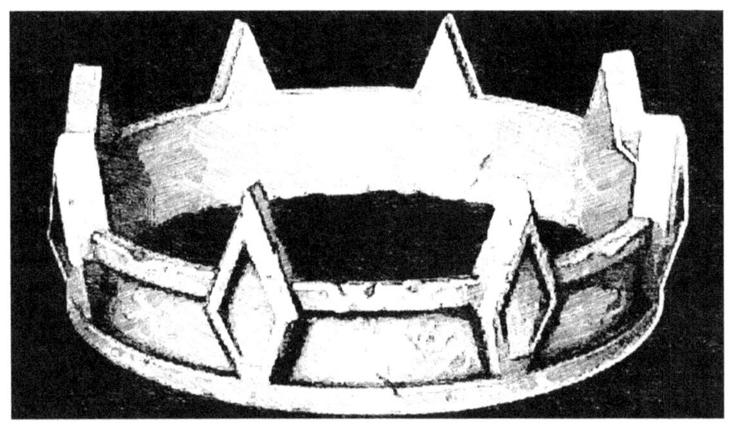

Invulnerable

J ULIE JUMPED DOWN FROM the wall.

"What's the situation?" Micheal inquired with worry.

"The village has been invaded. All the men have been bound. The women and children are being held at sword and arrowpoint, and the captors are loading up all the winter stores."

"How many are there?"

"Maybe three or four dozen."

"I wonder how so few could have taken control of the village in just a few hours." Micheal was confused by such an odd detail.

They returned to the others. "The village has been invaded," Micheal informed them. "Julie and I will go and begin our counter-assault. Wait by the gate, and we will open it from inside."

Micheal swung Julie back on top of the gate, then quickly climbed up to her side.

"What do you think?" he inquired.

"We take the perimeter guards, circling around to meet in the middle. Then make a coordinated assault on the main group. Let's go."

She jumped down. Micheal followed, then tacked in the opposite direction. He systematically neutralized all the perimeter guards, reuniting with Julie on the opposite side of the village.

"Ready?" he confirmed.

She nodded. They drew their bows and arrows and began their assault by unleashing a hail of arrows. To Micheal's surprise, every one of them bounced off. With the arrows being ineffective, they had to switch to hand-to-hand.

As Micheal engaged them, he quickly found that body blows were useless.

"Focus on their heads!" he yelled to Julie.

He re-racked his bow on his back and drew out his retractable staff. He began sweeping his way through the melee. With the way clear, he opened the gates, and the others came rearing for the fight while Julie began releasing the men.

The apparent leader of the invaders sounded a retreat, and they made a hasty getaway. At least they left without any of the village's supplies and about a dozen of their men.

"What are your thoughts?" Micheal asked Julie.

"Their invulnerability to most attacks seemed... superhuman. Except it was limited to the parts of them that were covered. That seems awfully familiar." She was clearly thinking.

"You mean like tripoly clothing?"

They went to the Great Hall, where the captives were being interrogated.

"Who sent you?" Ælfric demanded.

"Ælfric... Let us look at him," Micheal interrupted.

An inspection of the man's clothes confirmed Micheal's suspicions: he was wearing one of Micheal's tripoly shirts, which was like body armor, particularly against the weapons of these times.

"My Lord of Avalon, what interest is this vagrant's clothing?" Ælfric questioned.

"His clothing was once mine. It contains special properties which protect the wearer from harm. Whoever sent them must have recovered our other canister."

"And what exactly was in this... canister?" Chief Hildebrand asked with worry.

"Mostly this kind of clothing that protects the wearer from harm," Micheal explained.

"It is magical?" Josteinn looked in fear.

"Yes. This will make them formidable. And I can promise you they will be back."

"And what do we do against them?" Ælfric demanded.

"Assume that any part of the body that is covered is invulnerable, so target only exposed skin," Julie interjected.

"Julie and I must consult about what else they may have and consider how to counter it." He escorted Julie outside.

"So what else was in that canister?" Julie raised a brow.

"Some of our kinetic weapons. Along with a bunch of other generally harmless things." He was considering the potential usefulness of everything that was in there. "I mean... some of it would allow someone to convince others of their greatness. So they might be able to influence others to follow them or to intimidate them to fall in line." Micheal knew some of the things were like shiny objects.

"So what's our plan?" Julie shook her head.

"What's that about?"

"Sometimes I think it would be better for everyone if we just stayed in whatever time we happened to be in and live out our lives in a reclusive fashion, avoiding people as much as possible." She bowed her head.

"Don't think like that."

"It's true. Look at all the damage we've caused. I'm likely the cause of the Salem Witch Trials, getting 19 people killed in the process. We were responsible for the nuclear apocalypse, ending the Age of Atlantis, and killing over 3 billion people in the process." She was becoming upset.

"It was all part of the timeline. We didn't change any of the actual history."

"And that's supposed to make me feel better?" she flared, tears coming to her eyes.

He wrapped her in his arms. After she cried for a few moments, he said, "Jules, all we can do in this life is try to live the best we can. No one knows the consequences of their actions. Not even time travelers. We make the best decisions we can. You are a good person. There are so many people whose lives were better because of you." He began stroking her hair.

"I don't want to make friends because I'll just lose them. How many have I lost so far?" She cried into his chest.

"The only thing that matters to me is your happiness. If you want to stay and live out our lives in whatever place we happen to be in history, all you have to do is say so. You are the only thing I need. I love you, Jules." He kissed the top of her head.

After a few more minutes, she gathered herself together.

"I think they're waiting on us," she said.

"Okay," he wiped the tears from her cheeks.

"There were several magic weapons inside the capsule," he explained to the council. "It is unknown how many people the king of this group has at his disposal. Julie and I will track down this king. The rest of you need to prepare the village for their return. Now, this is what you need to do..." Micheal laid out their plan.

Magic

"Magic? ... Magic!" Julie balked.

"What was I going to tell them? The truth?" Micheal countered. "They are familiar with magic. I was simply trying to explain it in terms they understand." He justified, playing on their superstitions.

Julie was sick of all the mystical crap. All she wanted was to fix their fuck-up and set sail for warmer climates.

"So, where do you think these raiders were from?" Micheal asked, focusing on the task.

"They came from the sea, so I think Trondheim. So I think that's a good place to start."

"Should we take the Valkyrie?"

"Do you think it's wise to risk it falling into the wrong hands?"

"I think the advantages outweigh the risks."

As they sailed up the fjord toward where Trondheim would be, they came under attack from the shoreline. Julie accelerated toward the two enemy ships, pushing away from the shore. The ships were more like large canoes, about 20-30 feet long. Before the oarsmen could really get going, she rammed them, front on. The Valkyrie cut through like hot butter. Most of the men jumped in the water to avoid the collision. Then she put the reversing motor on to reverse them as both enemy boats sank into the freezing water.

The Valkyrie ran ashore on the sandy beach just before the village gates, and they took cover at the bow beneath the wolf's head at the front of the ship. They both fired an entire quiver of arrows, hitting hands, arms, and legs, crippling many of the men. They jumped down, rolling along the front line of the men. Julie thrashed her way through the forming squadron. She ripped a vicious sweep with their retractable staff, connecting a series of head blows and knocking out several men. Then she stroked low, sweeping the legs out from under those who ducked. She blocked a sword attack and parried into a spinning elbow to the head. She stopped the next man in his tracks, then tossed him into two more coming from her left.

At that point, the remaining men attempted to retreat to their boats. Julie lit some arrows and unleashed them onto the boats. As the flames erupted, consuming the tiny fleet, the men fled into the woods, leaving the injured behind, some two dozen.

As she and Micheal began sweeping through the fallout of the battle, the village gates opened. Not sure what to expect, Julie took a defensive stance. A group of maybe a dozen or so approached with their arms open.

"Thank you!" the leader said, bowing. The others followed suit. "Thank the gods who sent you to liberate us," the man said, still bowing.

Julie looked at Micheal. He surveilled the envoys, then the village. He looked at Julie and affirmed he believed them.

"Rise," he instructed. "Assist us in securing these men."

The villagers dutifully did as he instructed. The occupiers were rounded up and taken inside the village.

Most of the villagers just stared at them in awe.

"What's with them?" Julie asked in annoyance.

"Only a couple of us have ever seen a champion of the gods before," the leader informed them.

"Why would the gods send us?" she balked. "We are not of the gods."

"Many times, the hero knows not their purpose. We prayed to the gods for liberation. Then you arrived to free us," an older woman retorted. "Unless that is not your intention?" A look of doubt came over her face.

"Our purpose is to stop the tyrant," Micheal chimed in.

"Then you are the champions of the gods," the woman stated definitively. "Though it is unusual for it to be a woman, you are moved by the magic of the gods, as you demonstrated against a superior number," the woman fawned.

"Let's see if any of them will talk," Micheal said as they entered the hut where the men were being held.

They interrogated them individually, and the fifth man wanted to talk.

"My Lords, I beg your forgiveness and request your help."

"Our help!" Julie challenged.

"My village has been taken over also. Are you not sent by the gods to free the conquered."

Julie rolled her eyes.

"What is your name?" Micheal requested.

"Odo, My Lord," Odo bowed.

"And what is your name?" Micheal asked the village chief.

"Rainard, My Lord," he bowed.

"Rainard, maintain these prisoners, and we will take Odo to his village."

As they made their way to the Valkyrie, the villagers yelled praises to the gods. Julie considered all the things she and Micheal were capable of. From an outsider's view, she could concede that they would come off as impressive. But when she thought about all the work she put in and all the countless hours it had taken to become as skilled as they were, it was almost pedestrian. Anyone who had done that amount of training would be this good.

They boarded the Valkyrie. Odo looked at them and said, "I hope your magic is better than his."

<u>Copenhagen</u>

Micheal knew why Odo had been so impressed by whoever this king was.

"Micheal, can we talk?" Julie inquired.

"What's up?"

"So this unknown king has the kinetic staffs, my lightning sword, and the kinetic boomerang? What are we going to do against them?"

"I doubt they would be able to figure out how to use them."

"I think they already have. Why else would people think they're magic?”

"You're probably right. At least we know what we're up against."

"We better come up with a plan."

"We will, but you better get some sleep. We have a long way to Copenhagen."

"We're going to Copenhagen?"

"It's the only place that matches Odo's description."

"If that's true, this is the only king who rules from Norway to Denmark. This may be harder than we thought." Julie headed below deck.

A few hours later, they passed out of the inner passage beyond the Island of Smola. The full moon was rising in the east.

"Mani blesses our journey," Odo said as he stepped onto the bridge.

Micheal looked at the moon, which was lighting the way through the dark,

"You imagine the gods care who rules over we lowly people," Micheal challenged.

"Not all the gods agree on everything. King Ragnarr declared the god Loki to be his backer. So, who champions you? Word of your deeds has reached far and wide," Odo informed him.

"We know of no god's sponsorship. And to what deeds do you refer?"

"Travelers from the north told stories of the demon Fenrir's rampages through their villages and the lords from the magical land of Avalon sent by the gods to defeat him... When Lady Avalon demonstrated such incredible skill in my defeat, I knew you had to be the heroes of the war against Fenrir. And if you could defeat the demon of the night, I knew you could liberate people everywhere from King Ragnar's tyrannical rule. Why else would the gods gift you with this magical vessel," Odo said, stepping up to the rail, totally convinced of the validity of his beliefs about them.

The next day, the sun was setting as land came into view. Odo assured him it was his homeland. They centered the channel between Sweden and Denmark, then looped around Amager to the south. They parked in the channel between Amager and Zealand, about a mile south of the settlement.

Odo had detailed the village. It was large, maybe 40 acres, with a population of more than 500. It was built on piles near modern-day downtown Copenhagen. By comparison, their village was around 20 acres with nearly 300 people.

Odo led them to a secret access into the village. They made their way in and found a few men Odo trusted. They then began systematically neutralizing all of the occupiers. They would choke out or knock out a man, and then Odo and his crew would secure them. They worked swiftly through the village, saving the perimeter wall guards and the main gate barracks for last.

Over the course of the sweep, which took maybe half an hour, they took down nearly four dozen occupiers. Now, they were about to hit the guard barracks.

They snuck in and knocked out the century guards. They then were able to choke out about a dozen of the sleeping guards before one woke early and alerted the rest.

Micheal slid into the legs of the rising men, then spun into a capoeira cartwheel. He landed on his feet and delivered an upper-cut on the sweet spot of the first man's chin. He was grabbed from behind, so he threw the man over his shoulders, slamming him hard down on his back. Then he kicked the man in the sweet spot. He kicked a sword out of the next man's hand. He then caught another man's hand, stopping a knife thrust. He punched both men simultaneously in the face and then spun around, taking them both in headlocks and quickly choking them. He dropped them to the floor as he ducked the next attack. He turned, sweeping both men's legs, then delivered a drop elbow to one man's face and kicked the other in the head.

As he rose from the floor, Julie had taken down the rest of the men.

"Looks like the wall guards are all that's left," Julie said with certainty.

"Then let's finish this," he said as they exited the barracks.

"Meet you in the middle?" Julie challenged.

They quickly took down the main gate guards, scaled the wall, and raced around the perimeter, fighting through more than a dozen men each. The last five or ten guards abandoned their posts, fleeing into the village, but they were forced to surrender to the mass of villagers who had emerged.

"Ready to be worshipped again?" Julie rolled her eyes. There was a large crowd staring at them.

"You are always worthy of worship," Micheal tried not to smile. Then he dove off the wall, flipping and landing on his knee. He rose to find Julie by his side.

"Good people!" Odo began. "The gods have sent us salvation. Their heroes, the Lord and Lady of Avalon, have liberated us from the tyranny of King Ragnarr, the puppet of Loki. You've heard of the war against Fenrir. Lady Avalon defeated the demon singlehandedly. Now, they pursue the defeat of King Ragnarr. In a very short time, they took down our oppressors. Now, we should rise to the cause. We should rally to the cause of freedom and help our heroes liberate people everywhere!" Odo finished to raucous cheers.

"We wouldn't want to disappoint the gods, now would we?" Julie said mockingly.

"I guess we shouldn't waste any time then, should we? Micheal said. And they walked to the gate through the parting crowd.

<u>King Ragnarr</u>

After a night of interrogation and a feast in their honor, they learned the location of King Ragnarr's stronghold. It was near where modern-day Bergen would be.

Before dawn broke on the next day, they sailed west out of Copenhagen toward Bergen. They were accompanied by 100 men dressed in their tri-poly clothes, which they had recovered from the guards. This included Odo.

"We shouldn't have made so many tri-poly clothes," Julie said, as she and Micheal observed the men getting comfortable taking hits while wearing their clothes.

"It's not like we were going to have a Macy's around the corner to buy more or a factory to make more," he pointed out.

"Still, did we need so many?" she wondered.

"We never really lost a pod before. So we never really had this problem before," he argued.

"We'll have to be more careful in the future," she decided finally.

As the clock approached midnight, the village became visible in the light of the Aurora. The Valkyrie slipped out of the channel Askoy and the mainland. Julie was on high alert, ready for anything. But the next five minutes passed quietly. They secured the ship and approached suspiciously. It was quiet. Too quiet. The main gate was slightly ajar. They cautiously pushed the gate open.

"Where is everyone?" Julie asked Micheal nervously.

"I have a bad feeling about this. No way would they abandon this village." He seemed certain.

"You think it's a trap?" She was worried.

There was a sudden commotion behind them. Julie turned to see their army stampeding through the gate. She and Micheal spread apart to let them through. They were being pursued by a hoard of men.

As they were funneled toward the main hall in the center of the village, more and more men kept emerging. By Julie's estimation, there were around a thousand. They were vastly outnumbered, and now they were surrounded.

"The Lord and Lady from Avalon, I presume." A modestly tall man, perhaps 5'10", emerged from the crowd. He was a Norseman through and through. His hair was light red, almost orange. He had a long beard and appeared to be in his mid-40s. He was clad head to toe in furs, but his garb was of a finer quality. It had to be...

"King Ragnarr, I presume," Julie said shortly.

"At your service, My Lady," he bowed. "My Lord Avalon, I don't see why we should be at odds. We are both blessed by the gods." Ragnarr tried to convince them.

"I don't think that will work," Micheal began.

"And why is that?" the king challenged.

"Unlike you, we don't desire conquest," Julie countered.

"Conquest? I simply desire to establish order from the chaos.

To improve the lives of everyone." He cocked his head to the side.

"If you're so benevolent, why do you ship the majority of the men off to some distant place to be your occupying force? All you would need to do is show up and demonstrate how to 'improve their lives', and they would happily accept you as their sovereign," Julie mocked him.

"Let's talk of happier things." Ragnarr stared intently at her for a moment. "I can barely see a scar... That was my favorite of your great deeds. The Lady from Avalon, who killed the demon wolf all by herself, even with Fenrir's jaws locked around your neck... The wolf's cloak. Incredible size. The stories are true." Ragnarr appeared genuinely impressed.

"How about you let everyone return to their homes, then establish a great council of all the great chieftains of all the regions. Everyone would honor your great leadership," Julie suggested.

Ragnarr laughed. "A council? That would never work—too many alphas, not enough betas. As the demon wolf proved, there can be only one alpha. And that's me. The great god Loki saw fit to bestow great magic on me to help me establish peace amongst the warring tribes. And that is what I am going to do... My Lady. My Lord. Are you with me?" Ragnarr seemed to be indicating a final offer.

"Odo... You know what to do," Micheal said as he swung his staff into the first of the king's bodyguards.

King Ragnarr retreated behind his guards. Julie turned and began fighting her way through the mass of men who had gathered around them. She was trying to forge an escape route.

She spun her staff like a propeller, then began sweeping legs and cracking skulls with great flourish. She finally punched through the last vestige of the phalanx. Odo was right behind her. He led about half the men through the gap.

Julie and about two dozen men turned back to cover their retreat. At that moment, a bolt of lightning cracked into the heavens. Ragnarr was wielding her sword. She knew their only hope was to get to the king and disarm him. Julie began fighting through the melee. She drew her bow and began firing shot after shot, hitting her marks. Her shot at the king was sent awry by an attack from behind. She had to fight in close quarters for a minute. As she went to draw another arrow, the king's bodyguards closed ranks around him, taking the shot. She fired three shots in quick succession, taking down three of the guards. She was now only 100 feet from the king. She had to dive and roll to dodge a bolt of lightning. As she rolled to her feet, about 50 feet from her target, she stopped before drawing another arrow.

"Lady Avalon!" the king shouted. "I will kill Lord Avalon if you do not surrender!" King Ragnarr threatened, holding a sword to Micheal, who had been stunned by the lightning.

Julie lowered her bow, then dropped it to the ground, raising her hands in surrender. She was taken to the king by several men. Her hands were bound behind her back.

"If she makes one move, kill him," the king instructed his body-guards as he stepped over to her. He stared at her for a moment. A slight smile came to his face. Then he backhanded her across the cheek. She took it, then glared at him. Then he laughed.

"That's for your attempts to kill me," he informed her. "But, wow! What can I say? The real thing was better than the legend." He picked up her bow and looked at it with what appeared to be confusion or perhaps marvel.

"So what now? You kill us?" She scowled.

"Heavens no. I like your fight. I just want you to join me. How-ever, this little misunderstanding can't go unpunished. There are consequences for such actions," he was threatening.

"Like what?"

"We are going to sail the ship of the gods up to your village in the north and execute half the people. And the consequences will only get worse the more you disobey."

"You can't do that!"

"I can. And just know... this is all on you." He had them taken away.

CHAPTER 6: MAGIC WAR

A Hero's Quest

MICHEAL WOKE WITH A pounding headache. He was bound to a pole.

"Water?" he asked the guards.

One brought a bowl of water. Micheal realized he was alone. After a large gulp, he asked, "Is Lady Avalon alive?"

"She's alive!" the second guard seemed irritated. "Now, be quiet!" the man added.

Micheal wondered how bad the king's punishment was going to be. He knew it would come; he needed to escape. Over the next several hours, he efforted to that end... to no avail.

Julie was right. They needed to be more careful in the future. He closed his eyes and just focused on many things. Whether it was part of history or not, his actions still contributed to much death and destruction. While many of these effects were circumstantial, it was still true that they made many questionable choices. Now, another of those choices was about to yield dire consequences. Others would again pay for their actions. He knew this because he was still alive. The king would try to coerce them, just as the Empress of Atlantis had done, leading up to the nuclear war.

After a couple more hours of fruitless effort, he took a break from trying. His mind went to his family and friends 3800 years away in the 21st century. What would they think of his life since then?

He was once again his younger self at his parent's house on New Year's Eve:

"Micheal, I want to talk to you about something," his older sister said, indicating they should go outside.

They sat down on the swing set their father had built in their youth.

"What's up?" he asked as he began swaying a little.

"How are you feeling right now?" she seemed concerned.

"I'm okay," he shrugged.

"I'm not so sure," she challenged.

"What do you mean?" he looked at her.

"You put on a good face for everyone, but I recognize depression when I see it..." She paused, and he averted her eyes. "... You were never a normal kid. It was your genius. You may not know that I looked up to you as if you were my older brother from the time you could talk. You always seemed to know everything, and I always knew you would go on to change the world. Then Amanda got sick. I remember you told me not to worry. You said, 'I will find a cure. There's no way I can fail if I put my mind to it. I promise'. But you were 13. It was far too much to ask for you to cure cancer. And when she died, you never recovered."

He stopped swinging for a second but didn't reply.

"You shut down completely. You spent the last ten years blaming yourself for Amanda's death. You always wanted to be a hero, like in all those comic books we read together. But the hero always faces adversity. They fail; they fall down. What makes them heroes is that they get back up. Fight the good fight. You did that for Amanda. You were her hero. She would want you to get up. To be the hero again." Vanessa touched his shoulder.

"I failed her. I failed you, and the whole family..." he argued.

"You didn't."

"I broke my promise." He shook his head.

"That's not true."

"No? Is Amanda here now?" he replied sharply.

"You promised that everything would be all right, and it is. Amanda said you were her Superman. You inspired her to love life, and she did. She would want the same for you. She wouldn't want this." She alluded to his current life situation as she rose from the swing. "Be the hero Amanda knew you were. You just need to pick yourself up." Vanessa walked away.

He was returned to reality by a woman's voice. "Lord Avalon, wake up." The woman looked to be in her 40s. She had blue eyes and graying blond hair. She untied his bindings. As he got to his feet, she said, "You have to stop my husband. The power of the gods has corrupted him. He has stopped listening to me. He is a monster. I will lead you to Lady Avalon." The queen guided him out of the hut.

They covertly made their way across the village. Micheal disabled the guards.

"Julie, we must hurry," he said, releasing her bindings.

"You escaped your bindings?"

"The Queen. She is helping us."

Just then, the queen entered the hut. "My Lady, Hiln has sent you to protect us from Loki's tyranny. Stop Ragnarr for all of us," the queen pleaded.

"We will," Julie promised.

The queen provided a distraction as they slipped out of the village. They commandeered a long boat and began rowing out to sea. The sun broke over the east as they broke into the open Norwegian Sea. Barely a word was spoken as their endurance was put to the test. They pushed the pace all day, skirting along the coast. By the time the sun set, they had progressed about halfway to Namsos. They decided to rest a few hours on Vigra. He knew where they were because he could see that the strand of islands stretching to the northeast matched those near modern-day Alesund.

They must get going as soon as possible because King Ragnar had half a day's head start, and he had the Valkyrie. Micheal knew if the king had learned the ship's secrets, they would have no chance to reach Namsos in time.

"Micheal! The moon has risen. It's time to go," Julie said, waking him up.

"How long have we slept?"

"Five hours. But we don't have a minute to lose," she said, putting out the fire.

"You're worried we won't make it in time."

"We'll make it!" she retorted, preparing the boat for launch.

They rode through the night. As dawn broke, ominous clouds were streaming in from the west. The winds picked up, and the water became rough. They took shelter in the fjord, which led to Trondheim. They rowed furiously, but as time passed, the storm overtook them. They were fighting choppy waters not far from the village when a large wave caught them and flipped the canoe over. They were put through the spin cycle of a washing machine, and when Micheal hit something hard, everything went dark.

Endurance

Julie was being whipped around like a ragdoll in the vicious surf. She felt a hand grab her arm and pull her toward the shore. She was finally on the beach, but Micheal was not. She caught her breath and began walking into the surf, looking for him. The men tried to stop her.

"No! My husband is in there!" She ran and dove under a breaking wave.

She dove again and again, but she still couldn't find him. Finally, she was hit by something fleshy. It had to be Micheal's body. She reached desperately and finally got a grip on his arm. Suddenly, two other men were helping to drag him to shore.

They laid him on the beach. His eyes were open and lifeless. He had no pulse and wasn't breathing. She brought her fists down hard on his chest, then began CPR. After a couple of minutes, just when all hope seemed lost, she gave him a breath, and his eyes flickered. He turned his head to the side and coughed up some water. She pulled him into her loving embrace, overwhelmed with relief.

"Hi there." She stroked his cheek.

"How long was I out?" he asked, worried.

"Maybe five or ten minutes," she replied, helping him to his feet.

She noticed that the two men appeared stunned and confused. Apparently, they believed she brought Micheal back from the dead.

"The magic of the gods," she explained simply.

They were escorted to the village, where word of their latest deed spread quickly. They refreshed themselves in Trondheim for a few hours or so.

"What's our next plan? How are we going to get to Namsos?" Micheal asked Julie.

"With this storm, I don't think the seas will be an option," Julie concluded.

"Horses then?"

"I considered that, but that would take too long. Perhaps two days?" She shook her head.

"Then how?"

"Have you fully caught your breath yet?" She was studying him.

"Yes."

"Then we run it. What is it? A hundred miles. That's 14 to 15 hours."

"You're right. We have better endurance than the horses... Well, we better get going."

Before they left, Julie decided to address the townspeople:

"Good people! King Ragnarr is attempting to reassert control over this region. He intends to attack Namsos and slaughter half the survivors. And where do you think he'll come next? He travels by sea, and the great god Thor has seen fit to enrage the seas, giving us a chance to stop him. We will also need all who can fight to support us in this endeavor. Gather your horses and make for Namsos. With the aid of Tyr, we shall run nonstop until we have covered the distance. We will meet you on a field of victory! For freedom!" she finished.

The crowd erupted in cheers. Then, all watched in awe as they began their run. Micheal, as the human navigator, led the way.

The sun had set a couple of hours earlier, so it was around 4 PM. They ran all night. As the moon was setting, they reached an arm of the fjord of Namsos. They paused to catch their breath.

"So how much further? Twelve or thirteen miles?" she asked as she gazed over the water being illuminated by the last vestige of moonlight.

"Yes. We have an hour 'till first light. Let's try to get there before then." Micheal seemed determined.

"Do you think we can?" She was a little skeptical about that.

"I think so. Do you?" he challenged.

"I do," she said with doubt.

"Then let's go." He ran down the shoreline.

They were still a ways out when the first light broke, but they could see light from the village in the distance. Just a few more miles, and they would be there. Julie was exhausted by their 500-mile trek in 3 days, but her motivation was again boosted by her sight of the Valkyrie down by the shore. Were they too late?

In less than five minutes, they crept up to the back of the village. Micheal tossed Julie up to the top of the wall. From this perch, she could see King Ragnarr, lining the villagers up and beginning to summarily execute people. She drew her arrow, but just before she let loose, her hand was grabbed by Micheal.

"We only get one shot at this," he said. "We need to get to Ragnarr," he explained, then jumped stealthily to the ground.

They ninjaed their way quickly through the village. When they were about a hundred feet away, Julie saw that Saxa was going to be next. She was only 13 years old. Julie drew, but there wasn't a clear shot at King Ragnarr. The only exposed element was the hand he was about to slit her throat with. Julie let loose, and the arrow found its target. The king yelped as the arrow pierced all the way through his left forearm, causing him to drop the knife. Then he dove for cover as his bodyguards closed ranks around him.

They absorbed three more shots from her bow. She began fighting off attackers from all sides. A second tier closed ranks in front of the first, covering the king's retreat. The rest of the king's men followed him.

Julie looked back to see that Micheal had released the men of the village, and their counterattack had spurred the retreat.

"Thank the gods for your return. King Ragnarr had spoken of your capture," Odilia said after the gate was barred.

"You shouldn't be thanking us. This is our fault." Julie shook her head.

"How," Odilia challenged.

"We were the ones that lost our gifts from the gods. That's where Ragnarr got his magical weapons," Julie informed her. "And all this blood is on our hands." Julie collapsed next to Asta. She was only 16. The king had cut her throat.

The Battle of Namsos

The king had retreated to the Valkyrie, but they appeared to be regrouping. Micheal knew that as long as Rangarr was out there, Namsos would never be safe. They were in the council chamber preparing a battle plan.

"The focus of the battle to come will be me and My Lady against the King," Micheal began. "But we have the advantage. The King's weapons were gifted to us, apparently by the gods. The King found our other capsule, perhaps with the aid of Loki. He has learned their function very quickly. He is formidable," Micheal was explaining.

"If that's true, then this is our fault," Ælfric interrupted the briefing. "We took you as prisoners, which allowed Ragnarr to take these weapons into his possession," he explained.

"We've all made mistakes, but that's not important right now," Micheal countered. "What's important is stopping King Ragnar," he passed the mantle to Julie.

"We will need a few dozen men to cover our flank so we don't have to fight through their entire army. If we can get to Ragnarr quickly, the battle will be short," she admonished them. "Everyone get some rest. They'll attack at first light," Julie closed the meeting.

Micheal was out on the balcony, watching the Aurora. It was quiet, as it typically was before a battle.

"How are you holding up?" Julie inquired as she joined him.

"So many battles we have fought... You know, back in 2010, I never thought I'd be in a battle. Now I've been in so many. I remember them, blow-by-blow. It's worse in hindsight. I can slow it down and focus on every detail. I see their faces. What's worse is I don't even know how many I might have killed. Of course, we try not to, but sometimes..." He could feel the tears behind his eyes. She put her head around him from behind and lay her head against his shoulder.

"You, my love, are a good person. It is terrible when people die at our hands, but as long as we're doing the best we can to only kill when it's absolutely necessary, there's no wrong in it," she tried to comfort him. And though he tried to accept her reasoning, he examined all the times he might have killed. How many of those situations was he in because of careless decision-making?

"Come to bed." She kissed his cheek from behind and then led him to bed.

They suited up for battle but had to use period weapons as Ragnarr had confiscated all of their weapons. Micheal had a bow and sword, but his most important weapon this day would be his staff. As usual, he deplored taking life. So, neutralizing the enemy by non-lethal means was always to be attempted first.

Julie closed her eyes and focused on her center as they took their positions on the wall. Her breathing became slow and rhythmic. She always did this Zen routine before a battle.

Over the past 50 years, she had literally become a warrior. The dangers of time had forced them to become fighting machines; training nearly every day for 50 years had allowed them to master dozens of martial arts forms. While that didn't exactly match Batman's 127 forms, she still thought she could match blows with Bruce Wayne. After all, she had at least twice the practice. From her reckoning, only a few people in history were likely better skilled.

Gabriel, The Phantom, had honed his skill over the better part of a millennium. The same goes for her friend Melina. She could even concede that Katherine Cavendish, who was instructed by Melina personally, along with her centuries of training, was better than they were. But despite all of that, likely the only reason they had survived so many years and so many battles, was she never took any of that skill for granted.

Battles were phrenetic and chaotic. And even though she had single-handedly vanquished thousands of foes, it would take only one lucky shot, and all of that experience would be for naught. So, when the battle begins, she goes into a zone of focus and instinct.

Julie opened her eyes, and the next battle begins.

King Ragnarr walked methodically up to the front of the Valkyrie. Julie's sword was glowing in his hand. He began shooting lightning at the gate, and everyone dove for cover. They had expected such an attack strategy from the king and made sure the gate was coated in flame-resistant coating. But that would only hold out for so long.

Everyone took their positions. Finally, the gate caught fire. Ragnarr's army charged the gate. Their people hit the breaks in the walls, so the only thing that burned was the gate. When Ragnarr's men hit the gate, they were funneled into an ambush. In the gate zone of the village, there was a frenzy of hand-to-hand fighting. Once the majority of the king's army was through the gate, the next step of the plan was implemented.

She and Micheal dropped from the wall into the chaos. They quickly punched through the enemy hoard and out through the gate, flanked by over a dozen men. They rapidly progressed toward the king, who began firing bolt after bolt of lightning at them. After she was able to dodge a few, the king became irritated and cut a wide swath with electricity. He only served to harm his own arming, knocking many of his soldiers down cold. They were closing in, maybe a hundred yards from the Valkyrie, when dozens of long boats began landing on the beach. It appeared the king's reinforcements had arrived. Both she and Micheal could see that 300 warriors could definitely change the odds. They sounded the retreat.

Their rapid retreat ran them into some of the king's men, who were being repelled by the village warriors. Micheal and Julie opened a pathway for them. With the new arrivals, the village was outnumbered 4 to 1.

"Now what do we do," Ælfric demanded.

"Lock your shields in front of the opening of the gate. Force them to fight through hell, and we..." Julie indicated herself and Micheal "... will reach the king the old-fashioned way," she instructed.

Micheal looked at the odds, and they didn't look good. He and Julie had defeated over a hundred foes before, but this was several hundred. He doubted even they were that good. They would try, nonetheless.

They ran full speed toward the oncoming flood of human chaos. They needed to cover as much ground as possible. Micheal began by spraying the mass with a quiver of arrows aimed at their legs. Then Julie ran to his side. They locked arms, and he threw her high into the air. The hoard was temporarily transfixed by her soaring flip, and he used the distraction to knock out several more men. They were a little over halfway to the Valkyrie when one of the King's lightning bolts struck him, and he tumbled to the ground. When he stood up, he was hit by the kinetic disc boomerang, which sent him soaring through the air. He rose again to find himself surrounded by a dozen men. As he spun, surveilling the situation, he saw that the village phalanx was failing, and Julie was also surrounded by dozens of men.

He needed to get to her. He ran and jumped on top of the first man in her direction, then proceeded to run across the heads of the stunned soldiers. He dodged the kinetic disc but couldn't avoid the King's lightning. When he opened his eyes, he was relieved it was Julie helping him up. They pulled out their staffs and began circling back-to-back. As he analyzed the mob surrounding them, he considered how, even after so many battles, he had allowed his hubris to do him in. The village was being overrun. They were hopelessly outnumbered. It was only a matter of time before the overwhelming numbers won out.

Just when the mob began their assault, a loud horn blazed over the battlefield. Micheal looked southeast in the direction of the blast. Silhouetted in the first rays of dawn was a cavalry line. Their friends from Trondheim had arrived.

As they stormed the field, the King's army retreated toward

the fjord. With the pathway opening before them, they ran full speed toward the king, dodging bolts and discs the entire way. The reinforcements from Trondheim had nearly evened the odds, and the two armies began to engage each other.

Now Micheal and Julie were facing off against the King's bodyguards. They had to fight for every inch. While Micheal was engaged in combat by several men, he was blindsided by the disc and sent flying. Micheal immediately swept the legs of the men who attempted to take advantage of his vulnerability. He backhand flipped up to his feet. As he landed, he saw Julie get struck by a bolt of lightning.

The King was suddenly distracted by something on the fjord. Micheal looked past the bodyguards to see Odo leading a fleet of long boats, preparing to hit the King's men from behind.

"Let's go!" he yelled to Julie, who was getting back to her feet.

They used the distraction to cut quickly through the enemy hoard, then Micheal jumped, then sprang off the head of one of the King's men, then swung off the bow of the Valkyrie, and nearly leveled King Ragnarr, who had to jump off the front deck to avoid the impact.

Micheal landed on his feet, and Julie flipped up onto the main deck. The King and two other men were arrayed in a defensive stance, preparing for combat.

There was a loud horn blow from the landing long boats, it was echoed from the village.

"It should not have come to this!" King Ragnarr glared. "We could have been partners," he reasoned.

"The world is not enough," Julie countered.

"What does that mean?"

"In my 80 years, there has never been enough wealth or power to satiate a man of ambition. Someone like you," Julie explained.

"Eighty years?" the King looked back and forth between them.

"You believe the god Loki gifted you these weapons, and the first thing you try to do is subjugate everyone from the northlands. These weapons aren't gifts from Loki. They're ours. We lost them when our ship crashed on the shores. All you have to do is give them back to us, and then everyone can go home," Micheal offered.

"You're lying! Now it's time to find out who's the favorite of the gods!" the King yelled in conclusion as he climbed the stairs to the forward deck.

Michael glanced at the audience, now comprising both armies. Apparently they agreed with King Ragnarr—all other fighting had ceased.

Ragnarr raised the sword, and it was met by a lightning bolt. Then he began directing it at Micheal. Micheal dove over the sweep of electricity and rolled into a sweep of his own. Ragnarr leaped over the attempt. As Micheal slid to his feet, the King kicked him in a glancing blow to his arm. Then Ragnarr blocked his attempted strikes to his face. He was focused on the defense of his only exposed skin, both high and low. Micheal blocked a counter strike by a blow with his left arm, then tried to wrest it away from the King. The King fired a bolt of electricity, which connected, grazing past Micheal's cheek. Micheal tumbled down the stairs to avoid it. Ragnarr jumped from the foredeck, trying to bring the sword down on Micheal's face. He dodged it, then rose to meet the next bolt that Ragnarr fired. The flash shot into the graying sky. Micheal grabbed the King's arms and parlayed his momentum to throw him back up to the foredeck. As Micheal reached the deck, the King rose and fired a bolt at Micheal, who slid underneath it and kicked the sword out of his hand. They both caught it simultaneously, and after a momentary struggle, Micheal activated the sword, and a full-force shock of electricity seared into King Ragnarr's face, and he dropped like a rock. Micheal checked the King, who appeared to be dead—no pulse. Julie appeared on the foredeck; it was eerily silent. A woman's scream shattered the quiet.

Micheal and Julie looked over the mass of people surrounding them and saw a woman and a boy lying motionless on the ground, with burn marks on them. Clearly, they had been hit by lightning.

"Let's go!" Julie jumped over the bow, so Micheal followed her.

A pathway opened up, and they reached the pair quickly. Julie took the boy and began CPR. Micheal started to perform the same on the woman, who was most likely the mother. After a minute, the woman's eyes blinked, and she started coughing. After another tense minute, Julie proved successful, and the boy came around.

As Micheal and Julie rose, the masses around them went to the ground.

CHAPTER 7: ODYSSEY

Empire Falls

DECEMBER 23, 1778 B.C.

With the battle over, there were two days of mourning for the dead. The people from all over the region were unified in declaring that we were their new leaders, but we declined. We are currently on our way to returning the noble classes to their villages.

I worry about what Queen Valdis will think. I know what she said, but she still loved him once. It must be so difficult to lose someone you love to madness.

Speaking of madness, once again, we can't escape fame. Legend of our great deeds has spread to every village we visit. I suppose I'll have to get used to it. It seems a fate I can't change.

P.S. The small death is here.

The Valkyrie cut through the mirror-calm waters of the Bergen Fjord. A greeting party came out to receive them; Queen Valdis was at the head.

"Your Majesty, I'm so sorry it had to come to this," Julie said as the King's body was carried off the Valkyrie.

"Lord and Lady Avalon, the gods sent you to end his tyranny. Now, what shall become of us?" the queen questioned.

"All of the enmities are dissolved. Each village shall govern at their own will," Micheal decreed.

"And what of the Lords from Avalon?" Valdis inquired.

"When the winds of winter subside, we shall sail for home," Julie explained.

"An island of reputed beauty! Perhaps I shall see it someday," the queen bowed. "And I thank you for bringing him home..." she indicated Ragnarr. "... Now, farewell." And she turned to go.

They stood watching as the Bergen people carried the bodies of King Ragnarr and his two lieutenants into the village.

"Why did we do them this service after what they did to our village? We should have left them to rot!" Odilia declared.

"Despite everything, we knew Valdis would appreciate the gesture, and we were only able to escape here because she helped us," Micheal explained. "And everyone needs to learn to live and let live. This entire situation was the makings of one man's actions. We shouldn't blame the rest of them," Micheal admonished.

"My apologies. So where are we off to next?" Odilia asked apologetically.

"My home," Odo answered for them. "My Lady Odilia, I promise it's a place of great beauty." Odo had been sweet-talking Odilia ever since they had met eight days earlier.

"I can't wait to see it," Odilia sounded excited. "It's like a dream, flying over the water on the ship of the gods to an exotic new place."

Julie could tell Odilia was definitely into Odo.

The next day, Christmas Eve, they arrived in Copenhagen

"Odo, it's good to have you back," Dunstan said in greeting. "With the death of Chief Hakon, it has been decided that you should lead us," Dunstan informed them.

"Why me?" Odo seemed at a loss.

"Your leadership in liberating our village and defeating King Ragnarr, as well as your friendship with the heroes of Avalon, showed all of us that the gods favor you," Dunstan explained.

Odo looked over the gathering crowd, then said, "It is my solemn honor to be your new chief," Odo soaked up the adoration. "Please welcome our honored guests, Lord and Lady Avalon, as well as the lovely Lady Odilia," Odo introduced them.

"Welcome back, My Lord, My Ladies," Dunstan bowed.

"Thank you. We come bearing gifts," Julie indicated the ship. Men were sent to unload a massive supply of fish and other seafood. Much of it had already been cooked, and the village of over 500 had a massive feast.

"Merry Christmas, Jules," Micheal kissed her. "Oh, I have something for you," he went to retrieve a package.

"What's this about?" Odilia asked as she and Odo came to join them.

Julie considered for a moment. "On Avalon, we observe Sol Burðr Optar to celebrate the yearly rebirth of life. It is tradition to exchange gifts."

Micheal sat down and handed her a small package. She opened it. It was a fairly large piece of amber. "It's the most valuable item in the region," Micheal informed her. It had both their names carved at the top and bottom. In between were the numbers 51 and 45, which were buffeted around 6. It meant 51 years in the timeline together, 45 years of marriage, and six time locations.

"It's beautiful. It must have taken a lot of effort to make this." Micheal always put so much love and effort into his gifts to her. Now, it was her turn. Her gift felt cheap by comparison. "I'm sorry, Micheal. I didn't have time to come up with something better," she apologized in advance for her gift.

He opened the package and pulled the dagger out of the cloth wrapping. It had an 18-inch blade and was made out of some kind of steel alloy.

"Did you make this?" he asked with interest.

"No, it was given to me by Valdis. She didn't know where Ragnarr got it from, "Julie explained.

"You don't know what the inscription says?" Micheal pointed out some engravings on the blade.

"I don't know. It looked a little familiar, but I didn't remember how to read it," she admitted.

"If my memory serves, this was what Shem's area spoke after

Babel, and at that time, I was speculating this was a forebearer to Hebrew. See, it has the same structure as Hebrew. So if I'm correct, this says, 'The dagger which my father Abraham proved his obedience to God at the alter, and his faith rewarded with posterity,'" Micheal translated.

"What does that mean?" Odo chimed in.

"If I'm right, it means this dagger belonged to Abraham, which means it is a very important religious artifact from a distant land." Micheal didn't really state the details of the significance.

"You really believe it is? It says 'My father'..." she was a bit skeptical.

"Isaac... Isaac was the one who had it engraved. I mean, the timing does fit," Micheal pointed out.

"But how did it come to be here? There is a strong likelihood that Isaac is still alive. Jacob most certainly is." Then she thought they should probably finish this conversation in private. "I'm sorry..." Julie pivoted to Odilia, "... we're boring you. As I had explained earlier, we exchange gifts and reflect on the mini death of Sol and his rebirth, which brings warmth and life back to the world," Julie explained the altered version of Christmas.

"How else do you celebrate?" Odilia seemed interested.

"By having a great feast... This one reminds me of home. A great array of blessings from the sea." Julie had always loved her family's seafood Christmas Eve dinner.

When they left a week later, following their own special New Year's celebration, Odilia didn't come with them.

-January 11, 1777 B.C.

We spent the last week going village by village, dissolving any last vestige of the King's empire, but all of our efforts failed to alleviate my guilt over our indirect damage.

I feel like a living WMD. Everywhere we go, it seems chaos follows. Soon, we will sail for Egypt, and I'm a bit trepidatious. We know we will stick out like a sore thumb. What deleterious consequences will that garner? I'm starting to think we shouldn't go. But how can we not? Who would have believed I would ever get the chance to see Ancient Egypt? I'm more than excited.

P.S. Tomorrow marks 51 years in the timeline and Micheal's 78th birthday.

<u>Return to Avalon</u>

"Praise the gods! ..." Josteinn announced. "... for sending Lord Micheal and Lady Julie to see us through these dark times. It is a sad and joyous day that they must return to Avalon."

Julie stood. "I don't know if the gods sent us or if they have any other plans for us, but I will say I'm glad we were able to help. Everyone here has become as family to us, and we will miss you all. I know this village will be great, and perhaps we will return someday."

As she sat down, Micheal stood to take his turn. He had been trying to think of what to say. They have had to say goodbye so many times. "Saying farewell to people you care about is always difficult. And it's rare that you ever truly say goodbye the right way. I've lived through many more years than you would believe and have experienced many more things than you could imagine. The world is more complex than you could know. And while these kinds of separations may feel permanent, no one is truly ever gone. So, in closing, I will say farewell, and we will meet again someday." Micheal bowed and then indicated for the music and feast to begin again.

The next morning, they set sail from Namsos to a large, somber crowd.

"Do you think we will ever return?" Julie asked him.

"At some point. At least before we leave." He was sure.

"Do you think we should worry about those storm clouds?" She seemed unusually pensive. Then he saw him.

A man was flying in the sky. He had a hammer in his hand. As he rose toward the storm clouds, he began sending sparks of electricity all across the sky.

"I'm pretty sure that's Thor," Micheal decided.

Julie withdrew her sword and fired a lightning bolt into the sky.

"Do you think that was smart?"

Thor began to fly toward them.

"I wanted to draw him over here," Julie explained. Before he could admonish her, Thor arrived above them.

"The heroes from Avalon!" Thor exclaimed.

"And you are Thor, God of Thunder?" Micheal raised a brow.

Thor was levitating 20 feet above the ship. "I am."

"Everyone says the gods sent us. Do any of the gods back us? Do you?" Julie challenged.

"I have followed your progress. You are most impressive. Worthy to champion the gods," Thor answered with a nod.

"You saw, and yet you did not intercede?" Julie seemed upset.

"It's not for the gods to interfere," Thor retorted.

"If you really are a god!" Julie jabbed. "Cause many thought Ragnarr was."

He laughed. "I love your spirit, Lady Avalon..." Thor looked her up and down. "Perhaps you and your friend Odilia have that in common." Thor raised a brow.

Micheal had had enough of Thor's innuendos. "One more comment like that, and we may have to test your divinity." Micheal threatened.

Thor stared at him for a moment, then broke into a chuckle, "The heart of a champion, indeed... Well, it was an experience to meet you. And send my congratulations to Lady Odilia on her special day.

"And that's another thing..." Julie replied, "... you used your so-called divinity to take advantage of Lady Odilia."

"She seemed to rather enjoy our encounter. So, how could I be taking advantage of her? Besides, it's my right as a god," Thor argued. "Would you like me to demonstrate?" Thor smiled as he admired her again.

"That's enough!" Micheal's anger boiled over. He threw the kinetic boomerang at Thor. Thor dodged it, then came back laughing.

"Once again, give my best to Lady Odilia." Thor seemed to prepare to leave.

"What special day?" Micheal asked curiously.

"She is to be wed. Now... bring the rain!" Thor shouted as

he began to climb toward the heavens. Then electricity flashed across the sky, and the downpour began as he disappeared into the clouds.

As they reached the Norwegian Sea, Julie asked, "So, what did you think of Thor?"

"I don't know. Although I believe anything is possible, I have a hard time believing in these mythical gods. I think we're missing some element here." Micheal went over all the crazy things he had seen in his life and tried to imagine if it really was that unlikely.

"We've experienced some strange thing over the years," she seemed to read his mind. "I will just say, whether he's a god, an alien, or perhaps a time traveler... or something else... he seemed to pull it off."

Micheal shrugged.

Two days later, they arrived in Copenhagen.

"Micheal, Julie, welcome back," Odo said as they entered the Great Hall.

"Looks like a major celebration," Julie said of the decorations.

"It's our wedding day!" Odilia said, entering the Hall.

She certainly looked like a bride, for the times, at least. She wore a colorful blouse and skirt with a large bronze disc plate. Her hair was pulled back on the sides with combs and she had makeup highlighting her piercing blue eyes, as well as her cheekbones, surrounding her petite nose.

"You look amazing, My Lady," Micheal kissed her cheek.

"We are so glad you are here for our special occasion," Odilia beamed.

"We had a run-in with your favorite god," Julie cut in.

"Her favorite god?" Odo seemed confused.

"Thor..." Micheal informed him, "... he came to see us off from Namsos."

"He did?" Odilia seemed surprised. "So he was backing you," she concluded.

"The God of Thunder chose his champions well," Odo said in compliment.

"He said to congratulate you on your most special day," Julie informed them.

"He said that?" Odo seemed more than flattered. "How did he know we were getting married?" Odo seemed suspicious.

"He's a god," Odilia reasoned. "It's time, my love," she pivoted.

They swore their oaths before the gods, and the party ran into the night. Micheal and Julie spent the next day with the new couple, and then it was time to say goodbye.

"Odo, it has been a pleasure to know you. And the people chose well," Julie complimented. "Odilia, I know we didn't immediately become friends, but I found a genuine soul in you," Julie touched her arm.

"We did get very close, didn't we?" Odilia winked, and they both laughed.

"I will miss you," Julie took Odilia into her arms.

"As will I. Perhaps we will visit Avalon someday," Odilia smiled.

"I would love that," Julie responded.

"Odo," Micheal bowed, "there is no one better to lead these people and to care for Odilia." They put a hand on each other's shoulder. Then Micheal stepped over to Odilia. "My queen," he bowed and took her hands. "In the better part of a century of life, I have called 'friend' fewer times than fingers on my hand. Finding such a complimentary soul is rare, and I am terrible at saying goodbye. And this is the hardest one ever."

"Hugiun and Muniun will hold our friendship against time and distance. This does not end here. We will see one another again," Odilia promised, tears streaming.

"Yes, we will. Until then, farewell, Odilia." He kissed her.

"The sea calls us home," Julie interjected.

They boarded the Valkyrie and stood on the aft deck. The sails dropped, and the ship began slowly west. They watched until their friends were out of sight.

"Then into the west, we go," Micheal referenced Lord of the Rings: Return of the King as they turned to their future.

<u>Spring Equinox</u>

Two days and a night after leaving Copenhagen, the white cliffs of Southern England were blazing in the rising sun.

"We have until dawn tomorrow to reach Stonehenge, but we probably have to navigate River Avon in the daytime, so we have to hurry," Micheal informed Julie.

"I'm not so sure it's such a good idea. Isn't it already a big religious ceremonial event? Won't these people think we are intruding on their holy site?" Julie worried.

This wasn't the first time she had disagreed with Micheal about one of his desired experiences. Tomorrow was the Spring Equinox.

"We don't even have to interact with anyone, and we are unsure what language they speak. It could be Ancient Gaelic, or it could be something else. If it's Gaelic, we would be okay. But all we need to do is sneak to Stonehenge and watch the sunrise, then be on our way with no one the wiser," he tried to convince her.

"Yeah, like we're ever that lucky," Julie resigned herself to the task at hand.

By noon, they were breezing through the channel, north of the Isle of Wright, *en route* to the mouth of the Avon, east of the modern-day Bournemouth.

"Are you sure this river can handle the Valkyrie? It looks rather small," Julie paused at the entrance to the river.

"From what I recall, it's 50 feet wide at its thinnest, but it's usually about 100 feet. If we were in the 21st century, I would say it would be too shallow, but this period is wetter than ours. So by my calculations, it should be deep enough," he explained.

"That makes me feel better about this. How could you possibly account for something like precipitation?"

"It's based on the rivers we encountered in Norway. The weather patterns are not that different," he reasoned.

"We could moor here and walk it. It's only 30 miles. We could do that in 5 to six hours," Julie countered.

"I would rather navigate the Valkyrie up the Avon and spend the night on her rather than out there somewhere. And then it's only a mile to Stonehenge..." he was being stubborn. "... How about this. We take the Valkyrie upriver; the first time you think it's too risky to continue, we stop and go the rest of the way on foot."

Julie thought for a moment. "Fine. But the first time, I'm adamant, I don't want any argument," she stated firmly.

"Absolutely."

"So you get to captain, and I will be judging," she said as she prepared for a short ride.

As the hours passed, Micheal proved to be very adept at steering up the river. There were only a couple of questionable places, and they reached a sharp bend to the east as the sun was setting.

"I think we have arrived," Micheal slowed them down, mooring them to the north bank. "So tomorrow we set sail for Egypt," Micheal began.

"This is one of the things I've most looked forward to," Julie considered as the solar disc kissed the horizon.

Their conversation was cut short by the arrival of a crowd of people.

"Their language sounds familiar. It's similar to Proto-Scandic." Julie focused on the discussion amongst the crowds. And while there were differences, they were similar.

"Lord and Lady Avalon!" someone yelled from the crowd in Proto-Scandic.

Julie looked for a familiar face and found Katla there. She had been at Copenhagen when they were dissolving the king's empire. Katla fought her way to the front of the crowd.

"My Lady. Have you come for the festival of the sun?" she asked.

"Yes," Julie confirmed.

"We are so honored! Allow me to translate for you," Katla seemed to recognize that they might not speak the language.

"That would be very appreciated," Micheal agreed.

Katla stepped up onto the Valkyrie and faced the crowd. Then, the man who seemed to be in charge raised his arms, and the crowd went silent. After speaking for a while, Katla came over and filled them in on what she had told the crowd.

"I told them you are the heroes of the gods. I detailed some of your great feats and informed them of your desire to honor the sun with us," Katla explained.

"We are grateful, but we are a little surprised that you are here," Julie wondered.

"I am a trading representative for my people. We were in Copenhagen when the king attacked. We owe our freedom to you," Katla informed them. "Please join our celebration."

The party ran all night long. No one slept. When the first light of dawn appeared on the eastern horizon, everyone made a procession to Stonehenge.

Seeing the stones brought back memories. It had been almost 200 years but Katherine's eyes stared blankly from her dead body. George's scream echoed in her ears. The spirits of their death match to end the Age of Atlantis. A nuclear flash washed out the scene and Julie's steps faltered.

"Are you all right?" Micheal asked.

"Six years ago, this is where the world ended. 175 linear years have masked the truth of this place."

"I'm sorry Jules, I should have considered that."

"Non of these people even know. The world that time forgot."

"It's okay, we can leave." Micheal took her hand.

"Isn't it beautiful?" Katla asked.

"Quite impressive," Julie said, squeezing Micheal's hand. He looked at her. "We'll stay." She said in English.

They all began a ritual dance around the stones. Katla instructed them on what to do. Julie found it quite beautiful. They finished one final cycle; then, everyone fell flat to the ground.

"As our special honored guest sent by the gods, we would be honored if you took the place of honor in the center of the stones," Katla directed them.

"Are you sure?" Julie felt like they were intruding.

"Of course. It is a rare honor for such heroes to attend the Sun," Katla assured them.

They stepped into the center of the stones next to the altar. As the sun broke over the horizon, the light began to flood the center of the circle. They were situated on either side of the altar.

"Please take each other's hands," Katla prodded. The priest drew a dagger out of his robe. Julie became nervous.

"It's ok, My Lady. It's a small offering of blood to the sun," Katla tried to assure them.

The priest stepped forward and cut each of their wrists. Micheal locked eyes with Julie as their blood dripped to the altar. After a minute, the bleeding ended, and the sun was nearly a full disc on the horizon.

Another minute passed, and the final sliver of the sun broke the horizon. At that moment they became bathed in light, and a most stunning thing happened. Their amulets from Eden began to glow. The light seemed to begin to emanate directly from them. It suddenly burst into a cornucopia of colors that lit up the entire stone circle as if it were a rainbow.

The reaction from the attendees indicated that this was not the usual experience. It was one of the most magical, beautiful things she had ever seen. The effect began to fade as the sun slipped above the horizon. Then it was gone.

With the ceremony over, they said their goodbyes and sailed down the Avon. While she had originally been against this detour, Julie was incredibly glad they had participated in this special celebration.

<u>Odyssey (Knossos)</u>

Three days after Stonehenge, they sailed into a familiar place—the secret cove where they had hidden their technology and resources on Gibraltar before the bombs fell.

"It's been a long time," Micheal commented as they opened the secret port.

"The last six years felt like decades in the wasteland and frozen lands," Julie seemed relieved to be back in business with their disguised technology.

"We better be careful. We don't want the Egyptians to think we are gods, do we?" Micheal laughed.

"Absolutely not! It's going to be bad enough with how we are going to be so different; we will be like neon signs," Julie agreed.

"Okay. Let's start retrofitting the Valkyrie. It's probably going to take a few weeks," he estimated.

"I'm okay with that. We need some quiet time together before we go back into the fire, as it were." She seemed to be refreshed by the luxury of the secret facility. "So what do you think happened at Stonehenge?" Julie returned to the unusual reaction of their amulets.

"I've gone over everything, and the best explanation I can come up with is... now this is just speculation... is that the amulets are a balance between life and knowledge, and during the equinox, there was a balance of light from the sun. These things harmonized and caused the amulets to absorb the light energy. As the moment of singular balance was struck, the amulet released the energy as a spectrum. Then, when the balance shifted slightly, the singularity ended," Micheal finished. "But that's just a theory."

"Whatever it was... it was magical." Julie was marveling at the experience again.

A month passed, and they were just about to depart for Egypt.

"Hey, Jules, we've gotta hit the studio one last time before we return to the ancient world."

They went into the studio and just randomly picked songs for the pleasure of singing.

"... What song should we sing next?" Micheal asked.

"How about... *Don't Know Much?*"

"Linda Ronstadt and Aaron Neville," he confirmed.

The song brought him back to his childhood. They finished in perfect harmony.

"I think that song sums us up perfectly," Julie commented.

"Maybe. Except for the whole 'years are showing' line." They both laughed.

"Only..." she touched his cheek, "... I can see it." She traced the features of his face with her finger. He grabbed her hand and pulled her closer, searching her face, finding the truth in her features.

"The years have only made you more beautiful. The more I know you, the more I love you. And the more I love you, the more beautiful you become." He kissed her, and they made full use of the studio.

The next day, they sailed east toward Egypt. After a four-day journey, they were preparing to arrive in Egypt the next day.

"So, do we know who the Pharaoh is right now?" Julie asked him.

"That's not really clear. In our time, Egyptologists disagreed on who ruled when, with a margin of error of up to 300 years. Our best reference point is Pharaoh Sesostris, whom we met in 1952 B.C. He was on the King lists in the 12th dynasty. Most histories have that dynasty ending 25 years ago..." Micheal explained.

"So, who ruled after them?" Julie cut in.

"... it was the second intermediate period. And the Pharaohs and their domains are unclear. So, who knows who's ruling? And if it is the intermediate period, it's chaotic. Dangerous..." he had continued.

"I think we need to return to this once we deal with the immediate danger," Julie turned his attention to the storm closing in from the Southeast.

They were just west of Crete. Micheal guided the Valkyrie north of the island in an attempt to use it as a shield and bypass the storm. But as the seas only became worse, he steered toward a light on the darkening horizon. They locked the Valkyrie down as they began mooring the ship. Just as it was secured, they were boarded by a squad of guards. The leader spoke in some unknown language, which Micheal had to believe was Minoan. After they indicated no comprehension, the man paused a moment, then said, "Do you understand me now?" in Linear A Greek.

"We do," Micheal replied in kind.

"Will you please follow me," the man said, as more of a command.

They were escorted about an hour's walk to a grand palace through a city. Micheal tried to determine their location, but the city was so large it could only be Knossos.

They were announced in Minoan as they entered the throne room. The king sat on the throne. He appeared to be in his 40s. He had olive skin, black hair, and curious eyes.

"Welcome..." he began speaking in Greek. "... Approach," the king instructed.

They slowly made their way forward with their heads bowed.

"Be at ease. You are welcome guests in my lands," the king said, and Micheal looked up. "Where do you come from? What brings you here?"

"We are from a land called Avalon. We came seeking shelter from the storm," Micheal explained. "We meant no imposition. With your leave, we shall depart in the morning."

"I wouldn't dream of putting you out so quickly. You will remain my guests. Allow me to show you the hospitality of Knossos," the king said. Then, he added, "You must be weary from your long journey." He signaled for them to be escorted out.

Once they were alone, "What do you think?" Micheal asked.

"I think we are prisoners," Julie said. "Are we ever gonna get to Egypt?" She shook her head.

"Yes. We are just a day's sail away. But I do welcome the chance to experience the Minoan culture. And I doubt they could stop us whenever we decide to leave." Micheal was confident.

"You underestimated King Ragnarr. Aren't you doing that again?"

"King Lykos doesn't have our technology. He has no idea about our capabilities," he tried to convince her.

"I suppose." Julie wasn't persuaded.

The weeks passed, and they were given a grand tour of Crete. It was amazing and beautiful. They were also included in various cultural ceremonies, but Micheal was concerned—they were never allowed to go to the Valkyrie.

Julie became determined as the anniversary of their arrival into the 18th century came and went.

"Your Majesty. We have been honored by your hospitality, but I am afraid we must depart in the morning," Julie said as they ate dinner, catching Micheal off guard.

"I hope you have enjoyed our hospitality. And I do wish you good fortune on your voyages." The king's reaction was also unexpected.

As they were escorted back to their chambers, Micheal felt a hard blow to the back of his head, and everything went dark.

Micheal squinted against the pounding in his head. When the fog cleared, he saw Julie lying on the ground. He roused her and helped her to her feet. As he did, King Lykos appeared overhead.

"My Lord and Lady from Avalon, I desire your ship. However, I am a fair arbiter. Should you survive my labyrinth, I shall send you on your way with my blessing... Good luck!"

Lykos gave a signal, and Micheal could hear something coming. He realized they were in an arena maze. A giant male lion came around the corner. It charged them. Julie jumped over the pouncing beast, and Micheal slid to the ground, sliding under it. The lion came back around. Micheal signaled Julie, and when it pounced again, Micheal went to his knees and caught the beast's front legs just behind the paws. He leveraged its momentum to flip it and slam it hard on its back. Julie timed her landing to bring full force down on the lion's rear leg. Its reactive scream proved the effect. Both Micheal and Julie rolled away from the lion's reach. It limped to its feet, roared, then came at him. Julie stopped it short as it was about to reach him by grabbing its tail. Micheal flipped to its back and dug his thumbs into its eyes. As he jumped off, it scratched his leg below the tri-poly pants. Micheal signaled their next attack to Julie as the injured monster lashed out wildly.

Micheal charged the lion, shoving his forearm into its mouth. It hugged him with its front paws. At that moment, Julie kicked the beast hard to the spine, just between the shoulders. The forearms dropped limp, and the lion released his arm with a yelp. Julie's kick obviously did major damage to its spine. The lion was clearly crippled. Micheal quickly wrapped his arms around its head, putting it out of its misery in one quick twist.

The court sat in stunned silence, as with minimal injury, they dispatched both a black bear and a Bengal tiger. As they came to the end of the maze, the exit was blocked by a bull. The exit zone was about 20 feet across. The bull pawed the ground and then charged. They both jumped to avoid the horns, but Julie barely missed, and she fell to the ground. The bull immediately turned on her. Micheal jumped on its back and grabbed its horns. It bucked and threw him off, and he rolled to his feet. He immediately took a charge to the chest, knocking him back to the ground. As it was about to butt him with its head, Julie kicked it in the neck. It swung around and tossed Julie into the air with its horn. As she got up, it crushed her against the wall. Micheal ran over and side-kicked the bull's ankle. The bull turned back toward him. He rolled away from its stumbling charge. Micheal pulled Julie over to the entrance of the exit zone. It charged right at them. Julie slipped into the maze path. Micheal waited until the very last second to dive out of the way. The bull ran headlong into the corner of the opening. It was clearly dazed.

"Grab the bull by the horns!" Micheal yelled. "You take the right, I'll take the left!"

Micheal slid under as Julie flipped over the top, ripping the horns rapidly in the same rotation. The torque snapped the bull's neck. It fell hard to the ground, and Micheal helped Julie to her feet as the door opened.

"Who are you?" King Lykos just stared at them in awe.

"People you don't want as enemies. You're lucky we don't hold grudges," Julie said shortly. "We're leaving on our ship now. Any attempt to stop or delay us and you will find us your enemy," Julie warned.

Battered, bruised, and bleeding, they were escorted to the Valkyrie.

As they rounded the east end of Crete, with the sun setting on the horizon, Julie said, "I hope we have a better reception in Egypt." She was clearly disheartened.

Micheal embraced her from behind. "I promise it will be. It's going to be amazing," he assured her.

PART II: ANCIENT EGYPT

CHAPTER 8: SOBEKNEFERU

A FTER THEIR HORRIBLE EXPERIENCE on Crete, Julie was a bit leery of the reaction they would receive in Egypt.

"Cheer up, Jules, we're finally here," Micheal said as they entered the Nile near Rosetta.

She gazed out across the Delta as the sun sat low over the Eastern horizon. She slowed the Valkyrie to 20 knots. They raced past many small boats. All the occupants gawked at the impressive ship. Even at six in the morning, many farmers were out harvesting their fields.

"How long til we reach Giza?" Julie was curious.

"At our current speed, we'll get there in eight hours.

They were already conversing in Ancient Egyptian to help her refine her lexicon.

By the time they reached the coming together of the Nile and the Damietta branch, the noonday sun shined down on the pyramids of Giza to the south. The great pyramid was blazing white with a crown of gold. Julie slowed the ship to ten knots as the midday traffic on the river was crowded.

Over the final two hours on the route to Memphis, it became clear to her that there would be no anonymity, as they were the largest ship on the river. It was early afternoon when she brought the Valkyrie to a stop at a peer on the West bank of the Nile, banking the city of Memphis.

Julie had butterflies of excitement filling her stomach as they gazed at the impressive and beautiful city of perhaps 50,000 people. It was one of the two largest cities in this ancient world, Thebes being the other.

"Are you ready for this?" Micheal took her hand.

"You know I am," she said excitedly.

While the 90-degree heat was obvious, their temperature-controlled tri-poly clothing made her comfortable, even in her wolf's skin cloak.

"Halt! State your business," a man, likely the harbor master, demanded.

"We come for trade," Micheal replied, handing him a pouch filled with Amber.

The man seemed surprised by Micheal's reply in Egyptian. Then, he examined the stones with wonder.

"Go about your business," he waved them into the city.

"Can you believe this?" Julie asked as they walked down a main street. She was captivated by the towering temples and what had to be a palace.

The array of colors was striking. It almost didn't feel real. After a short walk, they came to a crowded market. The many merchant stalls were shaded by a panacea of color, billowing in the breeze like the sails of a fleet of ships. They definitely stuck out like a sore thumb. They were the subject of many stares and much speculation. She could hear many conversations discussing them. Most of the women were topless. Most of the people, in general, wore very little clothing.

"I will give you one of these for two of those," Julie held out a copper nugget in offer for two pieces of fruit.

"I agree," the merchant accepted happily.

They ate their plums as they walked through the market.

"Over here, My Lady!" a woman exclaimed from a small shop.

Julie saw some jewelry that looked interesting.

"Micheal, come on!" She pulled him after her.

"This one I think for you, My Lady," the woman showed her a usekh.

She examined the piece and then asked about another.

"This one is quite extravagant," the woman displayed it for her.

The first had been made with beads; the second was made of gold with gems placed throughout.

"I will take it... And this for my husband," she grabbed a ruby-eyed serpent bracelet for Micheal.

They haggled over the trade but came to an agreement.

They walked the market for an hour or so, acquiring several other trinkets.

"That smells good," Micheal indicated, a restaurant cooking fish over an open flame. "Two of those..." Micheal said, pointing to the fish. "...And two cups of pomegranate juice," he added as they sat beneath the cloth shade.

"The view is amazing!" Julie looked out at the Giza plateau.

She visited Egypt in 2008 and thought the pyramids were impressive then. But here, 3800 earlier, they were nothing short of spectacular. White cover stones created perfect pyramids that almost appeared unreal, and a gold top adorned the pyramids. She could understand how these people believed the pharaoh was a god.

"Isn't it?" Micheal replied. "Now, certainly, it was a trip when we were in the Age of Atlantis, but this is the first time we can really try to compare what historians believed what an ancient time was like and what the reality is." He scanned their surroundings.

"This pomegranate juice is amazing!" She was savoring the sweet yet tart flavor.

"The fish is pretty good also," he finished his last bite.

They paid handsomely, then just sat there watching the people go about their business. Julie noticed the children wore no clothes, and pretty much every one of them stopped in their tracks and stared when they saw her and Micheal.

"What are you?" a little girl asked.

"I'm Julie... What's your name?" she inquired.

"My name is Tiye. Are you a goddess?" the girl asked.

"No... I am from a distant land... It's a beautiful name."

The girl appeared shy, and then someone called her name, and she ran away.

"Do you know what that temple is?" she asked Micheal.

"It's devoted to Ptah, the god of craftsman," he informed her. "It's the patron god of Memphis."

Their conversation was interrupted, "Friends from distant lands, welcome to Kemet. My name is Senewosret-Ankh. I'm vizier to our Holy Pharaoh." Senewosret introduced himself. The harbor master was beside him.

She and Micheal rose from their seats.

"I am Lord Micheal, and this is Lady Julie. We are visiting from the Island of Avalon." She and Micheal bowed.

Senewosret looked confused, "I have never heard of this place." He raised a brow.

"It is far beyond the sea to the north. It is not some great power like this land. It is rather small," Micheal explained.

"If all of this is true, then how do you know our words so proficiently?" the vizier inquired suspiciously.

"Many years past, an explorer from Avalon visited this land. They brought this language back with them. As well as stories of the impressive nature of the land of the Pharaohs," Julie chimed in.

"It is obvious by your manners and dress that you are of some importance from this Avalon. It is customary for visitors of such stature to pay tribute to the Pharaoh. Will you accompany me and Bomani to the Pharaoh's court?" the vizier invited them.

"We are humbled by giving us such station, and we would be honored to give tribute to the Pharaoh," Micheal agreed.

"Follow me," Senewosret instructed.

They followed him to the docks, "Your ship, I presume?" the vizier led them to the Valkyrie.

"It is," Micheal confirmed.

"The Pharaoh's palace is two leagues upriver. Perhaps you might ferry us up to the palace," the vizier requested.

"We would be honored," Julie led the way while one of the men with the vizier was instructed to take care of the vizier's boat.

"Your ship is so grand!" Bomani was looking at the Valkyrie the same way they had been looking at Memphis.

"Where is your crew?" Senewosret seemed confused.

"We designed the Valkyrie to be operated by one person," Julie said as she stepped to the controls on the bridge.

"What is this ship made of?" Bomani was examining the railing on the deck.

"The main body of the Valkyrie is constructed out of a combination of metals," Micheal was intentionally vague.

"Like bronze?" the vizier supposed.

"Something like that," Micheal agreed.

An hour of curious chit-chat later, and they came upon a magnificent structure.

"Okay, through that opening. I will ensure our arrival," the vizier headed to the front of the ship.

The palace was quite grand. It seemed to Julie to be on par with Versailles in opulence. The gardens spanned a good half mile of the river. It had high banks to avoid the flooding season.

"Dock just there," the vizier directed.

So now they would meet the Pharaoh. But who would it be?

<u>Sobekneferu</u>

As they were about to exit the vessel, "Vizier Senewosret-Ankh, we came with gifts for the Pharaoh," Micheal informed him.

"What gifts?" The vizier seemed curious.

"We have this..." Julie laid a wolf skin down.

"... As well as this..." Micheal laid a sheathed sword down on the wolfskin.

"And also this..." Julie laid a chained headpiece down. It was made out of titanium and adorned with cut amber.

"These are quite spectacular! But the sword, I must carry," the vizier insisted.

Micheal bowed in agreement.

From the dock, they climbed a large staircase and passed through a gate that was flanked by two obelisks. They entered a grand courtyard with a grand reflecting pool. The entire courtyard was around 300 feet long and 150 feet wide. Columned walkways flank the pool. Then, they entered an inner courtyard with numerous statues. The entire palace was decorated with hieroglyphs.

They continued into a large foyer, which was even more lavishly appointed and illuminated by oil lamps. They were instructed to wait as they reached a doorway into a huge hall. The vizier disappeared into the chamber. A few moments later, he returned.

"Walk to the base of the steps and bow before the Pharaoh. Remain in that position unless otherwise instructed," the vizier explained.

Micheal noticed that Vizier Senewosret-Ankh gave two women servants the wolfskin and the chain, and he assumed the sword. The vizier led them into the chamber as Micheal heard them being announced.

"From the distant, exotic land of Avalon, Lord Micheal and Lady Julie!"

As they followed the vizier, the courtroom was flanked by the courtiers crowding between the pillars, trying to see these exotic visitors.

Micheal was a bit surprised to see a woman sitting on the throne. He quickly went through the king lists in his head. It had to be the Beauty of the Crocodiles, Sobekneferu. She looked about 40 years old. She had dark skin and slightly slanted brown eyes curiously gazing past her thin, pointed nose. She was fully decked out in the Pharaoh regalia and was being fanned with palm fronds by several servants. The chamber was huge, perhaps 150 feet and 100 feet wide. As they reached the bottom of the stairs, they both went to one knee.

After a moment, the Pharaoh spoke, "Rise."

They did as commanded but kept their heads bowed.

"The vizier tells me you are from beyond the sea, and yet you know our words," Sobekneferu questioned.

"We are of the seas. Far and wide do we journey. Many words can we speak," Micheal replied.

"You may look at me," the Pharaoh permitted. "I've never seen your like before. You are so pale." She seemed to be studying them.

"From our distant land, there are many times when the great light of the heavens is absent from our sight," Julie finally spoke.

"Let me see your faces," Sobekneferu said.

Micheal looked up at her. The Pharaoh came down the steps, examined him, and then went to Julie. "Your eyes are as the sea... You are a race of giants?" the Pharaoh inquired.

"Not all of us are so tall," Julie admitted.

"Only those of high stature," the Pharaoh concluded. "My vizier informs me you come bearing tribute." She looked past them.

"Yes, your holy eminence..." Micheal stepped aside, and the first servant came forward. "The skin of a fierce beast called a dire wolf..." the fur was held out for her to examine.

"The same as what you are wearing," the Pharaoh pointed out.

"... Indeed. And this is a wolf pin..." Julie indicated the silver pin. "... This is a loose crown of Avalonian silver, adorned with a rare gem called amber..." Julie continued as the other servant stepped forward.

Sobekneferu picked up the chain, staring at it with wonder. Then she looked at the crowns both Micheal and Julie were wearing.

"And finally..." Micheal began as vizier Senewosret brought the final gift forward. "... a sword from our land. It is made of steel silver and is engraved in our native language..." Micheal began as the vizier presented the weapon, with the hilt toward the Pharaoh.

She inspected the gem-encrusted end of the sword and the leather-bound grip. The sapphires glistened as she began to slowly unsheathe the blade.

"A god to rule men," Micheal said in Proto-Scandic, then translated into Ancient Egyptian. The Pharaoh closely studied the runes.

"We find your tribute pleasing. Repeat the inscription in your tongue," she implored him.

He did as instructed, and then she repeated the phrase in Proto-Scandic as she raised the sword above her head. Then she looked at them and said, "You will remain honored guests here at court. Senewosret-Ankh will see to it. Now... before we sit down to dinner, the vizier informed me of your very impressive ship. Will you show me?" Sobekneferu gave a signal, and an escort of guards instantly moved to chauffeur her on a litter.

The processional made its way out to the docks. As the Pharaoh stepped off the litter onto the docks, she commented, "The land of Avalon must be prosperous indeed..." Sobekneferu gazed up at the wolf's head at the bow. "... Can you build such a ship for me?" She looked at Micheal.

"It could be done." He weighed the options in his head.

"Will you give me a tour?" She stepped onboard.

"We would love to," Julie replied.

"Senewosret, we shall dine on..." she looked at them.

"... The Valkyrie," Micheal finished for her.

"Vizier, see that it's done."

Apparently, it was time for a sunset cruise.

Cruise The Nile

Julie took the wheel and pushed the Valkyrie off into the harbor. She guided the ship, that was crowded with much of court, down the canal and out into the Nile.

"Must be the power of the gods." The Pharaoh stepped up next to her on the bridge.

"The power of the gods?" Julie tried not to sound irritated.

"This vessel moves without oars or wind... This wheel controls the ship somehow?" Sobekneferu asked with interest.

"We are of the sea, so we have developed many ideas for ship design." Julie felt she needed to be careful.

"The Valkyrie... Correct?" the Pharaoh attempted the name.

"Yes," Julie confirmed.

"It is made of metal? I've never seen so much of it in one place before," Sobekneferu sounded surprised.

"We have our way of getting materials," Julie was saying.

The Pharaoh turned and stared at her. "I'm no fool, My Lady... You are scouting for an invasion," the Pharaoh accused.

"We are doing no such thing." Julie returned the gaze.

"It's all too perfect... This ship! Your gifts. Speaking so clearly in our tongue!" Sobekneferu was becoming animated. "... You leave in a short time and return with an armada of these ships to conquer Egypt!" The interrogation continued.

"This is the only one of these ships. And we originally intended to stay for a while. But if we are not welcome, we will leave!" Julie lost her cool.

"I would stop you!" the Pharaoh threatened.

"You couldn't if you tried... Where do you think the wolfskins came from? We could have eliminated you in an instant if we wanted to."

The Pharaoh seemed stunned that anyone would talk to her like that.

"... To think, I was impressed to find a woman ruling the greatest kingdom in the world..." Julie was prepared to fight if necessary.

"No one has ever spoken to me like that." Sobekneferu looked more impressed than upset.

"I am sorry, Your Majesty. We are guests in your land." Julie averted her eyes.

The Pharaoh stared at her for a moment. "You're rather defensive. Something happened, didn't it?"

Julie looked at the Pharaoh. "While we were at sea, we ran into a storm. We took shelter in Minos. The king took us prisoner and attempted to steal the Valkyrie. We were forced to fight our way out of his labyrinth of beasts. I was so excited to see the Land of Gold, but I guess it will always be a fight." Julie began to feel that her dream of seeing ancient Egypt was becoming a nightmare. She put her hand to her sword.

"Lady Julie, I've never met a woman quite like you before... You really are a warrior?" Sobekneferu looked at her sword and then back at her.

"I've been through more battles than you could believe." Julie closed her eyes and took a deep breath as she thought of how much blood she had shed.

"You said... 'How do you think we got these wolfskins?' You killed them yourself, didn't you?" The Pharaoh was looking at her in consideration.

"I got this for my trouble..." she showed Sobekneferu the Fenrir scar on her neck.

"You wish to remain in my lands?" the Pharaoh asked finally.

"Only if we are welcome," Julie replied a bit tartly.

"I am new to this role. I have had my guard up a bit. I would welcome another strong woman at my court," the Pharaoh said as Micheal and the vizier entered the bridge.

"Your Holy Eminence... How are you finding the Valkyrie?" Micheal asked with a bow.

"I am quite looking forward to my own vessel... I have decided to invite you to remain in Egypt. You will build a residence however you see fit," the Pharaoh said decisively.

"We are honored," Micheal bowed. "Now I think it's time for dinner," Micheal indicated the impromptu dining tables set up along the deck.

They sat with the Pharaoh, the vizier, and the highest-ranking courtiers who were set up on the bow deck. Seeing the pyramids of Giza as shadows to the setting sun was a true sight. It had been quite an interesting first day in Egypt, and now they were tentatively staying.

"So, what plan do you have for our residence?" Julie began when they were alone in their quarters. "Because I know you do," she added, shaking her head.

"While we were on Knossos, I came up with a general concept design, and then when the Pharaoh gave the invite, I amped it up a bit because I felt it should be able to handle a royal visit. So, these are the floor plans. I know it's a bit ostentatious, but you know me." He gave a sidelong smile.

She examined his designs, and then she recognized them. "This is river palace!" she returned the sidelong look.

River Palace

"River Palace? As in 'Wonders of the Ancient World' River Palace?" Micheal raised a brow. He had heard of River Palace as a child but had never seen it, so he didn't know what it looked like.

"I've been there... In 2008, when I visited Egypt. Of course, I visited River Palace. And when we were sailing up the Nile this morning, I had thought I might see it, but it was nowhere to be seen," Julie explained. "So apparently, we built it."

"And you're sure my designs are the layout of River Palace?" Micheal asked with consideration.

"It was a pretty unique design," she said directly. "That also explains the unique technologies present in the palace," she pointed out.

"So it's a hundred feet above the river?" Micheal asked.

"Yes... That's part of the wonder of it. How did they build such a massive thing so high above the river," she cocked her head at him. "So how are we going to do such a thing?"

He thought about it for a moment, then said, "We have the

m-pulse pads to move them, and we have the mining bores to cut out the building blocks."

"You really think the m-pulse pads are a good idea? That's pushing into the 'gods power'", she worried. "And we don't have any more convenient apocalypses to smooth things over," she added tartly.

"We do it at night. Sure, some might see magic involved, but I'm certain history will forget it all," he felt confident.

The following day, they sat down to breakfast with the Pharaoh. "So, how much land do you require for your palace?" Sobekneferu inquired.

"No land, shall we require. Except temporarily for construction," Micheal replied.

"No land?" the Pharaoh seemed confused.

"We plan on building in the river near the Delta," Julie informed her.

"Very well. You will have access to my best craftsmen," Sobekneferu offered, then went on to other subjects. "And what about my ship?" she inquired.

"We've located a deposit of enough metal for the project..." Julie was saying.

"... But just barely..." Micheal qualified the resource.

When they were about to retire to their chambers, the Pharaoh drew the sword they had gifted her and said, "Lady Avalon, you will teach me how to use this."

Julie bowed and said, "As you wish."

A couple of weeks later, they were ready to install the pilings. Julie had intentionally let Micheal finish the plans and pick the location, so as not to potentially create a paradox. Namely, her knowledge from 2008 affecting the construction of River Palace. Micheal chose a location approximately 20 miles from the sea, due to the breadth of the river there.

"We only have the night to get this done," he said as they dropped the massive columns into the pre-drilled post holes. "We have a steady stream coming in from the quarry," Micheal informed her.

"Someone is going to see us doing this," Julie worried.

"Would you stop worrying? It would take decades to build if we used conventional methods," he reasoned. "And besides, they already have a living god here in Egypt." He chuckled.

As the dawn broke over the Delta, the granite pilings had all been set a couple hundred feet down into the bedrock. They were interlocking columns 20 feet in diameter.

"Tomorrow, we will lay the foundation," he said as they boarded the Valkyrie to retire for the day. "So, how are the lessons going?" Micheal asked.

"She's making good progress... It has served another purpose, at least. She has concluded that we are definitely not an invasion. She thinks I must be gifted of the gods to have such skill, and she realized we could have conquered her in an instant," Julie shook her head. "How's her ship coming along?"

"The bore extraction of the metals has made the preparation process easy. The construction dock is ready at the palace, and I've already compartmentally assigned the different crews. It should be ready by summer's end. Oh, and it was a good move to give the palace some clean ground stones so we can eat the bread without grinding away our teeth."

In the cover of night, they laid down the foundation.

"Okay, let's drop it into the gap. Then, we shift the last section to the left, and voila—the foundation is set. We will take the next week to finish the column supports." He was confident.

Two weeks later, they returned to the Pharaoh's palace in Itjawy.

"I was beginning to wonder what my new friends were up to," the Pharaoh began as they sat down to dinner.

"The project in the Delta had some things that needed our attention, but now the craftsmen can finish the primary work and in a few months, we will oversee the completion," Micheal said.

"That fast? It does not seem possible," Sobekneferu challenged.

"Our sacred methods allow us to build at a much abbreviated time requirement," Julie excused.

"And I suppose you will still not share those secrets?" the Pharaoh accused. "I have inspected the building of my ship, and it does not even look like it could become a ship," she added.

"I inspected the craftsmen's work after we arrived, and everything is going to plan. Principal assembly is only perhaps a week away," Micheal assured her.

"I am still amazed to see so much metal in one place." Sobekneferu seemed jealously impressed. "You must serve powerful gods."

"All of the gods are powerful. This has been shown in great accomplishments of all different peoples, but Egypt exceeds all others." Micheal bowed.

"Your flattery betrays the clear superiority of the sacred methods of Avalon." The Pharaoh raised a brow.

"We are the exception, not the rule," Julie excused.

"Clearly." Sobekneferu left the table.

Once back in their chambers, "We always play to their superstitions, don't we?" Julie charged. "Do you ever feel guilty about the ease with which we lie and manipulate people? How do we know we aren't responsible for some of the distorted beliefs?" She looked away.

"It's human nature to believe in the supernatural. We can't take credit for that. Nor is it our place to try to discourage these people of their beliefs."

"I guess..." she finally agreed.

"Our deceptions are with the best intentions. So don't feel like a bad person because of that. Our unusual situation leads to moral quandaries. And we do the best we can. Okay?"

"Okay," she agreed.

"Now, let's get some sleep."

<u>The Uncertain Goddess</u>

Julie stopped the blade just millimeters from Sobekneferu's neck.

"Keep your sword up! Move your feet! You're exposing your guard," Julie pulled back. "Again!" she instructed.

The Pharaoh parried her next attack, which she successfully parlayed into a quick counterstrike. Julie parried and evaded, then met the next volley until they were sword-to-sword and face-to-face.

"Much better! Now, let's take a break." Julie stepped back and bowed.

They went and sat overlooking the sacred pond. After a deep gulp of water, Sobekneferu stared at her as if she were studying her. "Lady Julie..." she said, then hesitated.

"Yes, Your Majesty?" Julie prompted.

"Well...it is difficult for me to admit, but I was not completely convinced of my divinity or right to my father's throne. I knew some might question the gods endowing a woman as Pharaoh. Never in the millennia of our history did a woman take authority, but my father instilled my providence from my youth. So when my brother died, I knew it was my right. But those first few months, I allowed doubt to creep in. Then you arrived. Despite your obvious youth, you gave an air of confidence I had never encountered before. Then I learned you were a great hunter and warrior. You have been an inspiration and example that I look to emulate," she finished.

"I am flattered, your eminence. Both of our people hold women in high regard. You didn't require any reassurance," Julie demurred.

"But I did, Lady Julie. And I thank you for that. I also feel we have become friends. So few women understand the challenges of ruling, but I know you do. And I will value having a friend and confidante to advise me going forward," Sobekneferu said earnestly.

"You want me to advise you? What makes you think I know what it's like to rule?"

"I was raised to rule. I know it when I see it, particularly since you began instructing me. You carry yourself with an air of confidence. You are very decisive. It's clear—you have governed before," the Pharaoh stated with certainty. She then seemed to study Julie's eyes. "That's what I could see... Your eyes hold wisdom far beyond your years." She seemed to focus in wonder.

Julie averted her eyes. For a moment, she felt exposed, like Sobekneferu could see through the façade—the weight of a lifetime of experiences brought to bear on her soul.

Sometimes, when she gazed into a mirror, she could almost see the lifelines beneath her porcelain skin.

"It weighs on you, doesn't it?" the Pharaoh asked.

"What does?" Julie looked back at Sobekneferu.

"The responsibility of leading," Sobekneferu pressed.

Julie was tempted to lie. It had become so common. But then she said, "It's a lonely place at the top... People like the vizier get a sliver of what you feel when no one is above you." She looked Sobekneferu in the eyes.

"So I was right." The Pharaoh almost seemed surprised.

"I ruled Avalon for five years. Everyone looked to me, even worshipped me, their goddess on Earth. They expected me to save the day—to solve every problem..." Julie thought about all the decisions she had made as a goddess.

"How did you deal with it?" Sobekneferu asked with interest.

"I always tried to do the right thing... But sometimes it's not always clear what that is."

"You were a goddess to them?" The Pharaoh cocked her head.

"Yes. It was a bit much." Julie felt awkward.

"Do you know Ra?" The strange question came out of left field. "Because I think he knows you." Sobekneferu stared at her.

"My apologies, Micheal is waiting on me. If I may?" Julie bowed.

"I will see you tomorrow," the Pharaoh excused her.

Julie returned to their chambers.

"What's on your mind?" Micheal asked her in English.

"Sobekneferu said the strangest thing to me... She asked if I knew Ra. Apparently, he knows me?" She shook her head.

"That reference sounds like Ra is an actual being."

"Exactly... Just after I told her, in a roundabout way, that I ruled over Atlantis, it felt like she assumed I knew Ra." Julie was trying to work through it in her head.

"Wait. Why did you tell her you ruled Atlantis?" he seemed confused.

"She told me she looked up to me and knew I had ruled before... I swear, it was like she could see through my youthful façade and see the real me," she said defensively.

"Okay." He raised his hands in surrender. "So it sounds like this Ra was someone she would have had to talk to." He was considering, so she stayed quiet. "Clearly, Sobekneferu believes she is the incarnation of one of the Egyptian gods, so it's not out of the realm of possibility that she would think a regular person was a god... Unless the ancient gods are real?..." he suggested. "...Don't look at me like that. We already met Thor. Now, the Pharaoh mentions Ra. We don't know everything about history or reality," he argued bluntly.

"I suppose you're right. We need to try and figure out what the truth is," she decided. "On another note, apparently I'm going to be Sobek's special advisor."

"Special advisor?" He raised a brow.

"She's uncertain of how she's supposed to lead. Or how the people view her. She wants my advice based on my experience as a female ruler." She looked away nervously.

"Hand of the Queen?" he seemed to reference the book by George R.R. Martin. "I'm kidding. You'll do great," he tried to reassure her.

But she wasn't convinced.

CHAPTER 9: RA

The Satsobek

AUGUST 12, 1777 B.C.

As the summer comes to a close, the Pharaoh's ship is about ready to christen. There's a major ceremony planned in a couple of days.

River Palace is coming along quickly. Fortunately, the temp labor was able to finish the primary superstructure of all the major pieces of the palace. They worked it like a well-oiled machine. Despite how massive each section was, they finished just as the inundation receded. So now they have all returned to their fields as planting season begins.

The artisans have taken over, working on the hieroglyphics. All of the stories were coordinated between us and the Pharaoh. It's a massive task, but Sobek pooled every available artist, and they assured us it would be done before the next inundation.

It has been an adjustment to advise Sobek, particularly concerning military force. Some of the Nubian governors decided to test her authority, so she decided to put her newfound confidence to the test. She led her army into battle, and Micheal and I were at her side. We stormed the field on horseback and quickly routed the enemy. I was happy to see that my instruction had its desired effect.

When word came out that the Pharaoh and her female advisor laid waste to many men, the rest of the Nubian lords stood down.

I hope the word spreads and quells any other potential rebellions.

It took a while, but Micheal and I adopted an adapted Egyptian style. I keep my hair shoulder-length and straight. And I've perfected my eye makeup. My form-fitting body dresses complete the look. We look positively Egyptian... almost. We always make sure to include some Norse elements.

Julie temporarily put the quill in the inkpot and grabbed the mirror. She analyzed her reflection—the dark eye makeup only emphasized her eyes. They almost seemed to shine. The style of dress of the high class of the middle kingdom was rather revealing. Most women went topless, with a sheer wraparound, tight-fitting linen dress that came up short of the breasts. Others, like Julie, had nipple covers on their shoulder straps. As she contemplated any adjustments she might make, she caught Micheal's aspect behind her.

He was going full Egyptian for the Pharaoh's big day. He was wearing a Shendyt (basically a kilt) and had a leopard skin draped over one shoulder. He had the traditional eye makeup. That, combined with his dark tan, he nearly fit the Egyptian bill. It was made all the more convincing by his clean-shaven bald head. She was still trying to get used to it.

"It's just about time," he reminded her.

She picked up the quill again:

So now we unveil the Pharaoh's new ship. The Satsobek. It's made out of gilded steel and is shaped like a crocodile. It's about 150 feet long and 40 feet wide. The tallest points on the front, back, and center are a little under 20 feet about the water line, and it has the same filter system and drive systems as the Valkyrie.

P.S. Before I go, I have to mention that today is our 46th wedding anniversary.

Micheal was wearing his new gift from the Pharaoh—a leopard skin, dropped over his right shoulder. He felt a little exposed with his newly clean-shaven head. After so many years of a full head of hair, he had swung both extremes in less than a year. He hadn't cut it while they were in Norway, so it had become a bit long. Now, he had a smooth, bald head. But the most strange thing he had agreed to was the eye makeup. The black did help to deal with the blazing sun that beat down on both construction projects. It also had the effect of making him truly fit in a court.

"Honored guests from distant lands, I am humbled to present to her Holy Majesty—Satsobek!" Micheal announced, and the veils concealing the boat from dry-dock were let down.

The crowd gasped and cheered at the magnificent sight—the gold and silver glistened in the sun.

Sobekneferu stepped forward, admiring the ship, running her hand along the cherrywood guardrail of the gangplank. Micheal gave a signal and the dock was released, filling it with water.

"The Nile embraces Satsobek!" Micheal announced. The priests of Sobek began blessing the new vessel. When they finished, everyone from court was escorted on board, and the Pharaoh's captain guided the Satsobek out.

Showing off the ship's speed, they sailed up the river to Thebes. Pharaoh Sobekneferu was escorted through the streets in a processional. Massive crowds came to see the Pharaoh's court pass by. Micheal and Julie were riding horses behind the Pharaoh's litter.

"So, have you found out any more about Ra?" he asked Julie in English.

"She brings him up from time to time. I'm not completely certain, but I think Sobek believes that we are also gods incarnate. That's based on the way she talks about us in relation to the likes of Ra," Julie said with a shrug.

"Does she mention other gods?" Micheal looked over at Julie.

"She indicated last night that she has met a few other gods—Isis, Horace, Hathor, Anubis, and Set. But she is primarily interacting with Ra."

"You'll have to fill me in later," he said as they reached the docks.

The sun set a few hours after they departed for Itjawy. There was a collective gasp as all the oil lamps ignited sequentially as the sunlight faded.

"My Lord, Avalon, she is far beyond my expectations," the Pharaoh said as they sat for dinner.

"A ship to match your magnificence," Micheal returned the compliment.

"How do the torches do that?" Sobek was curious.

"Ra sends his power when Apophis tries to take the world. We harness that energy to light the darkness." Micheal gave a convoluted answer.

"That does remind me. I am sure Lady Julie has discussed this with you, but have you met Ra?" The Pharaoh took the bait.

"The pleasure has escaped me," he feigned regret.

"I'm sure you will when the time is right," Sobek said assuringly.

"What is he like?" Micheal inquired.

"Most of the gods are tall, like you. But those four are especially tall," she referenced the gods mentioned earlier.

"You mean Ra, Anubis, Horace, and Set?" he tried to confirm.

"Yes. I'm sorry. I presumed Lady Julie had mentioned them to you." Sobek looked to Julie.

"She did... So are they the only gods you have met?" he probed.

"One time, Isis visited my father, maybe ten years ago. She was about your height," she indicated to Micheal. "And one more thing, they always look young—like you."

Micheal was curious about this new goddess.

Ever since Julie told Micheal about Ra, they had attempted to use the sky-net to investigate these interactions, but the points and times were mysteriously missing from the data record.

As midnight approached, they sailed into the palace harbor. The Pharaoh had demonstrated she could go to Thebes and back in one day. This would only emphasize her authority. No one would likely cross her now.

A Palace Fit For Pharaoh

The months passed, and the royal artists laid the finishing touches on the hieroglyphics decorating the palace modules and the many statues. Micheal had attended to the obelisks and other carved stone monuments.

Now, they were traveling to their new home for the first time to stay. But Julie was nervous to use the m-pulse pads to place the palace in the sky.

"We've got a long night ahead of us," Micheal stated as they arrived at the expansive construction site.

"These modules are rather large. Aren't you concerned the vibration of the pads lifting them might shake them apart?" Julie was trying to consider all the possibilities.

"No. The bonding resin has made the bonds as hard as diamond. And the joints are meant to move a bit to absorb seismic events. So I don't foresee any problems," he tried to assure her.

In the twilight, they did a walkthrough inspection of all the modules.

"It's so crazy to think how I was, or am, part of the building of River Palace." Julie ran her hand across a hieroglyph depicting the Pharaoh's recent battle down in Aswan.

She tried to remember if she had seen it in 2008. She didn't think so but probably never passed it that day.

"Okay, it's been a long time since we've lifted anything this big with these pads..." Julie was saying.

"Not since the 24th century B.C.."

"... And I don't believe even the building blocks of the palace of the gods got this big," she pointed out.

"Well, here goes nothing..." he said as he activated the pads. They were on a single pad next to the central module.

The building began to lift off the ground. There was a bit of a rumble as the whole thing began to move.

"I need to increase the power." As Micheal pushed the throttle up, there was a bright flash above the module, and the pads below began to glow.

"Micheal! What are we going to do now?" Julie was slightly panicking.

"We place it as quickly as possible," he said calmly.

The module appeared as a giant glowing disc flying in the

night sky. The massive 600-foot diameter, circular central module looked like a UFO. It hovered above the columns, almost 200 feet above the water. After a few minutes of adjusting the alignment, they set the module down.

The same illumination occurred again when placing the Pharaoh's module, but it dragged on for over an hour because one of the columns were off by about an inch. They fell behind schedule and had to put off the rest for another day.

When they returned to the Valkyrie, "You know these strange lights are going to be known throughout the kingdom in a matter of days," Julie chided.

"So the gods helped build the palace," Micheal tried to dismiss the problem.

"This isn't a joke!" Julie was angry.

"It's okay, Jules; this was always likely to be part of such a rapid palace construction," he tried to reason.

"What do you think the real gods will think of all this?"

"That's an odd thing to say." He raised a brow.

"Clearly, we are on the radar of whomever this Ra actually is."

"We'll deal with Ra if necessary when the time comes." He seemed unconcerned.

"You're getting high on yourself again," she accused. "It's going to get us killed one of these days!" She went below deck.

Julie waited awhile, calming herself down, but Micheal never came down. She gave up after some time and fell asleep.

The next day, she arose a bit before dusk. She searched the entire ship, and he wasn't on board.

"Where would he go?" she questioned herself. "The palace." She took one of the m-pulse pads and levitated up to the main module.

"You made it," Micheal acted like he'd been expecting her.

"Are we going to talk about yesterday?" she asked sharply.

"I think you're getting all worked up over nothing," he said dismissively.

"No, I'm seeing all the same signs I saw in Atlantis all those years ago," she shot back.

"That was 50 years ago." He laughed.

"I've seen it several times, but this is the worst since then. Every time we get through some tough challenges, you get a big head, and your superiority complex comes out," she jabbed.

"Well..." he began.

"What!" she cut in. "You're just stating the obvious facts? No, Micheal, you may be very skilled and have a perfect memory, but you are no better than anyone else. But seeing as how you think you're so much better than anyone, you finish the palace by yourself, your eminence." She bowed elaborately. Then flew off on the m-pulse pad.

She sailed off toward the south with the Valkyrie.

Two weeks later, she returned to find the palace apparently finished. She docked at the landing platform and climbed the stairs to the main palace, which was a beehive of activity.

"Such a proud accomplishment, your eminence," she mocked, seeing Micheal leaning over the open courtyard to the river.

He didn't turn. "I deserved that," he sighed.

She wrapped him from behind.

"I'm sorry, Jules."

She kissed his neck from behind. "Did the extra work do you good?" She tried not to laugh.

"I don't know why I do that." He shook his head.

"Look at me," she ordered.

He turned his head.

"You're a good man. You just need to remember humility." She cupped his face in her hands.

"Do you forgive my shortcomings," he pleaded.

"You know I do... Now, why don't you show me to our private quarters." She smiled and raised a brow.

"As you wish, My Lady." He kissed her, and then carried her away.

Court At Delta

Micheal was happy he and Julie were back on good terms, but now they had to prepare to host the royal courts. The last two months had put the finishing touches on River Palace, and the "Gem of the Nile", as it would become known, was sparkly, shiny, and new.

The palace was twice the size of Buckingham by floor space but spanned nearly half a mile from east to west in the middle of the river and a quarter of a mile from north to south.

"The Satsobek is on final approach," Julie informed him.

"Let's go greet the Pharaoh." Micheal and Julie walked across the bridge to the main module, past the main court, and then over another bridge to the royal module.

"What do you think Sobek will think of this place?" he asked Julie.

"Anyone in this time period would be awed by this place, so I have no doubt she'll be impressed."

The royal module was 300 feet in each direction and three stories high. They waited at the entrance to the royal elevator, which was a simple dumbwaiter pulley system in a semi-open tube ten feet across.

Pharoah Sobekneferu and the vizier, Senewosret, had expressions of surprise on their faces as they arrived at the top.

"Welcome, your holy eminence, to River Palace." Micheal and Julie bowed.

"How extraordinary, Lord and Lady Avalon. The like I've never seen before." Sobekneferu began walking toward the back of the module.

"Vizier," Micheal bowed. And the tour of the palace began.

"This entire module is for you, Your Majesty. And these are your private quarters." They entered into a large multi-level suite on the north side of the module. "It's complete with a bath, as well as a privy. We have hired many servants to attend to your every need," he explained.

"Now, if you will follow me." Julie headed to the south side of the module. They crossed a bridge, which, like many of them, was cut from a single piece of granite. They averaged ten feet wide and a hundred feet in length. The bridge curved, following the curve of the primary, central module. They entered the sanctuary of Sobek. One of the two temple modules flanking the royal module. The temple modules were 150 feet in diameter and had ocular domes, like the Pantheon in Rome. In the center stood a statue of Sobek, the crocodile god. It was carved of green-tinted granite and was about 80 feet tall.

The Pharaoh marveled as they crossed the next bridge to the servant's quarters, saying, "It's hard to believe that this place, with its opulent furnishings floating above the flood plain, was built in just over two seasons."

"Many men working many hours," Micheal gave a copout answer.

"The Pharaoh arrives!" the door herald exclaimed as they entered the servant's module. It was a square 200 feet across with three levels.

"This module houses the service staff," Julie informed the Pharaoh. All the servants present went to their hands and knees.

"As you were," Sobekneferu released them from their pose, and the servants returned to their duties.

As Micheal led the way around the module, "You have the servants drinking water? Will they not get sick?" The vizier seemed concerned.

"The water that flows within this palace is pure... Sweet." Micheal stepped up to one of the fountains and drank deeply. "... And quite refreshingly cool," he added, wiping his mouth.

Sobek stepped up, eyeing the arcs of water.

"No, your eminence!" the vizier tried to stop her.

"Quite sweet," she said as she stepped back from the fountain. "Vizier Senewosret, it's just as the water on the Satsobek," the Pharaoh admonished him.

It had taken a bit for them to trust it, but eventually, everyone was willing to drink the "magic" water on the Satsobek and the Valkyrie.

They walked through one of the storage modules without stopping, and then they transitioned across one of the bridges to the entry module. Technically, it was the Temple of the Gods. It was another circular module 100 feet in diameter, with a partial dome open to the sky. It had a statue of every Egyptian god gracing the edges.

"Impressive likeness of our gods," Sobek commented as she made her way from one to the next.

Each statue stood 20 feet tall.

"We were honored by the graciousness of our acceptance into your lands. This palace combines the best of both our lands," Micheal explained.

They paused at the entry port, where they could look down onto the landing pad. A 500-foot square down near the water level at high flood. It had stables, boat houses, and such at each of the four corners and a massive obelisk in the middle—over 200 feet tall and capped with a pyramid of pure silver.

"Quite the stairs," Vizier Senowosret commented of the re-tractable staircases, providing access between the landing pad and the Temple of the Gods.

"A very complex piece of engineering. They can retract up to the palace level, preventing direct access from the ground level," Julie explained.

"How fascinating!" the Pharaoh exclaimed.

They then crossed the chamber to the primary bridge that accessed the main central module. The largest module, circular and spanning two football fields in diameter, featured a 200-foot hole in the middle. Here, a forever fountain cascaded water down into the river below.

As they opened to the grand courtyard, "Aside from the great pyramids of Giza, never have I seen such a monumental con-struction," Sobekneferu was amazed. Four small obelisks were marking the points of the compass. They were each 80 feet tall and crowned with gold.

They reached the fountain next to the west obelisk. The Pharaoh ran her hand through the water. "Your home is quite grand." She sounded a bit jealous.

"Our home is your home." Julie gave a bow.

"So, where do you stay here at the palace?" Sobek seemed to like the sentiment of Julie's statement.

"Right this way, Your Majesty." Micheal headed toward the rooms of the main module. "These rooms are for members of the main court," Micheal explained as they reached the top stair lead-ing to the second floor. "Each private suite has multiple rooms. There is a privy and bath for every eight suites." Micheal headed into one of the privies and then the bath. "Now, I suppose you'd like to see our private module." He led the way back down the stairs and, after crossing another bridge. "Here we are," he announced as they entered the courtyard. "The Lord's module is decorated in the style of Egypt, with the tales of Avalon," Micheal said. "As well as our style of words," he added, of the Norse runes. "The first floor is for dining, as well as for entertaining guests. The upper floor is our private suite," he explained.

"As you can see, it's not quite as spacious as Your Majesty's quarters, but it should be plenty for us," Julie chimed in. "Now for the final stop on the tour..." they crossed a bridge to the Lord's sanctuary. It had the same structure as the Temple of Sobek but featured the Norse gods.

"These are the gods of Avalon," Micheal indicated the statues. "On this side are the Æsir. On that side are the Vanir. On the wall, in the Egyptian style, and translated with runes, is the history of our people's gods. From the creation to Ragnarök," Micheal told them.

"Ragnarök?" Sobek seemed curious.

"The destruction and rebirth of all creation," Micheal explained.

"Who is this?" the Pharaoh asked.

"That is Thor, God of Thunder and the Sky," Julie answered.

"And him?" The Pharaoh moved to the statue at Thor's left.

"That is Odin, the All-father. Thor's father and King of Asgaard—where the gods dwell," Micheal informed them.

Pharaoh spent a bit of time exploring the sanctuary. "This looks like this animal's skin that I'm wearing," Sobek commented on one of the scenes from Ragnarok, featuring Fenrir the wolf-demon. She was wearing the wolfskin they had given her for the opening of River Palace.

"That is the demon wolf Fenrir. The doom of Ragnarok," she added.

"Wait..." Sobek crossed back into the Lord's module. Everybody followed her. She led them to a mural featuring Julie's defeat of Fenrir. "Is that not the same beast?" she looked inquisitively at Julie.

Julie looked away.

"You defeated the demon wolf?" Pharaoh deduced.

Julie instinctively touched her neck.

"It was not without a cost," Micheal interjected.

Sobek seemed to study Julie for a moment.

"Majesty, the court will arrive soon," the vizier changed the subject.

"Very well," the Pharaoh made her way to the royal module's throne room.

Micheal and Julie sat just below the Pharaoh as the courtiers arrived at the palace. Then, there was a grand celebration for the harvest and the beginning of the inundation.

Over the next few weeks, the river rose in the Delta until no dry land was in sight.

<u>Ra</u>

-January 12, 1776 B.C.

On this day, 52 years ago, I fell through time. There are so many feelings that this day evokes. The confusion of awakening in that field. The fear of being taken by that mob. The cold... I can still feel the chill of those horrible days.

As time has moved forward, other things have become attached. Missing my parents, my siblings, my friends, and even after all these years, I still miss Aiden. You'd think that the passage of time would lessen those losses, and with all the crazy things that have happened through the twelve different time periods I have experienced, I can momentarily be distracted from losses, but in the quiet moments, those absences are glaring. And whenever I have a crisis, I can't ask my dad what I should do. Or if Micheal and I go through a tough patch, I can't talk through my troubles with my mom.

As much as I love Micheal, sometimes I feel isolated. It can be very lonely. While I have made a few friends over the years, it always ends the same way. My life, through the ages, pushes ever forward. And their momentary friendships just become a more and more distant memory. There is one more loss that I ponder from time to time. Unless we make it back to the 21st century, I will never get to experience motherhood. And even if I do, that won't be for nearly two centuries from now. So it's likely I never will.

On another note, Sobekneferu left the palace last night to begin a progress of her kingdom. She took the court with her. After eight months of hosting the royal court, the palace feels empty. I think it's time we take a vacation from everything here. I have been continually surprised by how quickly we become accepted into so many different places and times.

Pharaoh... Sobekneferu has become so comfortable with me as her confidante that I have been able to see behind the tough veneer and have found a soft-hearted woman with an easy sense of humor. I think I will miss her. But that brings me to my final thought for the day...

She has never explicitly said so, but I think she believes I am more than human. She clearly thinks the gods are real and that they visit her occasionally. However, I have yet to see any evidence of this. In fact, any investigations into Ra or any of the other gods have proven fruitless. I have to conclude that either Sobek is crazy and just imagining them, or there are truly some supernatural beings beyond our ability to detect.

P.S. The one good thing about this fateful day is that it's my soulmate's day of birth. Happy 79th, my love.

"Home, sweet home," Micheal commented as they returned to River Palace after nearly a month away.

"It was nice to take a break from being lords in Egypt." Julie felt their tour of the Mediterranean, with a couple of weeks in Gibraltar, was essential for her sanity.

"It was certainly relaxing," he agreed.

Julie looked around. "Do you think conversing in English is smart? We didn't know Melina was learning it until she knew it."

"We will be more careful this time," he tried to assure her.

She still felt a little paranoid if they used it too much.

"We can worry about this later. I have a special gift for a special day," he said with a raised brow.

"Special day?" she was momentarily confused. "Oh! ... With everything..." she felt embarrassed. She forgot Valentine's Day.

"Don't worry about it," he turned her chin to look at him. He kissed her. "Now, turn around."

She turned, and he dropped a necklace down over her head. It looked like a small, truncated icosahedron—basically a small disco ball.

"Now, I know it's a little cheesy and obvious, but I realized I never gave you any kind of picture locket. So this is what I came up with..." He finished clasping the necklace.

She turned to face him. "What does it do?" She knew there was more to it than a pretty jewel.

"... When raised to eye level, it makes images of me. I had to compile different pictures of me over our time together. One for each side of the stone. So now you have me right next to your heart." He seemed to get a little embarrassed.

She turned his face to meet hers. "You're always in my heart..." She kissed him. "...Now, let me make it up to you." She dropped her shawl.

They used most of the bed chamber to express their love. Micheal carried her out to the balcony. As he laid her down, "You look so incredible in the light of the moon," he kissed her neck as he cupped her left breast with her hand.

She closed her eyes as he took another tour of her body with his mouth, finishing between her thighs. Her mind momentarily went blank as she reached the mountaintop. Once she returned to sanity, she was ready for more. She rolled him onto his back. She mounted up and began her moonlit ride. She locked eyes with Micheal, and they became one with the rhythm. As they approached climax together, she arched her back, taking in the full atmosphere. The Milky Way, the full moon, and their bodies in sync... They came together, and she collapsed on his chest.

When they caught their breath, she said, "Happy Valentine's Day, my love."

"Happy Valentine's Day, Jules."

"I love you so much."

"I love you, Jules." he began running his fingers through her hair. It was so soothing that she drifted off to sleep.

Julie woke to a strange noise. In the setting moonlight, there was a silhouette on the balcony.

"Micheal!" she woke him.

"You are an aberration in my land. The time has come for you to be gone," the being stated in Egyptian. It momentarily turned its head, and Julie could see what looked like a beak. Her first thought was ... Ra!

The shadow moved to attack. She and Micheal dodged the first blow. Julie grabbed her kinetic staff and went to the counter. As she began delivering strikes, she realized just how big Ra was. He had to be eight feet tall and was at least 400 pounds. He countered her with his staff. His quickness was amazing. His counter flurry finally connected. The hit to her gut knocked the wind out of her. Micheal defended her from Ra's finishing attack. Then she watched as Micheal wielded a sword, slicing gashes all over Ra's body. She was stunned, as all the cuts seemed to heal almost instantaneously. She sprung to her feet, sword in hand. Ra blocked her barrage of strikes, but she was able to spin inside him and plunge the sword into his chest. The fierce falcon eyes burned through her, then he backhanded her. She flew across the balcony. Micheal tried to move in and finish Ra, but he was able to counter, even with the sword in his chest. Ra pulled out the sword, and Julie thought, "He's too powerful..." She needed something more, but what was there? Then she thought... "m-pulse pads..."

She grabbed her smartphone and summoned the pads from their storage location below the palace. At that moment, Micheal attacked with the kinetic boomerang disc. Ra was knocked around a few times. Then he reached out his hand, and a green vortex opened. To Julie's horror, Micheal was sucked in. The m-pulse pads arrived above the balcony. She sent them from all sides, slamming Ra in the head, and he was stunned for a moment. She started circling the pads around Ra, sending them randomly to strike blows at him, knocking him off balance. She upped the attack, sending the pads in a train to force Ra off the balcony. She went and looked over the edge in time to see the splash in the river. She wasn't sure if it was over, but she had a more pressing issue—what did Ra do to Micheal. Julie took her smartphone and began scanning the world for Micheal. He was nowhere to be found.

Suddenly, Ra flew up and landed on the balcony. "I tire of this combat," he said menacingly. He reached out his hand, and a green portal opened next to her. She tried to run away, but it was too late. She was sucked in. She went through in a flash, and everything went dark.

CHAPTER 10: MAROONED

Micheal's head was pounding. The last thing he remembered was fighting against Ra (he was pretty sure that was Ra). There was a green flash, and he lost consciousness. It was still dark, and he did not know where he was—or when. That had to be a temporal portal. So what kind was it? If it was a well, he was at least 200-300 years afield, and he was stranded. If it was a Philadelphia portal into an eddy, he was within a century and could use his tether to return. But then he realized he first needed to find some clothes.

Julie began to regain consciousness. She felt the gritty feeling of sand beneath her naked body. She scanned the horizon, and there was nothing but the mellow glow of sand in the light of the setting moon. She was in the desert, probably the Sahara, west of Egypt, but the more important question was: *when* was she? Ra had thrown her through time. She didn't know when, but she was certain that Micheal was not here. What was she going to do now?

Micheal looked around and realized he was in a precarious location on some mountainside. The sun had set, and it was too dangerous to navigate in the dark. So he would have to wait until morning. He began to study the stars in an attempt to triangulate his location on Earth. He found the star Kocheb in Ursa Minor, which was the closest to celestial north in the 2nd millennium B.C. Then, knowing that the time must be between four and five AM, he found Errai, the pinnacle star of Cepheus low near the north horizon. Then he looked west and found Alphard near the horizon in the constellation Hydra. He ran the numbers in his head and determined he was between 28 and 29 degrees north latitude, meaning he was still in Egypt, maybe 50 miles south of Memphis. Except he was in a mountainous region. So he must be in East Egypt, or perhaps the Sinai. If that was true, he might be in trouble. Water was scarce in the peninsula, and crossing the desert landscape would take multiple days. The only thing to his advantage was that it was February so the temperature would be in the 70s instead of 100s.

Julie sat in the sand, just thinking about the situation. In more than 50 years out in the timeline, she had never faced such a daunting challenge—and she would have to face it alone. And Ra had sent her here. Would he show up to finish the job? Or did he send her somewhere where she would be trapped with no hope of return? While this was a vastly different situation than the one she faced in Salem, it had the same feeling—she was lost in time, separated from the love of her life, and the hope of a happy reunion was exceedingly slim. At least she knew the predicament this time around. But that knowledge came with a downside. The reality was—she wouldn't see Micheal again for a long time... if ever again. The thought brought tears to her eyes. She grabbed her Valentine's gift and raised it to eye level. The third image she saw was Micheal on their wedding day, over 50 years of love between them. How could she live without him? It was too soon to give up.

As the sun's first light cracked the horizon, Micheal began to make his way down the side of the mountain. Micheal had to be careful because any misstep would likely mean bruises and scratches without clothes in the rocky desert mountains. He was gingerly stepping down the hill. As he turned to the east to follow the trail, a bright ray of light pierced the horizon. He was momentarily blinded, tripped on a loose rock, and began to tumble down the hill. When he came to a stop, he was in pain from head to toe. He closed his eyes and ran an inventory of his body. Mostly bumps and bruises, except there was a long gash on his left calf, and his misstep seemed to have cut his right foot. But on the Brightside, he had made good time to the bottom of the mountain. And thankfully, "Junior" had escaped the naked tumble unscathed. Following his physical assessment, he was hit by an emotional evaluation. He closed his eyes, and he could see her. He thought of the images he had given her. He saw her walking down the aisle, her sparkling white dress and diamond crown. The look of the queen of his heart. Would he ever see her again?

Julie scanned the full horizon, trying to decide which way to go. She finally chose North. If she was lucky enough to be close to the north coast of Africa, she might be able to make the Mediterranean coast. She began making her way over the rolling dunes. As the heat of the temporal passage wore off, the chill of the desert night kissed her exposed skin, causing her nipples to intensely harden. She crossed her arms against the cold, as even the Sahara could drop near 40 degrees at this time of year. She prayed the sun would rise soon. Until then, she needed to keep moving. Half an hour later, the sky began to brighten. She continued dune after dune. She climbed one of the largest sand dunes she'd ever seen. It had to be over 400 feet tall. As she reached the crest of the dune, she could see in the light of the rising sun, that she was surrounded by a sea of sand for as far as the eye could see in all directions, and she thought, "If only I could drink sand."

<u>Sea of Sand</u>

Julie assessed her surroundings, and the first thing that came to mind was that she just became a movie cliché. The one where the character is stuck in an endless desert, droning "water". Only this was real. And with it being some 4,000 years in the past, there wasn't likely to be any random passersby to come to her aid.

She had decided that she needed to keep moving. She continued down the dune but stopped to consider whether she should keep going north. From this height, she could see for probably 30 to 40 miles; clearly, the Mediterranean was farther than she thought. After considering for a minute, she decided she would continue north for the time being and hope for good fortune to find the sea.

She walked for a few hours, and the chill of the night quickly evaporated into the heat of the sun. At first, she welcomed the change, but this was the Sahara, and even in the winter, the daytime highs would climb into the 70s, and there were no clouds in sight, which meant she would be at the mercy of the sun. And if the official high would be in the 70s, the solar temperature would be in the 90s. And worse, the temperature of the sand would blaze well above 100 degrees. She was becoming thirsty. She tried digging at the base of one of the dunes, in the gulley that lay between, but the ground was parched, and there was nothing—not even a couple of feet down. She decided to use the hole she dug to try and sleep. Exerting herself during the hottest part of the day would dehydrate her even faster. And with temperatures dropping into the 40s at night, she would have to keep moving to prevent herself from freezing to death. It was miserable under the sand, but she tried to sleep as much as possible. She only managed perhaps three hours of restless sleep.

As the sun set into twilight, she rose from her sandpit bed and began the long, dark trek by starlight. The moon had yet to rise as the big star-filled sky overcame the final rays of the sun. In the darkness, she lost her footing on the crest of a large dune and began to tumble several hundred feet to the bottom. She just lay there for a minute, staring up at the sky. She remembered something Micheal had talked about back in Boston—that the timeless nature of the stars made him feel a connection across time. She had never felt so alone. She was likely centuries apart from Micheal and millennia from anyone else who cared about her. She was alone in the middle of the largest hot desert in the world, with no clothes and no one to help her. The chill of the night began to take her. Maybe she should let it have her. The odds were against her, so what was the point? She was hungry and thirsty and lost. She closed her eyes, and the tears blurred the Milky Way. The cold seeped into her entire body. She shivered for a while. Then, a rush of warmth overcame her. At that moment, she felt something crawling on her leg. She sat up slowly. She could see it was a scorpion in the light of the moon that had just begun to rise. It was lethargic in the cold night air and probably was drawn to her body heat. In her despair, she thought about giving up, and here was this scorpion fighting for survival. She looked at the stars again.

"Micheal, I'm coming," she said aloud with determination. "But first..." she collected the scorpion from her leg. "Let's find you some shelter for the night."

She carried the scorpion to the windward face of the last dune. She dug out a small cave in the packed sand. She placed the scorpion inside and covered most of the opening with loose sand. With the insulation from the sand and the warmth a few inches down from the surface, it would likely maintain the scorpion for the night. Julie located Ursa Minor in the sky, which pointed that way north. She continued over the rollercoaster of dunes all night long. The constant exertion kept her from freezing, but she was still chilled to the bone when the sun rose. She traipsed through the endless sand until the heat of it began to burn her feet. She dug for water at the bottom of the next dune, but it was nothing but sand. It had been almost two days since she drank anything. Julie dug as deep as she could. She buried herself again and prepared for another day's terrible sleep. Despite the heat, she was deliriously tired and passed out.

Julie woke with a start as the evening chill set in. She could feel the rough sand on her sun-kissed skin. She rarely got sunburns, but two days in the unforgiving sun, with no clothes, had taken its toll. Her arms were dark brown in the fading light. She scanned the sky, deciding whether to continue north. She calculated that she had walked about 50 miles over the past two days. So she thought, how much farther to the sea? So she found the Little Dipper and began the laborious trek.

She continued all night, desperately hoping for an end to the sand, but there was none. She crested a towering dune as the dawn lit the Sahara and was devastated to see nothing but rolling sand as far as the eye could see, in every direction. She fell to her knees. She felt like an ant in the endless horizon of sand. Eighty miles north, and she felt like she'd gone nowhere. She looked at the sky, and it was nothing but clear. Not a cloud in sight. As bleak as it was, she decided to soldier ahead. But now she would trek east. As she walked, she began to see things. It looked like a small pool of water between the dunes, but when she reached it, it was bone dry. This happened several times. She was becoming desperate. She considered sleeping, but she knew she would never wake up if she did. She crossed perhaps 20 miles to the east, and still nothing. She was coming down to her last chance. Either she would find water soon, or she would die. She kept praying for rain, but the sky was hopelessly blue.

She was hallucinating now. She saw Micheal running toward her, and then he vanished. Now, she thought she saw a cloud on the horizon in front of her. She knew it would disappear as quickly as it seemed to appear. A few minutes later, the cloud was growing larger. She realized it wasn't a hallucination; it was a dust storm. And it was closing in fast. She threw herself down the side of the dune. As she rolled to a stop at the bottom of the hill, she turned and looked, and it was as if the Nothing from *The Neverending Story* was about to overtake her. She curled into a ball and cupped her face with her hands to shield her face from the sandblaster. The murky darkness became as night. She suffered through hours of choking agony as her sunburned body was whipped relentlessly by the sand. Finally, the blizzard of dust abated. Julie rolled to her knees and coughed up a lung of dust. She got to her feet and shook the sand out of her hair. She brushed off her body and made an effort to push on. As the dust began to move on, the blazing sun returned, torching her blistered feet. And she felt the shadow of Ra behind her.

She looked up, and Ra was there. She had no ability to fight. He moved to attack her and then disappeared in a cloud of dust. She tried to push on, but the delirious mirages began to come faster and faster.

Jessica was there, "It's okay, little sis. I'm here for you," she said. Then vanished.

She took a few more steps, and Cecily Penn sat at a table, "My Lady, Julie. Thee arrive promptly. Tea shall be served presently." Cecily smiled invitingly. Julie reached for the cup, and it turned to grains between her fingers.

Julie looked back up, and Cecily was replaced with Katherine. "My Lady Avalon... Or shall I address thee, Your Eminence, Aphrodite? ... Alas, it matters not! Thy death will I savor," Katherine laughed despicably and then thankfully evaporated.

"Jules!" she heard Micheal say.

"Micheal!" Julie efforted breathlessly.

"Thank goodness I found you! I searched the world, across time..." Micheal approached with open arms.

"Micheal... how did you find me?" She was confused and happy at the same time.

"Our love transcends any barriers." He smiled at her.

She reached out to him, and as she took two steps forward her vision blurred. "I love you, Micheal." She took one more step, lost her balance, and it all faded to black.

<u>Mountain Desert</u>

Micheal got to his feet and assessed his surroundings. There were rough mountain peaks all around him. Every direction looked the same. If he was where he thought he was, then north would be the logical course. He considered going east or west, but where was he precisely? If he were on Sinai, west would be best to get to the sea. But if he was on the Egyptian side, he could run into too much desert before the Nile. And if he went east, he would find the Red Sea but that would be going the wrong way. And on the Sinai, east would take him to a certain desolate death. North would lead him to a trading route. West might also, but the peninsula path was less traveled. So it would be north.

He began following a dry wash that ran through the canyon. He was slowed by the cut in his foot but made steady progress. It had been a while since he drank any fluids. Where might he find water? Around midday, he found a shaded spot and decided to get some sleep. He knew the desert would get cold at night. As he tried to sleep, he was tormented by his thoughts. Who or what was Ra? The portal had convinced Micheal that Ra was temporal in nature, which pointed to Ra being a time traveler, but he was so enormous that Micheal thought maybe he was an alien. The movie Stargate came to mind. So, if Ra was an alien, the portal might not be temporal after all. Maybe just spacial. That thought raised his mood. Maybe Julie was not gone forever.

He woke up before sundown. He held his arm out and counted his fingers from the horizon. It was two palms and two fingers, or ten fingers. That meant he had two and a half hours before the sun would set. He began moving in a northern direction through the canyons. He was very thirsty and began praying for rain. About an hour later, he saw some dark clouds in the distance to the south, and he thought maybe his prayers had been answered. But then he saw the lightning flashes. They intensified as the sun set. He kept monitoring the storm, but there was still no rain.

As night overcame twilight, he heard a crack of thunder. He looked to the sky, and there was still no rain. He continued for another half hour; then he heard a rushing sound like running water. It was getting louder. He looked up. There was still no rain, but now there were no stars and the noise was getting louder, coming from behind. From up the canyon! Micheal looked behind him, but it was pitch black. The rushing sound was becoming a roar. It had to be a flash flood. He immediately turned to his right and began climbing the side of the canyon. He stepped on some loose rocks and slid down a few feet. He felt the water on his toes rising fast. He attempted to escape it, but the rocks washed out below his feet, and he was pulled into the torrent.

Micheal fought to stay atop the water, but a current sucked him under. After whipping around a few times, he was able to get back to the surface. He continued the battle against the flow, but it was too strong. He was sucked under again. It was like being in the spin cycle of a washing machine. He spun so many times that he didn't know which way was up. He surfaced again, fighting to regain his breath. He felt the undertow take hold, and he was pulled back under. He whipped around again, then his face smacked against something hard, and it all went dark.

Micheal began to regain consciousness. His head was pounding, and the left side of his face felt swollen and sore. As his senses returned, the searing heat of the sun beat down on him. He struggled to his feet. His left eye was swollen shut. He wiped the dried mud off his naked skin as he assessed his surroundings. He was in the middle of a large, flat plain encircled by mountains. The plains stretched for miles in either direction. There was a shallow wash running to the west. He decided to follow it as he thought it might lead to a water source at a lower elevation.

As he walked, he thought about the irony of getting the rain he prayed for but way too much. And in the end, he was not able to take advantage of it. It actually made his situation worse. He walked all day across the plain. The wash was about to enter a narrow canyon as the sun was about to set. He was exhausted, so he decided to rest here for a time. When Micheal awoke, the moon was high in the night sky. He had slept most of the night, based on the location of the constellations in the sky. The hunger pangs struck him like a gut punch. His mouth was desperately dry after two days of this desert mountain nightmare. His best hope was that this canyon was pretty short, with a lake at the end of the wash. A few hours into a starlight trek, dawn lightened the sky behind him. This was going to be a desperate day. If he didn't find water today, he probably wouldn't live to see tomorrow, so he committed not to sleep until he found it.

The winding canyon seemed to be endless. He ached his way beneath the fire of the unrelenting sun. The hot desert sand caused his infected foot to be in constant pain. He pushed his battered, weary body ever on through the blazing heat. And as the sun kissed the horizon, his spirits were raised as the narrow canyon began to widen. He might be close.

As twilight gave way to starlight, he heard a slight noise approaching from behind. He instinctively dropped to the ground and felt the scratch of claws on his bare back as some kind of predator attempted an attack. He took a defensive posture and located the threat. In the mellow moonlight, he saw a large cat. It pounced again. He deflected its energy past him and got some scratches on his arm in the process. He turned quickly to face what he believed was a leopard. He raised his left arm to defend his throat from the powerful jaws which bit into his flesh. He barely remained on his feet, stumbling backward. The leopard bear-hugged him, slicing up his back, then dug in to hold on. Micheal summoned some of his last energy reserves to carry the leopard, which he gauged at about a hundred pounds, to a nearby rock, and he slammed the cat down hard, crushing its head against the rock. It released its grip and writhed around on the ground. Micheal took a large rock and put the cat out of its misery with one blow. Micheal collapsed to the ground.

He felt like giving up. How much worse could his situation get? Why should he go on? He thought of Julie. He couldn't give up on her. He would fight on for her. He struggled to his feet and began to soldier on. He pushed through the night by sheer force of will. By the time the sky lightened behind him, he was beginning to see things he wasn't sure were real. The sun rose in the sky. He stumbled into a shadow. The thought "the shadow of the sun" passed through his head—the shadow of Ra. He looked back, and Ra was there. Ra charged and swung at him. He dropped to the ground, but when he looked up, nothing was there. He got up and struggled on. A short while later, he rounded a corner and nearly ran into a giant black horse. It was Darkness, his first real companion on this temporal journey.

"Hey, boy. Long time no see." He smiled as he patted Darkness on the neck.

Darkness whinnied in agreement then ran away with the wind.

These hallucinations were a bad sign. It meant his mind was faltering. He didn't have much time. He was nearly stumbling down the hill when the temperature began to drop precipitously. The sky became as night.

"It's okay, Micheal." He turned to see Amanda, with Neptune in the background.

"You don't have to fight anymore," she said as she stepped toward him.

"I don't want to give up."

"You're not. Death is just a part of life. Just another path," she said with kindness.

He considered that. "I'm not ready."

With those words, the blazing heat returned. He prayed for water again. He desperately searched a small outcropping to no avail. As he stepped through a gap, he entered the penthouse in Atlantis.

"You're too late, eminence Koios," Gabriel Maximus stood in the doorway to the bedroom. "Now Aphrodite belongs to me," he laughed wickedly.

Micheal charged, and Gabriel stepped aside and revealed Julie tied to the bed, naked and strangled.

"Julie!" He rushed to her side, but everything vanished in a flash.

It was so vivid. When the flash cleared, he could swear he could see water. Could that be the sea on the horizon? His vision began to blur. When it focused again, she was there.

"Micheal, I always knew we would find each other again" Julie began to move toward him.

He stepped forward. "I love you, Jules," he reached for her.

His vision blurred and then faded to black.

<u>Oasis</u>

"That's it... Sip slowly," a voice said as Julie began to return to consciousness. She greedily gulped the water down as fast as she could. "Uh uh uh..." the man said as he pulled the cup back.

Her head was swimming. She took a couple of deep breaths and opened her eyes. There were palm trees above her. She turned her head, and the man was there.

"Slowly," he urged as he helped her sit up.

Julie was surprised to see that her rescuer was Caucasian. He looked young, perhaps early 20s. He had blond hair and hazel eyes.

"The desert is a dangerous place for a woman to be alone," the man commented. He spoke in Egyptian, but it was clearly not his native language.

"Water," she requested.

He gave her a pitcher of water, which she practically inhaled in one gulp.

"How did you find me?" she asked when she was finished.

"I was oasis-hopping across the desert when I found you, barely clinging to life," he explained.

"Where are we?"

"This oasis lies about 50 leagues west of the Nile River valley on the Oasis Trail to the northwest. Oases appear every 10 to 15 leagues along the way," He laid out the way back.

"Thank you for saving me," she remembered to thank him. As she was looking at him, he seemed so familiar.

"You're welcome, My Lady. Life is precious, and so is time. I wouldn't waste any more of it if I were you," he said, then began to walk away.

The statement struck her as odd.

She climbed to her feet. "Wait. What's your name?" she asked as she turned toward him, but she was shocked to find herself alone. She quickly scanned the area and nothing? Where did he go? He had literally vanished into thin air. Was he another hallucination? She rubbed her face to clear her mind, but she was still alone.

Julie assessed her current situation. The man had dressed her in a tunic-type dress. Most of the sand had been washed off her body. The blisters on her feet felt much better—she realized there was some sort of lotion or cream on the soles of her feet. She was in a shaded, soft grass next to a small spring. The spring was about 50 feet across. She cupped some of the water and tasted it. It was fresh and clean. She drank again until she felt bloated. It was greatly satisfying.

She examined the grassy area and found a linen sack full of food. Next to that was a pair of strapped sandals. Her rescuer had left her some supplies. She tried to think about who or what she was. Was he an alien? A figment of her imagination? Maybe an angel? Whatever he was, he was her guardian angel. Now, she needed to get back to Egypt.

She took a closer look at the general area, which became familiar. A large body of water was off to the east, with some slightly conical hills all around. It reminded her of the Siwa Oasis, which she had visited during her trip to Egypt in 2008.

She and her crew went to do a feature on the Siwa bottling plant in the remote desert oasis. So now she was sure that the body of water was Siwa Lake.

The Siwa Oasis was, indeed, 50 leagues west of the Nile. Basically, some 300 miles. She had a long way to go, so she better get going.

Julie followed the edge of the great sand sea to the southeast for most of the day. She reached the last vestige of the oasis a few hours before sundown. She lay under a tree next to a spring to get some sleep before nightfall.

She woke to the full moon's light and began the long foray through the vast desert. After two days' walk, she found the next oasis. After a brief respite from the dreary sand, she pushed on. Two more days, and she could see vegetation on the horizon. It must be the final oasis before the Nile.

Her four-day quest had probably taken her 200 miles, so she had another 100 miles to the valley.

The oasis was probably five or ten miles away—she could make it before sundown.

As she walked, she heard noises from all around her. She stopped to listen. There was no more noise, and she didn't see anyone. As she began again, a man stepped out from behind a rock.

"My Lady, are you lost?" he said. He was fairly tall for an Egyptian, maybe a few inches shorter than her. He had a scar on his left cheek and his teeth were yellow and black when he smiled.

"I'm perfectly all right," she went to step past him, but he put his arm out.

"Where are you going?" the man asked.

"What is a pretty thing like you doing out here all by yourself?" another man asked from behind her.

"You'll let me go, or you'll regret it," she warned. She stepped back and prepared for battle.

At that point, three more men came out to encircle her. All of them held either a sword or a knife.

They began closing in on her. She targeted the leader. She closed the gap and kicked the sword out of his hand, and it flipped through the air. She did a roundhouse kick, knocking him to the ground. She ducked a sword strike, diving to her knees. She caught the sword as it came down, just in time to parry the next swing. Then she went on the attack. She blocked a dagger strike by a different man and then kicked him in the stomach. She deflected the next sword strike, then spun in and elbowed him in the face. She caught the dagger jab from another man and parlayed it into the last man's shoulder. She punched him in the sweet spot, then dropped, driving the dagger into the man's foot, then kneed him in the face as she sprang to her feet.

She surveyed the wreckage—all were down for the count, except the leader who was graveling on the ground.

"You should find a new line of work." She stared at him for a second, then walked off.

A couple of hours later, Julie still felt she was being watched. As she reached the edge of the oasis, she finally stopped.

"Whoever you are, come out!" she demanded. She heard footsteps behind her. She turned around and was surprised to see a woman standing there.

"How do you do, My Lady." The woman bowed.

__Caravan__

Micheal felt moisture on his lips and happily drank what was being offered.

After getting a good amount, he asked, "Where am I?"

"We are approaching the Canal of the Pharaohs," a man said.

"Who are you?" Micheal inquired.

"Mbizi. We are but slaves for our master," Mbizi answered.

"I am no slave," Micheal said with certainty.

"It will do no good to fight," a woman said.

Micheal looked in her direction. She was naked. It was at that point that he remembered he had no clothes on. No one on the cart had any clothes on.

The caravan stopped as they arrived at what had to be the Suez Canal(The Canal of the Pharaohs).

"Looks like the giant survived," he heard a man say. The man was fairly short, perhaps 5 foot 3. He was wearing an obvious wig and a giant necklace. He was trying to project his importance.

Micheal sat up. "I thank you for your assistance. Upon our arrival in the Delta, I shall reward you appropriately." Micheal said confidently.

"Silence, slave! I will ask the questions," the man chided. "What is your name?" he asked sharply.

"Micheal, Lord of Avalon," Micheal informed him. He didn't know if that would hold any meaning. He didn't know if he'd gone forward, backward, or if he'd stayed in the same time.

The man and his assistants broke out laughing. Micheal just stared at them, and the laughter broke off.

"You own the River Palace in the Delta?" The man was studying him.

"As I said—take me home, and you will be rich. Very rich indeed." Micheal was now confident he had either gone forward in time or was still in the same time. He was gambling on the hope that the secret stash was still there.

The men discussed everything, then returned and said, "If you're lying, you're a dead man."

Three days later, they reached the main channel of the Nile in the Delta.

"Are you really a lord?" Shani asked a little tentatively.

"Yes," Micheal affirmed. "I am going to need some clothes!" he informed Hondo.

"Anything else?" Hondo inquired.

"I will need my necklace back. And Mbizi and Shani are coming with us," Micheal said firmly.

Most of the caravan stayed camped by the side of the river while Hondo and his assistants escorted Micheal and his new friends onto a boat. Micheal and Mbizi did most of the rowing. Before sundown, they made about 15 miles out of the 50 they had to go.

"Why did you bring us with you?" Shani asked as they ate their sparse dinner.

"I abhor slavery, so I intend to purchase your freedom," he explained.

"You mean to set us free?" Mbizi seemed confused.

"Where would we go? What would we do?" Shani almost seemed scared.

"You don't want freedom?" Micheal challenged.

"Well..." Shani stammered.

"Her parents died when she was young. She doesn't know any other life," Mbizi explained.

"There will be a place for you at the palace, but if you wish to leave at any time, you will be welcome to," Micheal assured her. "We can discuss this later, but we have an all-day row tomorrow. We should get some sleep," Micheal lay down to rest.

Before he could sleep, he saw the stars and thought of Julie. Where was she now? Was she all right? He closed his eyes, and she was there.

"What would you be doing right now if we had never fallen through time?" Julie interrupted his contemplation of the stars as she entered the barn back at Bostonian.

"I don't know... Probably wasting the night away doing this very thing—before I got my three hours of sleep so I could "zombie" my way through my deliveries," he said in resignation.

"As I recall, you were searching for some lost treasure. What if you found it?" Julie challenged.

Micheal looked at the sky again. "No... I would have failed... If it weren't this, it would have been something else... I never told you this, but do you know the flight to Orlando took seven tries over two days before I finally got out of JFK... And that was just a prelude of things to come." He shook his head. "What about you?" he turned the tables.

Julie looked at him in consideration, then sat in the chair beside him and gazed at the stars. "If everything went to plan, I would be a few months pregnant, going in for my first check-ups. Now, I don't know if I'll ever have children." He could hear the tears behind her words.

"I'm sorry for everything you've lost, but you will have children someday," he said with as much assurance as he could but decided against lamenting on her poor help from him. He just wished his affection for her was enough.

He came out of the memory to a field of stars. Micheal felt Julie's longing for children. They rarely brought it up because they still had many times and places to come. So, any prospects of children were centuries away.

The next day, after rowing much of the day, the massive palace loomed on the horizon. Suddenly, another boat took an angle right at them.

"Pirates!" Hondo yelled.

The other boat was moving too fast to escape, and they were rammed. Several men jumped into the boat, and Micheal went into action. He disarmed one man and sent him into the river. Then another man attacked him with a sword. Micheal parried a couple of strikes and sliced a grazing slash across the man's leg. Then he dislodged the sword into the river and hit the man over the head with the hilt of the sword. After he kicked two other men overboard, the rest scurried back to their boat and rowed off as quickly as possible.

Micheal handed the sword to Hondo and said, "If this man tries anything, kill him... Now, let's go. Just another hour or so."

The look on Hondo's face was a mixture of fear and wonder.

"My Lord. You're not going to exact vengeance, are you?" Hondo asked nervously.

"For the service of saving me in my time of need? For bringing me home? ... Of course not. I promised reward, and I will deliver," Micheal assured him.

A bit later they rowed past the massive pilings and slowly drifted to a stop at the elevator shafts up the entry hall.

"Everyone step onto the platform," Micheal instructed. He used the secret combination to self-operate the elevator. As the platform reached the top, they were greeted by armed guards.

"I am Lord Avalon. I return to the Delta," Micheal said in Proto-scandic.

"Welcome home, My Lord," a woman between the guards replied in kind, and she bowed.

She came back up. Micheal indicated the rest of his party.

"I will show your associates to their chambers," she changed to Egyptian.

"My assistants require new clothes," he indicated to Mbizi and Shani.

"I will see to it," she bowed again. "Right this way," she indicated for everyone else to follow her.

Hondo looked at Micheal.

"I will see you all at dinner in my chambers," Micheal announced.

"Yes, My Lord," the palace manager agreed.

Micheal made his way to the Lord's module. He stepped onto the balcony and immediately felt the emptiness. He was lost in thought when he heard a voice from behind him.

"My Lord?" the palace manager said.

He turned to her, and she went to her knees. "Rise," he instructed.

She complied.

"What's your name?"

"Nailah, My Lord," she replied.

"The palace is in good order."

"Thank you, My Lord. I have hoped for your return." She seemed to be excited.

"Your devoted service shall be rewarded. I shall host dinner in one hour," Micheal stated firmly.

"It shall be done." Nailah bowed, then left.

Micheal went and accessed the secret vault. He found the tachyon scanner and ran a few scans. It revealed good and bad news. The bad news was that he had been thrown through time. The scanner indicated the date was February 26, 1676 B.C. The good news was that the portal was a Philadelphia portal, which meant he could return. But first, he needed to search this time period for Julie. He wouldn't want to leave without her if she were here.

Micheal dressed in his Scandic-Egyptian style. Then Nailah returned.

"Dinner is served, My Lord," she announced.

As he entered the Lord's dining hall, all the visitors bowed.

"I offer you the bounty of my table," he indicated for everyone to eat.

The party went late into the night. Then he approached Hondo.

"Have you enjoyed yourself?" he asked.

"Yes, My Lord." Hondo bowed.

"I'm glad... However, we have some business to attend." Micheal signaled for Nailah to join them. Two servants accompanied her. "I think this should be an adequate reward for your service to me." The servants presented two boxes of gold. "They will be delivered to your room," he explained, as Hondo seemed stunned by the reward.

Hondo picked up a handful, examining the pieces.

"You have my deepest gratitude for your aid in my time of need..." Micheal signaled for the servants to depart, then said, "Enjoy the rest of the night. You are invited to stay three days, and then I will see you safely back to your caravan." Micheal turned to leave and then turned back, "And one more thing—Mbizi and Shani are to remain in my service," he added firmly.

"Yes, My Lord Avalon." Hondo bowed, and Micheal walked away.

A few days later, Hondo departed. Micheal summoned Mbizi and Shani

"Thank you, Nailah," he dismissed her. "Now that I have released you from bondage, you are welcome to stay in my service. However, if you desire to pursue other interests, I will support you in those endeavors."

"I would greatly desire to remain here," Shani replied earnestly.

"As would I," Mbizi agreed.

Before he could continue, they were interrupted.

"My Lord, Vizier Kazemdi seeks an audience." Nailah escorted a finely dressed man.

"Thank you, Nialah," he dismissed her and the other servants.

"Pharaoh Nebsenre celebrates My Lord Avalon's return with an invitation to the palace," the vizier informed him.

"I'm honored." Micheal bowed.

CHAPTER 11: QUESTIONS OF FAITH

<u>The Stranger</u>

"H AVE WE MET?" JULIE asked curiously.

The woman walked into the tree-shaded grass surrounding a spring. Julie followed. The woman finally looked at her with her piercing amber eyes.

"I have followed your progress," the woman said finally.

"For how long?" Julie was caught off guard.

"About a week," the woman replied.

"While I was out in a sea of sand, and you just watched?" Julie flared. "I almost died!" Julie was angry.

"It's not my place to interfere," the woman countered.

"And who the hell are you, anyway?" Julie demanded.

"Just call me 'Isis'," the woman, *Isis*, instructed.

"Another god of Egypt." Julie rolled her eyes.

"You don't believe in the gods?" Isis cocked her head.

Isis was relatively tall. Maybe as tall as Micheal. Julie examined

Isis thoroughly. She had olive skin, black hair, and amber eyes. A gold bikini top supported her chest, and she had a bright, colorful skirt to her knees. She wore a chain crown with an orb stone at the center that glowed like a rainbow in the evening sun.

"I've seen a lot of things in my time..." Julie trailed off as she really considered the possibility.

Isis stepped up and stared into her eyes. "You have, haven't you?" Isis traced Julie's face. "So many years... So much pain..."

Julie suddenly felt exposed, like she was onstage in front of thousands with no clothes. She fought the urge to step back.

"I can see it now. I see you. You've seen many battles, many tough decisions." Isis turned away from her.

"What makes you think you know anything about me?" Julie challenged, trying not to cry.

"We are more alike than you know." Isis turned back to her with tears in her own eyes.

Isis stepped over and cupped Julie's face in her hands. Julie thought she might kiss her.

"In my thousands of years of life, I've done many questionable things. The guilt can eat you alive if you let it. Never feel guilty for defending your life, or the lives of others..." Isis was saying.

"It's not just that..." Julie began to argue.

"... We make the best decisions we can. Even I don't always know the consequences, but we must learn to forgive ourselves," Isis cut in.

Julie couldn't stop the tears from flowing. Isis wiped them from her cheeks.

"This might help with your current predicament." Isis removed the chain crown from her head and placed it on Julie's.

"I can't take this..." She tried to stop her.

"Yes, you can," Isis insisted, then stepped back. "I will be watching," she said as a pair of translucent rainbow-colored wings unfurled. With a couple of beats, Isis flew up above her. "I wish you luck!" she added. Then, it flew quickly higher and disappeared in a flash.

A few days later, as Julie made the two-day trek across the open desert to the Nile River valley, she had plenty of time to think about the stranger who called herself Isis. It was such a challenge for her rational mind. She had seen and encountered many oddities since the fall. The universe and the world were far stranger than she had ever imagined a lifetime ago in the 21st century, but she and Micheal had always been able to satisfactorily explain what the science was behind the magic. But in the space of a week, Julie had encountered three beings with God-like powers. She couldn't forget about Thor either.

During the Age of Atlantis, Julie herself had successfully portrayed Aphrodite, so she knew it could be faked, but Isis and her mystery savior, at the very least, did not have any obvious technology. She had tried to look. And Ra was impossibly large. So Julie had to consider the possibility that, regardless of what they truly were, the mythical gods of Egypt were real.

By the time the sun was nearing the western horizon, she reached the shore of the Nile. She sat in the grass and prepared to eat her dinner when a large boat came from the south and took an obvious detour in her direction. She stood to assess the potential threat. The boat was perhaps 60 feet long and quite ornate. She saw a man move to the side of the boat. He was wearing some royal accoutrement. He might be the Pharaoh. The boat came to a stop. Julie stood, awaiting their actions. The man and his apparent second stepped off the boat.

"My Goddess of Isis, we are blessed by your return... I am Sosestris, and this is my vizier, Siese, at your service.

So this again, she thought in resignation. She might as well go with it.

Avaris

Micheal thought about the name Nebsenre in his head. It was on the Turin Canon—column nine, row 14. He was from the 14th dynasty. The Hyksos, he thought. While the Hyksos were normally attributed to the 15th dynasty, the 14th dynasty were Semitic from the Near East. So, if they weren't the Hyksos, they were likely related to them—or at least friends and allies.

"Vizier Kazemdi—you are my honored guests. I shall host you this evening and we shall travel to Avaris in the morning." Micheal indicated the vizier to sit.

"I'm curious. You hail from a place called Avalon. There have been no others before or since; your ancestors built this place a century ago." The vizier raised a brow.

"It lies beyond the sea. It is quite a perilous journey to get here," Micheal explained. "But the journey of the ancestors was not forgotten. So I decided to venture to this great land and reestablish our connection to this great palace."

"His eminence is eager to reestablish the friendship, so famously attested of your family," the vizier said with a nod.

In the night, Micheal extracted the hidden backup boat. It was about 30 feet long and ten feet wide. It was also equipped with a perpetual turbine-drive system.

They left shortly after sunup and reached Avaris in a respectable six hours. The city wasn't as big as Memphis or Thebes, but it was cleaner than either of them. All the buildings were brand new, built in the last ten or twenty years.

The River Spur in east Delta had been artificially widened to over a mile across to create a large harbor. They bypassed the main harbor and sailed into the palace. It was definitely smaller than Karnak in Thebes and the palace in Itjawy.

The vizier led Micheal into the throne room. The Pharaoh was seated in a throne at the top of the steps at the end of the hall.

"Your Majesty! May I present Lord Avalon!" Kazemdi announced as they entered the light.

The hall went quiet as they proceeded to the bottom of the steps. Micheal went to his knees in deference.

"My Lord Avalon, you may rise," The Pharaoh instructed.

Pharaoh Nebsenre had a lighter complexion than most Egyptians, clearly from Mesopotamia or the Levant. "It pleases me that My Lord has returned... There have been some impressive rumors of the mysterious Lords from Avalon," the Pharaoh stated complimentarily.

"Might I present your Majesty with a gift?" Micheal nodded.

The Pharaoh indicated agreement. Micheal indicated for Shani to bring the gift forward. She presented the gift on a small silver platter. Pharaoh Nebsenre's mellow green eyes lit up at the presentation of an amber goblet. The base of the cup was made entirely of titanium. The bridge to the cup was an amber orb that emitted a gentle orange glow. The main cup was a titanium frame, encasing dozens of amber pieces.

"I have never seen the like before!" Nebsenre proclaimed.

"It is called amber. It is native to my lands," Micheal explained.

"I much desire to learn more of the land of Avalon. I would also like to show you the grandeur of Avaris. Much like you, my ancestors hail from another land. I know you will appreciate our unique style here." The Pharaoh apparently felt some kind of connection because they were both originally from foreign lands.

"I would be honored." Micheal bowed in agreement.

As the early afternoon sun blazed over the delta, a procession led out of the palace into the streets. About halfway through the procession, Micheal stood side-by-side with the Pharaoh on his chariot of gold.

"We are not what you expected?" the Pharaoh asked.

"Change is a common occurrence between rulers of any dominion," Micheal was purposely deferential.

"If you mean to take over, you won't be successful." The Pharaoh read into something he had said.

"My forbearers could have removed an untested female Pharaoh, but they gave their allegiance to her... You are correct that should I wish it, I could displace you. But I hold no such desire. So long as I am a guest in your domain, I swear fealty to you," Micheal promised.

"I accept your devotion... However, I am curious why you are so certain you could displace me."

"I possess technology and know-how that exceeds anything in this land. It would allow me to proclaim myself a deity, through which I could command the allegiance of the masses," Micheal explained confidently.

"I will say one thing, My Lord Avalon, you don't lack confidence. I look forward to our partnership," the Pharaoh said, with an odd air that worried Micheal about his intentions.

Their afternoon parade through the streets of Avaris was well received. The Pharaoh soaked up all the praise and adoration being shouted from the masses. After a three-hour tour, they returned to the palace for dinner.

"My Lord, there's something I'd like to discuss... But first, where's My Lady?" Nebsenre began.

"There is no Lady anymore..." Micheal fought the tears that came at the thought of Julie, and he could not reign them in.

"I'm terribly sorry. How did it happen?" the Pharaoh asked sympathetically.

Micheal thought of which lie to give.

One of the first things he had done upon his return to River Palace was access the sky-net and search for Julie, but it had been thus far fruitless, and he feared he would never see her again.

"We were ambushed and severely outnumbered. I was able to vanquish the enemy but at great cost... That is why I decided to follow my forefathers," Micheal explained.

That night, Micheal had the strangest dream. He found himself in the sky above the Giza plateau. The sun was blazing in the sky. The blue sky turned black, and the river of stars stretched across the horizon, but the sun remained ever-resent. He looked down, and the pyramids turned into stars, then became Orion's belt. Orion formed into a transparent man. He drew his bow and let loose. The arrow whizzed past Micheal's ear. He followed its trajectory. As he turned, the sun disc became an eye, and another man formed around it. It was Ra. He reached out, and the arrow turned to cinder.

Ra sent a blast of flames, and Orion blocked it with his shields. Ra increased the intensity. While Orion was retreating, the star Sirius began to brighten and rose up as a woman with wings. Micheal realized it was the goddess Isis. She and Orion teamed up against Ra, repelling him. Ra then turned down and targeted the Nile Delta. His shadow turned the light to darkness. Orion and Isis dove down and shielded Egypt from Ra's wrath. Isis split the darkness with a beam of light from her crown. Ra was blinded, and Orion used his club to blast Ra back to the heavens. The sun disc was sucked into the river of stars, and then diminished into the horizon.

<u>Sesostris II</u>

Julie was led to a grand palatial suite in Itjway.

"We hope our meager offering will suffice," Sesostris groveled.

"It will do." She acted unimpressed.

"Should you require anything else, it will be acquired for you," Vizier Siese assured her.

"Thank you," she dismissed them.

Julie had been trying to figure out why the Pharaoh believed she was Isis. Then she considered the crown Isis had given her. It must be the way the Pharaoh knows it's the incarnation of the goddess. She knew that Sobekneferu was interacting with beings who claimed to be different gods. She also knew that the Pharaoh believed the gods came and lived in the form of a normal person for periods of time. She realized this was likely a holdover from the Atlantean Age. An echo from the past, as it were. There was something else she required, but she knew they couldn't acquire it for her. She needed to build a generator that could open a Philadelphia portal.

Through their discussions on their way from the upper Nile to Itjaway, Julie had learned this was Sesostris II, who was Sobekneferu's great-grandfather, according to Micheal. He had filled her in on his knowledge of the 12th dynasty. So that meant she was roughly a century in the past from their current present.

Ra apparently had the ability to open portals within a temporal eddy. Was he able to open temporal portals to the river of time? Or even more terrifying, the prospect of a rip current? If it was a Philadelphia portal, she might see Micheal again. He was gone forever if it was either of the other kind. She had to hold on to hope.

The next day, she went to the Pharaoh's chambers.

"I need your advice concerning some of the Nomarchs." Sesostris began. "Baufra in Xiost has been attempting to build alliances in the Levant, and there have been encroachments from the Nubians in Aswan," Sesostris explained the situation with some of the provincial governors.

"If we march to Canaan and demand ransom to leave, it will send a message to all of the Near East not to interfere with your kingdom," Julie instructed.

"It would require too much time. And with the harvest, we can't afford to pull so many men from the fields," the Pharaoh argued.

"You don't need very many men. I'll be the force to reckon with. Call up 1,000 men, and we will march on Canaan," Julie put forward her plan.

While she didn't really want to go to battle again, she thought a good offense was good defense. Now, she needed new weapons.

Remembering where Micheal had said there was iron and a few other valuable elements, she had the Pharaoh send some men to mine it for her. A week later, she had what she needed. She smithed the weapons and armor herself. She made a gilded steel chest plate, greaves, and shoulder guards. Then she made a pair of swords that connected to make a staff. She also crafted a recurve bow, along with some non-lethal arrows.

Julie woke up in her bed in her New York penthouse. She went over to the balcony overlooking Central Park. She decided to go for a run. As she ran, she noticed the blossoms near the Meadow, kids playing tag in the playground, the sky was blue, and fluffy white clouds were dotting the otherwise monolithic palate. A rocket sped through the air, and there was a bright flash. A wall of flames began consuming the buildings of Midtown. Julie looked back at the playground in time to see the children engulfed by the flames. She braced for the fire, but when she opened her eyes, she was unharmed, standing in a field of ash and bone. She turned to see Lord George Cavendish standing there.

"My Lady Avalon, not could I have done this without thy assistance," he laughed maniacally.

Julie awoke in a cold sweat.

The nightmares that haunted the dark throughout the years had escalated in Micheal's absence. She felt so hopeless. It felt like her sanity was slipping away. She needed to get back to Micheal.

They crossed the Sinai and arrived in Canaan a couple of weeks later. An army of some thousands came to greet them. The Pharaoh, his generals, and Julie went to parlay with the king from Canaan.

"Sesostris, I would appreciate it if you would take your small army and leave. There's no need for bloodshed." The Canaanite king seemed cocky in his own tongue.

"It has come to my attention that you have been seeking an alliance with Xiost. I would like you to stop," the Pharaoh tried in rudimentary Canaanite.

Julie had learned it in the wasteland.

The Canaanite king looked at Julie with interest. "What His Majesty is saying is, any diplomatic or trade ties must be with Egypt and not just part of it," she interjected in perfect Canaanite.

A look of surprise passed across the king's face. "And why should I listen to you? If this is all the Pharaoh can muster, I think we'll just take Egypt for ourselves. After we've dealt with this pathetic army." The king and his men laughed.

"Hammurabi, there is no reason we can't be friends, but your interference will not be tolerated. To show how serious I am, I will offer terms..." Sesostris was saying.

"You are in no position to establish terms..." Hammurabi cut him off.

"I would advise you to show a little more respect to the Pharaoh," Julie returned the favor. "The terms are to your benefit..." she paused to see his reaction.

"Very well. Let's hear these terms." The king seemed irritated.

"We will settle this with our best versus your best. Except you have 20 times our number, so you pick your 20 best men, and they will do combat with... me..." Julie paused at his surprised reaction.

Then, a smile came across his face. "You? ... A woman?" he balked.

"Unless you're worried..." Julie cocked her head to the side.

"Very well..." the king seemed confident.

"If you win, the Pharaoh's soldiers are yours, and he'll pay a heavy ransom for his return to Egypt..." she paused.

"And if you..." the king tried not to laugh, "and if you win..." he proffered.

"...You will pay restitution for your efforts, and all future efforts will stop. And we can all be friends again," Julie finished.

"My Lady, you certainly show confidence. But I look forward to claiming my new soldiers. Good luck. Or should I say goodbye, My Lady?" He smiled.

As they returned to their lines, the Pharaoh seemed worried. "Are you sure about this, your eminence?"

"Trust me," she said, as she headed out to meet her foes.

She sized up the men. Most were large—taller than her, and most were bulging with muscle, but she knew that her speed and skill were likely decisive. And she had the advantage of having armor made of advanced steel. And her other weapons were far superior to the enemy.

As she prepared for combat, the opposing armies closed in on each side to watch the battle. She looked to the west and saw the sun approaching the horizon. She waited a moment until the light was at the right angle. She began running at the enemy line, and as she neared, she turned her head to the left. The gem in her crown caught the light, and the prism array momentarily disoriented the warriors. She slid down and, in a fierce stroke of her staff, swept the legs of several of the men. She rolled to her feet and separated her staff into the double swords. The tempered steel sliced through multiple bronze swords like a hot knife through butter. She jumped over an oncoming attack and laid fierce blows with the butts of her swords, to devastating effect.

She drew her bow as she landed and sent a spray of bolts that hit with precision in the soldiers' soft spots. The arrows were blunt, but the impacts knocked the targets out of commission. In her opening flurry, she had halved her opponents. With her staff back in one piece, she went on the offensive. She helicoptered the staff and went into a series of lightning-fast strikes, halving the enemy again.

She stopped a sword strike with her left forearm then knocked the sword out of the man's hand. She punched him in the face and then the stomach. As he doubled over, she brought his face down on her knee. She ducked a sword she felt coming from behind and kicked the man in the chest in the same motion.

A spear that was thrown at her deflected off her chest plate. She used a roundhouse right on the next man's chin. The sweet spot cut her foes to three. One of the men who was down began to get back up. She evaded another attack and struck the man down again. She decided, for reassurance's sake, that while eluding the pursuit of the final three, she went and subsequently laid insurance blows on the other 17 men.

She had committed not to kill any of them. She just needed to decommission them. She paused upon completion as two men closed in on opposite sides. She waited for the right moment, then flipped up and helped them crash headlong into each other. She kicked them in the face as she came back down.

Her final opponent was a large man, perhaps 6'6". He threw his weapons and yelled, "Come on, little lady, let's do this straight up!"

She wasn't worried. She dropped her weapons and moved to attack. Her blows had little effect, and he kicked her in the stomach and sent her flying. She changed her strategy. She attempted to sweep him to the ground, but he was surprisingly quick. He dodged her next attack and hit her in the face, sending her reeling. She came back, letting him sidestep her. He grabbed her as she anticipated. She heel-scraped his Achilles, and he released her. She then got him in a headlock and used his momentum to suplex him. She slammed him hard to the ground, then flipped him to his back and choked him out. As she rose to her feet, the king approached warily.

"Who are you?" He was in a state of disbelief.

"You can call me... Isis." She stared down the enemy army.

They returned to Egypt with a chest of gold and a new diplomatic agreement with Canaan. There was no doubt in Sesostris' mind that Julie was indeed Isis. Now hopefully, she could work on her other problem.

<u>The Coat</u>

Micheal had spent a month in Avaris advising the Pharaoh. He was finally allowed to return to River Palace.

"My Lord, do you still have the dreams?" Mbizi inquired.

"Most every night," he confirmed.

Mbizi had come to Avaris to assist him in whatever he needed, and they had become fast friends. It had been a long time since Micheal made new friends, but Mbizi reminded him of T.C.

Micheal had become accustomed to his position as a Lord. Over the past 50 years, he had been one, in one sense or another. But on the downside, it was hard to get close to anyone when they would all bow down and kiss your feet. Mbizi always showed respect in front of others, but in private, he seemed comfortable being straight and honest with Micheal.

"I have brought you someone who understands dreams," Mbizi said as he escorted an old man into the chamber.

"My Lord, I have come to talk about your dreams," the man said.

"I'm sorry, what's your name?" Micheal asked.

"Joseph, My Lord. I was the chief interpreter to the Pharaoh some years ago. I used to be vizier," Joseph informed him.

Micheal looked at him with interest. "How is it that you would know about dreams?" Micheal challenged.

"I don't, but God does. The one true God."

Michael was now certain. He tried to verify, "Was your father Jacob, then Israel? And your grandfather was Isaac, right?"

"How do you know that?" Joseph seemed surprised. "Unless... you're the ones. The ones I was told about." Joseph looked at him more closely. "Where's your wife?" Joseph looked around.

"She's gone..." Micheal tried not to cry. "... You know our secret?" he had an idea.

"You come from the future," Joseph seemed uncertain.

"We do... But I was sent through a time portal by some being or person. I don't know where Julie is. But you are a prophet of God, right? Can you find out where she is?" he asked hopefully.

"I'm sorry, Micheal. I fear that's not in my ability." Joseph shook his head.

"Of course, you can't," Micheal said bitterly.

"God has a plan for all of us. You must keep faith," Joseph tried to console him.

"And what's that? Stranding us in the perilous reaches of time? We weren't chosen, like you..." Micheal was losing his cool.

"When my brothers sold me into bondage, I didn't understand God's plan for me either," Joseph tried to relate.

"Adam and Eve said we weren't chosen. We were just in the wrong place at the wrong time," Micheal walked onto the balcony. "... We're just nobodies, lost in time!" Micheal was dejected.

Joseph walked out to the balcony. "I don't know if you'll see your wife again, but I can say that definitively, you... both of you... are important... Don't lose faith," Joseph admonished.

"I can remember every moment of my 80 years of life, and I can say with certainty that while the bible appears to be based on actual history, I have trouble believing the claims of divinity," Micheal shot back.

"We all face trials of faith..." Joseph began.

"You have to have faith for there to be a trial..." Micheal cut in. He paused to see what Joseph would say.

Joseph just looked at him.

"I need my wife back, and maybe these dreams can help. Are you able to explain them?" he returned to the purpose of Joseph's visit. He turned his head to the setting sun.

After a moment, Joseph spoke, "Tell me these dreams."

Micheal recounted his vivid dreams, detail by detail. The golden disc, piercing through the skies, the orange glow was like Ra taunting him.

"A shadow of danger begins to darken Egypt's future. Only you are capable of restoring the light," Joseph explained vaguely.

"What? Does that mean I will find Julie? Is she Isis?" Micheal wanted clarity. "When does this shadow arrive?" he pressed.

"I cannot say about your wife, but you will know when the challenge comes. Your decisions will decide the fate of Egypt and, indeed, the world," Joseph warned.

"You can't say, or you won't?" Micheal was incensed.

"I'm sorry, Micheal, I just don't know," Joseph apologized and then left.

As the sun dipped below the horizon, the shadow of earth descending over Egypt felt like the weight of the world on his shoulders, and Julie wasn't there to help him.

The next day, Micheal went to see Joseph off. "My Lord, I thank you for your advice, and at so much trouble," Micheal nodded to Joseph.

"I have something for you," Joseph presented a multi-colored robe. "My father gave me this when I was 16. May it help you to keep faith. God does have a plan. Now, this is just me, but I believe you will see her again." Joseph began descending in the elevator.

Micheal closed his eyes and saw her face.

Three Wise Men

October 1, 1876 B.C.

Word of my demonstration at Canaan spread rapidly through the Near East and Egypt. All of the Nomarchs quickly fell in line, and several other neighboring countries sued for better relations with the Pharaoh. I have, however, had minimal time to focus on my main problem. Because Sesostris asked that I develop a plan to expand the arable land around the Faiyum Oasis, now that the implementation is fully underway, I have begun my efforts in earnest to find a way back to the 18th century B.C.

It has been a frustrating challenge. Egypt is short on several important elements I need to build my generators. I have decided to take the limited metal, make a small, sea-worthy ship, and sail it to Gibraltar. It has been four months, and there have been no sign of Micheal. He could be in any time, over a 200-year span across the eddy. I know how he thinks. He would first try to search the world to confirm if I am in the same time period. The first place we would try to rendezvous would be where we last saw each other. River Palace is in the delta. If one of us fails to show up within a week of the other, we leave a note. Multiple times, I have checked the most obvious places with no word. Upon determining we aren't in the same time period, he would try to get back to 1776 B.C. So that's what I will try to do.

I miss Micheal terribly. It has been five months, and I feel like I am just a hollow shell—like a tin man. Although I have lost not only my heart, but the essence of who I am. I hold onto hope that we will find each other again.

P.S. I have made a goal to reunite by my birthday.

Julie walked out onto the balcony to look over the oasis. The new palace at Faiyum had been gifted to her by the Pharaoh. She was currently hosting the Pharaoh's court, and since her arrival a couple of months earlier, she had made some needed modern upgrades.

"Your eminence, His Majesty requests you attend court," the vizier interrupted her thoughts.

"Thank you, Siese." She took a deep breath, then went to play her part.

As she made her way to the receiving chamber, the priests lining the hall bowed low before her. Then, the entire court bowed at her entrance to the dais, where she assumed her position to the right of the Pharaoh.

Various petitioners came before the Pharaoh. Then, three non-Egyptian men approached. After the Pharaoh allowed them up, the older man to the left of the lead seemed familiar. As she was trying to place the face, he locked eyes with her and seemed to squint in a confused fashion. As they conversed with Sesostris, she finally had the light go on regarding his identity. He looked like a significantly aged Shem, which made her examine his two associates with interest.

"...Most esteemed holy men of Canaan. You are my guests here in Egypt, but there shall be no preaching," the Pharaoh decreed. "You will also remain honored guests here at the palace for several days." Sesostris gave a signal, and the men were escorted away. Before they went too far, Shem shot her a knowing nod.

After court was adjourned, Julie sent for them.

"Your eminence, the men you sent for," Siese escorted them.

Once Siese left the chambers, Julie finally felt she could properly greet Shem.

"It's so good to see you, my old friend!" Julie said in Atlantean as she threw her arms around him.

"My Lady Avalon, I barely recognized you!" he answered in kind, indicating how she was dressed.

"Likewise. It seems time has finally caught up to you." She raised a brow.

"Indeed. It has been nearly 500 years since we first met," he pointed out.

"And you don't look a day over 550," she joked, to his amusement.

"Oh, and where are my manners...." Shem realized he had forgotten to introduce his companions. "... Julie, do you speak the Semitic tongue?" he asked in a mixture of Ancient Atlantean and Hebrew.

"I do," she confirmed in Hebrew.

"Well then..." Shem switched fully to Hebrew. "My Lady, Julie, this is my great-grandson, Abraham, and his son, Isaac."

She chuckled a little.

"Is something funny?" Isaac seemed confused.

"It's because they're in your scriptures?" Shem guessed.

"They are..." Julie looked at them again. "It's a true honor to meet you both." She smiled.

"What do we do in your scriptures?" Abraham asked.

"Well, you were 75 when you left Canaan. When you were 100, you and Sarah gave birth, miraculously to Isaac..." she gestured to Isaac. "Then God tested your obedience. He asked you to sacrifice Isaac, and both of you obeyed. An angel stayed your hand." They both looked stunned.

She did a calculation in her head. "How old are you?" she asked Isaac.

"I'm 41."

"That was only four years ago?" Julie was reexamining her faith.

Despite everything she had seen, her mind kept rationalizing it all. Particularly now, encountering some of the mythological gods. Were they all imposters of some kind? Or were they all gods? The Bible most definitely was based on history. She had encountered far too many biblical figures and witnessed far too many biblical events to think it had been made up. She also understood, from a scientific perspective, how they happened. Did that mean God, or whoever you believed God to be, wasn't behind these events? The Bible rarely explained the why.

"What am I to your time?" Abraham inquired.

"You're considered the father of the greatest religious movements of our time. Over half the world's population adheres to the Abrahamic Faiths," she explained.

"But you're lacking your own?" Abraham studied her.

"No... Well... I don't know." Julie searched for the right words. "It's more I am unworthy to be in such company." She looked away.

"What are you doing for the Pharaoh?" Shem asked.

"He thinks I'm the embodiment of the Goddess Isis. I've been advising his rule for a couple of months now," she replied with a shrug.

"And what about Micheal? Where is he?"

The question gut-checked her, and the tears came. "I don't know. We got separated four months ago, and now I don't know if I'll ever see him again." She bowed her head.

"What happened?" Shem was concerned.

"We were attacked by the Sun God Ra. He sent Micheal through some sort of portal, then sent me here—100 years in the past from where I was. Who knows when or where he sent Micheal." The tears were flowing steadily now. "Maybe we're being punished. Maybe we deserve it," she said in resignation.

"Why would you say such a thing?" Shem balked.

"It was our fault." The tears came anew.

"What was your fault?" Shem sounded worried.

"The war," she said simply.

"What war?" Shem pretended not to know.

"Three billion people died because of me," Julie shook her head, bowing.

"That's not possible," Shem protested.

"We made the bombs, and they were used to destroy civiliza-tion," she was explaining.

"You mean the nuclear bomb?" Abraham deduced.

"Yes," she confirmed.

"Why would you do that?" Shem seemed to accuse.

"The Empress of Atlantis had us abducted, and they implanted a small chip device at the base of our brains. It allowed them to cause crippling pain whenever they wanted," she was explaining.

"Why would they have targeted you?" Abraham interjected.

"Empress Selia had removed your sister, Jessalyn, from the throne..." she directed at Shem. "... When we arrived in the time period, we went to see her. That put us on the radar. They spied on us for a year following our scientific research. When they thought they needed our research, they came and coerced us into doing blind research for the government. We were usually able to determine what we had created or what we were making. When we discovered we had given them a hydrogen bomb... we made every effort to get it back, but... it was too late..." Julie broke off as the tears returned. She closed her eyes. "... That day haunts my dreams. And it's not just the war. In the last 50 years since we fell, I've killed so many people... And the fact that they were trying to harm or kill me doesn't make it any better... I see their faces, I hear their screams... I'm going to hell, aren't I?" Julie dropped her head. As she leaned against the edge of the balcony, Shem stepped up next to her.

"I know your heart. God knows your heart. You always have the right to defend yourself. I know you would never intend to kill anyone," Shem seemed certain.

"Then how come I'm so haunted," she wasn't convinced.

"Perhaps we can help you with that," Abraham said kindly. "Please sit," he indicated a chair.

Julie tentatively sat.

"What is your full name?" Abraham requested.

"Julie Alexandra Buckingham Hall." The Hall reminded her of Micheal again. How could she ever find him?

They all surrounded her and placed their hands on her head.

"Oh God, we bless Julie Alexandra Buckingham Hall. Julie, the unique challenges to your situation are known to your Father in Heaven. Suffering in your heart at the actions you have taken to defend yourself and others indicates your true nature. Your sorrow over the difficult decisions and their poor outcomes is further proof. We bless you that your mind will be calm and your heart will be whole. Beloved daughter, be at peace. This I say in the name of God, Amen."

As the blessing was bestowed, she felt a warm sensation wash over her, as if the weight of the world had been lifted from her shoulders.

"How do you feel?" Shem asked.

"Like I'm lighter than air," she said gratefully.

"You're not thinking about flying away, now are you?" Shem joked.

"Only if I see a rainbow," the reference was lost on them. "Never mind, it's a saying from my time," she dismissed the point.

"Can you still fly?" Shem asked seriously.

"We lost the rings," she gazed at a sky full of memories.

"Rings? How can rings make you fly?" Isaac seemed confused.

"We have spoken in the past about the way society was," Shem said.

"My dear Julie, would you perhaps share your angelic voice? It has been far too long." Shem smiled.

"How long for you? Three hundred years?" She shook her head.

"Pandora so loved Avalon," Shem commented.

"Oh, how rude of me. How is Pandora," she chided herself for not asking sooner.

"She died... Eight years ago," Shem informed her.

"That's terrible. How did it happen?" Julie asked, with sorrow in her heart.

"It was old age. She was surrounded by her family," Shem informed her.

"I'm so sorry," she touched his shoulder.

"I just realized I have something for you," Shem reached inside his sack and pulled out a small stone box. It was an expanded octagonal box about eight by four inches and around four inches tall. It had cut gemstones laid in various patterns. "This belonged to Pandora. She wanted you to have it." Shem handed it to her.

She looked at it with interest. She couldn't help but wonder: Pandora's Box. Was this the one from mythology? She decided not to open it until she knew more about it... just in case.

"Thank you." She set the box on the table, then went and picked up her lute.

"Before I play anything, I never did ask why you came to Egypt," she asked curiously.

"I had a vision telling me to come here. I didn't know why; I just obeyed," Abraham answered. "I asked Shem and Isaac to come with me. Now I'm sure you are the reason," he finished.

"You wasted a trip. I'm insignificant," she argued. "Micheal's gone, and I'm trapped here, probably for the rest of my life." She felt helpless.

"No one is insignificant to God. Julie, I promise everything will be all right," Abraham said directly.

"Now, let's hear that beautiful voice," Shem pivoted again.

"What do you want to hear?" Julie asked Shem.

"Well, your song, All of Me, became our song." She could tell he was living some memory from the distant past over again. She had seen the look on Micheal's face many times.

Julie played the smooth melody on the lute. As the night wore on, she played many tunes from that distant century when they ruled the music world. She finished with a new one she had written: "Lost". It was about their predicament, and until she found Micheal again, she would be lost.

CHAPTER 12: OPPOSITE SIDES

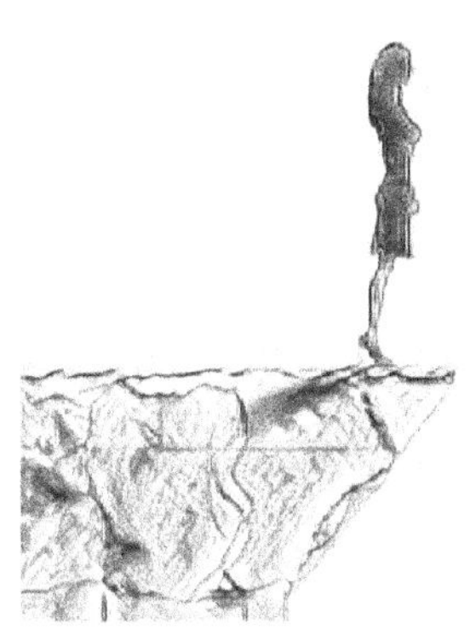

"**W**HAT IS THE NATURE of time?" Micheal said aloud to himself. He sat in quiet reflection on the balcony, watching the stars as they began their magical illuminations, as the last vestiges of sun faded into twilight. "The stars attempt to reveal their dichotomic nature. The constancy of their shine evokes ideals of permanence, while the distorted aspect of Cassiopeia belies the fact that the stars are in constant motion." He paused his oratory to examine the sky.

It had become familiar as they adapted to each time period, but Micheal could see the glaring differences between the centuries and millennia.

He always dictated his oration in English. On the occasions that he was separated from Julie, he periodically wanted to hear his native tongue.

"The fourth dimension is thought to be abstract, and yet I know now that it can be traversed in much the same way as the first three."

The thoughts about the nature of time, combined with those of Julie, brought him back to the first time he had ever seen her on TV.

Micheal's family had just barely gotten basic cable, and he had become a regular viewer of the only business channel available on their service. He was watching the morning show.

"The new technology stocks are booming. It's the dotcom economy. There seems to be a hot new internet stock every week. How do you know which one to buy? Who better to answer that than the top markets analyst at J.P. Morgan, and a teenager to boot! So she understands the new tech better than most... Julie Buckingham, welcome to the show," Mark said.

"Thank you, Mark; I'm happy to be here," Julie said.

Micheal's heart skipped a beat—he had never seen anyone so beautiful. For a moment, he was mesmerized. She was wearing a tight white blouse with her hair in tousled layers. Her piercing doe eyes shone like sapphires. He finally regained the use of his brain.

"... The EBITDA for the lion's share of the dotcoms is very excessive. It is unsustainable," Julie stated.

"So you think the markets are headed for a downturn," Joe seemed surprised.

"Inside of a year," Julie said affirmatively.

"And you're only 18," Joe marveled. "When I was 18, I was looking for a party, not advising one of the top finance companies," Joe joked.

"As long as it's a beach party, you can count me in," Julie laughed.

"We will discuss the markets and perhaps a party or two, with Julie who is joining us for the full three hours," Mark said as the show went to break.

Micheal came out of the memory from 65 years in his past. Even now, he still couldn't believe she had married him. But after 50 years together, he feared he would never see those pretty eyes again.

Julie worked tirelessly on constructing her seagoing vessel. Finally, as an anniversary gift to herself, it was ready. But now, her voyage would be delayed. Sesostris had a small crisis. Inundation had begun late and was lackluster. The Pharaoh had asked that she, the Goddess Isis, Bringer of Life, use her power to save the crops.

January 12, 1875 B.C.

I had to spend a few months attempting something I wasn't sure would work. I attempted to build some natural ion posts in Ethiopia to encourage the monsoons to kick in. Vizier Siese and I went to Ethiopia. I was able to identify some magnetically polarized rocks. Then, I recruited some of the local people who lived south of Nubia and taught them how to use the rocks to build monuments to the gods. The posts were built on the sides of a small canyon, making a kind of wind tunnel. Fortunately for me, though the effect was fairly minimal, it was enough. The taller the monuments became, the more the winds blew, which sparked the monsoon. This was followed by months of festivals celebrating me... I mean Isis.

So now I'm finally leaving today on my voyage to Gibraltar. Then, hopefully, I can reverse the door through time back to Micheal.

P.S. Unhappy 54th anniversary in time... Happy 81st, Micheal

Julie sailed up the arm of the Nile where River Palace would be built in a century or so. She tried to feel Micheal's presence as she passed through the exact location but felt nothing. Maybe he was gone for good.

Julie broke the coast's edge two hours later, where Alexandria would be built. Now, a thousand miles of the Mediterranean separated her from a chance to get back to the future.

Micheal used the sky-net to find enough metal to build a ship large enough to get to Gibraltar. He sailed an uneventful week and arrived at the secret hideout. He got right to work to tune the generators in an attempt to reverse the gate through time. He went back to the 17th century during their Philadelphia experiments.

"How do you know we can get back?" Julie demanded.

"In the Philadelphia experiment, the USS Eldridge, in an attempt to render it invisible, accidentally teleported to Norfolk from Philadelphia and about 40 years into the future. Based on the tachyon readings from our previous encounters in the Bermuda Triangle, I have determined that in that experiment, there was some kind of temporal tether that maintained a connection through time to the departure point. The door swings both ways, so when you activate the generators on the arrival side, it sends you back to the original jump point," Micheal explained.

"What, so we will go back to the same point in time? It will be like we never left?" Julie challenged.

"Not exactly... The crewman who detailed his experience on the Eldridge said he was taken to a holding facility for some hours, and when they returned from the 80s to Philadelphia in 1943, the same amount of time had elapsed on either side of the gate," Micheal countered.

"How long does the tether last? Or is it permanent?" Julie raised a brow.

"I don't know. The indications are that it fades over time. So who knows if it fades completely."

Micheal came out of the memory and began running scans with the tachyonometer. He adjusted the frequency until he found complimentary harmonics. So now he could go back, but he would return to Egypt first.

Julie sailed northwest for a couple of days until she could see the south end of Crete. Then, it would be the gap to Sicily. On the second day at open sea, the noonday sun began to be obscured by dark clouds rapidly approaching from the west. The wind began to pick up dramatically. Julie steered southeast to try and avoid the worst of the storm. She pushed as fast as possible for an hour, but the wind began picking up. She estimated it was around 50 to 60 miles an hour. The swells climbed to upwards of 20 feet. She was fighting to keep her boat upright. The pressure dropped rapidly. She felt her ears pop. The winds pushed up to 70 miles an hour. The sea swells began capping at 30 feet high. One broke over her ship. She tried to maintain orientation, but another swarmed her, capsizing it. Julie desperately tried to hold on, but the next wave hit hard, shattering the hull, and she was crushed under the surface.

Julie was disoriented. She swam away from the chaos, kicking until the water was relatively calm around her. She released some air bubbles and watched which direction they went. She followed them until she broke through the surface. She took in her first breath in several minutes. There were still 30-foot mountains in the sea all around her. She grabbed a large piece of debris and held on for the ride. After a few hours, the waves began to lessen, and the wind dropped to a stiff breeze. Exhausted by her bout with Mother Nature, Julie laid her body precariously on her makeshift raft and fell asleep.

She woke with a chill. She tried to peer through the darkness, but it was impossible with only starlight. After getting her bearings, she thought to herself—another desert, only this one of salt water.

She ran it just like it was the sand desert. She tried from dusk till dawn every day to stay warm, kicking with her legs and heading south, trying to reach the African coast. She slept in the middle of the day when it was hottest. Since the storm had passed, there had been no rain, barely a cloud in the sky. By the evening of the third day, she was desperately thirsty. She had yet to see land. She was losing hope, but she decided to push through the night. Just when she was felt like giving up, she saw the moon rising to her left. There was a stable horizon. "Land ho!" she thought.

She turned east and pushed with the last bit of energy that remained. A couple of hours later, she was there. She collapsed on the beach, and everything went dark.

Micheal saw the familiar outline of River Palace, silhouetted by the dawn. He sailed past the landing and parked at one of the elevators. Mbizi and Shani were there to welcome him back.

"My Lord Avalon, we celebrate your return," Shani said with a smile.

"Thank you, Shani," Micheal nodded at her.

"Did you find what you were looking for?" Mbizi inquired.

"Indeed I did," Micheal looked at them with consideration. "There's something I have to discuss with the both of you." He took a deep breath. They looked expectantly at him. "Now, this may sound crazy, but I have the ability to move between different points in time."

They looked bewildered.

"Allow me to explain. We met around this season about one year ago. I have a capability to go to that moment in time if I wish to."

They seemed to understand.

"You are of the gods." Shani's eyes went wide.

"I will be leaving this time. Both of your families are gone. I was wondering if you'd like to come with me?" he proposed.

"Of course, My Lord," Mbizi said with a bow.

"You don't have to... If you wish to stay here, your place is secure," he tried to reassure them.

"I am with you, Micheal," Mbizi reiterated.

"We both are, My Lord," Shani agreed.

"Then it is settled. But we need to go to Avaris to farewell his Eminence." Micheal was happy his friends would be coming.

They returned to River Palace two weeks later following a grand send off from Nebsenre. Then, it was a weeklong farewell festival for everyone at the palace, and they would leave the following day.

"Thank you for coming," Micheal said as Nailah entered his chambers. "I have been thoroughly impressed with your management this past year," he added.

"My Lord," Nailah bowed. "It has been a particular honor to serve My Lord Avalon." She bowed again.

"I have something for you," he grabbed the necklace off the

table. "This is a token from my land to remember me." He held it up for her to see. It was a choker made of cobalt, with five inlays of amber in descending size, from the center stone. The middle stone was engraved with their Egyptian cartouche, and it used a magnetic clasp. He circled behind her. She looked straight ahead as he encircled her neck. She gently explored the gift with her fingers.

"I shall treasure this." Then Nialah headed back to the festivities.

Micheal Mbizi and Shani sailed north up the delta to the Mediterranean the next morning. About ten miles north of the coast, they dropped anchor.

"So now, my friends, there will be a bright light, and then you will be disoriented for a time. You won't be able to see or hear. But it will be temporary, so don't be afraid," he admonished them.

He activated the generators, and they began producing a slight hum. A minute later, the vortex started spinning in the sky.

"Micheal?" he heard Mbizi say as he shook him.

He opened his eyes and sat up.

"We were worried," Shani said.

"I'm okay," he assured them. He stood up and pulled out the tachyon scanner. It confirmed that the date was February 21, 1775 B.C.

February 21, 1875 B.C.

I have resumed my role as Isis at court. The loss of my ship in the storm was devastating. I was a week away from my goal, and now it seems out of sight. It took months to build that ship, only to be caught in a hurricane-like storm in the Mediterranean.

It took weeks to get back to Faiyum. It would take months, through treacherous lands, to get to Gibraltar over land. I don't know if I can keep my sanity if it takes many more months or years to get back to the 18th century B.C.

I'm lonely... As a goddess, the only person I talk to on a regular basis is Sesostris. I feel isolated in this palace. I need a miracle. I need Micheal.

<u>Ascension</u>

Julie walked the palace gardens, a ghost of her former self. While Isis gave her access to the resources she needed to get back, the demands from the Pharaoh continually utilized more and more of her time. But now, the passing of her second anniversary without Micheal brought her firmly back to her true mission.

She entered her makeshift lab in the palace and then went to inspect the generators she had engineered. They were fairly compact, around the size of a basketball. She placed them in the ports of the magnetic gateway she had constructed to contain and focus the EM field. Now, she was on to the most essential part. It had taken a great deal of time and effort, but she had finally managed to get her hands on some magnetite—the last ingredient she needed to construct some kinetic energy extractors. She began the arduous task of finding the correct formula to draw energy from the air around her.

The days turned to weeks, and 111 tests later, she was beyond exhausted and frustrated. She took a break and walked the halls of the palace in Faiyum. The vast emptiness felt desolate. It had been nearly two years since she saw his face. Her stomach filled with butterflies that even if she succeeded, she might still fail. There was little guarantee that he was in the 18th century. If she got back, after two years, to find him dead or gone, could she live with that? She didn't think so. She sat next to the sacred crocodile pond. As the tears fell, she was visited by ghosts from her past.

"Tis a terrible thing… to lose those that thee love," King George said dispassionately.

"I haven't lost him," Julie argued.

"Thou dost not believe such is true," George challenged.

"We always find each other," she protested.

"Of what shall thee do when thou fail? Thou dost recall what I did… Thy loss of a part of thee, which makest the whole, tis as if thou shalt attempt life without thy heart, or perhaps thy soul?" George pushed.

"I will not fail!" she countered forcefully.

"Thee knows thou speakest false," he jabbed. "If not for thee, many billions should still live," he poked even harder.

"Shut up!" She was becoming angry.

"Thou art a murderer. Thou hast killed my family and the whole world with them," he continued his tirade.

"No!" she began.

"Indeed!" He cut her off. "Upon thy failure, thou shalt end thy life."

Julie scanned the gardens... King George was gone, but his words echoed in her head. What would she do if all ended in failure? She didn't know, and she didn't want to find out. She returned to the lab, and after going over the results of the 111 failures, she had an inspiration. She worked on the formula for the alloy one more time. Once she set the mold, she'd have to wait for it to cool. So she took a walk to stay awake. They felt particularly empty as she walked through the torch-lit hallways at night. Everyone was asleep, but she was so close she couldn't sleep.

Nearly a year had passed since she sank at sea. The vast time since she had been taken away from Micheal had emptied out her heart until it was as empty as the palace she toured. That emptiness was allowing other things to attempt to fill the void, like King George. She didn't want to admit it, but she was tempted to agree with him. After burning a few hours with her thoughts, she returned to the labs.

"Attempt 112," Julie said aloud.

She quickly assembled the KEE. She placed it in position, then said, "Then Isis said... Let there be light."

She pushed the button, and an arc of plasma flowed between the terminals. After so much trial and hardship, the excitement overcame her. She thought, what would Micheal say in this situation? And then it came to her.

"Julie! ... Tonight, I'm sending you back... To the future!" she could only laugh at the gusto with which she said it.

February 13, 1874 B.C.

This may very well be my final journal entry. I can't continue to live like this. I have performed my final test of the time gate. I am fairly certain that my calculations are correct. So, I will be going back to the 18th century B.C.

It has been two years since that terrible day. I know Micheal has made it back there... If he's alive. So if I don't find him there, I will just end it all.

Julie's tears splotched the ink on the page.

Today is "do or die", literally.

P.S. Tomorrow is the two-year anniversary since I saw Micheal.

Julie sent word to Sosestris that she would ascend in the morning. She walked the palace halls one more time and wound up in the Temple of Isis, built at Faiyum, after she saved the annual inundation from drought. It had recently been completed out of mudbrick. Accepting the statue of her, the Pharaoh had her likeness chiseled into a repurposed statue. As she marveled at her stone reflection, she realized it wasn't the first time she'd been deified; many temples to Aphrodite had been erected during the Age of Atlantis.

Now, using the scraps of material leftover from the construction of the time gate, she had built a couple of palm levitation gauntlets. And here, in her temple, she had been left alone by the priestesses, so she dared to test them out.

As she levitated up to face her statue directly, she heard something behind her.

"Doesn't it amaze you the things these people worship?" Julie recognized Ra's voice.

She rotated around in the air.

"My dear Isis, surprised to see me after your last attempt to cast me out?" Ra clearly didn't recognize her, so maybe this version hadn't encountered them yet.

"You claim to have Egypt's best interest at heart. But I know you—it's all about the adoration," she played along.

"And the people built 100 monuments to Isis, Bringer of Life, and she brought the waters to quench the Nile's thirst," he read the hieroglyphs on the temple walls. "It appears you have such motives."

"It was to help Egypt," she protested.

"Of course it was, my daughter," he mocked skeptically. "Why don't we rule side-by-side?" Ra suggested.

"I am leaving," she informed him as she flew down to the ground by the entrance.

"Why would you leave?" he examined her. "To find Osiris?" he seemed to conclude.

"Indeed," she said as she began to leave.

"You won't find him."

The words sent a chill down her spine. "I will, or you will pay," she growled, leaving the temple.

The next day, "It is so unusual to have two deities here at the same time," Sesostris seemed to marvel.

Julie glared at Ra.

"It has been too long since I've seen my daughter," Ra told Sesostris.

"It hasn't been long enough," Julie retorted.

"I am aware of the enmity between father and daughter, and I appreciate your truce on my behalf," Sesostris looked back and forth between them.

"It is time for me to ascend," Julie declared.

"I want to thank you for everything. Isis, it has been an honor," the Pharaoh bowed before her.

"This is not over between us," Ra warned.

Julie stared him down. "We will be ready," she promised.

She activated the generators. The slight hum began to accelerate in pace. Pharaoh Sesostris rose to his feet as she began to levitate. A green glow heralded the activation of the vortex. She looked at Sesostris, then at Ra. Then a bright flash filled the room, and she was sucked into the time portal. It felt like she was flying through a spinning green vortex, twisting faster and faster, building toward a climax. As the light at the end rapidly approached, she prayed her ordeal was finally over. The green glow flashed to brilliant white; then everything went dark.

CHAPTER 13: EMPTY SPACE

T HE MONTHS PASSED, AND the inundation came. Micheal had first searched the world, then waited every day for Julie's return. Pharaoh Sobekneferu had taken him as a confidante and advisor in her absence. So he'd spent half his time in Itjawy or on progress with the court and the other half at River Palace, their grandiose home in the delta. But the more time passed, the more empty the palace felt. It had been nearly 18 months since he last saw Julie, and he may never see her again. With his perfect memory, it wasn't possible to forget her face, but in his loneliness, he had been living in his head more and more.

Micheal looked away from the setting sun, and she was there in the doorway of the laboratory at the Homestead in Boston.

"Do you want any help?" Julie asked.
Micheal was speechless.
"Are you okay?" she proceeded to ask.
"I'm fine..." he looked at her big, beautiful eyes, then looked away in embarrassment. "... Um..." he stammered. "You can if you want," he said finally.
She had never offered before, and he was in a struggle between

wanting to say yes and wanting to say no.

"What are we making?" she asked, inspecting the device.

"It's an emulsifier," he said simply.

Julie cocked her head to the side.

"I apologize, but aren't there more important things to engineer than this," she indicated the device.

"Not many, actually. This is necessary to make the mouth pro-tectant rinse I have in mind," he said, still avoiding eye contact.

"Mouth rinse?" she seemed confused.

"This is the 17th century. The only dentists are butchers, and oral health is paramount," he reasoned.

"So what kind of rinse can make up for dentists?"

"It was an idea I first had when I was seven. I thought... What if I could find something that could kill the bacteria in your mouth and bond with the enamel in your teeth? You'd never need to brush. So now I'm going to see if it will work."

"Okay, so what can I do?"

Micheal came out of the memory. He decided to go for a stroll. As he walked the vast hallways and rooms, if felt abandoned. Without Julie, it was just empty space. That thought made him think of something.

"Micheal, how is everything?" his dad asked as they drove through the canyon toward Heber City.

"It's okay." He shrugged.

"The snow isn't causing you any trouble on your route?" his dad worried.

"Not too much... And I made an oath," Micheal replied in jest.

His dad chuckled.

"Have you been to the ice castles before?" Micheal changed the subject.

"Once with your mother, when they first opened," his dad said as they arrived at the castles.

As they walked around, the conversation bounced from one topic to another.

"... Science isn't counter to religion. They complement each other," his dad was saying.

"Clearly, whichever religion is the true one would have to work within the laws of physics. So I'm not sure which one has the most evidence." Micheal shrugged.

"It's not about evidence; it's about faith," his dad said with conviction.

"I don't have any faith," Micheal argued.

"I know you've struggled with this your whole life—it's that genius, analytical mind. But you at least have faith in that, don't you?"

"Not for a long time." Micheal paused as the emotions came flooding back. He stared intently at a frozen waterfall sequencing through a parade of colors, trying to prevent any tears from coming.

"It wasn't your fault, Micheal," his dad tried.

"My one supposed good quality failed her and everyone else."

His dad hugged him. "I miss her too... Every day."

Micheal returned to reality and just stared at the forever waterfall flowing over the courtyard's edge. After nearly falling into a trance, he went to the entry module. The statues brought on another memory.

Micheal was sitting at his desk in kindergarten, reading his latest book instead of paying attention.

"What are you reading?" Micheal looked up from his history book. "It's about Ancient Egypt," he told the kid.

The boy had dark skin and short, curly hair. "What's Ancient Egypt?" The boy looked confused.

"Micheal! Tyler!" the teacher, Mrs. Woods, yelled. She walked over and took his book. "The Pharaohs are going to have to wait, Micheal," she said, then went to the chalkboard.

The bell rang, signaling recess.

Micheal was kicking the soccer ball around when three other kids came and surrounded him.

"Give us the ball!" the leader demanded.

"I got it first," he retorted.

"What's a fatso like you doing with it anyway," one of the other kids said.

The third kid tried to take it from him. It became a tug-of-war until Micheal shoved the kid to the ground.

"Get him!" the kid on the ground yelled.

Micheal got hit in the shoulder. Then hit one of the kids, who started to cry. The kid from the ground got back up then got tackled by a new kid. Micheal tackled the ringleader and then punched him a few times. Then, all three of them ran away, and Micheal got up.

"I'm Tyler. Tyler Collinsworth," the new kid introduced himself.

"I'm Micheal Hall," he replied in kind. "Thanks, Tyler," he added. "You're new here, right?" Micheal asked.

"Yeah, we just moved from New Orleans. Do you know where that is?" Tyler asked him.

"Of course—Louisiana. That's cool," Micheal said with certainty.

"Hey, Mike. Can I call you Mike?" Tyler asked.

"That's cool," Micheal agreed.

"Cool. Wanna kick the ball around?" Tyler asked with a smile.

"Sure!" Micheal dropped the ball.

"My friends call me T.C.," Tyler—T.C. informed him as they began kicking the ball.

When Micheal came back to reality, he thought about how crazy it was to see his best friend the way he was over 75 years ago and how much he missed his friend. He walked out of the entry module and had to pause on the bridge because there was a sun path of shimmering gold across the delta to the west. It reminded him of another memory.

"Where are we going?" Micheal asked as he and his older sister, Vanessa, drove west of Ogden.

"Antelope Island. Have you ever seen a buffalo in the wild?" Vanessa asked as they crossed a bridge over the Great Salt Lake.

"We saw some on the road in Yellowstone," he informed her.

"I'm still mad that I missed that trip. So many good hikes." She shook her head.

"Speaking of hikes—we'll have to be sure to plan some for next year because you and Rob are going to get married when he returns from his mission. Right?" Micheal inquired.

"That's the plan... I mean, we have been dating since my sophomore year." Vanessa brought the car to a stop.

"Are you going to go to college?" Micheal asked.

"I don't know. I got accepted to BYU, but you know how complicated Dad's finances are. I can't get any grants or scholarships. Besides, if anyone in our family should go to college, it's you," Vanessa said, with a raised brow, as they climbed out of the 1981 Ford Taurus.

"We both know I'm not going to college," he retorted.

"Didn't you just take the entrance exam at the community college? You scored higher than anyone who's ever taken it. That's what mom said. And you're only 14. I've always known you were a genius," Vanessa was trying to convince him as they began hiking.

"Wow, community college! And it's not like we can even afford that. It would just be more of the same boring, rudimentary education that requires you to do a lot of work and waste much time for very little," Micheal balked.

"I would love to get results like that. And you scored 1600 on the SATs again! I just don't want you to waste your potential." Vanessa seemed annoyed.

They discussed things further as they made their ascent. By the time they reached the summit of Frary Peak, they were surrounded by the majestic views.

To the southeast, Micheal could see the Salt Lake City skyline against the backdrop of the Wasatch Mountains. Down below, on the island's east side, was the herd of American Bison—several hundred strong. As he looked west, across the lake, two golden eagles were soaring over the windswept desert island and a brilliant sun trail ran across the water, leading to the pale glowing orange globe.

As they took it in, they continued their discussion.

"I just want you to have a happy, successful life," Vanessa said.

He thought about arguing but decided against it. "Thanks, Vanessa."

"Of course. I'm your big sister, and I love you," Vanessa said with a smile.

"I love you too... Wow, the view was definitely worth the hike."

Micheal came back to his present. He passed through the servant's module. Many of the live-in staff had their families with them. Most husbands and wives had positions at the palace. Children couldn't access most of the palace. They were typically restricted to the servant's module and the primary module. Seeing the children reminded him of something.

Micheal and Julie had traveled to the New York border area to visit the Massachusett. Many of the children of the people took turns riding Darkness. None of the people had ever seen such a large horse before. After spending most of the day giving rides, some men wanted to go hunting. Julie remained in the village while they pressed north to Vermont.

They had a successful outing. One of the braves took down an Elk. Now Micheal had one in his sights. He let the arrow fly from over a hundred yards, and the bull fell like a rock. As they reached the animal, he saw his shot had likely pierced the heart. He was thankful for that. He knelt next to it and said a native prayer. Then, several others began preparing it for the long journey back. At that moment, the skies began to darken, and the winds began to pick up. About an hour into their trek, the rain began to fall in torrents and lightning flashed all around them. Micheal was riding Darkness at the rear of the party. Suddenly, a sound, like a jet engine, tore through the forest, accompanied by a piercing flash. Then, there was an explosive boom.

Darkness got spooked and rushed off in a mad dash. All Micheal could do was hold on for the ride. He finally regained control, but the five-minute flurry had them miles from the party, and the rotating clouds above made it impossible to determine direction. He found a rock wall outcropping, and they huddled against it, waiting for the storm to pass. They were on the leeward side, which shielded them from most of the gale-force winds.

"Now look what you got us into," he said to Darkness, who seemed to bow sheepishly. "Sure, you can run through a hail of bullets, but a billion volts send you running for the hills?" His horse looked at him. "It's okay," he said, patting Darkness on the side of the neck.

"You know, Darkness, you were the first friend I made in years... I've thought about that day. I would have never saved Julie if I hadn't met you." He fed Darkness a hand full of dried fruit. "And that's the best thing that's ever happened in my life. She makes me a better person. What to know a secret, Darkness?" His horse moved his head up and down. "Promise not to tell?" He smiled at the insinuation. "I love her..." he almost stopped himself. He had been in love with her for years but was always too afraid to say it out loud. "I love her, but she could never return such feelings. I'm just happy she's in my life." He patted Darkness on the neck. "We'll have to wait until morning," he told Darkness as he sat beside the wall to rest.

When the palace surroundings returned to focus, Micheal realized Julie wasn't in his life anymore. She might never be again. He crossed into the Pharaoh's temple. He stopped in the center. The torches had yet to ignite, and the only light in the room came from the mirrors, reflecting the sun through the oculus in the dome. The only god still in the light was the sun god, Ra. The image became the monster who took Julie from him. He was filled with anger as the shadow of Ra put him in darkness. As he considered what damage he might do to the graven image, the light faded to black, and the torches came to life. He walked around the chamber and stopped at Anubis and another memory came.

Micheal woke to the same awful reality he had been living in for the past two weeks since Amanda died. He had been sleeping for around 20 hours a day. It was his only respite from his perfect memory. He sat under the dark night sky with his thoughts. He was going over decisions he had made in an attempt to save his sister. He had promised her—and he had broken his promise.

"Micheal?" He heard Kimberly ask as she joined him on the garage roof.

"Kimberly?" he replied, his gaze still fixed on the heavens above.

She sat next to him. "What do you think happens when you die?" she asked.

"Why? You don't believe what the church teaches?"

"I used to... but then Mandy got sick... It's not fair!..." Kim began crying.

He put his arm around her, and they cried together. After a few minutes, he asked, "So, you want to know what I think about death?" He was a little confused.

"I know you, Micheal. You're all about facts, not some article of faith. I know you've researched the subject. So tell me the scientist's view."

"See the Milky Way," he began.

"Okay... what does that have to do with this?" She was confused.

"Based on the movement of the galaxies, we know there was a big bang. Now, based on the laws of thermodynamics, cosmologists will tell you that a god, or god power, or force had to have sparked the big bang. That's necessary for me to say because the question of a god is crucial to the question of death. Understand?" He paused.

"I think so..." She was hesitant.

"So now I've established that some form of a god is a fact. Then the possibility of a soul is also possible."

"And what does science say about that?" She was now more curious.

"Have you ever heard of '21 Grams'?" he asked.

"No."

"About a century ago, a scientist performed a controversial study attempting to measure the human soul. He found that at the moment of death, each of his subjects lost 21 grams of weight. While many are skeptical, some now believe 21 grams is the weight of the soul," he explained.

"What do you think?"

"Anecdotally, I agree." Then he continued, "Then you have the whole astral plane, where people claim they have astral projected. It's also where people say they go when they have out-of-body experiences, as well as the government-sponsored remote-viewing program." He paused.

"Remote viewing?" She raised a brow.

"A program to train people to be psychics. For military intelligence. Anyway, there was some evidence that it actually worked. Then, finally, there are near-death experiences. While most of these are difficult to test scientifically, the preponderance of eye-witness testimony can't be discounted too much. And near-death experiences have some verifiable evidence. People who die temporarily on the operating table are able to describe in great detail what was happening in the room while they were flatlining. So what other explanation is there?" he finished.

"So what's your final conclusion?" Kim asked.

He considered a moment, then said, "There must be a god and a soul. So where does it go? After death, I believe the spirit goes to another dimension. Whatever someone might call it, whether it's heaven, hell, nirvana, Elysium, or Valhalla, I think it's all more or less the same place, simply different dimensions," he explained.

"So that's where you think Mandy went?" Kim's tears came back. "Do you think it's a better place?"

"Yes. It has to be..." he pulled her into him. "...Maybe the Egyptians got it right... Death is just a transition to the next phase of life." He closed his eyes.

"I'm glad you came home again," Kimberly said.

"So am I." He closed his eyes. However, he didn't know if he believed that.

He opened his eyes and was face-to-face with Anubis. The thoughts of death were always with him. It had been 63 years since Amanda died and about 17 since he reunited with her when he died on Normandy. But the loss always felt ever-present whenever he thought of that time.

He made his way back to the Lord's module. He went and sat next to the window of the library. It took him back to 1697.

"My Lord?" Robert Rainsford interrupted his thoughts.

"Robert?"

"I do beg thy pardon." Robert began to leave.

"Might I trouble thee for advice?" Micheal stopped him.

"What is thy trouble?"

"I beg thee, sit." Robert complied. "How does thee in marriage?" Micheal asked.

"'Tis a wonderful thing. Mary occupies most of my thoughts..." Robert paused, then continued. "What is thy concern? Have not thee been happy in union of marriage these past five years?" He seemed confused.

"Many complications persist where my family relates to marriage," Micheal deflected.

"I imagine the complexities of thy house finding suitable partners, quite the challenge. Thou didst say as how her grace's younger sister requiring assistance, did lead to marriage. Might I then deduce, from said vow renewal, that though hast come to love My Lady?" Robert questioned.

"I have for many a year," Micheal admitted.

"My Lady did not?" Robert raised a brow.

"Aggrieved, she was. Much to overcome," Micheal explained.

"Now thou, 'tis as if thee be wed anew?" Robert asked.

"It does change many a thing." Micheal had thought about how things had changed with the new knowledge. "What if I should feel unworthy?" he asked honestly.

"Micheal, all men feel unworthy. Courage separates men who find joy and those who do not. I know thy brilliant mind forgets nothing, a burden for which I lack understanding," he paused. "Despite this, haunted could I be as well of memory. Marriage happiness is of the heart, not the mind," Robert finished.

Micheal's memory was interrupted by the doors opening.

"My Lord, Vizier Senewosret-Ankh…" palace manager Khepri announced.

"My Lord Avalon, Pharaoh requests your advice," the vizier declared.

Micheal bowed agreement without speaking.

"We leave in the morning," the vizier left the chambers.

Micheal had very little care for his location. It was exchanging one empty space for another. He looked at the rising moon and wondered if this was his life now. Without Julie, life had lost its meaning. He felt like an automaton, just going through the motions. If Julie were really gone forever, then the whole world would all become just empty space.

Micheal had spent the last few months advising Sobekneferu in Itjawy.

"Thank you, My Lord Avalon, for your advice," she excused him.

As he exited the royal chamber into the great hall, it appeared as empty as he felt. The size of the hall was similar to the size of the gym in his church when he was young. That reminded him of playing basketball in his ward for the stake league of church ball.

"Why don't you want to try out for the high school team?" his brother Brandon asked.

"I barely go to school. Why would I want to try out for the team?" Micheal retorted.

"I know how good you are. I could put in a word with Coach Henderson. Then we could play together your final year," Brandon suggested as he dribbled a crossover.

Micheal laughed at that. "I'm not good enough to play high school ball," Micheal balked.

Brandon shot a jump shot from 20 feet… Nothing but net! "Please. It's not like Granite is big or anything. You're one of the tallest kids in the school," Brandon argued while Micheal spun 360 degrees, passing the ball behind his back, then shooting a fadeaway jumper that rimmed out.

"I'm too fat and slow. I could never keep up," Micheal passed the ball back to Brandon. "Besides, I never fit in on a team," he pointed out.

"You don't seem to have any trouble with church ball," Brandon tried to convince him. "Or at least you didn't when you used to play," Brandon added. Then he cut past him and laid it in.

Brandon caught the ball and stopped. "Well, I don't really go to church much either." Micheal shrugged.

"I don't understand why you're acting this way. You weren't always like this." Brandon seemed upset.

"You'll never understand the burden I have to live with... You don't know how it feels to have every failure, every shortcoming, blaring out in front of you like a sea of neon signs, telling you how bad of a person you are. And everyone lying to you about your supposed brilliance." Micheal began to walk away.

"I never lie to you. The family never lies to you. You're just too stubborn and hard-headed to listen to anyone else but you," Brandon accused.

"Everyone lies about my intelligence. If I were really so smart, I would have found a cure for Amanda. What good is it if I can't use my supposed genius to save her?" He turned away so his watering eyes wouldn't show.

"It's not your job to fix everything. And just so you know, you're not the only one trying to help her," Brandon snarled. "You need to remove your ego from this situation," Brandon suggested.

"Don't worry about that; I'm leaving home. So you don't have to deal with my ego anymore." Micheal seemed to surprise his brother.

"What do you mean, 'you're leaving'? You're only 16," Brandon challenged.

"I dropped out of school, and I got my GED. The court just approved my emancipation. Once I save the money for a deposit, I'm moving out," Micheal informed his brother.

"Now you're abandoning the family?" Brandon seemed upset. "And you're throwing away your education?" he added.

"I'm not abandoning anyone. And high school, just like everything that came before it, is an abject waste of time."

"What about being an astronaut? I don't think NASA will accept a GED." Brandon shook his head.

"It was never going to happen anyway. I just need to get on with my life." Micheal averted his eyes.

"You're still just a kid. It's not like you could afford to support yourself." Brandon was skeptical.

"I haven't been a kid for a long time. And I start at the Post Office next week. I will make around $25,000, plus benefits," Micheal countered, then walked out of the gym into the foyer.

Micheal came back to the great hall. He walked to the end and stopped at the statue of Isis. The face reminded him so much of Julie. Then he could have sworn it spoke to him. He studied the statue. It reminded him of the statue of Aphrodite in old Atlantis, only it was much smaller. And that brought back another memory.

Micheal walked past the statue of Julie as Aphrodite in the process of being carved for the temple at the Palace of the Gods. He then proceeded to his temporary throne, where he was to select his chief priestess. As he sat there, the first candidate approached. She proceeded to remove her robe. While he was inclined to try to stop her, he wasn't sure if this was what they were expected to do, so he maintained his godly persona, hoping she would explain it.

"My god, Koios, I pledge to serve you in whatever way you like. I pledge to serve the pursuit of knowledge. I shed my clothes to demonstrate that I will not waste time or energy on unnecessary things and to demonstrate that my body is yours to use as you see fit." She stood only a few feet away while he asked a few questions.

Apparently this was how the cult of Koios operated. Over the next few hours, several dozen candidates followed a similar script. Then, the final perspective approached. It was Melina Hellas, the leader of the welcome party. She seemed a bit hesitant, but she finally shed her robe.

"My god, Koios, I pledge to serve you in any way you see fit..." she broke off, clearly nervous. All the other women seemed totally comfortable walking around naked, but Melina seemed different.

"Melina, are you okay?"

She seemed caught off guard by his question. "Of course, your eminence." She shifted her eyes.

"Do you pledge to serve knowledge and wisdom?" He tried to help her get back on track.

"Yes, your eminence..." She seemed to be trying to remember the script.

"Melina, come here," he ordered.

She nervously stepped up until she was standing right in front of him. She ran her hands down the sides of her body.

"It's okay." He gently stroked her cheek with the back of her hand. Then he picked up her robe and wrapped her in it.

She was averting her eyes.

"I appreciate your devotion, but I feel you are better suited for another service."

She looked up at him. "I would serve you." She began to remove the robe again.

He stopped her, "And I would be honored, but I can see your heart. Your tender heart is built more for love. But I applaud your courage for coming here. You are special, Melina. Now go, I'm sure Aphrodite would be honored by your devotion."

Her eyes lit up at his instruction.

He determined the reason she had been sent was because she had found them. But she was clearly different from the erudite confidence of the cult of Koios.

As he returned to reality, he was momentarily amused by how Julie had reacted to his priestess's practice of not wearing clothes. So Aphrodite had decreed that they must wear a robe when in the chamber of the Gods, lest they incur the wrath of her jealousy. Except for Elissa, his direct attendant.

As he looked around the palaces, both at Itjawy and River Palace, most servants wore little or no clothes. Then he reflected on Melina from all those years ago.

Despite everything, she was one of his best friends from the Age of Atlantis.

A few days later, the vizier came to Micheal to request that he try to help his granddaughter. She was sick, and they were worried she was going to die. He entered the room to find a girl of maybe 12. She was in bad shape. After a quick examination, he determined she had appendicitis, and worse, he was almost certain it had ruptured. He went and retrieved his personal medical kit. He used a local anesthetic to numb the abdomen and then performed an appendectomy. His worst fears were confirmed—the appendix had ruptured, and she was nearing septic shock. He cleared the cavity and began a morphine drip, along with antibiotics. The sight of her after the surgery brought back a memory.

Micheal arrived at Primary Children's cancer ward. Amanda had had a relapse and was lying in a hospital bed.

"Hey, Mandy!" he said as he entered the room.

"Micheal!" she said excitedly.

After he hugged her and kissed her on the forehead, "How are you feeling?"

"I'm okay." She was trying to be brave.

"Don't worry. You're going to be just fine," he lied. He had looked

at her charts, and it didn't look good. The treatments were no longer working, and she had been diagnosed stage IV, terminal, and all of his research had amounted to nothing. He knew he couldn't save her, but at least he could be a big brother to her.

"I don't want to be in this hospital anymore," she said sadly.

"Good, 'cause I have a whole day planned for us. Go get dressed," Micheal implored her. "And here, put these on." He handed her a wig and a pair of sunglasses. "We're on a secret spy mission."

She smiled and donned the disguise. They snuck out of the hospital and climbed into his black '92 Mercury Tracer.

"So what's our mission?" Amanda asked.

"To go to Lagoon and ride every ride they have. And have our pictures taken in Pioneer Village," he said with a smile.

He put his sunglasses back on and said, "Do you accept this mission?"

"You know I do." She smiled.

When they were about to go on the first ride, the Roller Coaster, Amanda worried, "The wig will blow off."

Micheal pulled off his own wig, revealing a clean-shaven head. "I know. It's the new style of cool."

She smiled and followed suit.

"Let's do this." They climbed in the front row.

They rode every ride and played many carnival games, winning many prizes for Amanda. When the park closed, they walked out the gate, put their spy disguises back on, and Amanda said, "Mission accomplished."

Micheal was glad he could give her this experience.

He stood in the palace gardens, reflecting on how watching Amanda go through all that taught him the true meaning of courage and how he misses her every day.

Micheal sat by the riverbank until the sunset. As he returned to the palace, the shadows in one section of the gardens had a familiar feel, and he remembered the situation with Kelsie Ambrose and their photoshoot in Tycho.

"...Do you really have to go? We're having such a good time," Kelsie tried to convince him.

After looking at her for a moment, he thought... "Why not? I'm going to find another drink."

"I'm going to get some air," Kelsie informed him as he walked off.

He returned, and she wasn't there. When she hadn't returned, maybe ten minutes later, he went searching for her.

"Kelsie?" he called as he searched the mansion gardens. It was dark, and he was getting worried. Then he saw her lying on the ground, curled in the fetal position. He rushed to her side.

"Kelsie!" he tried. "Kelsie!" he repeated.

"Make it stop!" she demanded, holding the sides of her head.

"What's wrong?" he demanded as he took her in his arms.

"It's a flood. It's a flood of memories. It's too much; I can't take it." She began to cry.

He thought about it. It's total recall. "Everything will be all right," he promised her. He carried her to his private suite, laid her on the bed, and went to work.

Kelsie, I'm here. Focus on my voice," he tried to soothe her as he brushed the hair out of her face.

"It's too much!" she complained.

"Just focus on me," he implored her.

It was a rough couple of days until she finally relaxed into him.

When she finally came around, "How are you feeling?" he asked as she looked up at him from his chest.

"Did we do anything?" she seemed to ask hopefully.

"No, I just tried to help you through your transition."

She closed her eyes. "I can remember everything." She seemed confused.

"It's okay. It'll take a little time to adjust," he assured her.

"They're coming back. They're all coming back!" she brought her hand to her face.

He wrapped her in an embrace from behind, then whispered in her ear, "Just focus on one thing."

She took several deep breaths.

"Just filter them out, one by one," he instructed.

She laid her head on his shoulder. A little while later, the storm had passed. "How did you know how to do that?" Kelsie asked with interest. "I mean, you're only 52," she seemed confused.

"I was born with it," he informed her.

"I've known you for years; how come you've never told me that?" She seemed surprised.

"I don't know. It's just a normal thing for me. Like breathing." He shrugged.

"That must mean..." she stopped, and he could tell she was sizing him up. "Well, thank you, Micheal, for everything."

As they were leaving the hotel, she kissed him in front of the paparazzi.

Micheal came back to the dark garden path. Whenever he thought of Kelsie, it was with mixed emotions. She was his best friend from the Age of Atlantis, but she also brought chaos to his marriage. All that, combined with watching her die... It was a complex subject.

The next day, Micheal accompanied Sobekneferu to parade for the masses. But one aspect brought back memories. They were giving alms to the poor, and that brought him into a memory.

It was November 15, 1991. Every year since he was three, his mom would take him downtown on this day to hand out blankets and sack lunches to the homeless.

"Now Micheal, when I was your age, I was living on the streets, just like these people," his mom told him.

"Why didn't you live in a house?" he was confused.

"I had been walking down by the river and got lost. I ended up in Philadelphia and didn't know how to get home."

"Isn't Philadelphia on the other side of the country?" He knew geography and was curious how she got to the East Coast.

"I don't know exactly," his mom seemed to consider something. "The point is Micheal, these kinds of bad circumstances can befall anyone. So it's incumbent upon us to help people less fortunate than us," she implored him.

As they walked around Pioneer Park, Micheal felt bad that these people had no homes. Thanksgiving was only two weeks away, and he was glad he had a house.

"Here's a blanket and some food," he said to an old man sitting next to a tree.

"How old are you, kid?" the man asked.

"I'm eight," Micheal replied.

"Why are you doing this?" The man raised a brow.

"Cause I want to help people. My mom says that's what we're supposed to do," he explained.

"You raised a good kid here," the man addressed his mom, who had approached from behind.

"I most certainly have," she agreed.

She took his hand, and as they walked out of the park, his mom asked, "Would you like some ice cream?"

"Yes. Mom, can I have mint chip?" he requested.

"Any kind you like." She smiled at him.

Micheal missed his mother's smile more than ever. And with Julie gone, his memories were the only place he'd ever see it again. Like always, he wondered how she'd ended up in Philadelphia. She'd always been vague about it.

The next day, he returned to River Palace. As he walked across the bridge, he saw a woman at the entrance.

"Julie!" He ran toward her. He reached out to touch her, and she turned to dust, blowing away in the breeze.

After thoroughly searching his module, Julie had clearly been an illusion—a product of his loneliness. The memories evoked by his private chambers were too much. He sought refuge in his sanctuary. As he studied the ancient Norse murals, Thor's image reminded him of something.

"So, this is the place?" Odilia said as she guided him to the ledge.

"It must have been amazing to be rescued by a god." Micheal examined the landscape.

"The gods have been very generous to me. They sent you and Julie to us." Odilia smiled at him.

"Odilia, I know you think we're of the gods, that Fenrir has been vanquished, but I'm not a hero..." he protested again.

She stepped over to him, "You're my hero. And I know if Fenrir is still a threat, you'll protect us," she said with absolute conviction.

"How can you be so sure." He turned toward the cliff's edge.

"Because there's a connection between us. I felt it when we met." She turned him toward her. "I know you feel it, too." She looked at him with those dark, blue eyes.

He looked away.

"Tell me you don't feel it," she challenged.

"It doesn't matter. I'm married to Julie," he said directly.

"We have nothing so formal in our society," she tried to reason.

"It's the most important commitment in ours," Micheal countered.

"I understand," Odilia relented. "You did promise to tell me more of Avalon," she reminded him.

"Very well..." he began. "Our home sits on a narrow stretch

of land between the sea and the lavender springs. The majestic snow-capped peak of Excalibur provides a dramatic backdrop." He was describing.

"How could you ever leave such a paradise?" she seemed confused.

"Avalon has become a part of us. No matter where we go, it's who we are," he spoke, with no deception in his statement.

As he came back to the history of the Norse, he reflected on how much Avalon had become a part of him. Then he realized Avalon lived inside Julie. And without her, there was no Avalon.

As he entered his chambers, she was there.

"Julie, is that really you?" he was hesitant.

"It's me. Thank goodness we finally found each other again."

He still didn't trust that this was real. He hesitated to reach out to her.

"Let me prove it," she admonished. "Close your eyes," she instructed.

He obeyed. After a moment, she had said nothing. He opened his eyes to the empty space of the chamber. These hallucinations were emotionally crushing. He realized the only place he would see her again was his memories. So he went inward again.

Micheal lay on his back, and Julie lay on his chest. You could see the stars flowing like a river to the horizon.

"Do you think we'll ever see one of those up close?" he asked Julie.

She rolled over in his arms. "You mean fly there in a spaceship?" she seemed to be analyzing the heavens while he was stroking her heavenly body.

"With everything we have accomplished, I think we will," she decided. "But we won't be able to, at least not until we get home..."

"...And that's 150 years away," he pointed out.

"You're worried we won't make it..." Julie rolled over on top of him, her tender perfection staring tenderly down at him.

"I promise... before this life ends, we'll see that alien sun... I know we will make it back... Because I believe in us." She kissed his chest, then moved to his mouth. "Because we are one," she said as she mounted up.

Their two bodies became one, bonded by love.

Micheal was pulled out of his mind by someone addressing him.

"My Lord, we are concerned about you," Mbizi said with worry.

Micheal only wanted to return to that Valentine's night to see her again, but then Shani said, "We don't think it's good for you to continue living in your past." She grabbed his hand.

He thought about it. "There's only one thing I can think to do. We must leave Egypt," Micheal decided.

"Leave Egypt?" Mbizi seemed surprised.

"There are too many memories. They haunt this place." Micheal closed his eyes and shook his head.

"We'll prepare the Valkyrie," Shani took Mbizi with her, and they left the chamber.

Micheal began gathering the most important things for the long journey ahead. As he finalized his suitcase, Julie entered the chamber.

"Where are you going?" she asked desperately.

"Away from this place. Away from you." He began to carry the case to the door.

"How can you leave? I've only just returned," she pleaded.

"You're not real. You're my sadness." He stepped right through the ghost and out the door.

They sailed upriver toward the sea for perhaps an hour. Then Micheal realized he had forgotten something in his haste to depart. They returned to River Palace. How the evening sun lit up the balcony spurred one last moment of reflection.

He ran his hand along the balcony of the terrace. This wasn't how his life was supposed to go. So, they would sail for Norway and leave Egypt behind. As he was taking another last look, he heard Julie's voice say:

"...Micheal..."

He needed to get away from this illusion.

CHAPTER 14: REUNION

J ULIE AWOKE IN FAIYUM in the gardens to find Isis sitting beside her on a rock.

"I've come for my crown," Isis explained. "I hope it brought you luck."

Julie handed it back. "I suppose it did," she considered. "Perhaps." She shrugged.

"I knew you were capable of representing me. That's why I chose you," Isis said as she flew up above Julie. "We will meet again, Lady Avalon." Isis disappeared in a flash.

Julie made her way to River Palace. She arrived a few hours before sundown. She accessed the Lord's module directly. After so long, she was finally here. At least, she hoped.

She quickly searched their quarters, and it was empty. She retrieved the tachyonometer from the hiding place. A thorough scan confirmed it was the 18th century B.C.—two years after their run-in with Ra. She searched the area again. There were no signs of anyone currently living here. As she was about to search the rest of the palace, Nailah knelt before her.

"My Lady, welcome back to the palace."

"Nailah, is My Lord in residence?" Julie asked hopefully.

"No, My Lady," Nailah remained on her knees.

"Is My Lord in Itjway," Julie tried.

"No, My Lady," Nailah replied.

"Thank you," Julie dismissed her.

Nailah hesitated for a moment, then left.

Julie looked at the balcony from a distance. She was hesitant to approach the haunting sight. She needed to take a break from her terrible memories. She went to the Lord's sanctuary. She looked at the murals and statues. She wondered all over again about who, or what, Thor, Isis, and Ra really were. Her life was in tatters because of Ra. What would she do now? She was walking suicide's knife edge before she left the 19th century, and now she thought maybe that is what she should do. If Micheal weren't back by now, he never would be.

Julie chose to revisit the crime scene, refusing to succumb to sadness. Upon entering the bed chamber, she spotted him standing there. It had to be a figment of her imagination, an illusion caused by her grief.

She closed, then opened her eyes and he was still there. She pinched herself and still, he was there. She slowly approached the balcony. She kept her eyes open for fear that if they closed this fantasy would end.

Then she tried, "Micheal...?" Her heart was beating in her chest, dreading the inevitable end to her latest hallucination.

Micheal turned to the manifestation of his heart's desire and pleaded, "Please. I can't take this anymore. Why are you haunting me?"

He began to walk into the bed chamber, trying to escape the ghost of her.

"Micheal, it's me..." the apparition declared.

"You're not real..." he closed his eyes, rubbing his temples in an attempt to focus his right mind. As he was focusing on his breathing, she touched him. She put her hands on his.

"Is it really you?" Her question seemed strange, and her touch didn't dissipate.

He opened his eyes. That perfect face was looking at him with the question he had. He dared to hope his most heartfelt desire had actually come to fruition. He slowly reached out and touched her cheek. It felt soft, like satin. She copied him.

"I've lived this moment so many times..." he said aloud. "... How do I know this is real?" he asked her.

"Because... I'm just as uncertain as you are. If we're both uncertain, it has to be real," Julie reasoned.

She was caressing his face. He took her hand and kissed her palm. He then made his way with his mouth down her arm to her neck. As he came up to her mouth, they locked eyes and stopped.

"Jules, I need you now." He took her mouth with his.

Julie's fears of this reality evaporating faded as Micheal efforted to remove any doubt. She felt strange and comfortable at the same time. Every rhythm of motion was familiar after 50 years of harmony, but the sensation of the touch of his skin against hers felt foreign. Like a desert dry wash, taking the tears of the seasonal monsoon. And just like the monsoon, two years of emotional torment and physical desire were unleashed in a flood of cathartic release. This reunion of souls became a marathon. Each of them seemed to fear that if they stopped, they might awaken from a silent lucidity. Finally, they ran each other ragged.

Julie sat cross-legged and Micheal was her mirror. She could see the questions behind his gaze but he didn't seem to know how to begin.

"I suppose I will start," she began. "When Ra sent you away through that portal, I feared you were lost forever. Then when he sent me across the centuries, I feared I was going to die. Then I though about you. I knew you would never give up. You would move heaven and earth to get back to me. And that hope was what kept me going. So I refused to give up until I found my way back to you."

"When did he send you?"

"I woke up in the sea of sand in the 1870s B.C. It ended up being exactly 100 years in the past. What about you?" she directed at him.

"I woke up in Sinai, exactly 100 years in the future—so the 1670s

B.C..." He trailed off. "Julie..." Micheal began, then stalled.

"Micheal, what is it?" she worried.

"I spent most of the last year since I returned, searching, and waiting for this day... I..." he trailed off and shook his head.

"It's okay," she prompted.

"... The longer I was without you, the harder everything became. I couldn't take the loneliness," he paused.

Julie worried he must have sought comfort somewhere. And though she could understand, she wished he could be as strong as she had to be. As he continued, she readied herself for the gut-punch.

"So I started living more and more inside my memories. Primarily of you."

This was definitely not what she anticipated.

"My lines of reality began to blur... Sometimes even now I have trouble knowing what's real." He kneeled before her and explored her face with his fingers, like he was unsure of her reality. She took his hands and placed them on her sides, then moved them encouragingly over the curves of her body.

"Close your eyes..." she instructed.

"...Trust your other senses. Focus on your sense of touch." Micheal allowed his doubts to surrender to trust. He slowly built a picture of her body in his mind through the sensations of her soft skin under his fingers.

"That's it," she encouraged.

The palm of his right hand found the familiar mound of her left breast. The pleasant firmness, the pronounced pinnacle of her nipple penetrated the gap between his middle and index digits, as well as the taught, undulating milky skin of her areola. His left hand explored her graceful neck. His index finger and thumb traced her clavicles to the familiar "V" of her sternum muscles. He followed them up to her jawline, then traced the trapezius back down and circled back to the hollow of the "V". He stroked softly up the trachea, fanning out to rest on her carotids. The gently pulse flowing below his touch brought life to his Venus De milo statue of Julie he had sculpted in his mind's eye. Micheal threaded her velvet tresses between his fingers. He leaned forward, maintaining his voluntary blindness and inhaled the potpourri essence of her, adding yet another layer of dynamism to her reality. He pressed her on her back and located the valley between her mountains with his ear. He listened to the symphony of her breathing, coming and going with her heartbeat. With all of that solidified in his mind, he rounded out his senseless cycle by tasting the delectable sweetness of her voluptuous lips, then traced down the contours of her body with his mouth, to the delicate flower between her thighs. As Micheal explored her intricate beauty of her lower lips with his tongue, he solidified the entire essence of her without the impediment of his dubious sight.

Julie let herself get lost in his search for sanity through her body. While she knew he needed to find himself again, she had her own demons to exercise. His blind exploration began to breathe new life. She surrendered to his touch, closed her eyes, and allowed her other four senses to guide her back to him. His hands were continuously tracing the lines of her body, then laid her on her back. His fingers preceded his lips down her skin. They lingered momentarily between her legs, sparking a new cycle of sensation. As his mouth replaced his hands, his fingers radiated out to her inner thighs, then he encircled her legs with his arms and began taking her on a voyage to extasy with his mouth. Julie helped elevate the experience to new heights by taking her breasts in her hands. She tweaked her nipples, then traced around them in smooth, gentle circles. He brought her over the top multiple times in multiple cycles until she was thoroughly spent. He muted the overwhelming sensations by gently pressing his mouth to her other lips. She threaded her fingers through the luscious locks of his hair. One final kiss down there and he rose up and opened his eyes to meet hers. She sighed deeply, maintaining eye contact as he slid up next to her.

He tucked her hair behind her ears, then said, "How can I trust to shut my eyes again for fear that I wake to find that this was the most cruel of dreams?"

Julie saw a hint of doubt tint his eyes. "I share this same fear. I promise to protect you in the night if you swear the same for me," she offered bravely, hoping to push away the lingering doubt that still remained.

He gently rubbed his nose to hers, then said, "I so swear."

He kissed her lips deeply. He finally kissed back and gazed at her one last time then laid his head on her chest. She wrapped him in a protective embrace, and they drifted into a slumber together.

Fifty Years

After three days in isolation together, they finally emerged from their private quarters. Julie walked into the fountain courtyard.

"My Lady Avalon," a finely dressed man with a dark complexion gave an elaborate bow.

"I'm quite sure we haven't met," she was confused.

"We have not... But I feel like we have... I am Mbizi. His Lordship has told me so much about you. It's an honor to finally meet you for real," Mbizi explained.

"My Lady Avalon," a beautiful young woman addressed her.

"I see you've met my most special friends," Micheal interjected. "You've already met Mbizi. And this is Shani. They are helping me manage the West Delta."

"It's a miracle the gods returned My Lady to you," Shani commented.

Later that evening: "... you did what?!" Julie couldn't believe Micheal had brought Shani and Mbizi back from the 17th century B.C. "Do you even know what the effects of that action is?" Julie challenged him.

He gave a look like he wasn't sure.

"Micheal! We can't take those kinds of chances!" She was exasperated.

"They had no family or friends left. They had been slaves," he tried to justify. "The temporal waves show limited turbulence. But you're right... what was I thinking," he relented.

Before she could scold him, they were interrupted. "My Lord, My Lady, Vizier Senewosret has arrived," Shani informed them.

"My Lady Avalon, a vision of beauty. It has been too long," the vizier said, kissing her hand. "Her Majesty was overjoyed to hear you had not suffered the worst."

They arrived at the palace in Itjway as the noonday sun brought extra warmth to the winter day. Julie wished it hadn't. Sweat was tickling her forehead and down her nose.

"Lord and Lady Avalon, it's so good to see you reunited once more," Sobekneferu said as they entered her private suite. "I look forward to your assistance with the many challenges facing Egypt," the Pharaoh directed to Julie. "And it was impressive how quickly you built River Palace. I would ask you to design and build my final resting place for my transition," Sobek said to Micheal.

"It would be my honor," Micheal bowed.

Later that evening they were summoned by the Pharaoh. "My pyramid is under way, but I am inclined toward something else. Your spectacular River Palace gave me inspiration. I would like a Nile burial chamber to honor my namesake—the great and powerful Sobek," the Pharaoh requested.

"I'm certain we might come up with something." Micheal was clearly considering ideas.

"Splendid! I can't wait to see your vision," Sobek smiled. Then she was looking past him. "Lady Julie, I would like your help in my efforts to bear a child. I realize I am late in my years, but I was unlucky in my efforts during my first marriage. Now that I am Pharaoh, I can seek other options." Sobek raised a brow.

"Why do think I would be able to help you with this?" Julie was confused.

"I have known since we first met that you are an emissary of Isis, Goddess of Fertility," Sobek stated plainly.

Julie thought *here we go again.*

A year passed and no luck yet. They were summoned to the palace chambers in Itjway.

"Lady Avalon, just who I was wanting to see." The Pharaoh motioned for Julie to come in. "I have some exciting news. I am finally going to have an heir to my throne."

This news seemed to stun and confuse Julie. Micheal was also concerned. Sobekneferu was 43 years old and with the state of medicine in ancient Egypt, this pregnancy could be fatal.

"That is incredible news!" Julie was congratulatory.

"What's the good news?" The voice was instantly recognizable...

it was Ra.

The Pharaoh bowed to him, then replied, "The future of Egypt grows inside me."

"The next god amongst men," Ra commented. "Now my Pharaoh, are you sure you want to take advice from people like these?" Ra indicated Micheal and Julie.

"They have been trusted advisors from the start," Sobek argued. "My god, Ra, I am surprised you showed yourself to them," she pointed out.

"They are not who you think. They are Isis and Osiris. They seek to ruin me," Ra said with conviction.

Sobek looked at them for a moment.

"Leave us," Ra commanded Sobek. She bowed to all of them and promptly departed.

Once they were alone, "It seems you found your way back from temporal exile," Ra began, "but I promise you will never replace me here in Egypt.

"We have no intentions to do so," Micheal countered.

"Of course not. Just like you were never going to betray me, but here we are," Ra accused.

"You mistake us..." Julie began.

"I make no error in my memory. I remember you from over a century ago. Then two years ago you had resurrected Osiris, so I had to act," Ra shot back.

"We are not Osiris and Isis..." Micheal began to argue.

Ra laughed. "Isis..." Ra indicated Julie, "...was advising Pharaoh Sesostris a century ago. Then both of you returned when I attempted to exile you to time. Save your lies." Ra was getting angry.

"We are just two normal people who fell through time," Micheal tried the absolute truth.

"Your lies will not stop me from exacting my vengeance."

"Then what are you waiting for?" Micheal goaded.

"Not in the Pharaoh's palace, but soon," Ra promised and then left.

"What are we going to do now?" Julie asked with worry.

"I don't know. Do you think we should leave Egypt? We could go back to Scandinavia," Micheal suggested.

"No." Julie seemed adamant. "If we let him run us out of Egypt now, we likely wouldn't be able to return to Egypt in the next few time stops. Then all the effort we spent on River Palace would be wasted. We just have to convince him we're not a threat," Julie argued.

"Then let's get ready," Micheal was resigned to the fight ahead.

August 12, 1773 B.C.

Nearly six months have passed since Ra made his threat and nothing has happened yet. I have not spoken to him in any of the few incidences when we have been in the same room together, but those situations have been increasing, the closer Sobek comes to term. To Ra's dismay, I have become her midwife.

Micheal has been at work full-bore, working on the Pharaoh's tomb. The main burial chamber is complete. The urgency exists because we will be leaving this time stop in a couple of months. Just after Sobek's baby is born, we will leave Egypt. If we can maintain the cold-war situation until then, the hot-war prospect might dissipate, and we won't have to use our new kinetic toys.

This brings me to my final and most crucial point: today is a significant milestone for me and Micheal. Today is our 50ᵗʰ wedding anniversary. Oh, how the years go by. Half a century of love has just flown by. The longer we're together, the more I'm sure we're made for each other.

I once thought the same of Aiden. How young I was. Aiden was the love of my first life. Micheal is the love of my whole life. I do occasionally think of Aiden, but a lifetime has passed since we fell. It has been about twice as long in the temporal ether as before I married Aiden.

Julie paused and looked at Aiden's wedding ring as she thought about him. She hoped he was happy, that he got to be a father. Time is so unfair and now it has become an intrinsic part of her life.

I am also reminded that we are back to par. We have around 150 years left to go. So the 55+ years in the timeline was a lifetime that we might have gone without. I will only say, I look forward to another couple of centuries with Micheal. The longer we are together, the more in love we become.

Micheal, I love you. Happy 50ᵗʰ.

"We need to do something special tonight," Julie said as they prepared to go meet Sobekneferu.

"It's going to have to be at Itjway," Micheal told her.

Julie had an idea.

"Sobek summoned you for her lying in," he informed her.

"My Lord and Lady Avalon," the vizier addressed them in formal fashion that indicated the Pharaoh's arrival.

"Lady Avalon, I hope you will deliver Egypt's future," Sobek said with a bow.

"It would be my honor," Julie bowed back.

"Now, as it pertains to my lying in, I have changed my mind. I feel there is no more appropriate place than here at River Palace." The Pharaoh smiled.

"It is our honor to host Your Majesty," Micheal stated honestly.

As the sun was setting, Julie entered the balcony. "I guess we are celebrating our 50th here at River Palace."

"Indeed. And that means we can keep the plan I had," Micheal indicated a table with a satin tablecloth and fine crystal setting.

"What's on the menu?" Julie asked. She was wearing a modern style cocktail dress, adorned with some of her more spectacular jewelry from her 1690s collection. Her dress was lavender through the bodice with a teal skirt that went to her knees. She was wearing a multi-colored diamond choker. It had a large, green diamond in the center, flanked by two peach diamonds, followed by two sky blue diamonds, all set in a platinum chain.

"It's a honeydew gazpacho with ice cream to start, then pan-seared scallops in butter-garlic cream sauce, followed by bacon mushroom cheese shells in alfredo sauce for the main course, and zesty lime crème brûlée for dessert. All accompanied by sparkling peach cider." Micheal described their meal like a chef as they sat to eat. It was the same meal as their wedding rehearsal dinner.

Micheal was wearing a double-tailed tuxedo. It was black with a turquoise shirt and a royal purple tie. He was wearing gold cufflinks with purple diamonds. At first it was odd to see him like this. They had primarily been Egyptian since they came here so for both of them to dress in a modern style made it all extra special.

"If you could watch one movie right now, which one would it be?" Julie began one of their favorite anniversary traditions of talking about pop culture from their time.

"*The Fifth Element*. Even after all these years, it's still one of my favorites... What book would you want to read?" he answered, then asked.

"*A Dance of Dragons*. It was going to be released maybe 2010 or 2011—the fifth book in the *The Song of Ice and Fire* series... What sporting event would you most like to see?" she asked.

"Probably March Madness. Especially if any of the Utah schools were competitive. Particularly BYU... Which TV show would you most like to see?" he raised a brow.

"*Heroes*. Especially season one..."

They continued the process for a while, until their plates were empty.

"I have something for you," Julie placed the small box on the table.

Micheal took the box in his hands. "Gold—the traditional gift for the 50th. Can you believe it's been 50 years since that incredible day?" He looked at her for a long moment. "I don't think I will ever understand what you see in me, but I thank God every day that you love me." Micheal opened his gift.

"Maybe this will help you with that," Julie indicated the gold amulet he held in his hands.

"What does it do?" he inquired.

"I wrote in one poem for every year of our marriage, exactly what I see in you. You press the button on the side, and it will project a poem in golden light. Then you rotate the wheel at the bottom to scroll through them," she instructed.

He projected it on the tablecloth. As he rotated the disc, the different poems were displayed in different languages.

"Are they all in a different language?" He seemed impressed.

"Yes. To remind you that no matter what language it's in, my love for you is universal." A tear came to her eye. "Even when I couldn't tell you directly, I got the idea from the locket you gave me in Mystique. That was one of the things that got me through those terrible two years."

Micheal came around the table. She rose to meet him with her lips.

"This is so amazing... You are so amazing," he said as he pulled back. "I love you so much."

"And I you."

"I have something for you as well." He went and grabbed a cloth-wrapped item tied with a bow.

The package was about twelve inches long, eight wide and two inches thick. It was relatively heavy. Julie pulled the ribbon loose, and as the cloth was unfolded, it revealed a book that appeared to be covered in gold. She opened the book to see an image of her sketched in gold. As she flipped through the pages, there were dozens of pictures of her.

"I searched my memories and found my favorite image of you from each of the 50 years we've been together. I've replaced the two years of our separation with my two favorite images from before we were married, in Boston," Micheal explained.

The images were magical. The first image was from their wedding day. All the images were so lifelike, it appeared as if he had used an editing filter to make photographs turn to gold. She knew that even with his unusual memory, this must have taken considerable time to make.

Fifty images of her in gold certainly brought back many memories from the past and only reinforced further why she loved him so much. As she neared the end, the third-to-last, it was an image of her in front of Homestead. She was holding a rifle with a look of shock. It was the day she woke up from her coma.

"This is one of your favorites from before we were married?" Julie was curious about the choice.

Micheal reflexively touched the corner of his eye where she shot him, then looked at her with consideration. "After I was able to get a pulse back into you, you were in a coma for about a week. I had pretty much resigned myself to the idea that you would never wake up. I thought when I returned, I would be burying you. Then you were awake... Looking back I realized how happy I was that you were. So, although you shot me and accused me of so many terrible things, that became one of the best days of my life," Micheal explained.

Julie became overcome with emotions. "I wish I could relive days over again like that in my head," she discovered a potential upside to remembered everything.

"You don't need to. All we need is today to live and love each other, each and every day. He picked her up and carried her to the bed...

CHAPTER 15: THE FIELD OF REEDS

A Prince of Egypt

J ULIE FELT SOBEKNEFERU'S STOMACH using a gauntlet to run a version of an ultrasound.

"Is my baby okay?" The Pharaoh worried.

"Your baby is perfect," she assured her. "Do you want to know if it's a boy or girl?"

The Pharaoh seemed momentarily surprised. "You can tell?"

"Yes," Julie confirmed.

Sobek looked at her with concern.

"It's okay," Julie was going to wrap up the session.

"No... I do want to know," Sobek decided finally.

"You're going to have a son," Julie smiled as she touched Sobek's stomach. "Just one more month," she added, as she felt the baby kick.

"My prince of Egypt. Impatient to begin his life," Sobek said in reaction.

"Your Majesty," Julie bowed, then left the chamber.

"So, how's everything going?" Micheal asked as she entered their chambers.

"It's coming along nicely, particularly for her age," Julie informed him. "How's her tomb coming?" Julie pivoted.

"The floating chamber is complete. The artists are now working to finish all the hieroglyphs. They should be done by the end of the month. And the pyramid is going up quickly, with a secret entrance that will access the main chamber," he explained.

"My Lord, My Lady... Your dinner," Shani escorted several other servants.

As their dessert plates were removed, Micheal heard an ominous voice, "Am I too late for dinner?" Ra asked, as he entered their private chambers.

"You're not welcome here," Micheal said, as he and Julie rose to their feet.

"We have unfinished business," Ra countered.

"There's no need for us to fight," Micheal argued.

"It's not going to be a fight—it's going to be an execution," Ra moved with astonishing speed on the attack.

Micheal ducked his strike and attempted to counter. Ra's reflexes were super-human. He dodged, then struck Micheal in the stomach. Even through the tri-poly clothes, it was devastating. Micheal flew through the air and slammed into the wall. He looked up to see Julie slice at Ra with a sword. She connected several times, spraying blood across the floor. Ra backhanded Julie, and she went flying. Micheal quickly grabbed the kinetic gauntlets that Julie had engineered, then rushed Ra. He connected to nothing but air and had to retreat to avoid more punishment. As Julie tagged in, Micheal saw that the gashes in Ra's skin were already closing up. Ra's super-human healing would make him very difficult to beat. Julie took a kick in the stomach and tumbled across the floor. Micheal charged, then pretended to lose his balance. As he went to the floor, he slid between Ra's legs.

Ra was momentarily confused about which action to take. Micheal unleashed two simultaneous blows to the backs of Ra's knees. Ra fell to the ground, and Julie came down on top of him.

Using her kinetic fists, she double-punched his neck. Ra gasped for air as Micheal piled on, delivering several rib shots. Ra kicked him off, and then Julie flew right into him. As they rose together, Ra stood to meet them.

"Enough of this!" Ra yelled and began trying to open a portal.

Micheal moved quickly and delivered a force upper cut, causing Ra to stagger. Micheal pressed the advantage by kicking Ra in his knee. He roared in pain, then hit Micheal in the chest, sending him flying again. Even injured, Ra was formidable. Ra caught Julie's attack and took her to the ground. He was straddling Julie, grabbing her around the neck. Julie was reaching for the control to open a Philadelphia portal. Micheal was slow to assist because he likely broke his leg when he hit the wall. He fought through the pain, forcing his way toward them. Suddenly, Sobek appeared behind Ra. She rushed to Julie and Ra before Senewosret could stop her. Ra backhanded Sobek, and she tumbled across the floor. Ra appeared stunned. Julie used his distraction to initiate the portal. Micheal charged at Ra as Ra turned toward him. He hit Ra with a full-force kinetic punch to his face. The impact sent Ra flying feet-over-head, propelling him into the time gate. There was a green flash, and Ra and the gate disappeared.

Sobek let out a terrible scream. Julie rushed to her. She was clearly sent into labor. Micheal moved her to a bed.

The labor dragged on through the night, and then Julie came to talk to Micheal.

"The baby is in a bad position and it won't turn. And worse, I think she's bleeding internally," Julie informed him.

"Can you get it to stop?" Micheal questioned.

"I don't know where it's coming from. If I don't act soon, the baby will die. But if I manually orient him, it will rupture her cervix, and she will most certainly die. If I do nothing, they will both die." Julie shook her head.

"Have Sobek make the call," Micheal suggested.

After it was explained to the Pharaoh, she said, "Save my baby."

Julie reached inside and began trying to guide the baby out. "Push," she instructed.

After an hour of trying, the prince finally came sliding out. Julie got him to cry, then handed him to Sobek. Julie touched Sobek between her legs, where an alarming amount of blood was pooling. Julie went back to Micheal and Senewosret and gave them the bad news.

"The bleeding won't stop. She won't last long. There's nothing more I can do," Julie said sadly.

"There is something you can do," Senewosret turned to Micheal. "As Osiris' emissary, you can grant safe transition."

Micheal looked at Julie, and they walked over to Sobek.

"My precious Sobekhotep," the Pharaoh said, gently touching her son on the face. Then she looked at Micheal, "I'm ready."

He kneeled next to her on the bed. Julie followed suit. She took Sobek's hand.

"You have my protection," Julie said softly.

"I thank you," Sobek replied, then turned back to Micheal.

He reached out and touched her chest. He closed his eyes for a moment, then opened them.

"I have weighed your heart against the feather of truth and found you worthy to enter my realm. Go... be at peace," Micheal blessed her.

The Pharaoh looked at him, tears streaming. She looked at Julie, took one last deep breath, cradled her son close to her chest, then closed her eyes for the final time.

<u>The Field of Reeds</u>

November 24, 1773 B.C.

Prince Sobekhotep died a couple of days after his mother. It pains me even to this day. After the muddy procession for the Pharaoh and the prince, the clock count began. We had 81 days to finalize all preparations for our departure from Egypt. The 70 days of separation for the mummification process, plus 11 days to wrap them. The death of Sobekneferu brings the end of the 12th dynasty. The second intermediate period, a time of turmoil, was about to begin. So we decided to spend our last year in this time stop in Norway, near where our departure point will be. It will be good to see our old Norse friends again.

Micheal spent most of the 70 days in Itjway overseeing the finalization of Sobek's tomb. There's a small pyramid, about 50 feet tall and 100 feet at the base. Two statues of the god Sobek guard the entrance to a small temple dedicated to Sobekneferu. Micheal hastily built a small pedestal and sarcophagus for Prince Sobekhotep. Tomorrow we travel to Itjway to conduct the burial ceremonies. It will last three days.

I have encountered death many times in the last 56 years. I have even crossed over a couple of times. It's fascinating to see all the different ideas about death. Sobek believed she was going to the Field of Reeds. If Micheal's sister Amanda was telling the truth, perhaps she is. So once again, I go to bury a friend. You would think after so many times, I wouldn't break down in tears but here I am, messing up my makeup.

Julie and Micheal boarded the Satsobek, which would now be Sobekneferu's funery. It would be buried in a chamber next to the burial chamber so Sobek would have it for her use in the Field of Reeds.

The Satsobek sailed out of the harbor at Itjway and into the Nile. The banks of the river were lined with people and became increasingly crowded as they sailed south.

"Who do you think that is?" Julie asked, indicating a finely dressed entourage standing on the docks.

"Probably the governor of Memphis, who will most likely take over this region because Egypt is about to split into three parts: upper, lower, and the delta," Micheal informed her.

They sailed on until they came to a canal leading northwest toward Faiyum.

"What do you think happened to Ra?" Julie questioned.

"I don't know. Even though he could likely activate the time gate to return to this time, I doubt he would know how it works. And we have no idea how he opens the Philadelphia portals. So he may be unable to return to this time and place," Micheal speculated.

"Do you think there's any chance he's dead?"

"No. He has some super healing capability. That coupled with his strength and invulnerability, I don't know if he could die."

Micheal was seemingly sure.

"Since all this Ra stuff began, I've been trying to figure out who Ra is... who Isis is... I mean, she could fly using wings of light. Are they really the Gods of Egypt? What else could they be?" She really wanted to know.

"They're clearly the gods of Egypt, but are they some kind of primordial beings who ushered in all of creation? I doubt it. They could be aliens," he pointed out.

"Like *Stargate*?" The thought of the movie made her think of multiple things at the same time. First, Ra in the movie was an alien, so that was definitely something to consider. Then, second, it had to be over ten years since she'd seen any movie, but as the Satsobek approached the tomb near Faiyum, the enormous crowds and colorful spectacle made her feel like she was in a movie.

They docked near the pyramid, then it would be the funeral. First, Sobek's body was ferried through the streets on a bier. A procession of servants and friends led the caravan, carrying grave goods, like shabti dolls, and food offerings for the Pharaoh. Just in front of the bodies, the Kites of Nephthys were wailing the whole time. They were dressed as Isis and Nephthys. They wore blue-gray with wings, and their breasts were exposed, their faces covered with sand. They were dramatically wailing, calling for the crowd to mourn their souls properly in preparation for their transition into the Field of Reeds.

The bodies were brought to the entrance of the tomb, where they were placed upright in their coffins. Vizier Senewosret began the honor of Sobekneferu's and Sobekhotep's lives by detailing all of their great accomplishments in life. Then, a parade of her friends and close associates told of her great personal attributes. Then, it was Julie's turn.

She stepped forward and began to speak. She hadn't prepared anything because it was a last-minute request from the vizier that she speak.

"Four years ago, I arrived in this land as a distant outsider. There was no reason for your Pharaoh to show me so much favor, but she told me it was right to extend the hand of friendship and welcome visitors from distant lands. She saw my strengths, and through her godly leadership, she fostered my abilities to their maximum potential to improve the lives of all of Egypt. I lament that her transition has come too soon. She sacrificed herself in this world, attempting to extend her grace onto her son, Prince Sobekhotep, with whom we also celebrate this day. I will miss their light in this world, but I celebrate their transition to the Field of Reeds. I was blessed every day that she called me 'friend'. Osiris take them, Isis protect them," Julie finished. She closed her eyes and stepped back, failing her efforts to keep the tears back. Micheal put his arms around her. Julie's speech closed day one.

On day two, the Priests of Sobek then conducted a ceremony with proclamations about how she honored her namesake god.

The third day saw priests chant spells while mourners presented offerings. The nomarch of Memphis was last, as he would succeed Sobek as Pharaoh.

The final day began with a ceremony to bury the Satsobek. It was placed in its chamber and then sealed inside. Then, the Priests of Anubis, the official overseers of the transition, came forward and performed the "Opening of the Mouth" ceremony. The chosen representatives of Isis and Nephthys began chanting the lamentations of Isis and Nephthys as the head chief began touching the Pharaoh and the princes' mouths, arms, legs, and other areas of their bodies with various instruments, such as the adze, a peseshkaf, and a serpent-head blade. This would reanimate their bodies for use in the afterlife. The lamentations, along with the spells being cast by the other priests, would call the souls back to reunite with their bodies and proceed on to the afterlife. This was followed by offerings of meat, accompanied by more spells. A symbolic final meal was presented to the bodies, then was delivered to the burial chamber. Closing spells were chanted while the inner coffins were closed and sealed. Then, they were placed in the outer coffins. Micheal and Julie assisted in moving first Prince Sobekhotep, then the Pharaoh, into the burial chamber. They stood watching as the sarcophagi were ceremonially sealed, permanently hiding the solid gold coffins.

Julie closed her eyes and listened to the blessings being chanted. They were instructing their souls on how to navigate the afterlife. Julie was filled with regret. All she could think about was how Sobek and her son wouldn't have died if it wasn't for her.

If they hadn't come to Egypt, the battle against Ra never would have happened. It was like she and Micheal were lightning rods for chaos.

The inner chamber was sealed, then the main entrance was as well.

After the procession of mourners exited, "Their majesties are on their way to the Fields of Reeds," Shani said with a smile. "Now we feast in their honor." Her excitement was matched by most of the people in attendance. "My Lady, you should not mourn Her Majesty. She has taken her place in the Field of Reeds with the gods. That is cause for celebration," Shani tried to raise her spirits.

"I've lost too many people," Julie said sadly. She gazed over the spread of meats, fruits, vegetables, breads, drinks, and desserts. Her stomach growled, but she had no appetite. Some Thanksgiving this turned out to be.

Once, many years ago, she believed that losing friends would start to get easier—but it was the opposite. At that moment, she felt completely alone.

A Long Goodbye

The next day, Micheal watched as River Palace became a dark silhouette in the twilight. Less than an hour later, it was now only a memory as they broke into the Mediterranean. In a couple of weeks, they would see the Norselands again.

As they cut up the passage toward Copenhagen, Mbizi looked up as snow began to fall.

"What is that?" his eyes were wide with awe.

"That is the snow we told you about," Micheal held out his hand to catch the falling flakes.

"It's cold!" Shani commented.

"And it will be for a couple more moons," Julie informed them.

"Ra takes longer to pass through the underworld here." Mbizi had taken particular notice of the shorter days as they sailed farther and farther north.

As they neared the harbor, they were intercepted by a patrol of three long boats, who then escorted them in.

Odo and Odilia stood in the center of a large greeting party. They each held a child in their arms.

"My Lord and Lady Avalon, it has been too long." King Odo

smiled and bowed.

Micheal returned the gesture. "My dear friends, I've missed you these last few years." He gave Odilia a big hug. "I see you haven't wasted any time," He raised a brow. "And who might this be?" Micheal went to a knee to get to the young girl's level. She had stark red hair like her mother and green eyes.

"Brenna, these are the warriors who defeated Fenrir." Brenna cowered shyly behind Odilia. Odilia's eyes went wide at something behind him.

Micheal turned to see Mbizi and Shani carrying some large containers.

"Your Majesties, these are some friends, Mbizi and Shani," Micheal introduced them. Nobody in the greeting party had seen people with such dark skin before.

"Come, let us feast in your honor," Odilia said, and they all headed for the Great Hall.

Even with lessons, their Egyptian friends were struggling to communicate in Proto-scandic.

"So, Shani, where do you come from?" Odilia asked as elk, whale, and kelp were served.

Shani seemed confused, so Micheal translated.

"A place next to the sea, lush and green, surrounded by endless sands," Shani described a place on the bottom of the Arabian Peninsula.

"Sounds beautiful," Odilia said longingly.

As the festivities ran long into the night, Micheal went outside for fresh air. He took a drag of some cool night air as a curtain of purple and green danced across the sky.

"Brings back memories, doesn't it?" Odilia asked as she joined him.

He turned to look at her. "I never thought I'd see you again," Micheal began.

"After all these years, I thought you'd forgotten about us." Odilia looked away.

"We had some unexpected challenges in Egypt..." Micheal trailed off as he thought of their two years apart.

"Do you want to tell me about it?" Odilia touched his shoulder.

He looked at her. "After spending nearly every day of the last 50 years together, Julie and I were forcibly separated for two years. It really messed with my mind. I didn't know if I would ever see her again." He was nearly in tears thinking about it again.

"I don't know what it's like to be with someone for such a long time, but anytime Odo leaves for some dangerous quest, I can never be sure if I will see him again," Odilia tried to empathize.

"Thank you for listening," Micheal looked back at the aurora.

"Will you be staying long?" Odilia sounded concerned.

"We will be in the area for perhaps a year," Micheal assured her.

"We will have you stay in the Ambassador's hut," Odilia decided.

"That's very kind of you," Micheal said. Then added, "We need some ice for dessert.

She raised a brow.

"Trust me. You will like this," he promised.

They ground the ice into a finely shaved ice, blended it with pomegranate pulp, and added a little sugar they had collected from their stash in Gibraltar. The result was basically a pomegranate slushie. Odilia tasted a spoonful, and her eyes lit up.

"What is it?" she asked as she took another scoop.

"It's a fruit from Egypt, where we spent most of the last five years," Micheal explained.

The special treat was extremely popular. Mbizi was gulping his bowl down with lightning speed, then pressed his hand to his forehead. Obviously, he had a brain-freeze.

"Open your mouth and take a few deep breaths. The sensation will pass momentarily," Julie instructed.

"That's what happens when you eat something this cold that fast." Micheal had to chuckle at Mbizi's expense.

"They are so smart," Shani commented to Odilia.

"Of course. They're of the gods," Odilia stated matter-of-factly.

"Indeed they are," Shani agreed.

The night grew to a close, and they retired to the ambassador's hut. It was the second largest in the village.

Julie woke up to Micheal singing "Happy Birthday":

"...Happy birthday, dear Julie.

Happy birthday to you.

How old are you now?" his smile grew wider.

"Don't even start!" she warned.

"Oh, come on. You don't look a day over 87," he laughed.

She playfully punched his shoulder.

"Sorry," he rubbed his arm. "Get up, my beauty. The whole village is preparing for your special day."

"That's just because it coincides with our departure," Julie argued.

"You know that's not true. Now let's go," he ordered.

It was like a big festival; people all over Scandinavia had come for their farewell. Copenhagen had swollen to around 5,000—three to four times its usual population.

"Chief Hildebrand, Queen Asdis, we're so glad you could come." Julie smiled.

"It was our pleasure to host you this summer past," the queen said.

"It was good to see everyone again. And your hospitality was amazing," Micheal said.

"Micheal, Julie, look who's here," Odilia came with Valdis from Bergen.

"I think this is the first time all of us have been together since the war ended," Odo commented.

"We're sorry we were away so long," Julie apologized.

"I'm sure the champions of the gods were doing things to help people," Queen Valdis said with confidence.

"While I have long questioned if the gods have any plans for us, I'm beginning to become convinced." Julie thought of the likes of Isis and other gods of old. Then she thought of the Christian God and how there had been so many events from Genesis, as well as some of the people claiming to be from the bible. Now, more than ever, she wondered what religion could best explain everything she had experienced firsthand.

The farewell dinner was a spread of Scandinavia's finest. Roasted elk and caribou stew followed by whale steak with a side of seaweed. Then, a specialty specifically for them, pulled wolf meat in gravy. The meal was accompanied by the last of their remaining canned juices from around the Mediterranean, including orange, grape, pomegranate, and apple juice.

"What's for dessert?" Odilia asked excitedly.

"This is called a chocolate brownie," Julie informed them as it was passed around the hall. "I think you will quite enjoy chocolate," she added.

The brownies were a topic of great interest as the night grew late. Then Julie rose, and Micheal followed her to the center of the dais.

"This has been a most special honor for me. On my day of birth... whenever another year passes, we take stock of everything about our lives. We examine what is important. And what truly matters are the people who give life meaning. I look around this room, and all of you have been so special to me..." she paused as a tear came to her eye. "... Saying goodbye is the hardest thing, but it is an inevitable part of life. We wish we could stay, but the sea calls us home. I will miss each and every one of you. Now, we would like to play and sing a couple of songs that help me remember those we've left behind."

She and Micheal picked up their instruments and began to play the end tune from *The Lord of the Rings: Return of the King*. Then Julie began her best Annie Lennox impression:

The beautiful lyrics flowed from her lips like silk.

She loved watching the reaction of the hall. They had never heard anything like it before.

Into the West was such a poignant song for goodbyes.

The tears came as the reality of another goodbye hit her. "That song has such an effect on me whenever we leave a place. And while the life we've chosen to live has made this an all-too-common occurrence, it is always difficult to leave so many friends behind. So, for my final farewell, I want to sing one final song. It's about our homeland."

With that, Micheal began playing Tina Melia's "Shores of Avalon". Then Julie began:

Her voice painted a vision of Avalon. Which felt very personal through Micheal's connection to Arthur.

Julie loved the melancholy tone of the song. She'd never heard it until Micheal sang it back in Atlantis, but it was the perfect close to their times in the Norselands.

They headed for the docks down a path lined with people. They were accompanied by Odilia and Odo, along with the leadership from Namsos. The weather was fair as the sun hung over the horizon in the late autumn evening.

Julie went to her knee to say goodbye to little Brenna. "Now you be good for your parents, okay?" She kissed the little girl's cheek, then stood back up. "Odilia, I'm so glad we had this time together. I will always keep your friendship in my heart and wish you a long and happy life." Julie embraced Odilia, and the tears fell like rain. Julie finally stepped back and held eye contact for one long moment, and then Odilia turned to Micheal.

"Having this time together this past year only emphasizes how special you are to me," Odilia began.

Micheal wiped the tears from his eyes. "In all the long years in my life, only one or two people have reached the depths of my soul like you have. While we must go, you have no idea how much I wish we could stay... This is the hardest goodbye I've had to say in nearly 70 years..." Micheal took a deep breath and closed his eyes. "... For me, I don't get close to many people..." he broke off.

"I understand how you feel. I promise I will never forget you," she said, embracing him, sniffling back her tears.

They just held each other for a while. Finally, they pulled back and shared a look for a few more moments, and then it was time to board.

At that moment, there was a crash of thunder, and a spiderweb of lightning snaked across the twilight sky. Then Thor landed hard on the deck between them and Odo and Odilia.

"Queen Odilia, it's been too long. Still beautiful as ever."

"Your eminence," Odilia bowed.

"And this is the lucky man!" Thor slapped Odo on the arm.

"Your eminence," Odo bowed.

Julie looked around, and everyone was bowing, including Mbizi and Shani.

"And what is the God of Thunder doing here?" Julie asked.

"Come now, Lady Avalon. How could I not farewell my champions," Thor feigned offense.

"Where was the God of Thunder when the Sun God, Ra, attacked us?" Micheal said sharply.

"Your trials in Egypt have made you stronger. And besides, that's not my dominion. I respect his boundaries; he respects mine." The answer indicated he knew Ra.

"How many other gods do you know from other domains?" Julie demanded.

"It's not important. Whenever you leave my domain, you'll be vulnerable to them." Thor shrugged.

"And how long have you known Ra?" Micheal came back.

"A few centuries. But it doesn't matter. Perhaps you should stay here," Thor suggested. "There's no one better to champion me," Thor tried to convince them.

"We have to leave." Julie scowled.

"No matter when you go to, you'll face the same dilemmas," Thor laughed. "I know who you are. I know what you're running from. You can't run far enough, Lady Julie." Thor seemed oddly serious, and Julie felt the sting of his words.

It had been a decade, but the flash of destruction was still vivid in her mind's eye.

"Worry not, my timeless beauty. You know what they say..." Thor indicated a blank, then said, "It heals all wounds." Then he smiled, raised his hammer over his head, then added, "See you next... time..." Then he rapidly ascended to the clouds.

Micheal looked over at Julie.

"That's amazing!" Odo finally said.

"Who, Thor?" Julie said.

"To see the God of Thunder and how you just casually talk to him," King Odo marveled.

"This isn't the first time we've met a god," Julie said dismissively.

"Thor came to see you off," Odilia said, touching Julie's shoulder.

"I suppose he did," she agreed with half a smile. She wouldn't let Thor ruin her farewell. "I will always remember you. All of you," she promised.

Everyone embraced one last time; then, they boarded the Valkyrie. Julie watched until her friends fazed into the horizon. Then, they sailed for the rocky Norwegian coast. A few hours later, the moon sat high in the November sky, and they quickly prepared everything for the jump.

"Both of you need to stand right there," Julie instructed Shani and Mbizi in Egyptian.

"We've done this once before," Shani said confidently.

"This will be a little bit different than last time," Micheal informed them.

"Ten seconds!" Julie warned.

"I'll see you on the other side," Micheal promised.

As the clock struck zero, the vortex burst to life above them. Julie looked up, and the moon was glowing green. She took a deep breath and closed her eyes. The flash cut through her lids. Then the tunnel had her. Some historical events flashed past her, and then everything went dark.

PART III: THE GREATEST STORY

CHAPTER 16: THE PHARAOH AND THE GODS

THE VALKYRIE SLID TO a stop under the main entry module of River Palace. The glossy sheen had faded over the past 320 years.

"Looks like it needs some TLC," Micheal commented as they climbed toward the palace level in the elevator.

"I don't know. It's survived the second intermediate period, seemingly intact." Julie shrugged.

The elevator came to a stop, and there was a welcoming party. At the center was a dark-skinned woman who was clearly in charge. She administered the challenge for verification and then introduced herself.

"My Lord, My Lady, I am Kesi, palace manager." She bowed.

"Very good. It has been a few centuries since our forefathers built this place, and it requires some special maintenance," Micheal said, scanning the entry module. "If you could come by the Lord's module this evening, I'd like to go over our plans," Micheal said.

"Of course, My Lord. Right this way." Kesi guided them toward the Lord's module.

After dinner, Kesi came as instructed. "It will take quite a bit of man power for this project, so if you could put the word out for more laborers," Julie instructed.

"My Lady, that will be very expensive," Kesi argued.

"The resources will be available, so don't worry about that," Micheal chimed in.

"I'm curious..." Kesi began.

"Yes?" Julie prompted.

"First, why has your family been absent for so long? And second, considering the length of absentees, it seems a lot of time and resources to maintain it over all these years." Kesi looked back and forth.

"First, our family are adventurers. We rarely stay in one place for very long. And second, when your heritage is responsible for such amazing places, those places should be maintained as a legacy of honor," Micheal finished.

"So, where do we begin?" Kesi asked.

Micheal and Julie went back to the recipe for the ceiling resin they used, beginning with Bostonian, back in the 17th century. They used their mining bores to collect the requisite amount of diamond powder required to protect the structure for a few more centuries. They mixed it with other elements in the same guise as the tri-poly alloys. The resin would bond with the stone, making it nearly indestructible. It would also resist weathering. While the resin was being mixed together, they put Mbizi in charge of crafting the paint rollers.

Over the next few weeks, the palace was systematically coated in protective layers. By the time they were nearing completion, their anniversary in time was drawing near.

"Kesi, we would like to celebrate the efforts of all the staff," Julie began.

"Make it a lavish affair. Spare no expense," Micheal added.

"There are a few specific things we'd like to have. Here's a list." Julie handed Kesi a papyrus scroll.

As Kesi departed, Mbizi and Shani entered.

"How's the progress coming along?" Micheal inquired.

"The palace looks as good as new," Shani announced proudly.

"It still amazed me that I live here," Mbizi commented.

"Well, it's time you earn your keep," Micheal dead-panned. "We're going hunting for some special items." Everyone laughed.

They sailed the Valkyrie up to the Mediterranean. They caught lobsters using a system of traps. By the end of the day, they had a mountain of them. They would feature in the festivities.

"I remember the first time you said we were going to eat these little monsters. I thought you'd gone mad. But then I tried some." Mbizi shook his head.

"Our world has certainly gotten bigger," Shani agreed.

"It has to when you service the gods," Mbizi quipped.

"Do you believe the gods choose people for special tasks?" Julie seemed serious.

"The gods can recognize when someone has superior capabilities. It only makes sense that they'd want to utilize that," Mbizi stated matter-of-factly.

"I wish the gods would leave me alone." Julie looked off into the distance.

After a quiet pause, Mbizi laughed. "Oh Julie, it's all for the better," he tried to convince her.

"I think we better get back to the palace," Micheal cut the discussion short. He hoped their challenges were for the better, but he had his doubts.

The next night, Mbizi was escorting Shani through the festival. "You are as a queen in this magnificent gown," Mbizi said.

Shani was wearing a new beaded gown accented by precious stones. She was also wearing a necklace arrayed in the colors of Isis.

"You smell amazing, my prince," Shani commented.

He wore his best wig with a tallow melt, scented in the perfume of susinum. He wore a bear skin across his chest that was gifted to him when they were in Norway. And that was accompanied by a necklace of amber, given to him by King Odo.

They walked to the edge of the fountain at the center of the main module. The water was falling in an array of colors that challenged the imagination.

"Can you believe this is our life?" Shani was scanning the chaotic party. Children were running around. All the people who usually had duties to perform had temporary replacements. It was interesting to see them just relaxing and acting like themselves.

"This is a long way from slavery," Mbizi agreed.

Their conversation was interrupted by the trumpets announcing the approach of the Pharaoh. Mbizi took Shani, and they found Micheal and Julie.

"Kesi, please keep the party going. We will go and greet His Majesty," Micheal instructed. "And you are with us." He indicated both of them, then led the way.

They split their way through the sea of people and made their way to the Pharaoh's module.

"Do we know who this Pharaoh is?" Shani asked.

"It's one of two people. It could be the female Pharaoh Hatshepsut, or more likely, his name is Thutmose," Micheal informed them.

They waited a few more minutes, and then the lift began to rise. The platform came to a stop, and the servants raised the gate. The Pharaoh and his entourage stepped off, then stopped at the sight of them. The Pharaoh was relatively tall—at least three cubits and two spans.

Mbizi stepped forward and said, "Your eminence, may I introduce Lord and Lady Avalon." Then he and all of them bowed before the Pharaoh.

"The Lord and Lady from beyond the sea have at long last returned." The Pharaoh sounded fascinated. "Rise," he commanded.

The Pharaoh proceeded to examine them more closely. "Manager Kesi led me to believe it had been over two centuries since any of your people last visited?"

"Our people tend to move and explore strange and distant lands. We were finally told of the great land of the river—Egypt. And of our forefathers' great home here, so we thought we would come settle down here for a while. And after over three centuries, the place might need some upkeep."

The Pharaoh looked around.

"We made no change to the appearance; simply added another coat to protect it for another few centuries," Mbizi volunteered.

The Pharaoh examined everyone again, then said, "I look forward to becoming better acquainted with you all. If I am not mistaken, it sounds like festivities are underway." He looked past them toward the bridge.

"We were rewarding the staff's hard work over the past three weeks," Micheal explained.

"Very nice, My Lord Avalon." Pharaoh indicated for him to lead the way.

Everyone bowed as they proceeded to the designated Lord's sanctuary adjacent to the Lord's module.

"Your Majesty!" Kesi bowed at the sight of him.

"My Lady, Kesi, a fine festival," the Pharaoh complimented.

At a signal, a parade of servants delivered a grand spread. It included lobster, scallops, and shrimp breaded with coconut; there were also many fruits and vegetables. The Pharaoh and his entourage examined the meal with apparent skepticism.

"We shall prepare something more to your liking if you wish?" Lady Julie offered.

"On the contrary. I would love to try some Avalonian cuisine." The Pharaoh delicately picked up a scallop between his thumb and forefinger, smelled it, then took a bite. His men followed his example.

A while later, "So, My Lord Mbizi, from where do you come? You do not appear to hail from Avalon," Pharaoh Thutmose inquired of him.

"I am originally from Kush, and she is from Saba," Mbizi indicated to Shani. "But we have been on a voyage with Lord and Lady Avalon since we met, some three years past."

"Have you voyaged beyond the sea?" One of Thutmose's generals perked up at the idea.

"We have indeed!" Shani chimed in. "To a land where magical white powder rains down from the heavens. Where the summer sun never sets and the long winter nights are illuminated by color, painted by the gods," Shani waxed poetic. She had fallen in love with the phenomenon, which Micheal had told them was caused by the Bringer of Light, Heimdall, rebuilding the Bifrost.

Mbizi wondered at the nature of the gods. When he was a boy, he knew Ra protected the day, Osiris watched over the night, and Isis brought life to the world. But he didn't realize how limited their power was until he learned about the gods of other places. He had yet to see Ra or any of the other gods of Egypt. But the Norse god, Thor, came before them in all his terrible glory, and he brought the thunder with him. Were the gods from different lands actually different? Or were they just called by another name in the other location?

"The gods are indeed wonderous," Thutmose agreed.

"How did your eminence fair in Syria?" Mbizi inquired.

"A great victory did we claim over the Mitanni," the Pharaoh boasted proudly, as he scooped up a dessert that Micheal called an "éclair".

His Majesty had been gorging on many of the treats made for this special occasion—as had Mbizi. Micheal and Julie certainly did possess divine knowledge.

"We surprised them when we ferried our armies across the Euphrates." Mbizi could tell the Pharaoh was most impressed with his own accomplishments.

"You are most blessed by Montu," Mbizi complimented.

"My Lord, Mbizi, you know the Lord of Avalon well?" the Pharaoh inquired.

"I have been his friend and advisor for the past three years," Mbizi stated.

"So he's to be trusted?" Thutmose observed Micheal making his way through the party.

"He is a man of great honor," Mbizi stated unequivocally.

"I look forward to getting to know you both better. I have already sent word. Court will be held here for the time being," the Pharaoh informed him as Micheal and Julie approached. "I thank you for allowing me to intrude on your festivities." The Pharaoh rose and headed for the door, followed by his generals.

"It appears the two of you have made fast friends." Micheal raised a brow.

"His eminence is very easy to like." Mbizi smiled.

"Perhaps we'll all be friends then." Micheal walked away.

Mbizi arrived late to bed. "How did I get so lucky?" he asked Shani. "To be friends to a champion, to be married to the greatest beauty in all the land. And now I may have the ear of the Pharaoh?" Mbizi marveled at his luck.

"No one is more deserving. Now come to bed," Shani said invitingly.

Instinct

Julie balanced her right foot on a small post in the main court-yard and wrapped the blindfold tightly around her head. She began focusing on her breathing—each push in, each push out—until she was at onewith herself. She began locating individual sounds and determining their sources, considering distance, weight, and the Doppler effect. Her focus initially settled on the cascade's sound as it fell into the river from the courtyard. The breeze rustled the vail shade that sheltered the courtyard from the morning sun.

Next, she detected the pattering of little feet on the courtyard stone. It must be a child at play. Then she heard it—the careful, deliberate steps of someone intent on attack. She breathed deeply and caught the faint whiff of body odor—slightly pungent with a musky quality to it. Then she felt a minute change in the air pressure coming to her left.

She quickly unsheathed her swords. The clash of metal indicated a correct detection. She flipped off the post, landing a defensive crouch. She cut a stroke to her left and heard another sword parry. Her left hand caught a wrist and she released backward into a kick-throw, tossing the attacker. The sound of a thud mingled with the clatter of her sword kissing the stone.

Then she continued her momentum over her head to her feet. She sensed a pressure change from behind and instinctively continued her backward momentum into her would-be attacker. His apparent sword strike missed around in front of her, ending with his arms embracing her in a hug from behind. She grabbed his hands and flipped him over. She finished with a strike to what she believed was his cheek. She heard the rush of two attackers coming from opposite sides. She delayed for two beats, then collapsed to the ground. The brush of the men's feet slid past her en route to an obvious collision. She extracted herself from the groaning men.

She was at her guard the entire time, unsure of how many attackers there were. She paused and just listened. Then she heard it—the faint sound of a foot on granite, attempting to stealth their way to her. She turned against the sound, pretending to scout the opposite direction. A couple of moments later, her prey took the bait—hook, line, and sinker. As the steps got closer, she did a backstep leg sweep, and the attacker was dropped to the ground. Then she did an elbow drop, which was answered by a grunt.

She regained her feet and attempted to detect any more environmental changes to her surroundings. She heard each defeated opponent groaning to one effect or another. Under the rules of the game, once you were defeated, you were supposed to stay in place until the game was over. After another minute, she became convinced she had won the game.

Just as she was about to remove the blindfold, she detected the slightest change in pressure to her right. She listened intently. There was a very slight footstep on the stone. She thought she knew instinctually where the attacker was. She stepped forward and cut a wide swathe with her blade. She was surprised when it missed, and there was no active retreat from her attacker. She tried again, but when she stepped forward this time, she was tripped by whoever was there. Julie rolled back to her feet, trying to detect the opponent. But after a few moments, he felt like a ghost.

Suddenly, the ghost became a poltergeist, knocking her sword out of her hand. As the clatter of the blade ceased, she began to wonder at the skill of her attacker. She began working a defensive pattern around her environment when she felt something tickling her ear. She kicked in the direction and found nothing but air. Then something tapped her on the nose, and she realized only one person would be doing this.

"Micheal!!!" Julie removed the blindfold.

And someone else was watching. "Very impressive." The Pharaoh stepped out of the shadows. "I have never seen such skill before?" It was stated as a question.

"Marshal skill is vital if you intend to voyage into the unknown," Julie explained.

"I'm surprised with skills like that; this Avalon has not conquered the world." The Pharaoh was examining them.

"Not all desire conquest," Micheal countered.

"All desire power, in one form or another," Thutmose stated definitively.

"I have never wanted such a thing," Micheal protested.

"I have studied the both of you, My Lord, these past few weeks, and I'll tell you now, I'm a very good judge of character. Would you like me to tell you what I've determined about the Lords from Avalon?" The Pharaoh looked back from her to Micheal.

"Your eminence," Juie prompted.

"That very differential manner proves the point. Your demonstrations of fighting skill say you can kill me and take my throne at your will, and yet you hold the pretense of subservient respect. The way you carry yourselves strikes a superior aspect. You feel above those around you. I spent much of my youth and formative years in this palace. And I've often pondered who could have built such a place." Thutmose walked over and ran his hand through the cascade. "... It was like magic. Most attributed it to the gods, but I knew there was more to it. Let me show you." The Pharaoh led them into the Lord's sanctuary. He stopped at the murals of the battles with Fenrir and Ragnarr. He seemed to study them for a moment.

"I knew the unusual people who built this place were the same ones in these images. Then I realized ... it was you." He looked into Julie's eyes, then at the mural, then back again. "Before you try to deny it, much of my youth, I dreamed of many harrowing adventures with the fierce-eyed maiden from these murals. I would recognize those eyes anywhere."

Julie felt exposed.

"So, no. I know you both. You desire power, which sets you above kings. So you answer to no one except perhaps the gods. Immortality is not so strange when you've met the gods." Thutmose touched the picture of Ragnarr shooting lightening from the sword.

"The gods?" Micheal questioned, looking at Julie.

"You didn't think you were the only ones who were special, did you? The gods actively back my impositions of security," Thutmose boasted.

"I would be careful from which gods I accepted patronage," Micheal warned.

"Who are we to question the gods?" the Pharaoh challenged.

"We've seen it go wrong before," Julie countered. "Just be careful."

"I will trust my instincts," the Pharaoh said, looking at both of them then exiting the chamber.

"Do you think he's talking about Ra?" Julie worried.

"It's been 300 years. Do you really think Ra is still around?" Micheal sounded skeptical.

"He was there in the 19th century. And who knows where we sent him. I'm beginning to have a bad feeling about this," Julie's stomach dropped.

"Well, I guess we better trust our instincts," Micheal concluded.

Karnak

"I can't believe we are going to get to see inside Karnak," Shani said as Thebes loomed on the east bank.

"Are you really so surprised? We've been high class for years now," Mbizi said dismissively.

"You must watch your pride, my love," Shani scolded.

They sailed into the main harbor, where the Pharaoh was there to greet them.

"Your eminence." They bowed.

"My Lord Mbizi. My Lady." Thutmose indicated for them to join him. "Did you know, my friends, that the gods have been known to frequent the Holy of Holies here at the palace?" Thutmose said casually. "I suppose when you're so close to immortals who have some sort of relationship with the gods, that's rather passé." The Pharaoh could read that they weren't overly shocked by the revelation.

"It is certainly different knowing the Lords of Avalon. They certainly converse with the gods," Shani informed the Pharaoh.

At that moment, a young man approached. "My son, Prince Amenemhat, shall be joining us," Thutmose informed them.

"Your Highness."

Amenemhat was perhaps 14 years old. He was around three cubits and a span in height and very much the image of his father:

light brown skin, downward-slanted eyes, and a slanted nose.

"My Lady, My Lord," the prince acknowledged them.

"The Lord and Lady of the west will be joining your initiation ceremony," Thutmose told the prince as he led them from the quay down the avenue of sphinxes.

They were all beautifully carved out of stone. There were dozens of them proudly saluting the honored guests who were permitted inside the sacred temple complex. They were followed through the first pilon by a bevy of servants bearing a great offering to the gods. The first pilon was blazing white in the midday sun and stood a good 30 cubits in height. It had banners blowing in a stiff breeze from the south. After passing through the second pilon, which was very similar to the first, the Pharaoh announced, "The great Hypostyle Hall... My predecessor was inspired but did not think big enough. Which is why I'm expanding it," Thutmose alluded to the craftsmen chiseling away.

"It's never quite big enough, is it?" a deep voice seeped from the shadows. Then, the face emerged into the light. Shani nearly tripped over Mbizi, who caught her, as she reacted with a start. The face was narrow, tapering to a snout, with teeth that reminded her of a jackal.

"Do I frighten you?" The creature seemed amused.

He was exceptionally tall, about four cubits and a span. His yellow eyes seemed to glow. Then she recognized him. It was the god Set.

"Your eminence. This is the Lord and Lady of the West," Thutmose spoke for them.

Set took a closer look at them, then said, "Just be careful not to get lost in the shadow of the rising Ra," he almost threatened. Then he turned to Amenemhat, "My prince, I endow you with divine essence to understand the land of lost souls, that you shall be forever found." Set emanated some light from his hands, which enveloped the prince. "A king of the living and the dead, you may become. Now leave me," Set commanded them.

They passed between the towering columns, ornately carved and standing 20 cubits tall. They needed to cross four pylons to move from the Hypostyle Hall to the Inner Sanctum.

After meeting Set, the next God wasn't as surprising. Standing tall in the center of the chamber was the Guardian Anubis. He was four cubits and two palms in height. And his red eyes seemed to cut right past his bared teeth to the heart of your soul. The sharp ears completed the intimidating look.

"The Prince comes for solidification with the Gods... Step forward." Anubis instructed with a voice of dark satin.

Amenemhat moved into the light. "I bestow upon you the gift of sound mind. May it be your guide through many challenges." As Anubis blessed the prince, he generated a red glow out of his hands. After a moment the light died, and Anubis nodded at Amenemhat. Who bowed in response. Then Anubis looked at them. "I see the truth of you My Lord and Lady of the West. Time has led you down a dangerous path. Kingdoms may rise or fall on your decisions. Use your time wisely." Shani felt like Anubis could read her like a scroll.

Reading itself was a bit magical. Micheal had given both her and Mbizi immense understanding of the world around them. Beginning the first year they met. And now they were better studied than any priest.

"How will we know which decisions are most important?" Shani questioned.

"Only time can tell." Anubis reached out with his hand and there was a flash of images then he disappeared.

They proceeded through a room where the central path was lined with priests who seemed to be mimicking The Avenue of Sphinxes. They waded through a series of veils to enter one final chamber.

Sitting on a golden throne in the center was The Sun God Ra. Shani was instantly terrified. He looked every bit as horrifying as Micheal had described him. Micheal had said he was five cubits in height, amazingly strong, and was unable to be injured. He also had the ability to control time.

Ra peered down his falcon beak at them with his inquiring glowing blue eyes.

"Your Majesty, who do you present?" An orb spinning above Ra's head began pulsating light.

"I offer Crown Prince Amenemhat, so he might be the next God on earth." The Pharaoh bowed in deference, everyone else followed suit.

"I endow you with the power of the day. The light of creation. By this power your divine provenance grants you future dominion over Egypt and all its empire. A God on earth." Ra emitted some kind of light from his hand, and something very strange occurred.

Suddenly the room went silent and there were colorful streaks of light that seemed to float in the air. Shani glanced to her side and the flames of the torches appeared to be frozen. Like they were made of solid substance.

Ra came methodically down from his throne and touched Amenemhat on his forehead. Then went and sat back down. His hands glowed again then everything seemed to return to normal.

The flames were dancing on their torches. And the streaks of light were gone. At that moment the prince collapsed.

"I have sent you but a small taste of real power. Rise now the divine Prince Amenemhat of Egypt." Ra declared.

As they all stood, Shani couldn't help but wonder what Ra had done. But her thoughts were interrupted.

"... And Lady of the West?" Ra looked to Thutmose as if in question, then continued. "Anyone the Pharaoh deems worthy of such a visit, I must get to know better... One note of caution. It is a risk to fly with the gods. Careful not to get burned." His eyes glowed brighter with the threat and the strange conditions as before returned.

The silence, the flames. Ra stood and walked casually out of the chamber. His steps made no sound. Shani kept absolutely motionless until he was out of sight.

She turned to her left and Mbizi, along with Thutmose as well as Amenemhat looked like statues. And the streaks of color were once again floating in the air all around them.

She stepped in front of Mbizi and waved her hand in front of his face. But he didn't seem to see her. As she looked around it was as if the whole world had come to a halt. She tried clapping her hands and there was nothing, no sound?

Then all at once the streams of light disappeared in a flash and there was a crack like thunder, which she thought might have come from her hands.

"The power of the gods is impressive, is it not?" The Pharaoh smiled at his son. "Now... Some of that power resides in you." Thutmose added. "Let's walk." The Pharaoh guided them out toward the South.

As they walked the magnificently ornate grounds of Karnak, Shani wondered about the power of the God Ra. Perhaps Micheal could explain it, but it was... Impressive.

CHAPTER 17: POWERS OF TIME

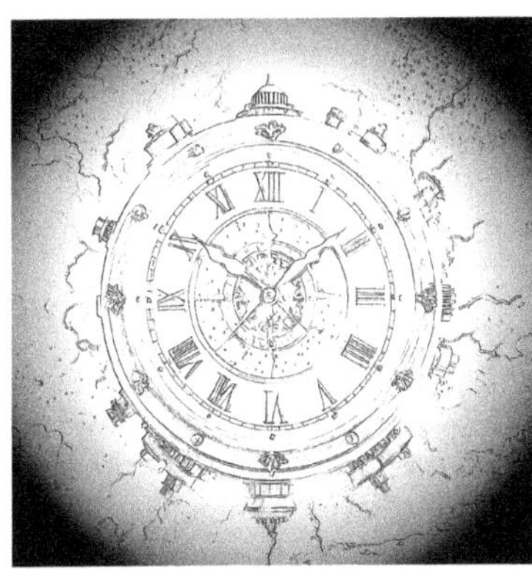

<u>Thebes</u>

"**A**ND NOW FROM BEYOND the sea, Lord and Lady Avalon!" The court, Harold announced as Micheal and Julie arrived at the palace in Thebes.

They were attending a celebration of Prince Amenemhat's divination. He was now officially a God on earth.

"Your holy eminences." Micheal and Julie bowed before both the Pharaoh and the Prince.

"Welcome, My Lord and Lady, to Thebes." Thutmose motioned for them to stand.

"We have a gift for your Eminence." Micheal signaled for a servant to bring the item forward.

Amenemhat looked expectantly at the offering. Someone removed a cloth, revealing a triopoly recurve bow.

"Wow! My very own Avalonian bow. It's just like my father's." He closely inspected the fine craftsmanship. It was a glossy silver, with Proto-Scandic runes engraved in the body.

Amenemhat tested the draw. It was only 30 pounds, but it shot with much more force. "A most spectacular gift." Amenemhat excused himself to go show it off to his friends.

"Your Eminence, there is a matter of some urgency." Vizier Neferweben interrupted their conversation with the Pharaoh.

"Micheal, Julie... There is a problem." Shani indicated they should follow her. They went out into the gardens overlooking the river.

"So what's wrong?" Micheal was concerned.

"First, we need to tell you. During the divination ceremony at Karnak, we met three gods." Shani was explaining.

"Three?" Julie looked at Micheal.

"First we met Set in the Hypostyle Hall, then Anubis was in the Inner Sanctum..." Mbizi began to answer.

"... And then..." Shani prompted.

"... Ra." Micheal realized.

"So he's back." Julie was considering. "And he brought friends." Ra was a difficult enough challenge by himself. If he were now three, that would be nearly impossible.

"There's something else." Micheal didn't like the way Shani said that.

"Each of the gods seemed to have some kind of mystical power. Set warned us about Ra. Anubis spoke of a vision about us. And Ra, that was where things went really strange." Shani was concentrating, trying to think of the right words.

"Describe what happened." Micheal prompted.

Following Shani's description.

"...Ra can stop time?" Julie was horrified. "Like Hiro Nakamura?"

"Apparently. Which means the next time he comes for us, I don't think we'll survive." Micheal allowed his negative sentiments to creep in.

"Wait... How come he never used it before? And why wasn't Shani affected?" Julie pointed out.

"I don't know, but we better find out." Micheal was determined.

The next day, Michael sat on their suite's balcony in the palace, delving into meditation to contemplate Ra's newly revealed temporal ability. He actively engaged in introspection.

He saw Melina Hellas.

"I would like to apologize," Micheal said as he landed in the gardens next to the sea at Melina's secret residence in Amazon. It straddled the border with Mystique.

"Koios! How?!... Of course... Your Eminence would like to apologize to me?" Melina practically laughed.

"When I chose you for this special gift, I should've come and offered it to you instead of imposing on you... We've known each other for a long time. And I consider you a friend. So I want to apologize if my gift has brought you hardship." Melina looked thoughtfully at him for a moment.

"I accept your apology, Koios." Then she walked out into the wet sand, where Oceanis kissed the shore. Micheal followed her in, removing his shoes as he went. "I remember it like it was yesterday. I was standing on the coast, watching you and Aphrodite about to leave. We had said our goodbyes..." Melina closed her eyes. "My heart was breaking, believing I would never see you again... Then it happened... The portal burst to life, and a host of images flashed past my mind's eye in that instant. I didn't understand any of it at the time. But I went inside my mind and looked at each image individually. Then, about a week later, one of them came to fruition. Followed by another, then another. I realized I was seeing the future. As time progressed, I began having dreams that did the same thing. I knew it must've come from you." Melina looked up at him.

"I always knew you were special from the first time I met you." Micheal tried to encourage her.

"I wasn't worthy of the power from the gods." Melina looked out to sea. "My whole life has just been a series of coincidences."

Micheal tried to find some sage words but said the first thing that came to him. "There is no fate but what we make." All his supposed wisdom once again came from the movies.

"What's that supposed to mean?" Melina challenged.

"No one is worthy of the power from the gods, and no one is unworthy. If we choose to give you such power, the only person who decides their worth is you." Micheal touched her on the shoulder, and they stared out at the great blue yonder together.

Micheal came back to himself. He kept his eyes closed and considered Melina. He was sure she had developed foresight through her exposure to temporal energy flows. Their energy signatures aligned with the Bermuda Triangle's temporal vortex, instigating their initial fall through time. What if temporal energy could affect the temporal vibrational frequency of different people in different ways when exposed to it? Maybe they could develop temporal-related special abilities, like Melina seeing the future. Or Ra opening time gates or even stopping time altogether.

Perhaps their use of Julie's portal is what gave Ra this power. There were always so many unforeseen consequences to the decisions they made. And now Ra had the ultimate trump card.

Micheal wondered what, if anything, he might have developed. Or if Julie had any special abilities. They had been exposed to far more temporal energy than anyone they knew about. Could they have some latent ability they just needed to discover and foster?

All of this still told him nothing in particular about who or what Ra was. Micheal zoomed out in his mind and looked at all the pieces of the Ra puzzle. Everything they currently knew about Ra. The puzzle was so incomplete. In frustration, he came out of his meditation.

"Did you find any useful insights?" Julie asked when he entered their suite.

"Nothing significant about Ra, but I do have an idea about us..." Micheal explained his conclusions.

"... So you think we might have... Superpowers?" Julie raised a brow.

"Clearly, they didn't call Melina the Oracle for nothing. And she told me it all started after we left the 29th century." Micheal shrugged.

"So, how do we find out if we have superpowers?" Julie seemed skeptical.

"I suppose we concentrate on one potential power at a time. Then observe what happens." Micheal thought logically.

"My Lord and Lady, his Eminence request your attendance." Neferweben informed them.

Micheal and Julie arrived at the throne room.

"Thank you, my friends, for coming. I know we have only recently come to Thebes, but it was for a particular purpose. Now, we must make our progress in preparation for my next campaign. And this time, my son shall join me. The progress will end in Heliopolis where we will seek the Sun God's blessing." It seemed they wouldn't have long to devise a plan to deal with Ra.

The soldiers of Upper Egypt and Nubia gathered to parade through the streets of Thebes on their way north. The Pharaoh and his son would ride in a chariot at the head of the column together.

Micheal and Julie mounted their chariot with Shani and Mbizi taking the one next to them. They would follow just behind Thutmose in a position of honor. The people of Thebes crowded the main road north as the Army began to march. They passed between two obelisks as the procession started. They were dressed in their finest linen and were armed with their full assortment of weaponry. As was usually the case, he and Julie always drew much attention from the public.

By now, most people knew they were from some exotic land beyond the sea.

The chariot parade got into a smooth rhythm.

"You never seem to tire of the public adoration," Julie seemed to observe.

"Well, unlike you, I can remember what it was like to be a nobody." Micheal pointed out.

"I haven't always been famous." She tried to lie. He looked sidelong at her. "Okay, so maybe I have." She conceded. "But you weren't a nobody." She lied again. "You were the heir to Camelot."

"I didn't really believe that at the time so that doesn't count. And any truth to becoming Lord Avalon came through all the trials of time." He thought about all the incredible obstacles they had overcome in the last 60 years. But that only served to emphasize the daunting challenge that stood before them. So, the decision became clear. "I think we have no choice but to leave Egypt." Micheal looked ahead of the city gates.

"There is no other option, is there?" Julie seemed resigned.

"We'll inform Thutmose before we reach Heliopolis." Micheal decided.

"Where will we go?" Julie asked.

"How about America?" Micheal suggested as they left Thebes behind.

<u>Horus</u>

As the southern army arrived in Heliopolis, Mbizi was both saddened and excited about the prospects of the future. Sad because they were now going to leave Egypt again. And just when he and Pharaoh were becoming particularly close. But also excited to get to travel across the world and see a strange new land. Somewhere on the other side of a vast sea.

"It saddens me that you shall not join me on this latest campaign," Thutmose said as Mbizi was placing the last of his most prized possessions in his case.

"We shall miss your company greatly. I..." Mbizi began.

"No explanation is required. Lord Micheal gave me the reasons. So how does it feel to be going into the unknown reaches of the world?" Thutmose asked curiously.

"I have come to understand why the Avalonians live such lives." Mbizi sometimes felt like Thutmose wanted him to expose some secret truth about Avalon. In the nearly three years since they arrived in this period of time. The Pharaoh had befriended him and then had been trying to get information out of him. So despite the fact that he, Micheal and Thutmose were all basically friends, there were always undertones of mistrust.

"I have to imagine that is also the secret behind their great wealth and immortality." Thutmose kept it light.

"Then perhaps when we return, I shall also be immortal." Mbizi played along.

"When you return, you must regale me with your great adventures." Thutmose prepared to leave.

"I wish you luck on your latest venture, my friend." Mbizi bowed.

"We have the gods on our side; how can we fail?" Thutmose smiled and then left the chamber.

Mbizi went and looked out over the palace gardens. The sun was setting in the West over the River Delta. He began to let his imagination carry him away to some new, mysterious land full of strange creatures he'd never seen before. Then, there was a flash behind him.

Mbizi turned to find a woman. A very tall woman. She was as tall as Micheal. And she was trying to hold up an even taller man. He was nearly as tall as the Sun God. They had to be Gods.

This God appeared to be injured.

"What happened?" Mbizi ran to their aid.

"It was Ra. My son is dying." The woman was distraught.

"Are you?..." Mbizi thought he knew.

"... Isis, yes. And my son Horus." Isis confirmed urgently. "There is no time!" She went on.

"No time for what?" Mbizi worried.

"Horus will die. But you could carry his essence." Isis looked Mbizi up and down. "You, My Lord of the West, are special. Do you accept this great honor?" Isis pleaded.

How could he say no to the Goddess of Life? "I accept." He went to one knee before her.

She touched his forehead, then touched Horus on the head. At that moment, there was a flash, and a horde of images raced through his head. Mbizi closed his eyes and let the energy flow through him. It felt warm, pulsating across his skin. It all increased to a climax, and there was another flash, and everything momentarily went dark.

A crowd of voices greeted him as he came around.

"How do you feel?" Isis asked through the tears.

Mbizi suddenly saw himself partially distorted from the direction in which Isis was sitting. "What's happening?" He was worried he was losing his mind.

"What do you see?" Isis inquired.

"I see myself..." He looked like a mirage he could see through himself.

"You have it then... The Sight of Horus." Isis informed him. When he closed his eyes, the images became like life. "You can now see through the eyes of anyone. If you focus on any person you can see and hear what they see and hear." She explained.

"So I just think about them?" Mbizi was still a little skeptical.

"Go ahead, try it out." Isis urged.

Mbizi thought about Micheal, and an image began to appear.

"So, who do you think is living in America right now?" He saw Julie ask.

"The descendants of the survivors of the apocalypse, obviously the ancestors of the Native Americans," Micheal replied. They were speaking Avalonian, but Mbizi could understand what was being said.

"Do you think we'll have trouble dealing with them?" Julie worried.

"I think we'll be okay. Would you stop worrying?" Micheal admonished.

"I just wish we didn't have to go." Julie seemed sad.

When Micheal moved in a little too close to Julie for comfort, Mbizi pulled out of the view.

"You now possess the Eye of Horus. May it serve you in the challenges to come. Learn to hone the skill, use it wisely, My Lord." Isis seemed to stare straight through him. Then she touched Horus, and they disappeared in a flash.

Mbizi decided to test it again. He thought about King Odo, and the he realized his old friend was long dead. So, he then focused on Odo's descendants.

"Why must you go?" A beautiful blonde woman questioned.

"We have to defend the fishing waters. The Vidar have been encroaching further and further into our area. Soon, it will become all-out war." The man said.

"But why does it have to be you?" The woman challenged.

"What kind of chief would I be if I didn't follow the great King Odo's example?" The apparent chief asked.

"You're not King Odo!" The Queen argued.

"Hella, I promise everything will be okay." The king went in for a kiss, and Mbizi pulled out of the view.

He thought about how this power from the gods could be useful. The next being he thought about was The Sun God Ra.

He saw steps leading down from the throne Ra was sitting on. There were two lines of priests on opposite sides of the carpet. Down the center of that carpet stood a procession of priestesses presenting Ra with offerings.

"Halt!" Ra commanded, and everyone stopped. Ra scanned the chamber, then paused, looking straight out over the room. He stood up, and the next thing Mbizi knew, The Sun God was standing right before him.

"My Lord of the West, you now possess The Eye of Horus." Ra looked human. He didn't have his falcon face.

"It was a gift from Isis and Horus," Mbizi told the God nervously.

"Indeed it was. Now, you will serve me." Ra emanated some light out of his hands and the room became saturated. Then, there was a bright flash, and everything went dark.

<u>Out of Time</u>

Micheal was kissing Julie, then he stopped in the middle.

"What's wrong?" Julie was snapped out of her malaise over leaving.

"I don't know. . . There was someone else here ..." Micheal wasn't making sense.

"Someone else? . . ." She was becoming worried.

"I think it was Mbizi ..." Micheal touched his forehead.

"What do you mean he was here?" Julie studied Micheal's face.

"It was like I could feel him inside my head. Like his presence. I don't know how to explain it." Micheal shook his head.

"Let's go talk to him," Julie suggested.

"Have you seen Mbizi? He's not in our chambers." Shani interrupted.

"He probably went to see Thutmose." Julie tried to assure her.

They all made their way to the Pharaoh's private chambers.

"His Majesty is in the receiving hall." The vizier informed them.

"Have you seen My Lord?" Shani inquired.

"Not since last night." Neferweben looked back and forth between them.

"Shani, you search the north half of the palace. Julie, you search the South. I will search the gardens." Micheal directed.

As Julie went from room to room, she wondered what Micheal had been discussing before. And then it happened. She felt a slight but weird feeling that there was another consciousness here with her. She tried to focus; she could almost hear their thoughts. It sounded like Mbizi.

She closed her eyes, and then she could see it. It was the gardens at The Temple of Amun-Ra in Heliopolis.

She went and found Micheal. "I know where he is."

"Where?" She turned to Shani entering the gardens.

"The Temple of Amun-Ra, I think Ra took him." Julie had felt that Mbizi was under duress.

"Why would you think that?" Shani was concerned.

"I think he is trying to reach out to me telepathically." Shani was clearly confused.

"Communicating from mind to mind over great distances... He did it to Micheal earlier." Julie looked to Micheal to affirm her explanation.

"It's one of the ways the gods communicate. Perhaps they gave Mbizi this power." Micheal explained in mystical terms.

"So how do we get inside the temple without Ra knowing about?" Julie wondered.

"This is what we are going to do..." Micheal laid out a plan.

They arrived at The Temple of the Sun just before the last twilight. Julie easily slipped past the first set of guards; Micheal did the same. They provided a light distraction to allow Shani to join them. They repeated this process two more times until they were in the inner sanctum of the temple.

They snuck into the side chamber where Julie thought Mbizi should be based on her memory of the alternate view in her head. She walked out onto the patio, which led to the gardens. She could hear the trickle of water. Then it went silent.

Streaks of color began to form in the air. Julie turned, and Micheal looked at her, and then his eyes shifted behind them. They turned, and Ra was there.

"We meet again for the last time," Ra said with a hint of menace in his voice. "But before you die, I just have a few things I'd like to say to you." Ra seemed to teleport right in front of them. Julie stood her ground. "The lovely Isis, so bold, so fierce. I've always loved that about you." He laughed.

"We tried to tell you before. I'm not Isis! He's not Osiris!" Julie said emphatically.

"Oh, so that's why I've had run-ins with one or both of you for the better part of the last 500 years. But now that I have killed Horus, you return to this old pretense." Ra shook his head. Then, he changed his face. "We all have the ability to disguise our appearance." He was apparently demonstrating.

"We are just time travelers; we are not Gods of Egypt." Micheal tried.

"Of course, you're able to travel through time; we all are... Oh, and by the way, I wanted to thank you for that last encounter. You gifted me this ability to control the speed of time. Which now will allow me to eliminate anyone who might be a threat to me." Ra then demonstrated by evidently stopping and starting time. And tying them up in the between times.

"We'll leave Egypt; we will go to the lands to the west across the great Sea. You will never have to see us again." Julie promised.

"I'm supposed to believe that after more than a thousand years, you're just going to abandon your claim to the throne, my daughter? I think not!" Ra raised his hands over them, and his palms began to glow.

Julie looked up from the table on which she was lying, and a beam of light burst down, piercing into her chest. It felt at first like a searing heat followed by a biting cold. Her vision began to blur, and it felt like every one of her cells were being torn apart at the seams.

Julie felt herself come out of her body. She looked over to see Micheal floating beside her. After they made eye contact, she looked down at herself. Her lifeless eyes were staring back at her.

At that moment, the horizon around them darkened, and then light began to flow to them from every side. Julie reached out to meet Micheal's hand. The light coalesced around them. It burst into a white out, and everything went dark.

<u>State of Flux</u>

Shani followed Julie into the inner sanctum of the temple. She felt strongly that Mbizi was to the right. She entered a private chamber, and he was there.

"We've come to rescue you, my love." Shani threw her arms around him.

"You should not have come. You are in danger!" Mbizi was trying to keep his voice down.

"Micheal and Julie are here also; we need to hurry." Shani urged.

"The Sun God sees all, and he's always nearby," Mbizi warned.

"Come!" Shani pulled Mbizi after her, into the inner sanctum. She scanned the chamber, and no one was there. She tried to scurry across the wide-open room. Mbizi stopped so abruptly that Shani lost her feet and fell hard to the floor. As she began to get back up, dim streams of color began floating in the air. The torches no longer flickered. And Mbizi was like a statue frozen in place. Clearly, Ra had stopped time. She looked around, but the God must be somewhere else nearby. He likely had Micheal and Julie. She wasn't sure what to do. What could she do?

Then she thought about what Micheal and Julie would do if she were in trouble. She had to try. Shani entered the chambers on the other side of the inner sanctum; the first one was empty. She began searching from room to room. She came to the final chamber, and they were there.

Micheal and Julie were bound to two separate altars. Ra was emanating some kind of purple light out of his hands. Micheal and Julie appeared to be being roasted. And they were both screaming in agony.

She began to move toward Ra when a green glow started to pulse out of Micheal and Julie. The intensity began to increase. Suddenly, the green light came together, and a bright beam shot into Ra, sending him flying through the air. Shani herself was knocked to the ground.

The ribbons of color vanished as time seemed to begin to move again. But it didn't last long. The torches re-froze as Ra rose like the sun he controlled.

"Why won't you just die?!" Ra roared.

He tore through the chamber, knocking around the furniture until he found a sword. He walked over and raised the sword high, about to bring it down on Julie. "There's more than one way to end you... Survive this!"

Before he could swing, Shani stepped in and yelled. "Stop!"

Ra hesitated, then turned his gaze on her. "My Lady of the West..." He trailed off with a confused look on his face."... How are you doing this?"

"Why are you doing this? I have always worshiped you, but The Sun God should bring light and life, not be ending it." Shani was devastated to see one of the great gods of Egypt acting so viciously. And against her friends.

"You should not interfere in the business of the Gods!" Ra moved right toward her. She instinctively stepped backward and tripped to the ground.

Ra swung the sword at her. In reflex, a rush of energy flowed through her. She saw Ra become transparent; the sword went right through her but didn't cut her.

She got to her feet and ran to the other side of the room. The confusion on Ra's face turned to anger. "Who are you really?" Ra demanded. He had her cornered. She tried to slip past him, and he caught her by the throat. "It doesn't matter... This is your end!" He began trying to crush her neck.

She grabbed his wrists and tried to repeat what she had done before. At first, nothing happened. Then she felt the energy begin to surge again. In her mind, a series of images started to pass in front of her in sequence. It felt like she was watching moments pass into days, months, and years. She saw the seasons pass—the ebb and flow of the inundation. She saw crops grow from nothing in mere moments. It was like she could feel the flow of time moving through her.

The cycle seemed to reverse back to the moment. She was back face-to-face with Ra. Her hands began to glow white. The light started to encompass Ra's arms and then spread over his entire body. There was a pulse, and it felt like she had pushed off Ra. At that moment, he disappeared, and she fell to the ground.

A breeze blew in from the gardens, signaling that time was no longer frozen. She looked around, but Ra was nowhere to be found.

"Shani!" Mbizi appeared at the doorway.

"I don't know if Ra is gone." Shani looked around again.

Mbizi closed his eyes briefly and then said, "I don't see him anymore."

Shani stepped over to Mbizi. "What do you mean?" She was confused.

"I was given the power of Horus. I can see through anyone's eyes. I can't see anything when I think of Ra. That means he must be gone." Mbizi explained.

"I'm so glad you're okay." Shani threw her arms around him.

After holding each other for a time, Mbizi said. "Come on, let's help Micheal and Julie."

They went and untied them. Julie was shaking as she sat up.

"Is everyone okay?..." Micheal asked, then said. "... We need to go." He stumbled to his feet, wrapped his arms around Julie, and led them out through the gardens.

America

Even though Ra was gone, they still decided it was a good idea to get away for a while. Two weeks later, with a short stopover in Gibraltar, the Valkyrie sailed into New York Harbor.

"Home sweet home." Julie joked.

"How close is it to what you remember?" Micheal played along.

"It's pretty similar. If you expanded the park and removed the buildings, you just might be close." Julie tried not to laugh. Then she got more serious. "I can't believe this is Manhattan. Even the small city from the Second Age of Atlantis is lost to time." She remembered a short stopover in the 20th century BC.

"I suppose an Apocalypse and 500 years can do that." Micheal pointed out.

They were making their way through the thick undergrowth.

"Halt!" Julie heard a man yell in a language that sounded very much like Atlantean.

"We come in peace." She said in Atlantean as they all turned to the greeting party, holding out their hands in deference.

Those who welcomed them looked like Native Americans. There were five of them. The leader examined them one at a time, then asked. "Where you come from?"

Julie could understand him, but it was like an American talking to a Scotsman with a thick accent.

"We come from a place called Avalon." She said.

The man lowered his bow and then instructed the others to do the same.

"Welcome, I am Mahigan. Our village is not far." He indicated they should follow.

They walked for about 15 minutes through a thick forest in what would have been Chinatown until they came to a slight clearing. There was a large group of people, perhaps several hundred strong. In the middle was an oddly familiar face. It was the good Samaritan from The Sea of Sand.

"Hello again, My Lady Avalon." The man said.

He indicated for them to sit in the shade, out of the heat of the summer day.

"You look awfully familiar..." Micheal seemed to be studying him."... David!" He apparently remembered.

"You must have an outstanding memory, My Lord Avalon."

"Micheal?" Julie now wanted to know.

"This is the David who was helping Noah that day back before the flood." Micheal's statement stirred the mental juices.

"So 400 years ago...?" Julie questioned.

"When you didn't recognize me, I thought it was better not to remind you." David shrugged.

"Are you a God?" Julie asked directly. David laughed.

"I could ask you the same question... Aphrodite." He cocked his head to the side, inspecting her. "You look even younger today than you did almost 2000 years ago, the first time I ever saw you in Atlantis." He sat back more comfortably.

Julie looked to Micheal, unsure how to respond.

"How old are you?" Micheal asked casually.

"Somewhere north of 8000. As to me being a God? All I will say is that I am to these people." He looked around the tribe.

"Why have you been helping us?" Julie raised a brow.

"Time rogues have always fascinated me. Following our run-in before the flood, I studied you. You are both inherently good and exceptionally intelligent. Your skills are essential for events to come." David's tone became more serious.

"What events?" Micheal wondered.

"Time is tricky, My Lord; I can't reveal anything without altering everything. And it's too important. But there is something I did come here to show you. That does pertain to the future." David stood up.

"What is it?" Julie was skeptical.

David looked back and forth. "What day is today?"

"I don't understand, on which calendar you mean." Micheal seemed confused.

"No calendar is required. It's the summer solstice." David said with a raised brow. "May I see your amulet?" He asked Julie.

"Why?" She was suspicious.

"I'm not going to take it; I do know where it came from." He held out his hand. She hesitated, then slipped it from her neck. "Sacred knowledge... Eternal life..." He read. "... And therein lies the dichotomy, does it not? I mean, what choice would you have made?" He studied the amulet. "Follow me, it's just about time."

He led them to an altar in the middle of an open field. It was a large circular stone divided into 28 segments. It spanned around 20 feet across.

David instructed them to stand in the center of the sun wheel. He oversaw the ceremony and directed the tribe to begin a sun-dance. He passed their amulets through the tribe from one member to another. Each transition was done in rhythm to the constant beat of the drums. The smooth choreography was nearly hypnotic. As the pace of the dance picked up, the necklaces returned to David.

He held them high, one in each hand. And he made his way to her and Micheal. As he passed them back, he indicated for them to hold them high. At that moment, which appeared to be high noon, the light began to saturate the amulets, and the rapid drumbeat abruptly stopped.

The light split into a rainbow spectrum that illuminated the entire area. A cool wind blew in from the east, and the temperature seemed to drop from around 80° to about 60° in mere moments. It almost felt like the sun was in an eclipse.

Julie looked out at the tribe, and all were on their knees. The effect lasted a few minutes, and the sun began to return to form.

"My Lord and Lady of the West. Join us on the altar." David instructed.

Once Mbizi and Shani were standing with them, the sun came back in full force. The drums and dance began again. Then David raised his arms to the sky, and there was a bright flash. With that, the strangest thing happened. It felt like they had shifted through a portal and were suddenly back on the Valkyrie.

"Sorry to cut your visit here short. Not that you can't go back if you want to. But how do you think these people will view you after that demonstration?" Julie knew David was right.

"I have to ask what this was all about?" Julie challenged.

"I knew you would come to this place on this day. It was the perfect opportunity to open the second seal." He looked at her amulet.

"Second seal?" Micheal interjected.

"The first of four seals was opened at the stone circle in the North Islands over 300 years ago." David spoke of their visit to Stonehenge on the spring equinox in the 18th century.

"What happens when we open all four seals?" Micheal seemed leery.

"It's not my place to say." David shrugged.

"Of course, it's not." Micheal shook his head in annoyance.

"Your path through time has many perils as well as discoveries.

And you must walk it." With that, David promptly disappeared in a flash.

"So now, what do we do?" Julie raised a brow.

-January 12, 1446 BC

"We return to River Palace following an epic journey traversing the globe. After spending six months visiting various tribes in North America, we spent another three months island hopping through the Caribbean. Then we ventured up the Amazon and made a run of the South American coast to Cape Horn. By then, it was February, and we decided to stop over on the Antarctic Peninsula for Valentine's Day.

"Luckily, the Drake wasn't too terrible. The Valkyrie seemed to handle the 6-meter swells just fine. Our penguin-themed celebration of love was definitely unique. After our trip to the bottom of the world, we ran the Ring of Fire North to the Gulf of Alaska for our transition to the northern summer. We reached Japan in July. Then, it was a race across the West Pacific to beat the heart of typhoon season.

"By September, we were diving at The Great Barrier Reef. The aborigines didn't know what to make of Micheal and I. Mbizi and Shani, however, fit in well enough that it helped with our acceptance. Following a couple of months down under it was time to cross the next ocean.

"We spent some time in the subcontinent. We are both relatively fluent in Sanskrit, which helped with communication. Then, we spent a few weeks in the homelands of Mbizi and Shani, at the bottom of the Arabian Peninsula and Ethiopia. Then, it was a month circling Africa on our way back to Egypt.

"Our return was the reverse of when Thutmose first came to River Palace. Court was already being hosted, and we were given a grand welcome back.

PS: It just so happened to be a bittersweet day. Micheal's 87th birthday. And our 60th anniversary in time. Happy birthday, my love.

CHAPTER 18: MOSES

Chariots of Fire

"Yah! Yah!" Micheal's driver pushed the chariot faster as they raced through the course. He knocked his next arrow and fought the bumpy vibration to find his mark. The bolt struck pay dirt, and they whipped around the next rock outcropping. Micheal hitched his bow and drew his sword, then proceeded to slice through the next two targets. As they came around to the backside of the course, he lined up a javelin, showing off his dynamic marksmanship. Repeating the feat a second time a few moments later. He then went back to his bow for the home stretch. He went rapid fire, plowing through target after target. Culminating in a blazing stop in front of his friends.

"IMPRESSIVE! NOW LET'S SEE if Amenemhat can do anything." Thutmose showed clear signs of doubt about his son. And there was obvious jealousy that Micheal had performed so well. The prince was an accomplished charioteer but was not likely to match Micheal.

A few minutes later, the marksmanship challenge was over, and a slow run through the course proved Micheal to be the winner.

"I propose a race to the Tower and back." The Pharaoh suggested.

The Tower was a rock formation about 5 miles out in the East Desert.

"No drivers." He added as he stepped onto his chariot.

The horse minders promptly changed out the horses on all 12 chariots. The dozen consisted of Micheal, Mbizi, the Pharaoh, the Prince, five of Thutmose's favorite generals, and Amenemhat's three best friends.

With the fresh horses ready, Micheal stepped up and took the reins. He had raced horses a few times and knew a 10-mile race would be challenging for the horses. This would be all about pacing. So he would keep a steady pace regardless of what everyone else did until the last few miles. He would see what everyone else was doing at that point, and hopefully, his warhorses, which he knew were trained and bread for endurance, would have enough left in the tank for a sprint to the finish.

The chariots all took their marks next to one another.

"My Lord, maybe a superior marksman; however, I think this shall prove the elite charioteer." The Pharaoh was determined.

"Don't expect it to be me." Mbizi was ever doubtful of his chariot skills.

"I have heard your son is quite the racer." Micheal indicated Amenemhat.

"The Prince is far too eager to prove himself; he will overestimate his skill." Thutmose shook his head.

A flag was raised. Then, a trumpet sounded, and the race was on.

Micheal got off to a slow start and found himself in 10th place. A couple of the prince's friends gunned it off the start and pulled to a large lead. The Pharaoh went out comfortably in the middle of the pack, probably about ten lengths ahead of Micheal. Mbizi was right behind in 11th.

Micheal clocked his 1st mile at a little over three minutes. A few moments later, Thutmose's generals got tangled and crashed out. Micheal had to pull a quick maneuver to avoid the same fate.

He reached the halfway point to The Tower in eighth place, registering just over eight minutes. The lead break were probably half a mile ahead at this point. The main pack was around a furlong afield. And Prince Amenemhat and his father were side-by-side at the head.

As the lead pair reached The Tower, there was a collision in the main pack. The other of the prince's friends and one of the generals crashed out.

So now the leaders were on their way home. The Pharaoh picked up the pace as he rounded The Tower in third. His son was a few lengths behind. The Pharaoh's favorite general was in fifth place, not far behind that.

At this point, Mbizi sidled up next to Micheal. He looked back and saw the old general gaining in last place. Micheal eyed Mbizi, cracked the whip, and began pulling away as they approached The Tower.

Micheal did a time check and saw it was about 18 minutes. He came around The Tower and saw that the Pharaoh had extended his lead to around 1/4 of a mile. But the leaders were beginning to falter. Their lead was down to 3 furlongs.

Micheal urged his stallions for more speed and began to close the gap to the general. He also thought he was making up ground on the Pharaoh as Thutmose blew past the former leaders.

Micheal saw that the old general was falling further behind and Mbizi tried to make a comeback.

Now, just ahead, the chief general made several attempts to block Micheal's advance. Micheal finally outmaneuvered him and scraped past.

As Micheal reached the midway point back, he overtook the original leaders, falling off as their horses were exhausted. Micheal checked the time and the situation.

The clock read 25 minutes. The Pharaoh was in first place, perhaps a furlong in the lead, with his son a few lengths behind. Micheal was now in third. He looked back. Mbizi had passed and was now about 20 lengths back in forth. The two generals were doing battle in fifth and sixth. Amenemhat's friends were attempting to limp home in seventh and eighth.

With less than 2 miles to go, Micheal pushed his steeds for everything they had left.

As 2 miles became one, he had closed the gap to the Prince. He was now within shouting distance. And he was less than 20 lengths from the lead. He pulled up next to Amenemhat. The Prince tried to bump Micheal to the left. Micheal veered in that direction but was able to get to a gap first, moving into second.

His horses seemed tired but now with just half a mile to go he could see Thutmose and the finish line. He asked for more speed, and his stallions answered.

He began to close in with a quarter mile left. The Pharaoh fought desperately to hold him off. They bumped into each other, and Micheal took the lead with one furlong to go. He was now one length ahead.

As the finish rapidly closed in, Thutmose burst back, so they were side-by-side again. They began trading off the lead. Micheal and the Pharaoh stared each other down in a battle of wills.

Their bumping contest must've slowed them because, out of nowhere, it was a four-horse race. Prince Amenemhat was on Micheal's right, and Mbizi pulled up on Thutmose's left.

Everyone pushed the pedal to the metal as they closed the final football field run to the finish.

Micheal and the Pharaoh used the final burst to push slightly back in front. Micheal was only ahead by a nose. But at the last second Thutmose edged him out at the finish line. And it seemed that Mbizi may have beaten out the Prince.

Everyone pulled up to slow their horses. As Micheal came to a stop, the two generals crossed the finish in short succession, with the Pharaoh's favorite in the lead.

Micheal gave his steeds some grateful pats for their noble effort while they began to inhale water brought by the minders.

Then, as they all gathered, Amenemhat's friends limped across the line.

"Your Eminence is a true chariot master." Micheal gave a bow to Thutmose.

"My Lords were a true challenge." The Pharaoh said proudly.

"An impressive showing, Your Highness." Micheal bowed to the Prince.

"I almost got you, My Lord Avalon." Amenemhat gave a frustrated grin as he shook his head.

"And where in the world did you come from, My Lord?" Micheal laughed as he slapped Mbizi on the shoulder.

"I just tried to take all of my cues from you," Mbizi admitted.

"Quite the day of games. Let us return to Heliopolis and celebrate into the night." The Pharaoh said with great excitement.

The Pharaoh's Advisor

"My Lord of the West, what may I help you with?" Thutmose asked Mbizi as he entered the chamber.

"I know this may be a tenuous subject, but I want to ask if you might ease the restrictions on the Levantine people?" he asked nervously.

"What do they matter to you?" Thutmose looked at him suspiciously.

"I... Have seen through their... Eyes. I... Understand their plight." Mbizi momentarily made eye contact, then looked away.

"You, My Lord..." The Pharaoh rose from his table and walked toward Mbizi, staring at him with interest. "... Have the sight? Don't you?"

Mbizi looked up at that. "The sight?" He wasn't sure if he should tell Thutmose.

"The sight of Horas." The Pharaoh touched his shoulder. "My friend, I have met The God of the Sky. He sees all. And he has gifted this ability to you, hasn't he?" The Pharaoh was getting excited.

"That is more or less what happened," Mbizi confirmed.

"Well, my friend, I know you will be happy to advise me on what is happening inside my kingdom and outside." Thutmose smiled.

"But of course." He said uncertainly.

"We are friends; I promise I won't abuse this." Thutmose tried to reassure him. Mbizi wasn't so sure.

"So what about those in servitude?" He tried again.

"I assure you, I will look into it. But first, do you mind looking into a few things for me?" The Pharaoh pressed him.

"What do you want to know?"

Over the next few weeks, Mbizi reported on the happenings with the Hittites, the Mitanni, the Assyrians, the Minoans, the Nubians, and many other foreign lands. He had also observed the actions of several Nomarchs across Egypt, demonstrating his proficiency with The Sight.

While they were traveling the world, he would practice in each place they visited. He started to learn that he could think of a person, a place, or a thing, and he could see them in his mind's eye. He regularly used this to go back and see some of his favorite views from such places. Through this process, he gained an understanding and appreciation for people from near and far. He felt he could begin to think more like Micheal and Julie.

"So, how is the Pharaoh?" Shani asked as he entered the chambers.

"He's being a king," Mbizi said in frustration.

"He still won't move on the servile class?" She shook her head.

"It's not just that. I spend a lot of time looking through the eyes of kings; they are pretty much all the same. They become obsessed with their own power. And the ways to control people. As well as maintain or increase their power." He was annoyed that Thutmose was beginning to act more tyrannical.

Slavery, a prevalent aspect in every culture he encountered, was something he harbored no illusions of ending. His goal wasn't to abolish it but to improve the lives of those in similar positions to his past. However, Thutmose's growing obsession with spying on potential rivals to his power increasingly consumed him. He had ignored Mbizi's numerous requests for better treatment of the lowest class. And now he felt like his friend was using him.

"Come here, my love." Shani pulled him to her.

She kissed him on the ear. He closed his eyes and took in the pleasant scent of her as she moved to the side of his neck. He reached down and grabbed her firm behind, pressing her against him. As they passionately locked lips, they ravaged each other's bodies with their hands. His shendyt dropped to the floor. Then he slid her kalasiris down from her breasts until it was at her ankles.

He turned her around, bent her over, and took her from behind, holding a firm grip on her chest for support. He worked out all of his frustrations, culminating in an explosive release. They found their breath in concert, and then Shani wanted more.

She returned him to form with her hands, then mounted on top of him and began riding her way toward ecstasy.

While Mbizi was lying in a state of utter contentment with Shani in his arms, his mind began to wander.

He closed his eyes, and his thoughts strayed to The Goddess Isis. He suddenly saw an extraordinary sight. He realized he was seeing the land from an extremely high perspective. It was like being on a mountaintop, except without one. He decided that she must be flying the birds.

"My Lord of the West..." She spoke in her Goddess voice. "... Take heed and prepare yourself, for a storm is coming." She warned.

"What kind of storm?" He sought clarity.

"Much is not certain. But Egypt will experience much turmoil." Isis went silent, and Mbizi took one last long gaze over Egypt from a goddess's perspective.

He had seen it a couple of times before, but not from this angle. Cutting through a nearly endless sea of brown was a narrow run of green and black. It was the fertile Nile River Valley. The river itself sparkled in the evening glow. And the Valley branched into a much bigger area ahead. As the angle of Isis's view became more slight the whole river turned to gold and he could see The Pyramids of Giza, their pinnacles glinting like evening stars. Then he broke the connection.

He sat up in his bed. Shani rose and embraced him from behind, laying her head on his shoulder. "Mbizi, what is wrong?"

He closed his eyes and sighed deeply. "Isis told me that more trouble is coming our way." He looked out at the setting sun.

"Why must the gods fight each other endlessly?" Shani seemed irritated.

"I don't think it's the gods this time. At least that's not the impression I got from her." He was tempted to reach out to Ra to see if he was involved somehow. But he knew that would only bring terrible things with it.

"I suppose we must prepare for these troubles then." Shani seemed resigned to their situation.

"Everything will be okay. I know that with us together. Along with Micheal and Julie. There's nothing we can't handle." He pretended to be confident. But he was already beginning to dread the future.

Moses

Julie slipped out of bed after the Pharaoh sent word that he would be holding open court and wanted them there as a display of power to anyone who might present themselves.

"What do you think? The red and green? Or the blue and gold?"

She asked Micheal.

"The blue and gold says goddess more than the other." He affirmed what she was already thinking.

"Why do you always agree to help them put on a show?" She challenged as she stepped into the soft linen.

"He doesn't ask very often, so I don't think it's a big deal." He shrugged into his tiger skin.

"Are you worried that nothing has happened since Isis warned us to prepare?" It had been about three months since the warning had come from The Goddess of Life. And while they had used that time to prepare for a prolonged emergency both at River Palace and on the Valkyrie. Nothing had happened yet.

"We use our time wisely, preparing for any situation, whether a natural disaster or something more sinister. We stand ready to face it." He came and fixed her chain crown. "You look positively divine." He smiled through the words.

They stood on the east side of the throne and Mbizi and Shani stood on the West, of course. They advised their dozens of petitioners, and then the herald announced two petitioners that sent a chill down Julie's spine.

"From the land of Midia, the prophets Aaron and Moses!" She and Micheal exchanged a nervous glance.

"What would you ask of His Majesty, the Pharaoh of Egypt?" Moses looked every bit the 80 years the Bible said he should be. While he was rather tall, perhaps five-foot-nine. He looked frail. He had a long white beard and seemed to require his staff for support. Aaron, who appeared to be of similar age, stepped forward.

"The Lord God of Israel sent us to recount his words: Let my people go into the wilderness and offer a feast unto me."

Thutmose considered for a moment. "I do not know of any God of Israel. So why should I grant such a request? Surely the people of Israel can make their offerings between their labors." The Pharaoh suggested.

"The God of the Hebrews met with us. We ask Your Majesty to allow us to journey three days into the desert so we might make sacrifices unto our Lord God. Or else he will fall upon us with pestilence, or with the sword." Thutmose's face reacted like he received the statement as a threat.

"So the Midian prophets, Moses and Aaron, would have me release the people from their burdens? There are many people who dwell in Goshen. If I let them go, who should do their work?" The Pharaoh was clearly irritated by this 'request'.

"The God of Israel gave dire warning..." Aaron began.

"And where is this God?" The Pharaoh cut him off. "I know The Sky God, I know The Goddess of Life, I know The God of Death, I even know The Sun God. But I know not this God of Israel. I will not let your people go.

Moreover, if your God is truly powerful, let Him aid your people in brickmaking. I hereby decree that they will no longer receive straw. Yet, I expect no decline in quality," declared Thutmose. Following his signal, the guards escorted Moses and Aaron out of the chamber.

Thutmose abruptly ended the court session and asked them for counsel. So the Pharaoh, Mbizi, Shani, Micheal, and herself went into his private chamber.

"The gods have been absent for three years. You all represent the nearest connection I have. What advice can you provide in regard to this God of Israel? Should I be fearful?" Thutmose had taken the threat seriously.

"I can speak for Isis..." Julie began."... She speaks from on high, saying Egypt will suffer much turmoil." She relayed the message.

"She has spoken to you?" Thutmose seemed nearly incredulous.

"Your eminence, we know this God of Israel. I feel it would be wise to offer some kind of appeasement." Micheal suggested.

"My Lord Avalon, I understand that you are more experienced in the ways of people from around the world. But I have witnessed the power of The Gods of Egypt. I would not betray them for those of another land." The Pharaoh chided.

"My Lord of the West, what say you?" Thutmose pivoted.

"These Hebrews were given refuge in Egypt. Not so long ago, they were guests. Then put into bondage. They are a significant number of your subjects. Is it not prudent to grant some clemency toward their God? I have witnessed the power of other gods, and many are comparable to Egypt." Mbizi recommended.

"I can't believe all of you would turn on me like this." Thutmose scanned all of them.

"You asked for our counsel. Clearly, we only desire what's best for your eminence." Julie tried to soothe him.

"Leave me, all of you. I must do my own extant to Amun-Ra. I know he will not allow any such intrusion into the domain of Egypt." The Pharaoh ordered. They all left and moved to her and Micheal's quarters.

"So the Exodus is what Isis was warning us about. Do you think it's wise to try to talk Thutmose out of his original course of action?" Julie challenged Micheal.

"Obviously, I don't want to alter the timeline, but I felt like I didn't want to lie to him." Micheal looked thoughtful. "We both know that an event like this carries a lot of temporal force behind it. Likely, short of killing a major player, the flow of time will force the outcome." He reasoned. And Thutmose's reaction to their advice did seem to suggest that.

"You know what is coming?" Shani questioned.

"It will certainly be chaotic," Micheal confirmed.

"Maybe we should leave Egypt altogether." Julie decided.

"I understand your reticence. But are you willing to pass on the chance to live through the greatest story ever told?" Micheal's nature of experiencing the history was difficult to refute most of the time. But could she withstand the ten plagues?

"Fine. The other question is, should we reach out to Moses?" She considered how he might view them. "I mean, what have we done to help those in slavery? We befriended the Pharaohs, but they all sanction slavery." Julie felt guilty that they were, in a way, a part of that system.

"Unfortunately, slavery is the norm in most cultures throughout history. So either we try to change thousands of years of known history, forever marooning ourselves in time, or we have to accept that we are not gods. And we can't wave a magic wand to fix all the evils of humanity." Micheal's clear reasoning still didn't fully convince her of the correct course of action. "Now, as it pertains to Moses? For now, I don't know if our involvement would be a good thing." The situation was complicated.

"Perhaps it would be best if Shani and I made such efforts," Mbizi stated after observing quietly for the duration.

"Okay, but do it very delicately. And we must make several more specific preparations now that we know what is coming." Julie rose and signaled for Micheal to follow. "We only have two days to go to River Palace and back. Cover for us with Thutmose." She requested. And she and Micheal quickly departed.

<u>Common Ground</u>

Shani and Mbizi started their journey the following day, exploring the servile cities surrounding Pi-Ramesses, the city built to honor the Sun God Ra. This magnificent city rose from the ruins of Avaris, the former Hyksos capital. Most of the people they encountered bowed down to them as they walked.

An elderly man bowed and said, "How might we serve the Lord and Lady of the West?"

Shani was a bit surprised at such a reputation. "A man named Moses and his companion Aaron came before Pharaoh. Are they here?" She asked.

"They have brought nothing but trouble." The man seemed fearful, looking around nervously.

"We only wish to talk with them." Mbizi reached out a hand to stop him.

The man looked back and forth between them. "Right this way, My Lord."

They were led to a small house inside the city. Moses and Aaron rose to their feet at Shani and Mbizi's entrance.

"You can arrest us, but God will provide for us." Moses stood defiant.

"We are not here to arrest you. We only wish to talk." Shani said.

"And why would we trust some of the Pharaoh's closest advisers?" Aaron challenged.

"Because we desire the same thing you do..." Mbizi showed a hidden mark of servitude. "... We were once slaves, as your people are. And even before your arrival, I was attempting to convince

His Eminence to ease restrictions on your people."

"What would you like to know?" Moses relented.

"What will your God do if his Eminence refuses to let your people go?" Mbizi asked directly.

"I do not know. I simply do as the Lord commands me." Moses shrugged.

"I have witnessed the power of The Gods of Egypt. It is vast. What makes you believe your God can stand up to them?" Shani felt a chill of doubt run down her spine at the memory of Ra.

"I don't know what you've seen. But I can state with no doubt, that there is only one God." Moses was clearly certain of his beliefs.

But Shani knew what she knew as well. "We have seen things most people would never believe. We can do things beyond what a man or woman is capable of. I know we are not Gods, but we have gifts from them. It will take much to convince us of your God's supremacy. And it will take more than that to convince the Pharaoh. He has consorted with them for most of his life." She tried to make them understand the difficulties ahead.

"Consorted with the Gods of Egypt?" Aaron seemed curious.

"There are no Gods of Egypt. And if there are, they are false." Moses stated sharply.

"Moses!" Aaron touched him on the shoulder in reproach. "You say the gods gifted you powers. What kind?" Aaron seemed honestly curious.

"The Goddess of Life, Isis, transferred a power from her son Horus, The God of the Sky, into me." Mbizi touched his four head. "It's called The Eye of Horus. It grants me the power to see through the eyes of any person or animal in the world at this moment in time." He looked up.

Aaron and Moses exchanged a look.

"That is what gave me a harsh perspective about how your people were being treated." Mbizi finished.

"So, is there any chance the Pharaoh might acquiesce to your appeals?" Aaron asked hopefully.

"His Eminence was quite upset by your threats. It is now unlikely he will budge." Shani answered.

"Then what was the reason for this visit?" Moses inquired.

"Our good friends are hesitant to seek you out. They worry about the events yet to come." She informed them.

"They know of us? Tell me, do they wear special amulets around their necks?" Moses was suddenly much more excited.

"They do," Mbizi confirmed.

"It's them!" Aaron seemed to have the same gusto.

"Who do you believe our friends to be?" Shani inquired.

"They are the Lords of Avalon. They are traveling through time. Called to assist the Lord our God in his plan." Aaron explained.

"They certainly do move through the centuries. But they never mentioned any such calling from the God of Israel." Shani looked at Mbizi.

"Would you be able to arrange for us to have an audience with the Lords of Avalon?" Moses was adamant.

After considering for a moment, Mbizi said. "We will send for you tomorrow." Then he left the house, pulling her behind him.

"I don't know if they will be happy about this." Shani worried.

"I have to do what I think is right for these people," Mbizi stated with certainty, then headed for Heliopolis.

CHAPTER 19: PLAGUES

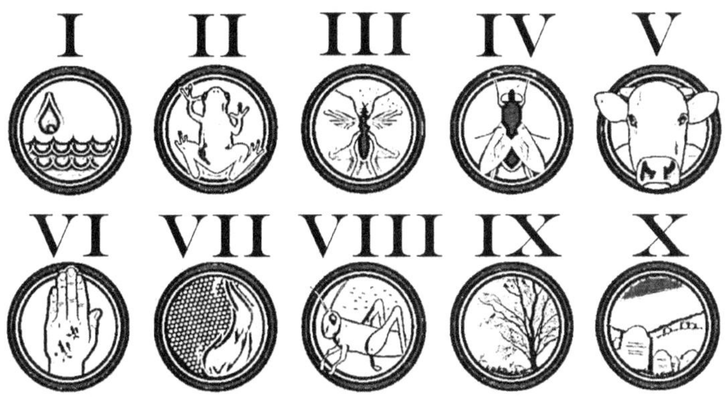

Blood, Frogs, and Lice

"S O THE FIRST ROUND was yesterday. How soon do you think the first plague will begin?" Julie asked Micheal.

"I don't know, let me think. They have to go before the Pharaoh again, have the battle of the serpents; then it's water to blood. So I would say we have at least two or three days." He ran through Exodus 7 in his head. But his thoughts were interrupted.

"Micheal, Julie. Please don't be angry with us." Mbizi pleaded as Moses and Aaron entered the chamber.

"You are the Lords of Avalon?" Moses seemed surprised.

"We are." Micheal looked sidelong at Mbizi.

"You are advisers to the Pharaoh?" Aaron almost accused.

"We have advised many rulers," Julie said plainly.

"You adopt the customs of Egypt..." Moses indicated their attire. "... And make friends with those who enslave the people of God..." He was becoming angry.

"How dare you judge us!" Julie flared, cutting him off. "I don't care if you're the great prophet. You have no idea what our lives are like! God never spoke to us in a burning bush. We were never commanded to do anything! The last 60 years have been one hell experience after another. I have been tortured and killed multiple times! I've seen every friend I have ever had taken in the most horrific ways possible! And I've seen more than one apocalypse! I have been forced to be separated from all of my family. Only to have to survive centuries through many hostile places and times and the whole while hoping I don't do something to change the fate of events that are to come! Until you know what that is like, I don't want to hear any criticism from you!" She stormed out to the gardens.

Moses and Aaron were in stunned silence.

"You know, when Adam and Eve made the request. We almost said no. It was already going to be tough enough without all of the prophets having expectations of us..." Moses raised his hand.

"I suppose we are having difficulty understanding. Perhaps you could give an example?" He softened.

"We have been through dozens of different periods in time and across numerous cultures. And there are horrors and injustices everywhere. How do we know which to stop? And if we do, will we kill countless more by altering events to come? We know we can live normally and interact. But making major changes? It's so much more dangerous." Micheal tried to explain.

"Could you not pray to God for such knowledge?" Aaron wondered.

"Despite countless attempts, I have never received such an answer. As Julie said, we are not prophets." Micheal retorted.

"Are you not called of God?" Moses seemed confused.

"No. Adam and Eve even admitted as much. They were shown that we were going to be progressing through history. They requested that we help the prophets going forward in whatever capacity we could..." Micheal was explaining.

"You have the Pharaoh's ear. Could you not assist in our efforts?" Aaron pleaded.

"While much that takes place is shrouded in the mists of time. The Book of God is quite detailed in regard to some events. We must use that as our guide to know how much intercession we make. If anything seems to be going askew, or if anyone else is interfering with the events we know must come to pass, we will act. That is all I can promise you. I would tell you to trust in the Lord." Micheal indicated that they should probably leave.

"And so we shall." Moses led Aaron out of the chambers.

When they were gone. "I'm disappointed in both of you." He shook his head at Mbizi and Shani.

"I am terribly sorry, my friend. I did not know there were so many expectations of you." Mbizi hung his head.

Micheal thought of saying something, then decided against it. He exited to the gardens to look for Julie.

He found her on a bench overlooking the river and sat beside her.

After a long few minutes Julie broke the silence. "Do you ever think he's right?... About us, I mean?... Back when we first fell, I had such trouble dealing with slavery. But we've pretty much ignored it since we arrived in this century. And we even befriended the Pharaoh." She just stared out at the flowing current.

"If we stay in Egypt, we really don't have much choice but to befriend the Pharaohs. We are the Lords of Avalon. We could abandon River Palace and leave it all behind. But I doubt we could ever escape this sort of dilemma. And you know as well as I do that more or less every culture in the world at this time involves slavery in some fashion. So I don't know what we can do about that."

Slavery had been there during the entire Egyptian era in which they had interacted. It was just more pronounced since the Israelites had been subjugated.

"His Majesty requires your attendance." One of Thutmose's ministers interrupted the conversation.

As the court session pushed toward evening, Moses and Aaron appeared before the Pharaoh. They demanded for him to let the Israelites go.

Thutmose looked back and forth between them, then said. "If the God of Israel is so powerful, will you give us a demonstration of his power?"

Moses told Aaron to cast his rod to the ground. The rod spiraled into a serpent, a cobra, to be exact.

"Mere parlor tricks." The Pharaoh signaled for his priests. They came forward and threw down their rods, six in all. And likewise, they became serpents as the priests chanted spells.

The Pharaoh's serpents surrounded Aaron's. The Israelite rod serpent rose up then brought its mouth down over the first Egyptian viper. It then proceeded to systematically swallow the other five.

The snake slithered over to Aaron, rose to his hand, and became a rod once more.

After watching the famous showdown, Micheal tried to figure out how this was all possible. Not only that God could potentially make a piece of wood transform into a cobra, but that the Pharaoh's priests could do the same. There was also the fact that when the competition was over, all that was left was Aaron's rod. And it was precisely the same size as it had been when this all began.

Moses looked at Micheal, then asked Thutmose to release his people, to no avail.

"I shall meet Your Majesty at the river's edge in the morning. There you shall witness our Lord God's true power." Moses led Aaron out of the chamber.

The next morning, all prominent court attendees met at the river's edge in the Palace Gardens.

Thutmose turned to Micheal. "My Lord, do you still think I should acquiesce to these... Heathens?"

"Your Majesty has already decided." Micheal didn't even try.

Thutmose just looked at him for a moment, then looked past him.

Micheal turned, and Moses and Aaron were being escorted. They came to a place where they were face-to-face with Pharaoh.

"Your Majesty, will you let my people go?" Moses asked.

Pharaoh considered for a moment, then said. "Show me your God's true power."

Moses took Aaron's rod and plunged to the tip into the Nile. The river began to bleed in all directions, spreading as far as the eye could see. Then he said.

"The Lord God of the Hebrews sent me to petition you to let his people go into the desert to serve him, and you would not hear. And he said: you shall know that I am the Lord. For I will smite the waters of Egypt with the rod in my hand, and they shall turn to blood."

As Micheal watched another event from the Bible unfold, he tried to think of what he thought that said about God or faith or religion.

The Old Testament applied to many Christian faiths, and the Torah was also the Scripture of Judaism. So, just because he had personally witnessed many of the events of the Old Testament, and had also met many of the people from the Old Testament, that didn't narrow down which of the Judeo-Christian religions would likely be correct.

There was the fact that he had also met multiple mythological gods who had demonstrated superhuman powers. Did that mean that the various mythos of antiquity were correct?

During their travels through time, Micheal and Julie had come to find that the history and the reality of the world were far more complicated than they had ever imagined.

"Remove them from my site!" The Pharaoh commanded. "Leave me! All of you!" He yelled to the entire court.

Everyone began to make their way out of the gardens. Micheal turned with Julie.

"Avalon, you remain. You as well, Lord West." Thutmose instructed.

They all went and joined him next to the river. Everyone just stood there, waiting on the Pharaoh. He was just staring at the crimson current as if he was trying to figure it out.

"Lady Avalon, have there been any other communications from the gods?" He finally asked.

"There has been no further contact, Your Majesty," Julie admitted.

Thutmose clearly didn't like that answer. "My Lord of the West, can you look through any of the God's eyes? Attempt to summon them for me?" The Pharaoh seemed to be getting desperate.

Mbizi focused, with his eyes closed for a minute. "I cannot sense any of the gods." He stated in disappointment.

"So now the gods of Egypt cower before the God of Israel?!" Thutmose was stewing. "If the gods have abandoned me, then I no longer require your counsel at this time. I will send for you if I so desire in the future." The Pharaoh dismissed them with a wave of his hand.

They sailed the Valkyrie through the bloody river to Goshen, where they planned to visit Moses and Aaron.

"Surely Pharaoh will have to recognize God's might now." Aaron was trying to convince everyone.

"Perhaps, but his eminence is a stubborn man." Micheal tried to temper expectations. "Moses, we came to tell you that we are returning to River Palace. If you should require anything, or if you would like to come visit, you are welcome." Micheal and the rest of his party prepared to leave.

"So you're not going to do anything?" Moses seemed dejected.

"Pharaoh won't listen, even to us. But we may still have a role to play yet." Micheal stated with an air of mystery.

"Can you at least tell me everything works out in the end?" Moses pleaded.

"This is where I'm supposed to tell you to have faith." And Micheal led the way out of the house.

"Have you ever seen so much red?" Micheal asked as Julie drew samples out of the river.

"It looks like shark week on the Discovery Channel." Julie joked as she finished filling a vial from the Nile.

"Do you think it's actually blood?" Micheal was never clear whether the Bible said "water to blood" or "water as blood".

"I suppose we'll find out when we look at it through a micro-scope," Julie said, examining the sample.

Micheal thought it looked convincing enough.

They arrived at River Palace, and Kesi seemed relieved that they were there to deal with the situation.

"My Lord! The gods are punishing us." Her eyes went wide, and she lowered her head.

"Kesi, do not fear. Our preparations should be more than enough to get us through."

"Yes, My Lord." She headed off toward the main module.

"Mbizi, if you can, do a regular search for any of the gods who might come back to Egypt." Micheal requested.

"Of course, Micheal. I'll let you know if anything changes." He and Shani headed for their quarters.

"All right, Jules, we have work to do." Micheal led Julie to the secret elevator. They were the only ones who could access it.

"It's not really much work to analyze the samples through a microscope." Julie raised a brow.

"I have an idea I'm going to need your help with." He opened the door to the secret chambers beneath River Palace, deep below the riverbed.

"So what were you thinking?" She looked at him as she prepared for research.

"I thought we could turn the obelisks into bug traps. That might help to deal with many of the plagues."

Micheal drew a diagram of how they could adapt the KEEs inside the crowns of the obelisks to make them attract insects and electrocute them.

"Okay, so how are we going to access the crowns?" Julie turned her head down but maintained eye contact.

"After nightfall, we use M-Pulse pads to levitate up and make the adjustments."

Julie laughed at his suggestion.

"Do you have a better idea?" He tilted his head, mimicking her movement.

"What's one more thing?" She shrugged.

The next night, they put their plan into action. Micheal wore all black and floated from the Lord's module balcony to the main obelisk on the landing platform. He had to use a small M-Pulse pad to minimize the chance of being seen. He then used a special tool they had engineered for just this kind of situation—a magnetic spanner. He used this device to cause the crown of the obelisk to levitate. He then began connecting a few extra KEEs. The whole operation took about an hour. The entire time, he was monitoring and was fairly sure he wasn't seen.

"So, how did it go?" he asked as Julie returned to the balcony.

"You should have taken the courtyard. I'm almost certain someone saw me." Julie appeared to be irritated.

"I think it will be worth it." Micheal tried to reason.

"Yeah, sure, just give me a minute to get my old Aphrodite costume out of the closet." She wouldn't look at him.

"I think you're overreacting. Even if someone saw you, they're not going to think we're gods." Micheal kept it light.

"Why not? Atlantis thought we were. The Norse thought they sent us. Everyone here thinks we are their proxies. Hell, pretty soon, I'm going to believe it myself!" Julie exited the chamber.

The next day, they were finishing breakfast. "My Lord and Lady, you have visitors." Kesi interrupted.

They made their way to the main throne Hall. As they entered, Moses and Aaron were waiting for them. The visitors bowed before them.

"Rise," Micheal instructed in Hebrew. "Prophets from distant lands, what brings you here today?"

"The Lord said the blood would last seven days, so we decided to come seek your counsel." Aaron began.

Micheal looked back and forth between them. "You didn't come here for counsel. You came for a break from responsibility."

They seemed to shrink at the statement.

"Don't worry; everyone needs a break from time to time. You are welcome to all the amenities this palace has to offer." Micheal signaled some servants to show them to their quarters.

Later that evening, Moses and Aaron came to their chambers.

"This is quite the palace you have here. We thank you for your hospitality." Aaron seemed to be making small talk as they gazed out over the blood-red Nile Delta.

"My Lord and Lady Avalon, I would like to apologize for my conduct the other day. I have no right to judge you. The Lord has made clear to me that you have an important role yet to play. I beg your forgiveness of my shortcomings." Moses turned explicitly to Julie.

"Of course. With our uniquely different experiences, it's easy to have misunderstandings." Julie was very amicable.

Over the next few days, Moses and Aaron relaxed around the palace. Micheal was walking with Moses on their final evening, in the Lord's Sanctuary.

"These murals are very impressive, very lifelike. This one looks very much like Lady Avalon." Moses pointed at Julie's image.

"It was quite the battle." Micheal touched Julie's face.

"Micheal... May I call you Micheal?" Moses checked himself.

"Of course." Micheal nodded.

"I realize that you were not called of God. And that you might occasionally lack faith. But when I look at what you have been able to accomplish despite all that. I feel you are where God wants you to be." Moses touched his shoulder.

"Perhaps... But it would be nice to have a more certain future."

Micheal still wondered at the nature of God.

Moses and Aaron left for Goshen the next day.

A few days later, the waters became clean again. That signaled the coming of the second plague. So Micheal ordered that the stairs to the landing platform be lifted, and the palace would go into lockdown, as he knew the frogs would be coming.

The days passed, and the landing platform became overrun

by frogs. With the second plague effectively neutralized, they extended the lockdown, restricting any and all access to River Palace.

Now they began preparations for the third plague. They ordered all personnel to be bathed fully. And all clothing, bed linens, and any other fabric element to be cleansed. The death of the frogs indicated that they had only a short time to clear the stench of death before the lice would descend.

The measures taken paid off. No lice infestation came to River Palace. After a couple more days, it proved that their preparations had mitigated the first three plagues. But what about the fourth?

They stood on the balcony. "When do you think the flies will come?" Julie asked, looking out toward the sunset.

"It will be soon. Then we'll see if the obelisks work." Micheal looked at the pinnacle rising from the landing platform.

"How many more plagues will the God of Israel send?" Shani asked.

"There will be seven more, and they will keep getting worse," Micheal stated.

"And the gods of Egypt will allow that?" Mbizi questioned.

"They won't be able to stop it," Julie said as she approached Micheal.

He wrapped his arms around her, then said. "Whatever comes, we will weather the storm."

And the sun disappeared below the horizon.

Flies, Cattle, and Boils

Mbizi came to Micheal's summons.

"Mbizi, I have a task for you."

"Yes, Micheal?"

He wondered what the God of Israel would curse them with this time.

"Send word across the West Delta that all livestock: cattle, pigs, goats, and sheep. They are to be brought to River Palace for slaughter. All meat will be stored here for distribution." Micheal's order came as a shock.

"All of them?" Mbizi sought clarification.

"Any that are not slaughtered will die in a few days, and they will be wasted."

Mbizi understood. He crossed the bridge from the Lord's Module. A massive swarm of flies began descending from the sky.

The central courtyard began emitting lightning that connected from one pinnacle to the other. The swarm started flying straight into the bolts of lightning. A large portion of the swarm were fried and fell down into the river.

Mbizi knew Micheal and Julie were behind the lightning trap for the flies. Their knowledge of events to come was most definitely shielding the palace from all kinds of effects from these plagues.

Mbizi and Shani boarded their ship, The Isis, and departed on their voyage to deliver the order across the delta.

"You know many people won't want to follow this order," Shani said as they approached the first village.

"If they refuse and their livestock dies, they will not receive compensation or a portion of redistribution," Mbizi explained.

The Isis came to a halt at the village dock.

"My Lord West, we are honored by your visit." One of the elders said in greeting.

"Summon all of the villagers," Mbizi ordered.

"Right away."

All the people of the town gathered around.

"Good people, My Lord Avalon has ordered that all livestock, cows, sheep, pigs, and goats, be delivered to River Palace for preservation. A boat shall arrive tomorrow, in the afternoon, to collect them. All shall be compensated for your burden." Mbizi explained.

"How shall we survive yet another loss? These plagues have left us destitute." One of the men in the crowd demanded.

"These times are difficult, but Lord Avalon will provide for all in need," Shani said with enough confidence to quell the rising discontent.

As Mbizi scanned the village, he saw swarms of flies attacking everything. He realized they had to hurry. By the evening, they arrived in Sais.

The Nomarch, Kafele, gave them a warm welcome. He was in charge of the fifth Nome.

"What brings the Lord and Lady of the West to Sais?" His worry was evident.

"Lord Avalon has decreed that all livestock in the West Delta be taken to River Palace for a mass culling." Mbizi tried to be delicate.

"My Lord, can you not see our suffering? And now Lord Avalon wants our livestock?" Kafele looked angry.

"Lord Avalon was inspired. His order is for the benefit of every-one." Mbizi pressed the Nomarch.

"Very well. I shall trust My Lord's instincts."

Kafele gave the order to his advisor, who departed immediately.

"My Lord, I wish to apologize for my outburst. It's just that these plagues have brought chaos to the land. And I don't know how much more the people can take." Kafele lowered his head.

"My Lord is doing everything possible to mitigate the people's suffering." Shani chimed in.

"Do you understand what is happening?" Kafele shifted his eyes between them.

"There is a disagreement amongst the gods." Mbizi decided to explain.

"The gods are displeased? What can be done to appease them?" Kafele seemed alarmed.

"It's not for man to settle such quarrels. The gods work on their own time." Shani gave a stern look.

"Prepare for further difficulties. The troubles have only just begun." Mbizi admonished, then guided Shani out of the chamber.

Over the next few days, they spread the word from nomarch to nomarch. Now, they were approaching River Palace from the west.

The Grande Obelisk of Avalon had a brightly glowing pinnacle of lightning frying an in-coming swarm of flies.

Mbizi could see masses of livestock being slaughtered in the fading light of dusk. The smell of roasting flesh filled the air.

"My Lord and Lady of the West. I want to commend you for a job well done. Nearly all the stock from the West Delta has come in time. All except for Osaze in District Three. He has countermanded the order." Micheal informed him.

"I'll go see to it myself." Mbizi declared.

"It's too late for that. By morning, all of the livestock will be dead." Micheal spoke with surety.

"So what do you want me to do?" He was annoyed that Osaze had lied to him in Hermopolis Parva.

"In the morning, I want you to use The Sight to confirm if my prediction is correct," Micheal instructed.

The next morning, Mbizi went to Hermopolis in his head.

"My Lord, all of my cattle died in the night. I beg you to help me with my burden." One of the many petitioners coming before Osaze.

Mbizi switched to a man in a field. An entire herd of goats were clearly dead, spread across the ground.

He shifted to another man with his stock of swine who had perished.

Mbizi reported his findings to Micheal.

"So it seems we have little time to prepare for one of the worst so far," Micheal warned.

"What is coming?" Shani reflected the way he was feeling.

"The next plague will be boils," Julie answered as she entered the chamber. "We've been working desperately to make as much ointment as possible to deal with it." She presented a white cream.

"What does this do?" Shani scooped up a bit of the strange substance on her finger.

"It is designed to counter both itch and pain. Hopefully, it will work on these boils." Mbizi could see the doubt in her eyes.

The next evening, Lord Osaze arrived at River Palace.

"My Lord Avalon, I beseech you. We need food. All our livestock have died." Osaze pleaded.

"You were warned of the consequences if you disobeyed my order and chose to anyway. So now you pay the price." Micheal stared him down from his throne.

"My Lord, please, show mercy. I was a fool. I doubted the veracity of your warning." Osaze admitted.

"Your failure of leadership has caused your subjects to appeal to me for aid. Any assistance must naturally be taken from others. Those who were obedient." Micheal was clearly annoyed by Osaze's defiance.

"I beg of you." Osaze went to one knee.

"I am willing to grant clemency. But it will cost you. Fifty percent of next year's harvest will go to River Palace. With that understanding, I will return your region to favor... I would advise you to remember that our special status with His Eminence is not without merit. We have capabilities here at River Palace that are not available anywhere else. We also possess knowledge beyond a normal man. So if I decide to deliver an edict, It will be followed, or you will forfeit all of next year's harvest. Do I make myself clear?" Micheal glared down at Osaze.

"Yes, My Lord Avalon." Osaze bowed in deference, then quickly departed.

The next morning, Mbizi woke to terrible sores all over his body.

"Shani, please tell me that ointment works." He watched as she rubbed some on her arm, which was covered in boils.

"It's definitely better than without it." She closed her eyes with relief as she worked it into her skin.

Mbizi began rubbing the ointment into Shani's back until it covered her entire body. After ensuring his wife was cared for, they turned their attention to him.

When they were done, he still felt sore, but the itch was gone, and the pain had been dulled. Once again, he was glad the gods favored them.

"Julie was right. This is the worst one yet." Shani laid down and closed her eyes.

"Now I'm dreading what comes next," Mbizi admitted. "Do you know what comes next?" He decided to ask.

"I don't know. I was afraid to find out." She said without moving.

"I suppose it's time to find out. Come, my love." He grabbed her hand, helping her to her feet. Then, they headed off to learn the bad news.

Hail, Locust, and Darkness

"The early harvest order has begun to bring in massive amounts of food for the stores. Our distribution efforts have increased the willingness of everyone to obey our latest edict." Julie was discussing their preparations for plagues seven, eight, and nine.

"So what are the next punishments from the God of Israel?" Shani inquired. She and Mbizi had emerged from their isolation.

"We have been gathering as much food stock as possible from the early harvest," Julie informed them.

"So first they attack the meat supply, now they are going after the grain?" Mbizi shook his head.

"There is going to be fire from the sky, followed by a plague of locusts, and then there will be three days of darkness," Julie revealed the future.

"So it just gets better and better." Shani sighed deeply.

"We have been hardening the vulnerable elements of the palace to provide the best chance to weather the coming storm." Julie examined the awnings over the Main Module.

"How's the hardening going?" Micheal entered the courtyard.

"Just about ready. How much time do you think we have?" Julie went to greet him.

"A day, two at the most." He kissed her. "Thanks to your ointment, everyone is at least functional." He seemed to be inspecting her boils.

"I look hideous, don't I?" She winced at his touch.

"You look beautiful." He brushed the hair out of her face.

"Thank you for lying. Now let's get back to work." She led him to the next thing that needed checking.

That night, the Vizier arrived to request their return to Pi-Ramesses. The next morning, they sailed off on the Valkyrie, filled with supplies ordered by the Pharaoh. The Lords of the West followed with more supplies on the Isis.

The sun moved near the western horizon as they neared Pi-Ramesses.

An alert triggered on Julie's phone. The sky-net detected a large debris field in space on a collision course with Earth. She steered the Valkyrie close to the Isis.

"Take cover!" Julie yelled to Shani. "We have two minutes until the fire will rain! Stay inside until the danger passes!" Julie hit the lockdown and joined Micheal in the cabin.

Only seconds later, a loud sonic boom cut through the air. Then, a bright streak lit up the evening sky.

"How long will the storm last?" Julie looked at Micheal, who was hypnotized by the spectacle unfolding before them.

"Probably ten minutes at most." He never broke his gaze.

Julie was entranced by the devastation raining down on Egypt. At that moment, she realized she was likely witnessing the worst sky-fall event in recorded history. It was both awe-inspiring and terrifying at the same time.

A cacophony of sonic booms created an orchestra of sound to accompany the aerial light show of thousands of streaks of fire. Then, suddenly, their role as observers became one of participation.

There was a bright flash followed by one of the loudest noises she had ever heard. The Valkyrie had taken a direct hit to the forward deck. The ship shook violently, causing Julie to tumble out of the protection of the awning. Micheal ran out and grabbed her; then he rolled her out of the way of another meteor.

They continued for a few more minutes. Then, just as they approached the palace harbor, a large meteor plunged into the river, sending an enormous wave directly toward them.

A quick pulse from the starboard thrusters and the Valkyrie turned headlong into the oncoming surge. Their ship, as well as the Isis, were both sent rushing into the palace harbor.

The waves pushed the Isis into the Palace Gardens, but the Valkyrie took a hard impact against the landing, then began to get sucked into the backwash. The meteorite impact vaporized a large volume of water, and they were caught in the rush to fill the void in the Nile.

Julie pressed the engines to the max, attempting to counter the vacuum. It was just enough to prevent them from sinking into the turbulent undertow.

"Get ready for the repulse of equilibrium!" Julie yelled, seeing the torrents coming violently together.

The second surge sent them right back into the Palace Harbor. The water slowly stabilized.

The Valkyrie could finally dock at the palace and the world was becoming much more quiet.

"What's the status of the debris field?" Julie asked Micheal.

"The main field has been absorbed. The projections show another few hours in a much-diminished shooting gallery." He said, focusing on his smartphone.

"Does the sky-net know where that came from?" She pulled out her phone.

"I just tracked it. There was a long-period comet that was ripped apart by Jupiter about six months ago. It mostly disintegrated during a very close pass with the sun last month. It finally came apart completely about a week ago." Micheal showed her the video from the sky-net.

Julie followed Micheal to the deck, and they emerged to a scene of devastation. Plumes of smoke were rising in every direction, as far as the eye could see.

"This is probably one of the worst sky fall events in recorded history." Micheal seemed almost fascinated.

They exited the Valkyrie to the gardens and found Mbizi and Shani beside their beached vessel, the Isis.

"The God of Israel must be furious," Shani concluded, as she never took her eyes off the bright streaks still cutting across the sky.

"Let's go check on the Pharaoh," Julie suggested.

"What about the Isis? Are we just going to leave it here in the gardens?" Mbizi scanned their ship, sitting in the middle of a path.

"We'll deal with that later." Micheal began leading the way to the palace.

"It's about time you arrive; we are in crisis here!" Thutmose glanced from one to the other, apparently searching for answers.

"What do you want us to do?" Julie asked.

"Use your connection to the Gods; bring them to Egypt's defense!" The Pharaoh was desperate.

"The gods are silent," Mbizi stated directly.

"Of course they are! They clearly fear this God of Israel!" Thutmose glowered. "Lady Avalon, can you summon Isis?" He then tried.

"It doesn't work like that. I serve her, she doesn't serve me." Julie tried to dissuade this avenue of thought.

"Then what good are any of you?" The Pharaoh demanded.

"We can advise you... And I would advise you to appease this God of Israel." Micheal admonished, but it clearly fell on deaf ears.

"Never! The Gods of Egypt will come to deal with this foreign God." Thutmose had a flare in his eye.

"Is there anything we can do to help you?" Mbizi asked, trying to temper the Pharaoh.

"My Lord, can you look through the eyes of this Moses? Are the people of Goshen suffering as much as we are?"

Mbizi complied. He began describing the scene.

"They are marveling that the fire from the sky did not come for them."

"What do you mean?" The Pharaoh demanded.

"It appears that the land of Goshen was not impacted by the destruction that rained from above," Mbizi explained.

"Damn the gods for abandoning their people!" Thutmose's head dropped as he scowled. "Enough! I've heard enough."

Mbizi came back to himself.

"Since I can't depend on the gods, at least tell me I can trust in you. Did you bring the requested supplies?" The Pharaoh pivoted to her and Micheal.

"Our cargo holds are indeed full. There is just one problem."

Micheal explained the Isis.

"How in the world did this happen?" Thutmose seemed exasperated.

"One of the sky missiles hit the river as we approached the palace. The water surged into the gardens, carrying the Isis with it." Micheal explained.

"I will marshal the men necessary to return it to the river." Thutmose was about to send word.

Julie stepped up and said, "That won't be necessary! We already sent for something to deal with the situation, your Eminence."

"In the meantime, we can have the cargo from the Valkyrie unloaded." Micheal indicated their ship.

"Very well." Thutmose agreed.

Later that night, the M-pulse pads arrived, and they used them to take care of the Isis. The next day, they were advising the Pharaoh when Moses and Aaron came to make their appeal.

"... The Lord God of the Hebrews spoke to us, and this is what he said: how long will you refuse to humble yourself before me? Let my people go, that they may serve me. If you refuse to let my people go, I will bring a plague of locusts into your coasts tomorrow. And they shall cover the face of the earth, so you will not be able to see it. They shall eat the residue of all that remained from the hail. They shall eat every tree that grows for you out of the field. They shall fill your houses and the houses of all your servants. All the houses of Egypt. This plague will be the likes of which neither your father nor your father's father would have seen from their time until this day." Then Moses and Aaron exited the chamber.

The Pharaoh asked for everyone's opinions.

"Father, how long shall this man be a burden upon us? Let the people go so they might serve the Lord their God. Can you not see that Egypt is destroyed?" Prince Amenemhat pleaded.

Everyone else echoed the Prince.

Thutmose did not speak. He sat thoughtfully. After a minute, he signaled, and Moses and Aaron were brought back into the chamber.

"Very well, go, serve the Lord your God. But, who amongst you shall go?" The Pharaoh seemed to relent.

"We must all go. With our young and old, our sons and daughters, with our flocks and herds. For we must hold a feast unto the Lord." Moses looked at Julie; she shook her head.

Then Thutmose said. "May the Lord be with you. I will let you go with your sons. Go now, all that are men and do that which you desired." And with a wave, Pharaoh had Moses and Aaron removed from his sight.

After they were gone, Amenemhat seemed to believe his father had appeased them.

"Perhaps all the chaos will end now." He said hopefully.

"This isn't over. The request was not met." Julie informed the Prince.

The Pharaoh sat there staring at the ground like he was contemplating something. At Julie's rebuke, he looked up and said, "The gods will come!" Then he rose like he was about to leave.

Julie looked at the Prince, who seemed just as frustrated as she was. At that moment, she realized Amenemhat was the firstborn son who would fall victim to The Angel of Death. She had an urge to enlighten the Pharaoh of this fact.

But instead, she took a deep breath and said. "Your Eminence, how much will you suffer before you relent on this prideful intransigence?"

"Lady Avalon, I will not show weakness before the gods. I have just come to an understanding. The gods are permitting this to continue as a test of my loyalty. I will not bow to any other gods! When they see my sacrifice to their authority, the gods will come and deliver Egypt from our strife." Thutmose made a quick exit.

"Lady Avalon, are the gods really testing my father?" Prince Amenemhat seemed doubtful.

"I'm sorry, Your Highness, the gods will not intercede in this matter." Her guilt made her avert her eyes.

This was always one of the most challenging things about time travel. The knowledge that someone would soon die, particularly someone she knew, sometimes led to the temptation to change the outcome. She had really come to like the Prince.

"Maybe I can convince him to cede to this God of Israel." Amenemhat's eyes show doubt in his statement.

"I hope you can. It's only going to get worse from here." Julie locked eyes, then looked away, and the Prince headed after his father.

Over the next day, Julie, Micheal, and the Lords of the West worked to set up kinetic energy barriers to deal with plague number eight. There was a steady wind blowing all day out of the East. As the last pieces were put in place, a buzzing sound began to rise from the desert to the east. A few minutes later, the eastern sky began to darken. Until, in the mellow light of dusk, Julie could see that it was insects.

Using her electric gauntlets, she ignited the East energy field. The locust descended on the palace and began frying on the energy field. There was smoke emanating off of the lightning bolts.

After a few minutes, the swarm began to flow around the palace. After the mass had passed by, Julie ended the light show. She turned to find the Pharaoh and his son just staring at her.

"Impressive, Lady Avalon; I have never seen such power from you before."

"Your Eminence, it is only recently that we have acquired this power. We believe that the God, Set, must have delivered these gauntlets." She showed them her hands. Then she closed her eyes, realizing she had just indicated that the gods were still helping him.

"So, the gods haven't forgotten me. Perhaps my steady faith will bring them back to my rescue." Thutmose seemed to have a pop in his step as he headed off.

"Lady Avalon, didn't you say the gods would stay out of this?" Amenemhat was confused.

"These are but token help. I assure you, it will get worse." Julie shook her head.

The next day, Julie looked at her phone. The sky-net had sent an alert that there was a large eruption on Santorini and that the ash cloud was moving toward Egypt.

"Micheal, I think plague number nine is already inbound." She showed him the satellite feed.

"Well, we've already battened down the suite as best we can and have stocked up on enough supplies for a few days. We had already assumed it would be a dust storm or a volcano. We should seal off as much of the palace as possible." He suggested.

"The Pharaoh wants all of us in the throne room," Shani informed them.

"This plague of locusts has devoured nearly all of my harvest." The current petitioner was at the front of a very long line. Then, he was interrupted by the Vizier.

"Your Eminence, the prophets."

Moses and Aaron came to a stop at the foot of the stairs.

"I have sinned against the Lord your God. And against you. I pray for your forgiveness this time. Please entreat the Lord your God that he may take away this death from my land." Thutmose seemed sincere. But Julie didn't trust it. As only the other day, he was steadfast in his attitude of resistance.

"Very well." Moses seemed a bit leery but agreed to the request.

After they were gone, the Pharaoh rose from his throne and said, "I will hear no more today."

He signaled as he headed toward his private chambers, and all his principal advisors followed.

"Neferweben, remind the taskmasters that the Hebrews are not to leave." Once the vizier had departed, Prince Amenemhat protested.

"Father, why can't you see that this is not the gods testing you?"

"I have known the gods far longer than you, my son. They will deliver us from this foreign tyrant." Thutmose looked at Julie and saw her disapproval. "My Lady Avalon, you disagree?"

"If you are wrong about the gods, eventually, this God of Israel will do something to hurt you directly. It will become a personal punishment specifically for you." She wanted him to believe her but knew he wouldn't.

"I, like you, realize this is all building up to a final conflict. That is how I know The Sun God will come down from the heavens and restore order to Egypt. I know it will be soon." Thutmose looked around at everyone. "If there is nothing else, you are all excused." The Pharaoh turned to his shrine devoted to Amun-Ra.

Julie and her friends entered their connected double suite.

"The darkness is inbound; in an hour or so, the light will turn to the dark. It will last three days." Julie studied the screen on her phone. "Shani, Mbizi, here are your lights to resist the darkness." She handed them each a kinetic orb.

"These are magic from the gods?" Shani studied her orb closely.

"Don't lose them," Julie ordered, and then Mbizi and Shani exited to their chambers.

Julie went and found Micheal gazing out at the noonday sun. It was becoming a rusty orange as the first flakes of ash began snowing from the graying sky. Then, as the minutes passed, the sun became an opaque circle, fading slowly to black.

As the hours dragged on, it sounded like a thunderstorm was raging all around them. She knew three days of this would strike fear into all of Egypt. But she also knew it would take one more terror to cow the Pharaoh.

The Passover

Shani woke to the comforting glow of her Orb of the Gods. It had been nearly three days since the roar of thunder swallowed the sun. Even with the knowledge that it would soon be over, she still couldn't help but tremble at each crack.

"Shani, we need to get to Micheal and Julie. Thutmose has just sent for us." Mbizi was apparently looking through the Pharaoh's eyes. They arrived in the Pharaoh's murky chamber to find Moses and Aaron before Thutmose.

"If you betray your word once again, there will be dire consequences," Aaron warned.

"Go and serve the Lord. Only leave behind your herds and flocks. Your families my go with you," Pharaoh said.

"You must allow us our offerings to the Lord. Our cattle must go with us. We will leave none behind. For we know not what the Lord requires," Moses demanded.

"Leave me! See me no more! For in that day, you shall die."

"Very well, I will see you no more," Moses said, and he and Aaron left the chamber.

"So, My Lord of the West, do you believe the word of this prophet?" Thutmose turned to them.

"Clearly this god is powerful. He even shut out the sun for days," Mbizi tried to convince the Pharaoh.

"I believe his last insult will stir Ra from his final apathy." He had failed.

"Father, this is madness. You should end this now," Amenemhat pleaded with his father.

"Your lack of faith is troubling," the Pharaoh chided him.

"Of course, I believe in the gods, but they are allowing our torment to continue," Amenemhat was becoming frustrated.

"There is no shame in recognizing obvious truths..." Shani reinforced the prince's plea.

"We will bide a bit longer," Thutmose declared, then exited his bedchamber.

The end of the 9th plague brought an uneasy calm over Egypt. Over the next few weeks, Shani and Mbizi took a tour of the East Delta. The first stop was in Goshen to visit Moses and Aaron. They spent a few days there, then moved on to various villages and palaces. One of the most interesting things was how much respect everyone had for the prophets of Israel. People from all over Egypt were coming to pay tribute to the Israelites to appease the great Lord of the Hebrews. They received many gifts of jewelry and trinkets made of gold and silver. During a sight link, Mbizi saw that Lord and Lady Avalon had returned to River Palace but were en route back to Pi-Ramesses. By evening, they had arrived at the Pharaoh's palace. Mbizi began observing things all over the world for Thutmose. While they were waiting for him to work, Shani sat with the Pharaoh and his son.

"Well, Lady West, it seems the god of Israel has given up. Two weeks without a plague. I supposed the Hebrews value their livestock more than freedom." Thutmose appeared to be in a good mood.

"Lord and Lady Avalon have no doubt told you they don't think this is over yet. I believe this god of Israel may be preparing one final punishment. You have said they can leave; why not allow then their herds and flocks?" Shani's eyes locked with the Pharoah's. His eyes narrowed.

"Those herds belong to me!"

"If you really believed that, you would have taken them by now. I think you fear the god of Israel." She kept eye contact and tilted her head.

"You dare accuse me of fear!"

Shani slightly averted her eyes at his intensity and was instantly struck by an unusual shadow behind Prince Amenemhat. She was momentarily transfixed by the silhouette on the wall, which had ears like Anubis.

"Lady West! You will answer me!" Thutmose demanded.

She looked to the Pharaoh, then back to the wall, and the dark form was gone.

"My Lady, are you all right?" Amenemhat was looking at her with concern.

"Oh..." she snapped out of her trance.

"I'm okay, Your Highness." She turned back to Thutmose. Before she could return to their discussion, Mbizi emerged.

"What have you seen, Lord West?" Thutmose sat up, looking intently.

"Mbizi detailed the lands, ranging from Mycenae to Babylon.

"And what about Goshen?" The Pharaoh seemed impatient.

"The Hebrew people have been observing some special festival at the direction of the prophets. Something to do with a first-born lamb, unblemished. I saw thousands of Egyptians paying tribute to this Moses, as well as the people." Mbizi was explaining.

"Why are my people honoring these prophets?" Pharaoh tilted his head and furrowed his brow.

"The Egyptian people believe Moses is backed by an angry god and hopes to appease him with offerings. They hope these punishments will end."

Mbizi's head dipped, but he maintained eye contact.

"It has been nearly two weeks since any punishment has been delivered." Thutmose seemed to be in a positive mood.

"It feels like something terrible is coming, and this is the calm before the storm." Shani felt a chill run through her at her statement.

"What have you seen?" the Pharaoh demanded.

"Not seen, felt." She took a deep breath to settle her stomach. "This feeling of dread has been growing as each day passes," she explained.

"Have you heard these prophets indicate anything about what they think is coming?" Thutmose directed to Mbizi.

"Nothing I understand. The only thing they said was that they were celebrating a festival called "the Passover".

"Thank you, Lord West, Lady West," the Pharaoh dismissed them.

The next morning, Thutmose had convened a meeting with them, Lord and Lady Avalon, the vizier, and the prince. They debated about this Passover and any other ideas about the calm period. Pharaoh stubbornly refused to accept all advice about the potential threat. Shani saw a strange form lurking next to the prince as this debate was going on. Her reaction must have shown. After Pharaoh dismissed everyone, Mbizi stopped her.

"What is wrong?"

"It's the prince. It's like there's a shadow following him around, and every time I look at it, I get a feeling of foreboding," she explained.

They walked over, and the prince was in conversation with Micheal and Julie.

"I just want you to know that whatever comes next, it has been my honor to know you, Your Highness," Julie said.

"It sounds like you're saying goodbye." The worry was clear on the prince's face.

"You never want to live with regret for something you didn't say." Micheal touched Amenemhet on his shoulder.

The whole scene had an odd feeling.

"In that spirit, it was nice to relate to someone other than my father these last few years. Both of you have taught me much about how to be a good and just leader of people. There are so few people who understand the complexities of ruling. You were like an aunt and uncle to me."

The prince looked like he was holding back tears.

"We feel the same. One final thing—time is so precious. You

should spend some time with your father and mother today. No talk of troubles, just quality time with your parents," Julie advised.

"Good idea, My Lady. I think I'll do that." Then Amenemhat turned to her and Mbizi.

"Both of you have been good friends..." as he talked, Shani kept being distracted by the shadow hovering over the prince.

"So I want to thank you for all the advice over the years, and it was an honor for you to witness my deification." Amenemhat finished.

"You are like a little brother to me. And whether it was racing chariots or testing our skill with a bow, you have always been a worthy opponent." Mbizi gave a slight bow.

"Your Highness always knows how to make me laugh or impress me with some skill, but I am most impressed by the type of leader you have become. How much you care about the people under your charge. And finally, in the spirit of this discussion, no matter what happens, it's been a pleasure to know you." And those words sent a commotion through her stomach. The shadow seemed to descend onto Amenemhat, then disappeared inside him. One final warm look passed between the prince and the four of them. Then, he headed off after his father.

"What was that about?" Shani thought they knew something they weren't telling them.

Lady Avalon shook her head, "There are some things it's better you don't know." Julie shifted her eyes to Micheal.

"Neither of you have younger siblings, correct?"

This question was odd.

"I don't," Shani confirmed.

"I was first-born in my family," Mbizi was just as confused as she was.

Julie looked at Micheal, then said, "I want the both of you to travel to Goshen tonight. You will spend the night with Moses." She then nodded, indicating her instruction. Shani had considered inquiring but decided to obey the command.

A few hours later, they were at the door of the prophets.

"This is unexpected. We have some rather important rituals to attend. Perhaps we might visit another day, Lord and Lady West." Moses seemed to want them to leave.

But Shani felt there must have been a reason Lady Avalon had sent them there.

"I think you should know that Lord and Lady Avalon instructed us to sleep here this night. It was odd. We don't know why." She shrugged her shoulders.

Moses' eyes widened, and he looked back and forth between them. Then he said, "Inside, quickly," and ushered them in.

"We are just about to perform a special ritual."

Moses and Aaron brought forward a couple of stark white lambs. After completing a prayer, they cut the throats of the lambs and caught the blood in two large bowls. "What are you doing this for?" Shani inquired.

"It's for all of our protection. The god of Israel will pass through the land this night. When he sees the blood of the unspoiled sacrifice on our door, he will pass us over," Moses explained.

"What will happen if there is no blood?" Shani had that dreadful feeling come back to her stomach.

"When our people were enslaved generations ago, the Pharaoh, in an attempt to prevent a prophecy from coming to pass, ordered every firstborn of the Hebrews to be slaughtered. So this night, that same punishment will be brought upon all the houses of Egypt."

Shani realized why she was getting that feeling from the prince.

"We have to warn Prince Amenemhat!" She began to pull Mbizi behind her.

"You don't have time." Moses raised his arm to stop them. "Lord and Lady Avalon sent you here for your protection." Moses's head dropped slightly, and he locked eyes with her. "My Lady, if you go out there, you will die."

Shani went and sat down in a corner, away from everyone else. She began to stew over all the things in her head. She was angry with Micheal and Julie for keeping this from them. Her heart was breaking for Amenemhat. He had done nothing wrong, but now he was about to die. Her anger returned, but this time it was directed at the gods—all of the gods. They all seemed to go around killing the lowly humans whenever it suited them. Mbizi came and sat with her. He pulled her into him.

"They should have told us." She laid her head on his shoulder as the tears flowed.

"At least we got to say goodbye." Mbizi just held her for a little while. When she had calmed down, she saw that Moses and Aaron had the bowls of blood carried to the door.

Shani and Mbizi went to see what they were doing. Moses took a cloth and dipped it in the blood. He prayed, then brushed the cloth on both sides of the door and above it. He said another prayer.

"What is this for?" she couldn't contain her curiosity,

"This is how God knows that believers reside here," Aaron answered.

As she watched the blood run down the sides of the door, she felt utterly helpless to save her friend. Shani hardly ate her dinner, as her appetite had abandoned her. She laid her head on Mbizi's chest and tried to sleep, but the arrival of this "angel of death" disturbed her dreams. She lay there and could feel death approaching from the sea. She could literally feel the shadow as it passed by. Her restlessness finally got the better of her.

"Mbizi," she shook him awake.

"Yes?"

"Can you look at Amenemhat and his father?"

"Of course." He sat up.

Shani took a deep breath and prepared for the bad news.

Mbizi was just a shadow in the darkness. Then he spoke. "I can't see the prince, so I'm switching to the Pharaoh.

"Come quickly! It's the prince!'" Mbizi repeated Vizier Neferweben's words.

"'Get Avalon!' Thutmose ordered. And he is rushing through the palace." Mbizi paused for a minute.

"He just grabbed his son and screamed... Micheal and Julie just arrived. They are trying to help Amenemhat."

Mbizi was quiet for a few minutes. "Micheal said, 'I'm sorry. He's gone'. Pharaoh replied. 'Damn the gods! How could they abandon me like this!' After looking at Micheal and Julie, he said, 'I know you did everything you could, but you're still connected to the gods. I want you out of my sight.'

'I'm so sorry, Your Eminence,' Julie said. Then she and Micheal left.

'Bring me Moses!' the Pharaoh just ordered."

Mbizi continued, but Shani didn't want to hear anymore.

"That's enough." Shani took comfort in Mbizi's arms as she mourned the death of the prince. After a couple more hours, she finally felt the ominous presence leave Egypt. Right around that time, there was banging on the door.

"Open up in the name of the Pharaoh!" the visitor demanded.

Moses opened the door.

"His Eminence requires an audience."

And with that, Moses and Aaron left with the escort.

"I guess it's safe to return to Pi-Ramesses." Shani headed off toward the Isis. Mbizi was right behind her.

"I'm going to give them a piece of my mind!" Shani felt her anger rising again.

CHAPTER 20: EXODUS

MICHEAL AND JULIE RETIRED to their suite and began packing to leave the palace.

"Micheal?" Julie asked.

"Yes?"

"Sometimes I have trouble with the actions of God. When I was in Sunday School and I first read the Old Testament, I thought most of the stories had to be allegory. But now, as we know, the Bible is fairly literal. We've seen the flood of Noah wipe out many good people. Then, situations like this, where thousands of innocents lost their lives to punish a few men. Every time these things happen, I wonder how, if God really is God, he can't figure out some other way." Julie looked up with tears in her eyes.

Micheal stopped what he was doing and went and took her in his arms. "I know how difficult these situations are." After a moment, he pulled back.

"We have a lot still to do," Julie agreed.

Micheal returned to his work and his thoughts. His rational mind told him that everything he had witnessed confirmed that the Bible was written from history. But then he considered all of the old gods and some of their amazing abilities. The Bible may have been written exclusively about one deity among the ancient world's many gods: the God of Israel. However, this does not necessarily imply that this deity is the ultimate or only "God".

Micheal was brought back to reality by Shani and Mbizi entering their chambers. He was a bit surprised that Shani immediately slapped Julie.

"You should have told me!" Shani accused. "You knew what would happen, didn't you!"

Tears came back to Julie's eyes. "You don't want that burden," Julie said.

"And you just let it happen." Shani was still upset.

"Shani!" Micheal stepped in. "You don't understand the stakes..." Micheal began.

"I understand you let our friend die, when you could have stopped it!" She took a step in his direction.

"Are you a god?"

Shani stopped cold.

"What does that have to do with this?"

"You don't have the experience and knowledge we do. When you know what future is written, your decisions are akin to a god. You can save a life you know is meant to end, but the consequences would ripple through centuries. Thousands, perhaps millions of people, may no longer be born. Your choice removed them from the timeline. Do you have the right to make such a change? Could you live with yourself? Knowing your selfish choice to save your friend, who was meant to die, ended countless lives? So I ask again—are you a god? We cared for the prince as well. The burden of future knowledge is an awesome responsibility. Next time the fate of future lives conflicts with your personal feelings, perhaps we'll let you test your divinity."

Micheal went and comforted Julie, who was falling apart. After a minute, Shani approached. Micheal stepped back.

Julie said, "Shani, I'm sorry!"

Shani hugged Julie.

"My Lords and Ladies, his eminence has requested your attendance," Vizier Neferweben interrupted the scene.

They entered the throne room.

"...leave the Land of Egypt! Take the People of Israel with you! And take your flocks and herds as well. Bless me also."

After Moses and Aaron left, Thutmose spoke. "My friends, I should have heeded your advice. Clearly our gods have abandoned us to the mercy of this "God of Israel", and while I value your counsel, your connection to the gods is intolerable at this time."

"Of course, your eminence, we understand. We will leave Egypt temporarily and give you some space... But with permission, we will return for the prince's funeral," Micheal proposed.

"Very well," the Pharaoh agreed, then dismissed them with a nod.

Once back in their chambers, "Where are we going?" Mbizi asked.

"We will meet the Hebrew people on the shore of the sea. There are some miraculous events we still wish to witness." Micheal resumed packing.

A couple of hours later, they sailed toward the sea, making one stop in Goshen to let Moses know their plan. By evening, they passed out of the East Delta into the Mediterranean Sea. The Isis was right behind them.

"So, it's a twelve-day journey around Africa. That means we have a few days to spare. Are we going to stop at Avalon?" Julie asked as she joined him on the bridge.

"Most definitely. I know I'm ready for a break from all these "ten plagues" of Egypt." Micheal set the course for Gibraltar, then sat on one of the benches just outside the bridge. Julie came to join him.

"What I've been wondering is, why have the gods of Egypt went silent during this time? Where do you think they go?"

Micheal began analyzing this new quandary. "I don't know. Maybe they are from some other dimension. Like in the *Percy Jackson* book series."

Julie put stock in one potential theory. "That could make sense. The Garden of Eden certainly seemed to be something like that."

Micheal stared at the setting sun, and that brought a new quandary. "After what happened against Ra last time, do you think we'll see him again? It has been some time."

Micheal hoped the Sun God was gone for good.

"I get the feeling he's not gone for good, And the new powers he demonstrated makes me wonder if he was just holding back before or if he's evolving over time."

Julie gazed at the West horizon as the sun was swallowed by clouds moving their way.

After the stop at Gibraltar, the circumnavigation of Africa took 16 days. Now the Valkyrie and Isis were drifting toward the west coast of the Gulf of Suez. They docked at a point where the mountain and the plain met at the sea.

"Do you think we're in the right place?" Julie asked as they assessed a potential place to set up camp.

"It looks right to me. And I think that's the guiding pillar." Micheal pointed out what looked like a dust devil to the north.

"I thought it was supposed to be a pillar of fire," she seemed confused.

"Exodus said it was a pillar of cloud by day and a pillar of fire by night. Now, let's set up right here." Micheal directed to a small, flat clearing next to the sea. In just a few minutes, both of their tents were set up, and they placed another one for Moses and Aaron.

During the stopover at Avalon, they retrieved some of their compact inflatable tents, engineered in the Age of Atlantis. These tents, made from a soft, flexible tri-poly alloy, offer easy set-up and take-down. Initialize the valve to inflate or deflate them.

Knowing it would take several hours for the mass to migrate down the valley, Micheal asked Mbizi to see what the Pharaoh was doing. His friend dictated the scene as if he was acting out a play:

"Thutmose is just arriving at the Temple of Amun-Ra in Heliopolis... He's entering the inner sanctum...

"'Why have you betrayed me?' Ra asked, wearing his full bird appearance..."

Micheal had to quell the urge to react. He didn't want to interrupt Mbizi's flow.

"... 'Me, betray you? You abandoned me to the whims of this God of Israel, and now my divine prince is dead!' Thutmose accused.

'How dare you speak to me in such a fashion. You are no god yet! Ra stepped up to the Pharaoh. He towered over him.

'...Any more belligerence, and you never will be! Now, you will pursue the Hebrews who are trapped by the sea and return them to my domain. I will go and ensure that they do not escape. Now go!' Ra commanded."

Mbizi shook his head, ending the connection.

"Go get Julie and Shani. We need to figure out what we're going to do," Micheal instructed.

Everyone sat down in the tent.

"So, Ra has ordered Thutmose to return the Hebrews to Egypt. And apparently, he is going to come here to make sure they can't escape. So we are going to need to stop him," Micheal began.

"I thought we weren't supposed to interfere with the events of history." Shani's head tilted to the side and she furrowed her brow.

"There's nothing in the Bible about Ra or anything else trying to stop the escape of the Hebrews." Micheal returned the stare.

"So what do we have at our disposal?" Mbizi interrupted the contest.

"You have the sight. Shani has some kind of counter to time-stopping that can also repel Ra temporally, and we apparently have resistance to temporal energy attacks. On top of that, we have our fighting skills, tri-poly alloy clothing, and kinetic energy weapons. The boomerang, our lightning gauntlets, and a kinetic staff," Micheal ran down their inventory.

"We team up to neutralize him. Julie and I will use our gauntlet. Mbizi, you will use the staff. And Shani, you use the boomerang. If Ra stops time, Shani will unfreeze us, and we will do a coordinated attack. Hopefully, the lightning will stun Ra, allowing us to trap him somewhere where he won't be able to keep coming after us." Micheal wasn't sure how that could work. Ra's abilities made it impossible to know if anything could stop him.

By the time they retrieved their weapons from the ship, the head of the caravan was coming to a halt a short distance away, so they went to greet Moses.

"Moses. Aaron. We've already set up a place for you," Micheal indicated the tents.

The tents were about 20 X 20 feet with seats and tables built into them.

"Join us for a while," Aaron said, accepting the accommodation.

"Very impressive. I've never seen anything like it," Moses said as he went inside.

"There's something we need to tell you," Julie said as she took a seat.

"The Sun God has returned. He has ordered the Pharaoh to come and bring you back to Egypt," Michale continued the story.

"God said we must camp here for eight days." Moses seemed unconcerned.

"We already knew about the eight days by the sea. But the Bible says nothing about the gods of Egypt interfering. Ra is coming here to prevent your escape." Micheal was unsure of how these events should play out.

"Perhaps that is why you're here." Moses scanned the room.

The next week passed without incident. They all marveled at the pillar of fire by night and the manna by day. It tasted sweet. It reminded Micheal of these glazed croissants he used to buy from a local bakery in Salt Lake City. The main difference being that one piece of manna, about the size of a fist, would satiate your hunger, replacing a meal. It would go bad if it were left uneaten by the next morning.

They started to wonder if Ra was ever going to show. Then it happened.

Micheal suddenly saw streaks of light fill the air, then realized Shani was holding his hand.

"Ra stopped time. We need to go," Shani was urgent.

"He's over by the pillar," Mbizi added.

They ran the one-mile distance to the pillar.

"It has been quite some time," Ra said, with his back to them.

He turned to reveal his beaked face; his eyes pulsed with yellow light. "It seems, Lady West, that you possess some type of push ability. So, while I know a few years have passed, to me, our last encounter was just days ago. But I would like to let all of you know..." he scanned them. "...that I have come to a different conclusion regarding you. Whatever your relation to Isis and Osiris, I am convinced you are simply time travelers. So I will make you a deal. What do you say we let bygones be bygones, and so long as you stay out of my way, I'll leave you alone." Ra extended his hand, indicating they should return to where they came from.

"There's only one problem with that—we can't let you prevent the Hebrews from leaving," Micheal said.

"What do you care about these people? While you may not be gods, you possess the powers of them. They mean nothing to you." Ra tilted his head to the side.

"In the time we came from, the Hebrews left Egypt at this time. We can't allow the history to change. And I do agree with you on one thing: as a god, these people are meaningless to you, so why do you want to stop them?" Micheal challenged.

"As a god, these people belong to me. All the insignificant people in this world belong to me. The four of you as well. All should worship me, and no other god. Not this God of Israel, nor the Anunnaki, or the gods from any other region of this world. All should worship me." Ra took a step toward them.

"All of us insignificant people shouldn't mean anything to you. Maybe it would be best if you returned to the heavens and tended to the sun. Aren't you the Sun God?" Micheal was mostly serious.

"I tire of this debate. As the power behind the sun, I cast many shadows. If you remain in this one, you will suffer the consequences."

Ra stepped toward them and was stopped mid-swing as the kinetic boomerang slammed into his chest. Micheal moved to attack with his lightning and took a massive impact to the chest. He had to roll away from the next swing of the massive war hammer. He was glad his trip-poly clothes softened the first blow. He still felt the bruise as he flipped back to his feet. Then he ducked the next swing, which came from Anubis. He activated the gauntlets and hit Anubis with a pulse of electricity. The Protector of the Underworld dropped like a rock. Micheal took a moment's reprieve to assess the situation:

Julie and Shani were double-teaming Set while Mbizi was laying strikes with the staff on the Sun God. Micheal grabbed Anubis's hammer and swung it full force at Ra. The god went down but immediately came back up to his feet. Micheal then turned the hammer on Anubis, who was getting back up. Anubis dodged the strike, then spun past the hammer, laying a punishing blow to Micheal's side. Despite his protective clothes, the blow was painful as Anubis had clearly used a sharp dagger. Micheal wielded the hammer again, but Anubis took hold of the handle and over-powered Micheal to the ground. They rolled over, and Micheal tumbled to his feet, but Anubis maintained control of the ham-mer. Micheal saw Julie shock Set while Shani was on the ground, reeling from a strike from the God of the Desert. Then he saw Ra attacking Mbizi with what had to be temporal energy.

Micheal immediately sent a bolt of lightning into the face of the Sun God, interrupting his attack. Mbizi collapsed to the ground. Micheal barely remembered Anubis charging from be-hind. Micheal spun on his heel, fading from the rush attack, and unleashed another shock. As Anubis came crashing down on top of him, he directed the god's energy to continue with its momen-tum, and the God of Death tumbled to Ra's feet. Micheal quickly got up and sent another bolt at Ra to join the fight with Julie.

At that moment, there was a flash over the entire area, and the ribbons of light in the air disappeared. The pillar of fire began spinning rapidly. The next thing Micheal knew, he had a massive headache, and his face felt wet. The light was suspended in the air again, and Shani was trying to help him up. He fought through the pain and got to his feet. Julie was in the grip of Anubis and Set while Ra was shooting a beam of light at her chest. Micheal and Shani moved quickly to her aid. He unleashed two sprays of electricity, hitting Ra and Set. Julie fell to the ground. Micheal slid to Julie. She was coughing. When he touched her, a purple glow came over her. He then looked up to see Anubis mid-swing with his hammer. Before he could connect, the kinetic disc knocked him to the ground. Julie sat up, and Shani joined them. Anubis and Set were helping up Ra. Shani ran and grabbed Ra by the wrists. Micheal reached out, grabbing her ankle to try and pull her back. At that moment, a surge of energy seemed to pulse through him and into Shani. Her hands burst with light that emanated out, enveloping the entire scene. A rush of wind raced through, washing the light away, and the gods vanished with it. Micheal turned and saw that the world around them was moving to the beat of the clock again. He heard Shani scream and looked to see her draped over Mbizi, who still lay unconscious on the ground.

<u>Parting Seas</u>

Mbizi felt himself come out of his body. He saw himself getting hit by a beam of light emanating from Ra's hand. The Sun God was taken down, and Mbizi saw his body fall to the ground. He stared at his own face in horrid wonder. After a minute, he looked around and saw odd-colored light emanating from everyone around him. Then Micheal, Julie, and Shani came to his side. Micheal and Julie grabbed each other's hands and touched his chest together. A deep purple glow began to encompass his whole body. Suddenly, a beam reached out from his body, reeling him in. He felt himself reconnect with his body, and everything went dark.

Mbizi woke the next day in his tent.

"How do you feel?" Shani was holding his hand.

"I feel like a hippo trampled me."

"Do you have much experience with that?" Shani laughed at her own joke. "You scared me for a while," she became serious.

"We fought the gods and won. I'd call that a win… Where are the gods anyway?" He looked around.

"I pushed them through time again," she almost seemed sad about it.

He grabbed her chin to make her look at him. "They were the ones in the wrong, not you. We were protecting these people."

"We may need to do it again!" Julie entered the tent. "The Pharaoh has arrived with his army of chariots."

"I guess I should get up," Mbizi's head began to pound as he sat up.

***

He stumbled outside and into a scene of people crying out to Moses, who stood on a rocky outcrop beside the sea.

Moses raised his staff high in the air. Suddenly, a powerful wind began to howl out of the east. Mbizi was stunned when the waters of the sea started to split. Eventually, there were two seas—one on either side. He stumbled down into the gap between them. The walls of water stood as high as the temple at Karnak. Mbizi was mesmerized, considering just how powerful this God of Israel must be to do something like this. By nightfall, the masses were walking through the canyon of water. A strong east wind howled past them on either side as they walked. Mbizi wondered if that was the arms of this god holding the waters back. When he reached the sea's eastern shore and joined his friends with the prophets on the outcrop, he could see the incredible view of the Hebrews crossing between the divided waters and the pillar of fire standing sentry on the western shore.

Mbizi could see the end of the migration. In a couple of minutes, everyone would be through. At this moment, the fiery pillar ascended to heaven in a flash. Mbizi decided to see what Thutmose was seeing:

He looked from one wall of water to the other. It gave Mbizi the sense that he didn't trust it. After a short hesitation, the Pharaoh said, "After them!" A trumpet sounded, and then the chariots raced into the canyon of the sea. The Pharaoh didn't go with them. He stood in his chariot, observing the charging attack. As he watched the stampede of chariots rapidly cover the ground fade into the distance, Mbizi shifted his view back to his own eyes.

As the thunder of hooves grew louder, the remaining Hebrews began to run as quickly as they could to the safety of the Eastern shore. The last of the people climbed the hill to the normal dry ground of the Sinai. Moses stepped to the edge of the outcrop and extended his staff toward the dust cloud gathering in the watery canyon. At that moment, the eastern wind ceased, and the walls of the sea began to collapse in on themselves.

Mbizi went back to Thutmose's perspective. He could see the chariots stumbling back toward him, but they were in a race they couldn't win. When the closest soldiers were still a few rods' distance from the shore, the water overtook them, and the sea swallowed up the Pharaoh's army.

Mbizi couldn't help but feel bad for his friend. Even though they were chasing the Hebrews, this time, it was Ra's fault. As camp was being set up, Mbizi had an odd sensation in the back of his mind. It was Isis. He headed up in the hills beyond the shore.

"My Horace," Isis flew down from the East. Her wings sparkled in the moonlight. "I just wanted to extend my gratitude for the banishment of Ra and his lieutenants."

"I was wondering why the Goddess of Life allowed the God of Israel to punish the people of Egypt." Mbizi was angry that Isis didn't do her duty.

"Is this not the outcome you desired? Did you not wish to see the Hebrews freed from bondage? As you once were?"

"There had to be a better way."

"His eminence is a stubborn man, and my father has been

corrupting his ear for several years. But now, thanks to you, I can begin to repair the damage."

Mbizi looked up at her. "So you're going to take Ra's place?"

"I will ensure that Egypt's future is prosperous and help restore what was lost. Now, be grateful that you have helped free these people. Leave Egypt to me."

The orb on her forehead pulsed. She spread her wings and took to the starry sky in one motion. Despite everything, Mbizi was still in awe that he regularly interacted with the gods.

"There you are," Shani came up the trail. "What did Isis want?"

"What all gods and kings want... Power."

"She has to be better than Ra," Shani reasoned.

"I guess time will tell."

<u>Amenemhat</u>

May 28th, 1446 B.C.

"I have much to cover today. When we joined the Exodus, I forgot to bring my journal and so much has happened. The terrible misery of the ten plagues gave way to the wonders of the famous miracles of the exodus. We battled the Gods of Egypt in the shadow of the pillar of fire. Then we walked on the seabed through a canyon of water, and finally, a smoking mountain announced the Ten Commandments. There are many others, such as manna from heaven and split rock. Every time we experience something from the bible, I can nearly bring myself back to faith. But some of the ways these "miracles" manifest themselves leaves room for doubt.

Julie gazed out over the Delta from the balcony at River Palace.

"Some things that the Gods of Egypt can do are not too dissimilar from what the God of Israel has done. Is it possible that Thutmose is right and that the God of Israel is the same type of entity that Ra and Isis are? Tomorrow, we go to Thebes for Prince Amenemhet's funeral. From the Bible, we knew this was coming, but does that necessarily mean that the God of Israel is the true god? I have so many conflicting thoughts and feelings about our experiences. The ten plagues brought death and destruction to Egypt. And who truly suffered? The innocent. Supposedly, the tenth

plague punished Pharaoh personally, but the method was so un-fair. The prince was a good man who was killed to get to his father. While Thutmose is generally a self-absorbed, power-hungry ruler, I can still understand his reticence to appease the God of Israel over his own gods. So now it's time to say goodbye to yet another friend.

"Will it ever get easier? Sixty years in the temporal ether has seen so many come and go. I've decided the best course of action is to focus on the good times with each of them. To that end—safe journey to the Field of Reeds, Prince Amenemhet."
-Julie Hall

"Are you ready?" Micheal's voice interrupted her solace.

"I think so."

"There's one more thing," Julie turned to face him.

"It appears we've had a visitor." Micheal held out the Goddess of Life's chain crown, and he was wearing a matching crown, except his had feathers on either side. In the middle was a glowing Bennu or phoenix. It was most certainly the crown of Osiris.

By early evening, the lamp glow from Karnak was welcoming their arrival. The Valkyrie drifted to a stop, and the masses went to the ground as they disembarked. Vizier Neferweben bowed and then led them to the Pharaoh.

"So it seems the gods decided to grant me their favor again," Thutmose greeted them bitterly.

"Isis promises new life for Egypt. She aims to rectify Ra's failure," Micheal seemed to improvise out of nowhere.

"She has sent us to oversee the prince's transition. She will provide new life for you as well, Your Majesty." She added.

The Pharaoh seemed unconvinced.

The procession led from Karnak to the Valley of the Kings, and the Isis was featured as the vessel to carry Amenemhat from the living side of the Nile to the shores of the afterlife. The symbolism continued when they reached the burial site. Julie's Isis throne was erected on the east side of the tomb, and Micheal's Osiris tomb was on the west side. As the representatives of the gods, they oversaw the ceremony. The sun approached the horizon, and Micheal stood and gave a blessing, welcoming Amenemhat to the underworld. The disc kissed the desert in time to his closing, and the gem on his crown began to glow intensely. Then, all at once, it burst into an explosion that illuminated the entire valley. What appeared to be a phoenix soared into the sky and then descended to Amenemhat's sarcophagus. It signaled the end of the ceremony, and the prince was sealed in his tomb. While the masses departed for the festival, Julie, Micheal, Shani, and Mbizi remained with the Pharaoh and Amenemhat's mother.

"My Lord Avalon, you carry the blessing of the God of the Underworld," Queen Satiah seemed unsure.

"Osiris knows the heart of every man. Your son's heart was pure. His fields will be evergreen," Micheal reassured her.

"Ra sanctified him as my successor," Thutmose was defiant.

"Ra abandoned Egypt to a rival god. He has abandoned you once more," Julie didn't hide her contempt.

"And where was the Goddess of Life? Did she not abandon Egypt as well?" Thutmose scowled.

"Ra demanded total obedience. Isis can now lead Egypt into a new era," Julie countered.

"Really? Then where is she?" The pharaoh opened his hands.

At that moment, a light showered the valley and Isis descended from the twilight sky. Her wings shimmered like a rainbow, illuminating everything. She came to a soft landing just a few feet from the six of them. Julie greeted her with a bow, and the rest of them followed suit.

"Be at ease, my loyal friends. I've come to bless you in your time of sorrow," Isis touched the queen on her head.

The look on the queen's face led Julie to believe this was the first time she had met Isis.

"Why didn't you do anything when Egypt was under assault?" the Pharaoh challenged.

"You do not speak so brashly, Your Majesty." Thutmose shied away from her piercing stare.

"I could not cross my father, but now that he has returned to the sky, I have taken his place. Egypt will be full of life once more." She placed her hand on Pharaoh's head. "Do not weep. The prince has transitioned to a new phase of his life, and I will fill your sorrow with a new son and heir. I promise you a long life to see him grow. You will raise the next god on Earth."

Thutmose seemed set at peace by her blessing. Tears streamed down both cheeks.

Isis stepped over to Mbizi and Shani. "My Lord and Lady of the West, I'm grateful for your service of life and wish you good fortune on your journey ahead." Isis touched both of their cheeks. Isis looked from Shani and Mbizi and then moved toward Julie and Micheal.

"My Lord Avalon, you have done my husband proud. Osiris lives through you." Isis kissed Micheal on the forehead, then removed Osiris's crown and nodded to him. Then she stepped over to Julie.

"You, Lady Avalon, have been a most loyal servant in the cause of life. You have truly been my voice on earth. It brings me great sadness to see you go, but I look forward to seeing you next time." Isis emphasized *next time*. She took Julie's face in her hands, leaned in, and kissed her forehead, then removed the crown. Isis stepped back, scanned the group, then spread her translucent wings,

"Egypt will be restored to glory." Then, with a few flaps, she soared up to the stars.

They all took the ship Isis back to Karnak.

"Well, Your Majesty, it's been an honor to serve you," Julie said as they dropped off the Pharaoh and queen for the festival.

"You're not staying for the celebration?" Thutmose asked.

"We've said our goodbyes to the prince, and after everything that's happened, we feel it's time to return to the West."

"You've been invaluable as advisors, and I have enjoyed our friendship, but I think you're right—the events of the last few months feel like a transition to a new phase of my rule. I shall put my trust in the Goddess of Life. Egypt will come back stronger than ever." Thutmose bowed to them, and his wife followed suit.

"It was our honor. You shall rise like a phoenix. Micheal bowed, and they all did the same.

They boarded the Valkyrie and the Isis and pushed off from the dock.

"I know I could use a break from all of this "god" stuff," Julie said in English.

"We still have to return to Sinai," Micheal reminded her.

"But after that, we need to go to Avalon to do some research," Julie decided.

"What do you think we should research?"

"A way to beat Ra—once and for all. I know we haven't seen the last of him."

They sailed through the night and arrived at River Palace by daybreak.

"Kesi, prepare everything for a week-long festival. We will be returning to Avalon at week's end," Julie instructed.

As the week grew older, the Nomarchs from the West Delta came to pay tribute individually. The palace was hectic. People from all over Egypt came to bid them farewell, including vizier Neferweben. The party ran night and day, and the number of guests swelled the population from a few hundred to several thousand. A buffet feast was set up on the final day, and all servants were given the day to enjoy the party.

They brought Kesi in for a private farewell.

"You've done an amazing job these past four years. We know our family's palace will be in good hands." Julie handed Kesi a drink.

"I was honored to host the Lords of Avalon. I pray your family shall not be absent for so long this time. We never would have survived the plagues of Israel if not for you. All of Egypt celebrated your contribution. The gods picked well." Kesi bowed.

They emerged to a crowd of friends and well-wishers. Mbizi and Shani were waiting for them. This time, they took the stairs down the landing platform. Vizier Neferweben was at the boarding ramp.

"Safe voyage, my friends." He bowed.

"The sea beckons." Micheal nodded, then headed up the plank.

"Farewell. The journey is long, but we are finally going home." Julie bowed, then boarded the Valkyrie.

A few hours later, the Egyptian coast began to fade with the dying light.

"Another chapter closes," Julie said as Micheal joined her on the bridge.

"Not quite." He raised a brow.

"Moses and the Israelites are another chapter," Julie said definitively.

As the Valkyrie drew closer to the Isis, the moon lit the darkening sea of their voyage.

Ark of the Covenant

A week after leaving River Palace, Shani was focused on the rough seas. They were passing south of a rocky coast, which Julie had told her was near the bottom of the world, about as far from Avalon as there was. Even though Shani trusted what Micheal and Julie had taught her about the world, sometimes she still had difficulty comprehending the concept of the world as a sphere—basically the shape of a pomegranate. Shani was impressed by the incredible power of the Sea God Nun. There were flashes of lightning along with a terrible wind from the east. Mountains of water were dwarfing the Isis. Shani's original beliefs became challenged by the knowledge she had gained since meeting the Lords of Avalon. But it had occurred to her that this new information didn't necessarily mean that the gods she had worshipped from childhood were not the true gods. The gods are magical; they can alter their appearance at will. That fact led her to conclude that the God of the Sea of Egypt and the God of the Sea of Mesopotamia were the same deity. Or the God of the Moon of Egypt was also the God of the Moon of Mycenae. Shani took a deep breath to settle herself and calmly guided the Isis through the maelstrom. As the sun emerged from the east, piercing through the spotty clouds, she wondered about Ra. As far as she knew, he was in between times. But the patron God of Egypt found a way to bring the sun back every morning. Shani was thankful for such favors, but her ambivalence still persisted.

Five days later, the coast of Sinai rose slowly out of the sea to greet them.

"Welcome back, My Lady of the West," Aaron kissed her hand.

"It has been 40 days. Has Moses still not come down from the mountain?" Shani looked around.

"We don't know what's become of him."

"It seems you're throwing quite the party." Mbizi indicated, the mass of people dancing before a calf made of gold.

"Aaron, what have you done?" Julie seemed livid.

"The people begged me."

"Your god explicitly said, 'No other gods before me.'" Shani realized the offense.

"Yes, we all heard the voice of your god admonishing you," Mbizi added.

"What should I do?"

"It's too late. God already knows. Moses will return shortly." Micheal shook his head.

There was a flash of lightning on the edge of the mountain; then thunder roared across the plain. Shani saw Moses holding two blue tablets as the group approached the golden calf. He smashed them down on the ground, and the party came to a sudden halt. The tablet sparked and ignited a flame. Then Moses stepped forward.

"Cast the unholy idol into the fire!" Their group approached Moses.

"You did nothing to stop this?" He scanned them.

"We've only just returned. We had no part in this," Shani explained.

"Aaron, what have you done?!"

"The people feared what became of you. They asked me to make them an idol that they may worship."

"You've brought them to great sin against God. The punishment will be harsh."

The retribution of the God of Israel was indeed harsh. Over the next few days, Shani watched as the Hebrews were forced to drink their idol as a powder within their water. Then Moses ordered a culling. The "righteous" Levites took up arms and slaughtered whole families. By the time it was all said and done, some 10,000 people had been buried in the ground.

"What kind of god demands so much blood?" Shani was disgusted with Moses.

"In only 40 days, my people directly disobeyed God's sacred edict. Better a few sinners die than the entirety of my people find eternal condemnation."

"I know they disobeyed; I just feel the punishment was too severe."

"After all you've seen, you still don't believe in the one true God?"

"The God of Israel is just one of many. I have met a multitude of gods. All of whom performed miracles. So how could I believe in just one?"

Moses studied her for a moment. "That is fair enough, and I know you don't have to believe to serve God's purposes for you. Your path is wrought with danger, but you have a strong spirit. Your part in the plan is of paramount importance."

"What part?" Shani didn't like feeling like the gods were counting on her.

"When the time is right, you will know. Now, there's a project that I need all of your help with. Let's go find the others." Moses led off toward the foot of the mountain. "Bezaleel, Aholiab, I need your leadership. Micheal, Julie, I need your skill and resources."

Everyone gathered around.

"The Lord bids us to build a sacred tabernacle and a holy ark to contain the word of God. Now, these are the Lord's instructions." Moses gave precise dimensions and materials to use for the project. He had two tablets carved out of stone.

"I must return and speak with God," Moses announced and then began the trek up the mountain.

"Aholiab will oversee the construction of the tabernacle. I will personally craft the ark out of wood. Moses said you could provide the gold and craft the necessary elements." Bezaleel instructed Micheal and Julie. He had been placed in charge of all the projects.

"Do we have that much gold?" Shani asked Micheal.

"We can acquire the requisite resources." Micheal led off into the desert.

They walked about half an hour until they approached a strange object. It was coming out of the ground. It looked like a column, but it was made of metal, and it penetrated the ground at an angle at the end of a ditch.

"What is that?" Mbizi asked.

"We call them mining bores. They are where we get all of our resources," Micheal explained.

"Are they from the gods?" Shani was examining the object.

It was at least five cubits in width; the end was perhaps three cubits above the ground. Julie touched some odd illuminations on the top, and a smaller column, as if by magic, began to rise out of the larger one.

Julie seemed to understand they had questions.

"These catches collect the valuable materials. This one has gold." She opened some kind of door, and the shiny metal began falling on the sledge they had tied to the mule.

"This one contains silver," Julie extended another small column.

"You never showed us these before." Mbizi protested.

"That's because there was never a need before," Micheal shrugged. "These drones have served us for a very long time. Most of the time, they're an afterthought. They supply Avalon and River Palace with the necessary resources. We don't even see them very often," he explained.

Shani studied Micheal and Julie, trying to decide if they actually were gods. When she compared them to gods she had met personally, they measured up pretty closely. They were exceptionally tall; they seemed to have immediate influence over everyone they came in contact with. In times of conflict, their super-human combat skills were mesmerizing. Even in the heat of battle, she would find herself stopping to marvel at their amazing feats. And finally, they had access to magical devices such as this "mining bore".

They denied their divinity, but what else could explain how they could manipulate time, just like Ra or Isis?

The mule sledge was completely loaded with gold and other metals. They dragged it all back to the main camp. Over the next few days, the gold was crafted into a magnificent sculpture of two winged cherubim. They flanked what Bezaleel called the mercy seat, which would act as the lid for the ark. Shani and Mbizi were assigned to plate the box with gold. They were given 50 small cylinders of gold. Each was a handbreadth in diameter and about the same in height. They were very heavy for their size. Micheal had told her that each one weighed 175 debens. By comparison, she only weighed about 500 deben, or about three times more than each cylinder. They were supposed to make the plating about a third of a digit in thickness. The lid, or mercy seat, was to weigh an equal amount. Shani did all the math calculations and determined that when the ark was complete, it would weigh an incredible 20,000 debens. Transporting such a massive object would probably require magic.

Mbizi heated the gold until it was soft. Then, using a stone press, they flattened the precious metal into sheets approximately one digit in thickness. Then, they layered all four sides of the box between sheets of gold. They placed the segments over a fire until the metal was about to melt and then pressed each one together with the stone press. The result was five panels of shittam wood coated in gold. The panels were about three digits thick.

The next few days were used to fix the panels together using the four corner posts. The posts had foot extensions about a handbreadth in length and rings for staves. They relied on a pulley system to move the massively heavy panels, each weighing about five times more than Shani.

"Have you ever seen so much gold?" Mbizi marveled.

"Obviously, Micheal and Julie have access to all kinds of gods' technologies and resources. We always knew that normal people couldn't build River Palace."

"So you still believe they're gods?"

"It's obvious."

"We've known them for years. We've seen their secret hideaway in Avalon. If they were gods, they would simply tell us."

"Are you sure about that?"

Mbizi didn't speak. Shani turned in the direction he was looking. The lid to the ark was magically floating over the ground at about her eye level.

"You might be right." Mbizi now agreed.

Shani and Mbizi then began coating the five-cubit length staves with gold. While they were doing that, Micheal and Julie expertly carved elaborate designs into the body of the ark. The weeks of labor had produced a most stunning holy box. They called it the "Ark of the Covenant". And now, the four of them carried the 20,000 deben container to present to Aaron. Shani could feel the energy pulsing through the stave. As they placed it on the mount in the tabernacle, just in front of the altar, the entire Ark glittered in the torchlight. It was the most mesmerizing thing she had ever seen.

"Well done, all of you. Truly a box worthy of God." Aaron proceeded to sanctify the Ark with prayers and ceremony. Shani took one last look before leaving. They were told that the Ark would now become sacred, and only the holy priests and the prophets would be able to look upon the Ark without being struck down dead by the God of Israel. She certainly didn't doubt the threat after everything that happened with the ten plagues of Egypt.

A month passed, and Moses finally returned from the mountaintop. He carried the two sapphire stone tablets he had departed with, but now they were engraved in Hebrew with a list of laws the faithful would be required to follow. The tablets were extraordinary.

"I see you completed the tabernacle," Moses indicated.

"And the Ark of the Covenant is in place in the Holy of Holies," Micheal added.

Moses gave a speech to the masses of Hebrews, instructing them what their god commanded. Then, he came to talk to the four of them.

"I know you intend to take your leave of us once and for all, but there's one final thing I would show you." He signaled all of them to follow him. He removed the lid of the Ark. At that point, Shani remembered Aaron's warning and began to flee.

"It's okay, Lady West. God has permitted you." Moses stopped her. "I have a few things to share with you all," Moses said once they were in the inner sanctum.

"Lord and Lady Avalon, I know you both struggle with your faith, but God is pleased with all of your efforts in service of him. Just continue to follow your heart, and you will see home again. That's a promise... Now, Lord and Lady West, I know you don't believe God is the one true God, but he has chosen you for an essential task. The fate of the world will depend on your decisions."

"What does that mean?" Shani suddenly felt nauseous.

"At some point in the future, you will be faced with a difficult choice. Your decision will determine the course of history."

"You're a prophet. What will be my decision?"

"I cannot say. You will have to do this on your own... Now it is time to say farewell."

Moses gave them a nod.

As the Isis drew farther and farther from shore, Shani tried to study her heart's inner thoughts, but she heard nothing. She hoped that she would know what to do when the time came. After all, the future of the world was depending on her.

CHAPTER 21: EXIT TO AVALON

M ICHEAL GUIDED THE VALKYRIE into the secret cove, followed closely by the Isis. The secret underground facility beneath Avalon in Gibraltar had survived the double apocalypse relatively intact, but 500 years of dust still covered most of the sections. They had visited a few times for a few weeks but only used a few of the sections. Now that they were planning a multi-year stay, they would need to clean and refurbish the entire facility.

"Now, I know both of you have seen some of our more advanced technology, but this compound may give you the impression that we are gods, or, at least, of the gods. Neither of these would be the truth. We've tried to introduce you slowly to our more strange devices. They might seem magical at first, but we will try to impart understanding. It will be essential for our preparations."

Micheal guided them to the deeper hidden sections of the bunker. The main sections were relatively small and were primarily for living. The entry section was on the dock level, running the entire 200-foot length of the facility. It contained everything needed for servicing their ships, from spare parts to cleaning elements. The section was 50 feet deep and extended out in front of the main compound. The storage section sat on the same level, extending another 200 feet behind the entry section. The main compound was 200 feet by 200 feet, three 20-foot-high levels above the storage. The top level was a fabrication factory. The level below that was a recreation center, and the level above the storage was living quarters in the front, and laboratories in the back.

"So this area is where we study different things in order to make many useful technologies. We call them the labs."

"You intend to teach us more about the world so we might assist you in this study?" Mbizi asked.

"Yes. It will be a challenge, but I know both of you are more than capable. Now, up these stairs is a leisure area for relaxing and physical activity. We likely won't be going outside a whole lot."

"This will just be another unusual experience," Shani chimed in.

"And now, for what will likely be one of the most difficult places for you to grasp, this is what we call a factory. We use these... devices... to make many helpful items."

Micheal began pulling the sheet covers off of all of the assembly lines. Five hundred years of dust and weathering showed their evidence.

"How long has this place been here?" Mbizi asked.

"About 700 years," Micheal said.

"Why didn't you show us this place the last couple of times we came here?" Shani was examining one of the robots.

"Because of the way you are looking right now."

"So why are you showing us now?" Mbizi turned to him.

"We are certain we have not seen the last of the Gods of Egypt, and we don't want to be caught at a disadvantage again. As it pertains to you, we think you need greater enlightenment to prepare you to face the gods."

Six weeks later, the whole facility was up and running. Micheal sat in the music studio, strumming a guitar.

"May I interrupt?" Julie entered the studio.

"Always."

"It's been a while since we made music together."

"Is that what you want for your birthday?"

"I think 90 celebrations is enough."

Micheal set the instrument down and stepped over to Julie. He tucked her hair behind her ear, then said, "Oh, I fully intend to see what 91 looks like." He searched the depths of her eyes. "I can see it."

"What do you see?"

He put his hand on her neck, his thumb caressing her throat. "I see the pain of Salem, I see the Goddess of Love, I see the strain of half a century of battles, I see the guilt of billions, and I see the weight of history on your shoulders."

A tear came, and Julie looked away. Micheal turned her back to make eye contact again.

"But more than all of that, the timeless beauty of your eyes cast a mere pale shade on the flawed perfection of your soul." He wiped the tears away. "And finally, I see the pure love you continue giving me after nearly 60 years." He paused for a moment, taking in the totality of her soul, then took her lips in his.

Julie made quick work of his clothes, and he returned the favor. Then she jumped up and wrapped her legs around his hips. He found the sweet spot, and they found a rhythm as he pressed her against the wall. After a few minutes, Micheal carried her over to the sofa in the corner of the studio. She suddenly reversed him, and he was on his back, looking up at heaven, sweat dripping from her nose. Then she kissed him. She increased the tempo of their harmony. As they built pace together, she arched her back. His hands enjoyed the softness of her body, and then they arrived at the summit together, and Julie collapsed on top of him. After a minute, Julie sighed deeply, then rolled over in his arms.

"Do you ever think about having kids?"

"Occasionally"

"I don't think it's ever going to happen." There was a hint of sorrow in her voice. "I mean, I'm 91. Over 60 years ago, I was planning on being a mother. And as amazing as some of the things we've been able to experience in this crazy life may be, I can't help but feel cheated. What good is immortality if we can't experience all aspects of life."

"What has made you think about this now? You've only ever mentioned it a few times.

"And you never bring it up."

"I felt there was no point. When it was at least a couple centuries away."

"Do you want children?"

"I've said I did on multiple occasions, so, once again, why now?"

"I don't know. I thought about turning 91 and just got a flush of introspection. I thought of everything I'd never get to do. We already had over a century to go, then we missed our jump in the 20th century, and the road grows 50 years longer."

"We'll make it home..."

"Will we? I'm not so sure. Do you really think we'll never miss another jump?"

"That was a unique situation."

"Really? Because I would say our Sun God problem is pretty similar to the Cavendishes. I mean, isn't that why we're here?"

"Jules, I don't know everything that is going to happen in the future, but I promise everything is going to be okay."

Micheal began running his fingers through her hair.

"I've told you before, don't make promises you can't keep." Julie began to rise.

Micheal sat up and wrapped his arms around her waist to stop her. He set his chin on her shoulder.

"To me, it's a promise already kept because we've shared a timeless love over 60 incredible years, and whatever comes in the future, that's something no one can ever take from us. You promised to love me from now until the end of time. So, yes, everything will be all right." He kissed the side of her neck.

Julie turned with tears streaming. They locked eyes; he wiped her cheeks.

"I love you, Micheal." She kissed him passionately, and they went for another round.

<u>Enlightenment</u>

Two moons had come and gone since hey had arrived at the secret chamber of the gods. Mbizi was sitting in the labs, trying to comprehend what was before him. A glove was sitting on the table, and several small balls were floating above it.

"Allow me to demonstrate." Micheal picked up the glove, and with some kind of magic, the balls came with it. "These orbs are connected to this glove by a force that cannot be seen. I can manipulate this connection by touch. I tap here, and the first pellet is activated. Then, if I want to send it, I simply flick the same finger in the direction I want it to go."

Micheal showed the same action as he explained. The ball flew extremely fast, hitting a predetermined target.

"Then a simple tap on the side of the finger in use summons the pellet back to you." Like magic, the ball came right back to the glove.

"When you want the pellets out of the way, you simply tap your thumb and little finger, and they go into storage on the back of your hand, like this." The balls seemed to adhere to the back of the glove, just behind the knuckles. "You should practice until it all becomes natural to you." Micheal handed him the glove, then left.

Mbizi spent a couple of hours working with the glove. The whole time he was trying to figure out just what was allowing the glove to control the balls. Unseen forces and energy flows still didn't bring understanding.

"What are you doing, my love?" Shani entered the chamber.

"Learning to control some divine magic."

"So, just like me, you still haven't accepted their protests against godly influence?"

"Just look at this place. Come with me."

They went up the stairs to the factory. One of the "assembly lines" was actively making some strange small balls. There were different "machines" that were moving by themselves. He would have thought them to be living things if he hadn't been told otherwise.

"I know they told us this was all just a more advanced version of a rope-pulley system, and they tried to explain the exact process that we are witnessing, but just look at all of this and tell me the gods aren't involved."

"We are certainly privileged. My understanding of how the world and everything in it works has not diminished my awe of the gods. In fact, the more I learn, the more I want to worship the incredible gods that make it all work."

More moons came and went, and the Lords of Avalon continued to open his and Shani's eyes to the reality of the universe.

"Today, we are going to help replenish the eye in the sky," Julie announced.

There was a large metal pinnacle that looked like an obelisk. Mbizi understood that the eye in the sky was a swarm of tiny orbs in the heavens that collectively watched the world from above, and through some kind of magic, Micheal and Julie could see what the eye in the sky could see. He wondered at the power of the Sky God Horace.

"Time for launch," Julie said as she tapped her fingers on one of the strange glass tablets in her hand.

A small roar came from the pinnacle, and Mbizi could feel the earth begin to shake, and the metal object began to rise toward the clear blue sky. On the bottom, there was a light that could nearly match the sun. He became transfixed, watching as the pinnacle became smaller and smaller until it disappeared.

Mbizi reflexively attempted to see through the eye in the sky with the sight of Horace. Suddenly, a most peculiar sight appeared before his eyes. At the top of his view was total darkness. It was very much like the night sky. There were many visible stars. Below was the most beautiful blue glow, curving like a rainbow. Below that was an amazing mixture of colors. Dark blue, green, white, and brown. Mbizi didn't know what he was seeing, but he couldn't stop staring.

"It appears I have an intruder," a voice broke the silence. Mbizi tried to come back to himself, but the connection remained. "You can't escape that easily." The being was clearly holding the connection.

"Who are you?" Mbizi asked.

"You haven't forgotten after all these years? No, you're someone else. You understand Egyptian, but you're at the pillars of Hercules."

"Are you the Eye in the Sky?"

I am the Sky God and King of Olympus, and you possess the power of Horace."

"Isis chose me to inherit this power from our Sky God."

"Then Horace is dead?"

"Ra killed him."

"That is not possible," the mysterious King of Olympus protested.

"Ra can stop time."

There was silence for a moment.

"Then there is no time to lose. Beware, Son of Horace, war is coming." And the connection was severed.

"Mbizi?" Shani touched his shoulder.

"I just talked to the King of Olympus."

"The King of Olympus?" Julie was staring at him.

"That's who he said he was."

"Did he tap into your mind?" Micheal inquired.

"First, I saw through his eyes, then he saw through mine. Is he the Eye in the Sky?"

"He's not what we were working to fix, if that's what you mean." Julie looked at Micheal.

"The King of Olympus is Zeus," Micheal answered on cue.

"You really think so?" Julie seemed nervous.

"Norse, Egyptian, why not Greek?" Micheal shrugged.

"Who is Zeus?" Shani asked.

"In Greece, Zeus if the God of the Sky and Lightning, and he is the King of the Gods of Olympus," Micheal explained.

"What did he say to you?" Julie turned to Mbizi.

"When I realized he had detected me, I tried to break the connection, but he stopped me. He thought I was Horace. When he found out I wasn't, he asked about Horace. Apparently, they knew each other. I told him Ra had killed Horace. When I told him why that was possible, the king became scared and broke the link. Oh, and he said war is coming. Do you know what he meant?" Mbizi was becoming worried now.

"I don't know, but whatever it is, we need to make sure we're ready." Micheal seemed to be formulating a plan. "On top of everything we were already doing, we need to try to develop our temporal powers. And Mbizi, I have a big ask of you—I need you to reach out to as many gods around the world as possible. See what we can learn from them."

"I would be happy to. Where do I begin?"

"I will make you a list."

"I hate when this happens." Julie seemed annoyed.

"And once again into that breach." Micheal shook his head.

Three Years in Avalon

January 12, 1442 B.C.

Today is Micheal's 91ˢᵗ birthday, which marks 64 years since we fell. In all that time, we've rarely had a moment's rest. So the last three years in Avalon have been quiet nourishment for our souls; while many of the gods we have talked to portend a coming time of chaos, we have been enjoying the simple life. We have been preparing and doing much research on temporal energy to discover how it seems to change anyone regularly exposed to it. Though we didn't know it at the time, the first indication of the effect came when my old friend, Melina Hellas, developed the ability to see past, present, and future events. And she never jumped through time. She was only present at our arrival and departure from the 33ʳᵈ century and then at our departure from the 29ᵗʰ century.

Shani and Mbizi both have time-related powers. And Ra has demonstrated many different temporal powers. So clearly, exposure to temporal energy can cause some kind of reaction in the human body, allowing some level of inter-control over temporal energy, which brings me to us.

Micheal and I have never discovered any overt influence over time. The incident when Ra tried to kill us is still a mystery. Micheals' memory could only provide so much information to study. A more helpful manifestation of these powers is the one Mbizi inherited from Horace.

In the past three years, he has tried to reach out to as many gods from various pantheons as possible. Zeus was gone, and none of the other Olympians were there either. There was more success in other places. The list includes Rhea and Ariadne from Minoa, Arinna from the Hittites, Kiririsha from the Elamites, there was Shangti and Xi-Wang-Mu in China, the Indus Valley gave Kali, Shiva, and Vishnu. There was even someone calling themselves the Great Creator in North America. But by far, the most active of pantheons was from Mesopotamia.

There were many Anunnaki. They matched Ishtar's Babylonian Gods. It seems these beings are the ones she was interacting with back in the Age of Atlantis. Several even visited Avalon. The most impressive of these encounters was when Marduk and Inanna came together. Marduk was the King of the Anunnaki and was twice as tall as Micheal. He had a dark complexion with glowing red eyes and a beard. He was only wearing pants, and his muscular torso looked like it was carved out of stone. The most imposing of the two, however, was Inanna. She was at least 11 feet tall and wore nothing but a crown. I only came up to her hip. She also had a large pair of black wings protruding from her back. Her hair matched her wings, and she had glowing red eyes. She wasted little time trying to seduce Micheal and Mbizi. Ultimately, they visited for an hour or so and claimed to have no fear of Ra, but they were in the minority. Most of the gods fear him. The revelation of dozens more mythical gods has only deepened the mystery of their nature. And it has only added to my hesitancy at opening my mythical gift from Pandora.

"I think we are ready to start the scan," Julie said as she activated the chamber.

"Aren't you being a little suspicious? You don't honestly believe this is *the* Pandora's Box?" Micheal had been trying to convince her to open it since they were reunited.

"The more these mythical gods have shown up, the more leery I become, especially after Zeus."

"We know Pandora was not the Pandora from Greek Mythology."

"You know as well as I do that the mythologies are just that. But clearly, they were based on actual beings. So who knows if the story of Pandora's Box isn't based on my decision to open this."

"Just for the record, I think Julie is wise in this matter," Shani said.

The chamber ran some scans.

"It's generating a tiny number of tachyons and has a fairly strong high-band EM signature. I think it's some kind of transmitter."

"Do you think it has any temporal effect?" Micheal wondered.

"I don't know. Some of these readings are pretty low, but that might change if we open it."

"So, are we going to open it?" Micheal prodded.

"No. I want to do more research."

"Okay, what do we do now?" Mbizi asked.

"Now, we've been in this compound for too long. We're going to take a trip, and when we get there, Mbizi, I need you to reach out to someone."

"Who?" Shani questioned.

"You'll find out when we get there."

"Get where?" Micheal raised a brow.

"A beautiful place for a honeymoon."

Three days later, they arrived in Bermuda.

"At least we'll have the island to ourselves. There are hardly even any animals here."

Micheal found a place to dock. Then, they found a natural beach nearby and relaxed for the rest of the day. The next morning, they returned to the beach.

"Now, Mbizi, I need you to reach out to the god David." Julie was a little nervous about contacting David. Based on the last few encounters, David didn't seem like the type who liked to waste time.

There was an emerald flash, and then he was there.

"Julie Hall, what can I do for you?"

"What do you know about a coming war between the gods?"

David looked at her for a moment. "What do you care?"

"So there is one coming?"

"I know you've decided to stay out of what's coming."

"Why would you say that? We came here to talk to you specifically."

"You came here for sentimental reasons. I could have just as easily come to Avalon. You are ambivalent about destiny."

"I don't believe in destiny."

"You fear it."

"I fear nothing."

David just seemed to be studying her. Then he scanned the others. He reached out and touched the Fenrir scar on her neck. She was determined not to retreat.

"All the battles, all the times you've overcome the odds or done amazing feats, or the moments when history, or even time, was shaped by your influence."

"What's the point?!"

"You can't lie to me, Aphrodite: I can read your soul."

"I'm not Aphrodite."

"Millions of people worshipped you. You answered prayers with love. You bound unions of matrimony. They built statues of you."

"I didn't do any of that."

"Belief made it happen. What qualifies someone to be a god? All those people had faith in you."

"They were all fools," Julie was becoming annoyed.

"Were they? What about all those people you saved from terrible fates?"

"It was all meaningless." Julie was on the verge of tears.

"Because of Aphrodite, people saw their child take their first step; a father heard his daughter say 'dada' for the first time. People had years of family get-togethers, earning educations, starting businesses, creating art, or falling in love."

"Then they all died."

"Everybody dies. What really matters is that they lived."

"Why are you telling me all of this? What does it have to do with everything?"

"You feel like if destiny calls you to be the savior of the world, you will fail. And that's what you fear."

"Do I have a destiny? Has God called me to be a savior?"

"There is no destiny. Only choices."

"But we know what will happen in our future. Isn't that fate? Or destiny?"

"You may be from *a* future, but the future has not been written. There is no fate but what we make for ourselves. You still have to choose."

Julie closed her eyes. She could feel the weight of the future bearing down.

"What do you know about Ra?" Micheal finally asked.

"I have known Ra for millennia. There was always a mutual respect, but now he has unmatched power. What would *anyone* do with it?"

"Are you going to stop him?" Shani seemed hopeful.

"I don't have that power."

"What do you know about this?" Julie produced the box.

"Where did you get that?" David seemed genuinely curious.

"Shem gave it to me 400 years ago."

"Pandora guarded it jealously... I don't know much about it, except it holds great power. It is very dangerous."

"So I was right not to open it."

"Whatever is inside that box strikes fear in the gods."

"Well... David... Thank you for your time, and your advice." Julie felt she was pressing her luck, occupying his time.

"Julie, I know you've struggled for many years to understand your place in the story of time. Don't concern yourself with fate or destiny. Trust this..." he indicated her heart. "... It will lead you true." David stepped back. "That's good advice for the rest of you too." He vanished in a flash.

After a two-week beach vacation, they returned to Avalon to make final preparations for the next jump.

<u>Chosen?</u>

Shani finished combat training and went to the factory. She watched the assembly lines, making various useful items as if by magic. But the years at Avalon had brought an understanding of many things. She now knew that one of the mining bores would deliver various kinds of materials. Then, the processors would liquify them and send the proper amounts to the molds. After all the necessary components were ready, a computer system would tell the assembly line how to assemble the components into a finished project. And just like that, a small box appears, as if by magic.

Understanding the process didn't make it any less magical. Just like learning that Julie and Micheal were the fallen Gods of Atlantis, Aphrodite and Koios only increased her respect for them. They had been worshipped in the distant past but lost much of their power when divine weapons were used to destroy Atlantis. And still, while they are forced to live as humans, they continue to accept responsibility for time. And protect the innocent. While they humbly protest their own divinity.

One question that had been on her mind since Bermuda was about destiny. The God David had told Julie she wasn't chosen. Shani wondered if *she* was.

She'd come a long way since she met Micheal. The scared slave girl was now powerful. Her travels through times had caused the gods to gift her some of their power. She had gone toe-to-toe with the Sun God multiple times and lived to tell about it. And now, years of training and education had made her a formidable warrior and high-class lady. The only reason an orphan girl from Saba could rise so high was because the gods had chosen her. If there was no fate but what we make for ourselves, then Shani decided, she would accept the god's sponsorship, and prepare to face Ra or whoever was the biggest threat to the just rule of Egypt, or even the whole world.

Mbizi reached out to her from outside of Avalon. She went to his location. Shani arrived on the west beach. The sun was low toward the horizon, and a picnic was set up.

"Our time here draws to a close. Soon, we jump to the future. I thought we could have a nice relaxing evening," Mbizi indicated for her to join him on the blanket.

As they ate their burgers and fries, they talked.

"I've been thinking a lot about destiny," Shani looked at Mbizi.

"Do you believe David—that there is no destiny?"

"Do you remember the day we first met?"

"The sea had overflowed its shores and swallowed your village."

"It must have been what Julie calls a 'tsunami'. It washed my family away, and at eight years old, I had to survive on my own for weeks."

"Yes, and then our caravan came and took you in."

"Looking back now, it feels like fate. First, I met you, and we grew to love each other. Then, we just happen to pick up a god. He sets us free, and now we have become important in a way we never would have. Doesn't that sound like destiny?"

"You were always destined for greatness."

"What about your destiny?"

Mbizi touched her cheeks, "My destiny is to make love to you this instant." He kissed her passionately. She gave it back, and they stumbled, tumbling to the sand. Shani kept the vigor up. They rolled in the shallow waves until she ended up on top. She threw off her soaked top and then met his lips once more. She found he was ready, so she mounted up while he searched her body with his hands. They found a rhythm between the waves. Mbizi suddenly thrust very hard, coinciding with a huge wave that carried them higher up the beach. As the water receded, they continued toward the mountaintop, reaching the pinnacle as the next tidal surge washed past them. Shani rolled over, and she and

Mbizi sat side-by-side. She lay her head on his shoulder and took in the beauty of the golden trail crossing the sea to the sun kissing the horizon. The whole world seemed to be shimmering gold.

The next day, they boarded a smaller boat and set sail for a place beyond the sea called "Florida". They had briefly visited a few years back when they first went to America. They spent a few days setting everything up, and now they were set for the jump. The moment arrived, and Shani was pulled into the swirling green. She was flying through the portal when she felt everything slow down and then finally stop. Shani found herself swimming in light. Then a voice spoke.

"Lady of the West." Shani instantly knew it was Ra. "When are you going?"

"I will never tell you."

"Come now, child, I don't want to hurt you. I want you to join me."

"You've tried to kill me and my husband and my friends. You're evil."

"You don't understand the difference. Do you honestly believe Isis is any different? Our struggle for power spans millennia. Everything was beautiful and peaceful before my daughter stole my throne."

Ra was a blurry image. Then he came into focus.

"Isis never tried to kill us."

"That was all an honest case of mistaken identity. I'm prepared to let the past stay in the past."

"What about all the other gods from around the world? They're all terrified of you."

"If they choose to join me, they won't have anything to fear."

"That's exactly my point."

And with that, the light accelerated around her. She came to a bright flash at the end of the portal, and everything went black.

PART IV: THEOMACHY

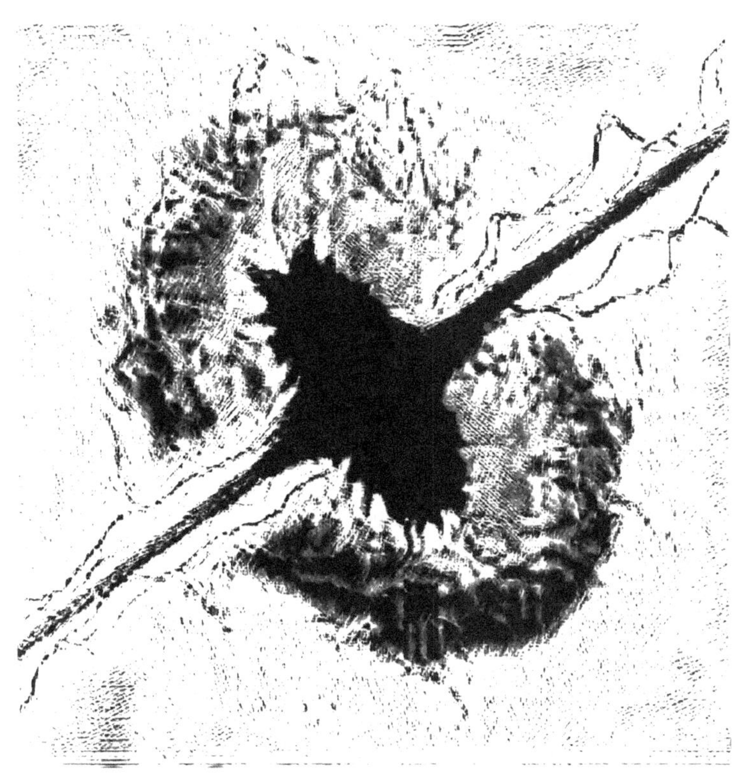

CHAPTER 22: MISSING

M ICHEAL CAME OUT OF his malaise and tried to assess his surroundings.

"Julie?"

"I'm here." She was covering her eyes with her hand.

"Have either of you seen Shani?" Mbizi sounded concerned.

"I'm just getting my senses back," Micheal admitted.

"How far could she be? I've searched the entire area I woke up in."

"She should have landed about 50 cubits from you," Julie informed him.

"Maybe she went to use the bathroom?" Micheal suggested.

"Have you tried to see through her eyes?" Julie asked.

Mbizi closed his eyes, bowing his head slightly. "I can't find her anywhere?" Mbizi said with urgency.

Micheal connected to the sky-net and began to search for Shani. After several hours, he came up empty. The main shortcoming of such a search was that it had to be targeted to a narrow band, and if the person in question were not in direct sight of the sky, it wouldn't be able to detect them.

"What are we going to do?" Julie asked.

"We need to secure the pods. Then we can try an expanded

search."

"We have to keep looking!" Mbizi insisted.

"We've searched for hours and covered a lot of ground. I've done numerous scans with the sky-net, and you've attempted to locate her with your power. We'll try again in a few hours, but it's vital we do not lose our technical advantage."

Mbizi looked like he felt betrayed.

"I understand how you feel better than anyone." Micheal looked at Julie.

"Shani is well trained. She's easily capable of taking care of herself. But why don't you continue looking? When we have hidden the technology, we will come to help you."

After a moment, Mbizi said, "For as long as it takes."

"Absolutely."

Mbizi headed off.

"What do you think our chances are?" Julie asked.

"We would have found her by now. For how thoroughly I scanned the area, there would be no place for her to be hiding. And the fact that he can't see her..."

"What do you think could have happened? We have been so meticulous in our calculations."

"It's, of course, possible we made a mistake. It's not like we're perfect, but that's why we go over the numbers countless times."

Julie looked at him, then said, "You're thinking about the Cavendishes, aren't you?"

"They caught our wake both times and skipped a stop. What if there was some unknown influence on the conduit? Shani might be in the 11th century by now. Or even the 14th century. There's no way to know."

Julie sat there, shifting her eyes back and forth.

"Why don't you just say what you want to say?"

"I've advised against bringing them with us. I know they are friends, but we've said goodbye to many friends. And now we've gone so far as to train them in martial arts and given them modern knowledge of math and science."

"They are no more dangerous to history than we are. And with more capability, that wherever Shani happens to be, she'll be okay."

"I don't think that knowledge is going to appease Mbizi."

"I think the pods are secure. I've just signaled for the Valkyrie to sail to our location. It should arrive in Massachusetts Bay tomorrow."

"I think we should go help Mbizi."

"Good idea."

They headed off in the direction they had gone. After about five minutes, Mbizi was running up the path.

"I think I found a major clue. Come with me."

They followed him to a small village.

"I carefully surveyed the settlement until I saw that," Mbizi whispered as he indicated a small hut in the center.

"What is it?" Julie asked.

"From the other side, I saw what appears to be one of the devices used to connect to the sky-net."

Julie looked at Micheal. "Do we try to go ninja on this one? Or do we just go talk to them?"

"I don't know if they speak any language we'd understand. I guess we go, ninja."

They returned to the landing area to prepare.

"So, what's the plan?" Mbizi was fidgeting.

"The moon sets around 3 AM. That will give us good cover. Julie will search the northern structures, and I'll search the south. Mbizi, you will go for the phone in the central structure. Remember, just neutralize the guards."

"I want to look for Shani."

"Julie and I have much more experience in these searches. I promise, if she's in the village, we'll find her."

They dressed entirely in black, and as the light of the moon went out behind the horizon, they began their sweep. Micheal pushed aside the first animal skin door to find ten sleeping people of various ages, gently illuminated by the light of the night coals that rested in the firepit. A quick search of four more huts found a similar arrangement. Julie reported the same discovery. They gingerly crossed the open ground to the center structure.

"I got it," Mbizi whispered.

"She's not here," Micheal shook his head to quell his friend's reaction.

"We need to go." Julie immediately headed back the way they'd come.

Following quickly after, Micheal found Mbizi had successfully neutralized both sentries. As they neared the edge of the settlement, a small figure emerged from the shadows. It suddenly stopped in their path. A second later, the girl screamed and then ran away. After that, it was a mad scramble through the dark forest. A fifteen-minute sprint later, they were back to the shore.

"*In through the nose, out through the mouth*," Micheal thought the instructions to recover his breath.

When they had calmed down, Micheal just listened for a while.

"I don't think we were pursued."

"We better keep an ear out tonight," Julie suggested.

"How do you know Shani's not there?" Mbizi had tunnel vision.

"All the perimeter shelters were full of sleeping villagers. If Shani had been there, she would have been under guard."

"This is Shani's device." Mbizi held it out.

"Let me have a look," Micheal began his examination.

It was Shani's phone, but now it was just a hunk of glass.

"The kill switch has been tripped. That means Shani is at least 20 miles out of range."

"But this means she has to be here somewhere." Mbizi tore up the path.

They searched all the next day without luck. Near sundown, they approached the shore when a couple dozen warriors surrounded them.

"To the ship!" Micheal charged at the east side of the cordon.

They unleashed arrows, but they just deflected off. He plowed through with Julie and Mbizi on his heels. Using their parkour skills to outrun the men, the Valkyrie drifted to the shore as they broke into the clearing. Micheal felt arrows bouncing off his back. Then he turned on the speed, leaping on the deck. Their pursuers came to an abrupt halt at the sight of the ship. Julie got them underway. Micheal became light-headed, and then everything faded to black.

The Search

Mbizi wanted to get back to the search, but Micheal had been struck in the side of the neck by an arrow. Julie was performing surgery. An hour later, his friend was stable. Mbizi spent hours running scans on the sky-net, all ending in failure. With no other ideas, he reached out to friendly gods.

"My Lord of the West, how can I help you?" Isis was somewhere in the heavens.

"Do you know where Lady West is?"

"I've not seen her in nearly 200 years."

"So she's not in Egypt?"

"How did you get separated?"

"When we arrived in this time, she wasn't with us. We found her communicator."

"I'm sorry I can't help. I've been preoccupied with Ra. Good luck, My Lord." Isis severed the connection.

Mbizi didn't know why he thought a goddess would help him. Ever since she chose him to carry the legacy of Horace, he'd felt a connection to her. But maybe it had all just been random. It's not like Isis had ever done much to help them through any other challenges.

Mbizi searched for other gods like David, Marduk, Inanna, Zeus, and Thor, but they were all apparently out of range. He went to Julie.

"I understand the situation with Micheal, but we can't abandon the search for Shani."

"Until Micheal is recovered enough, I can't leave the ship. But we could sail up and down the coast, and you could go from tribe to tribe looking for her."

"How would I communicate with them? I don't speak dozens of languages like you."

"You have images of Shani on your device, correct? Just show them her image and indicate to ask if they've seen her."

Julie waved her hand, palm up, then pointed at her eye, then at her communicator. With a plan in place, the real search began.

The first stop was a place called Nova Scotia. Mbizi trekked inland for about half an hour when he was intercepted by two sentry warriors pointing arrows at him. He held up his hands and gave a greeting. A look of confusion passed between them.

"I'm looking for someone," he decided to try. They said something he didn't understand. "I have a gift for you," he said as he slowly reached for his bag. Their eyes were fixed on his hand, their fingers ready to loose their arrows. He deliberately slid his fingers into the pouch, retrieving two silver necklaces. He bowed, extending the offering. A moment passed, and Mbizi glanced up. The men were cautiously lowering their bows. They closed the distance in sync, accepting the gifts. They seemed pleased with the offer and signaled for him to follow them. Five minutes later, they entered a small village.

A few dozen people came from all the different huts, eyes wide, scanning him. His escorts said something to everyone else.

"I have a gift for all of you," Mbizi added. He retrieved a bag of chocolate balls and proceeded to eat one, then gave the bag to his nearest escort. They passed his new offering around to the crowd of people. The gesture seemed to relax his hosts, so he addressed why he was here. He pulled out his communicator and showed an image of Shani. He tapped his chest twice, pointed to his eye, then at the screen. As he said:

"I'm trying to find her."

All eyes went wide. Mbizi opened his arms, palms up, circled the people with his right hand, then pointed at his eye, then at Shani. One of them reacted by addressing the crowd. After conferring for a moment, the leader faced him. Their eyes dropped, and their mouth turned down. Clearly, none had seen Shani. Mbizi gave another sweet parting gift and left the way he came.

Weeks passed, and he followed the same routine in village after village.

"This is where I grew up," Julie guided the Valkyrie to a stop on the north riverbank. "In my time, we call this place Richmond." She closed her eyes, and a tear came down from her lids, and then she led the way down the plank. They climbed an embankment, then went a couple of rods distance. "This will be my home 3300 years from now," Julie was gazing intently, as if she was seeing her future/past.

Mbizi thought about his past. He realized he was now five centuries further in time. Some of the concepts were still difficult to wrap his brain around. Most people didn't even live half a century, and now he had seen parts of a history ten times that long. Becoming a time rogue gave Mbizi a new perspective on life and purpose; seeing how fleeting human existence is sparked a whole new set of questions: Is there a meaning to life, or are we just pawns of the gods? Will anyone remember anything we do? Or only our personal posterity. If the only people who would take note of his existence were his children, he needed to find Shani even more. It had only been just over a month, but he was filled with constant worry. He felt he understood more about how Micheal reacted to his separation from Julie.

"Do you think you'll ever see home again?"

"Only in my memories." Julie closed her eyes and faced up as the cold, wet flakes began falling down. It was starting to snow.

Mbizi decided it was time to look for villages. He returned to the Valkyrie in failure as the last golden light of the sun sparkled off the fresh coat of white.

"Mbizi, you need to prepare yourself for the likelihood we will never find her."

Micheal's words were a gut punch.

"I'm not giving up!"

"That's not what I said. I just don't want you to become consumed with this."

"What if it was Julie?"

"You've already seen that situation; I barely survived it."

"This is different. We know Shani is here somewhere." Mbizi held up her communicator.

"But you don't detect her; the sky-net has failed so far, you've asked every village for a thousand miles... I don't know what else to do."

"We keep going till we find her," Mbizi decided. He refused to give up. No matter how long it took or how far they had to go, he would find Shani. He knew she was here somewhere. Shani would never give up on him, so he would go to the ends of the earth for her.

"We need to talk to the tribe we stole the communicator from." Mbizi began prayerful meditation to the goddess Renenet, asking for good fortune on his quest to find Shani. Mbizi had not honored the gods often enough over the past few years, becoming prideful in his understanding of the world. Perhaps reasserting his faith would change his luck.

Tunnel Vision

Nearly a year of searching went in vain to find Shani. Julie felt there was no point in continuing the nonstop voyage, but Mbizi insisted. So, here they were, 200 miles inland, on the Yellow River in China. They continued the strategy of body and sign language, along with the images of Shani. They had been receiving many stares. Julie imagined that no one in these parts had ever seen people like them or Mbizi.

A blockade formed in their path, and they drifted to the north shore. There was an archery greeting party. The rest of the day was spent on horseback. They arrived at a palace in a large walled city.

"Where are we?" Julie asked.

"We have to be somewhere around modern-day Anyang. I think they call it 'Huanbei,'" Micheal's auto-map and historical knowledge informed his answer. "But it could also be Yin," he added.

All their weapons were confiscated. The only major weapon they brought was a bow and arrows, meant to be a gift for the ruler. Julie had been listening to the people talk the entire way here and didn't understand almost any of it. Ancient Chinese must be quite different from Mandarin Chinese.

They followed their escort's example, bowing before the king. The king said something, and when no one responded, Julie, Micheal, and Mbizi were made to look at him. He repeated his request, indicating the bow and arrows. Julie decided she needed to respond. She touched her chest, pointed at the bow, then indicated the king.

She spoke in Mandarin, "A humble gift for Your Majesty."

The king seemed to understand and began inspecting the offering.

At the same time, a figure standing in the shadows stepped forward and spoke in the king's ear. The king looked back and forth between them, then said something loudly. The entire hall emptied in moments. Once they were alone with the king, a second figure joined the first, and they emerged together. Julie could now see that the first figure was a woman, the second was a man. The woman was wearing an elaborate headdress concealed by a dark cloak that she now dropped to the floor. She took a step down the stairs and then spoke in modern Mandarin.

"The servants of the Egyptian Sun God are not welcome in our domain."

"We do *not* serve Ra!" Julie protested.

The woman came down to the main floor and circled them.

"You are Lady Avalon. You have been advising the Pharaohs for six centuries, haven't you? Egypt is Ra's domain. Therefore, you must be in league."

"We have opposed him at every turn," Micheal said.

"I find that hard to believe. Ra is most formidable. If you did oppose him, you would not be here." The other man said. He wore a long mustache and a chin beard.

"How do you speak Mandarin Chinese?" Julie finally recognized the oddity.

"Do you think you are the only time travelers we've met?" the woman answered.

"What's your name?" Julie asked.

"I'm Xi-Wang-Mu, and this is Shangti. This is our domain. Why have you come here?"

"We're looking for someone." Julie showed the image of Shani.

Xi looked at it for a moment. "We can't help you."

"Now, you've overstayed your welcome." Shang blinked and was suddenly in front of them.

There was a green flash, and they were all on the deck of the

Valkyrie.

"Egypt is a long way from here. You better get going," Xi suggested.

"I know you serve the Sun God. If you ever return, consider us enemies," Shang warned.

Xi and Shang teleported to the shore and observed until they were out of sight.

"I think that went well." Julie breathed a sigh of relief.

"We sure know how to make an impression."

"Where's Mbizi?"

"Meditating."

"That's productive."

"He reminds me of me when I couldn't find you. I got tunnel vision."

Julie went and wrapped her arms around Micheal.

"I was lost without you. He's searching for meaning as much as anything else."

"I understand, but this endless quest isn't helping anything. I'm charting a course for Egypt."

During the three-week voyage, Mbizi became more and more distant. He would spend hours and hours looking through the Eye of Horace, hoping any random eyes might see Shani. And when he wasn't meditating, he would run all sorts of scans on the sky-net. Julie worried he'd be consumed by his tunnel vision.

CHAPTER 23: ALONE

S HANI WOKE IN A field of leaves. Her head was aching, and it was painful to look at the sun. She took a deep breath to steady herself, then found her feet. She scanned the area. The trees made a colorful palette. Then she realized she couldn't see Mbizi. Julie said he'd be around 50 cubits away from her, but it was an empty forest for at least 100 cubits in any direction.

"Maybe he went to the shore. It should only be a few hundred cubits." Shani oriented herself east and began walking.

The minutes passed, and she saw no end to the trees. A cool breeze sent a chill down her spine, and she started to feel sick to her stomach. Something wasn't right.

"Mbizi! Julie! Micheal!" she yelled, as the panic was creeping in. Had her encounter with Ra in the timestream altered her exit trajectory?

Shani pulled out her communicator. Just as she was about to call Mbizi, she saw movement to her right. She dove away as three arrows hit the tree behind her. She rolled to her feet, taking cover behind another tree. Three more arrows sprayed the tree. She was about to flee when she realized her communicator was gone. She tried to retrieve it when more arrows flew her way, repelling off her back. Shani was trying to decide what to do when several more warriors broke into the clearing. All she could do was run. It was a blur of branches and leaves as she weaved a path through the woods. The cries and rush of her pursuers were closing in from behind. Shani broke into a clearing and immediately had to slide to the ground.

At least ten more warriors were directly in her path. Her heart skipped a beat as the arrows flew just over her face. She sprang to her feet as her original pursuers and the new arrivals began to engage in combat.

She ducked an attack from behind, sweeping the man to the ground. The battle intensified as more men joined from both sides. Shani drew her blades and began engaging anyone who tried to prevent her from retreating from the field. She blocked a sword with her forearm, then drove a blade into the man's arm. She spun between two more attackers, drawing blood from both. Three more closed in from around her as she neared the edge of the battle. She ducked an axe, then kicked another warrior in the chest. A spear thrust caught her neck below the chin. She grabbed the pole, yanking the attacker off balance and smashing his face with her elbow. A punch to the back reminded her of the last enemy. She spun on her heel and brought the man's face into her knee in one motion. The way was finally clear, and Shani sprinted into the trees.

Shani ran as fast as she could until her hands started shaking. She felt her strength wavering. Her chin was tickling. She scratched it, and her palm came back blood red. Then she remembered. Her lids became heavy, and everything faded to black.

Shani opened her eyes to the chill of a starry night sky. She looked around. The dark woods appeared the same in all directions. Rather than risk the unknown forest, she would stay put until morning. With hours to kill, she reflected on her situation. Clearly there was something wrong. She had arrived in the wrong physical location. Now, she worried she might have landed in the wrong temporal location. If that were true, she might be completely alone. What would she do then? The worst evidence that she was alone was that Mbizi hadn't connected with her mentally. She also knew how the sky-net worked. If Mbizi's God power failed for some reason, Micheal and Julie would scan the area and locate her. Shani felt more alone than she had since she was a young orphan, trying to survive on the streets after her parents were killed. She closed her eyes and pictured their faces. Even more than 20 years later, she could see them vividly. She felt comfort, knowing they were happy in the Field of Reeds.

<u>On the Run</u>

The stars began to fade into the dawn sky, and Shani tried to figure out which way to go. Then, it was decided for her. She detected a war party coming up from the south. She ran a good while to try to put distance between them. By midday, she arrived at the shore of a large lake. There were islands scattered across the surface. She looked at the water and decided it was clean enough. She began cleaning the dirt and blood off her neck. The gash was sensitive to the touch. Julie had told her that meant it was becoming infected. It had been years of revelations for Shani, learning about the wonders of the gods. Micheal had shown her some of the messengers of Sekhmet, the Goddess of Pestilence. Shani prayed to the goddess but didn't expect any help. Sekhmet was the daughter of Ra, so being on the wrong side of the Sun God might hamper any assistance she might otherwise receive. She gazed at the sun and felt ambivalent. While all the gods are to be respected, having been targeted by some of the gods made that more difficult. Shani thought more deeply about Ra's offer. He had said he wanted her to help him. That Isis was just as bad as he was. She was having difficulty believing that. Ra's interruption of her journey through time is likely what got her into this mess. Her stomach drowned out all the thoughts running through her mind. She ate one of the meal bars she had for emergencies. As she was washing it down, several boats began approaching the shore. It was time to run again.

Shani reached the edge of the lakeshore as the men began exiting their boats. With only a few minutes' head start, she broke into the cover of the woods. After a few hours, she stopped for a quick drink at a river. She had barely caught her breath when she heard movement in the trees behind her. She forded the river, then went into a sprint again. As she continued, the terrain began to go uphill. The mountains on both sides got taller. It also narrowed her options for escape. The temperature dropped with the elevation. Shani knew she had to get out of the mountains before sundown. Based on everything Micheal and Julie had explained about time, she felt she must be somewhere on the eastern seaboard of America. The mountain range called the Appalachians was not very large. Shani followed the ravine into a pass between the mountains. She traced a river until she reached a waterfall. At that point, she thought she should divert. As she progressed, the trail headed downhill. Encouraged, she picked up the pace. She just might make it out before night. As the sun touched the horizon, she reached a large river. This would be a good place to spend the night.

Shani woke, and the first light of dawn was lightening the eastern sky. She realized she had a new threat chasing her. The skin around the gash on her neck was sore and hot. If the infection spread, she would become unable to continue. So she needed to push herself today and hope to find help somewhere.

A day of steady pacing brought her to a large lake at least a league long. She spent the night at the north end of the lake. When the sun came up, Shani felt tired. She felt her forehead, and it was hot. She stumbled to a point where a river flowed out of the lake. There was a small boat about ten cubits in length and maybe two cubits wide. She climbed in and allowed the current to pull her toward the sea.

As Shani flowed with the current, time began to have no meaning. Days likely passed between her waking recognition. In one of her final recollections of conscious view, she saw a dark shadow stalking the side of the river. It reminded her of Prince Amenemhat. Maybe it was the shadow of death. Shani became delirious. Her fight against this darkness failed, and everything faded to black.

New Friends

Shani woke to what looked like a thatched roof. A woman was standing over her. She said something Shani didn't understand and then offered a cup of something. It was hot and had a bitter taste. As the cup emptied, the woman took it back. She seemed to ask a question.

"I don't understand," Shani said in Egyptian.

Her neck began to itch. She instinctively tried to scratch it. The woman grabbed her wrist and shook her head. The woman's kind eyes set her at ease. Shani relaxed, and the woman touched her forehead with her hand and then smiled. She was an older woman. She brought over a bucket, and using a ladle, she offered water. Once Shani drank her fill, the woman indicated she should sleep some more. Feeling much better, Shani took the suggestion.

The next time she woke up, she was alone. She saw the bucket of water and helped herself. With her strength returning, she found her footing and grabbed a cloak off the wall. Shani's stomach fluttered as she pushed the animal skin door aside and slowly stepped outside.

She was in a small village next to a body of water. It might be a large river because an island was separating two arms that appeared to be slowly moving east. Dozens of people were just going about everyday tasks. She felt a touch on her shoulder. She looked over, and her nurse was standing next to her.

Months passed, and Shani slowly learned the language. She had primarily spent time with Winema—the one who had healed her. They were sitting on a riverbank under a misty spring rain.

"I know you haven't wanted me to talk about my past since we've been able to communicate, but there are some people I need to find."

"Shani, I've come to love you as a daughter. I know that sometimes it's hard to accept what we lose. My birth daughter was tragically taken from me. I want you to take my place as chief when I die." Winema was going further down that road than ever before.

"You've become like a mother to me, but my husband is out there somewhere. I would never forgive myself if I didn't try to find him."

"I had hoped you'd become one of us, but I understand. Tell me about home."

"A great river, much like this one, flows into a great delta that meets the sea. My husband and I live in a... hut... that is many-fold the size of this village. I am a ruler of the western delta and so the title I am known by is the Lady of the West. The land is called Egypt, and it stretches far beyond what the eye can see."

"Where is this Egypt?" Chief Winema's eyes went wide.

"It's beyond this sea." Shani indicated toward the Atlantic.

"I want to help you. Is there anything I can do?"

"I would need a very large boat, called a ship."

"If you know how, we can help you build it."

"This is what we need to do…"

Over the next few months, they felled, then split hundreds of trees, clearing a large stretch of the forest. Slowly, the two ships started coming together. The larger one was for her. It was 25 cubits long and 10 cubits wide. The one for the tribe was 15 cubits long and six cubits wide. It was time to add the final special piece to the puzzle: a perpetual drive system. It was a concept Micheal had detailed explicitly for her. Shani knew she'd never be able to do the complex engineering that Micheal and Julie could, but she could grasp this. The system would use a one-span turbine on the front and a 1-cubit propeller on the back, utilizing a gear system to amplify the turbine force and accelerate the larger propeller. A simple separation break would nullify the system. Shani knew the only flaw was that she had to carve the components out of wood, which meant they'd be vulnerable to break.

The months long process saw her first year come and go. The ships were complete, but the snow had arrived. Shani would have to weather another winter in America.

Spring finally came, and the ice on the river finally melted away.

"The Gaia is fully loaded and prepared for your departure." Winema entered the hut.

"I don't know how to thank you."

"Your contribution to our people has been thanks enough… I hope it's okay to admit I was glad the ice kept you here that much longer." Winema touched Shani's cheek.

"I did enjoy our time together." Shani took her hand.

They headed to the river, and the whole village came for the sendoff.

"I suppose this is it." Shani took Winema in a firm embrace.

"Will I ever see you again?"

Shani pulled back, wiped the tears from Winema's eyes, and said, "Perhaps, in time. You never know where the winds of tomorrow will take you."

"May Gaia bless you on the voyage to come."

"No matter where the seas lead, I will always be your friend." Shani boarded the ship and set sail with the tides. A few minutes later, her friends vanished into the horizon.

<u>Voyager</u>

Shani had been able to craft a vital tool Julie had taught her about. It was called a 'sextant'. She used it to determine where she was north/south on the earth. She was at about 47° north. The straight of Avalon was 36° north, so she needed to cross the Atlantic Ocean in a southeastern direction. She followed the coast until she was headed in the proper direction. It had taken a few days, but she was finally entering the open ocean. Five days after her last sighting of land, Shani found her latitude: 40° north. Her perpetual drive system was doing wonders for her passage. The Gaia was moving at about half the speed of the Isis, but it still wasn't fast enough to outrun a storm closing from behind. The next several hours were spent in a battle with the gods Set and Nun.

The storm finally passed, and Shani lay exhausted in the afternoon sun. She looked at the all-encompassing sky and reflected on the gods. Was the storm a warning from Set after their last encounter? Or was she too insignificant to garner such attention?

Then she thought of Mbizi. She was sure she had fallen into another time. She still had no idea when, and even if she determined her location in time, she wasn't a Lady of Avalon. Was there any chance she could master a time transfer? The endless open sea in every direction only emphasized how alone she was.

Five days later, she saw the Straits of Avalon. One quick stopover and she would have a definite upgrade in the Isis.

As Shani approached the strait, three rowing galley ships blocked the path. She steered north toward Avalon. The ships turned, attempting to intercept. The Gaia was much faster, so she thought she could outrun them. Two more appeared from the north as she slipped past the lead vessel. Shani tried to redirect south. The second of the new ships was closing fast. She held her breath. It was getting close, but she just might slip the attack. The sea was opening up in front of her. Shani let her breath go; she had made it. Just then the Gaia shook viciously. She looked back, and the other ship was cutting to her right. She was pulling away, but the Gaia was slowing. While the other ship had just clipped her, it must have damaged her propellers. She dropped the sail and caught the wind, but it only stalled her slowing. Fifteen minutes later, she was preparing to be boarded. The ships boxed her in. The boarding party of about 20 began searching the ship. A man dressed more elegantly than the rest approached. He said something she didn't understand, but it sounded like Phoenician.

"I have nothing of value," Shani tried in Egyptian.

"This very unusual ship is precious and now belongs to us. As do you," he replied in Egyptian.

"No one owns me!"

He grabbed her chin, looking at her face.

"Yes. I think you will fetch a handsome price."

She knocked his arm down, and he instantly drew a dagger to her throat. After a moment, he laughed.

"I love your spirit."

One of his men approached. "No one else is on board, and there are limited supplies."

"Quite impressive. A single woman operating a large vessel all by yourself? Perhaps you will fetch more than I thought." He gave an order in Phoenician. Then, five men forced her to their ship.

Two weeks and two failed escape attempts later, the ship arrived in Byblos. In shackles and chains, she was brought to market. When she'd been enslaved as a child, there was really no use to resist, and now she felt just as helpless. Despite her knowledge and training, she was just property to be bought and sold.

Shani stood naked, being prodded and probed by potential buyers. After a lengthy bidding war, a wealthy Hittite merchant purchased her for a very large sum.

Before she could be taken away, everything stopped, and the streaks of color filled the air. Then Ra approached.

"My Lady of the West. How unfortunate to see you brought so low."

"This whole situation is your fault. You altered my passage through time."

"That was not what I intended."

"It doesn't matter. If you mean to kill me, just get it over with."

"Why would I do that? I want you to join me."

"I'm not interested."

"Join me, and when the world is mine, you can have any land you wish."

"All I'd have to do is help you kill all the other gods. No thanks."

"What do you want?"

"To find my husband and my friends. Can you help with that or not."

"Unfortunately, no. They're not in this time period as far as I know."

"What time period am I in?"

"It has been 163 years since our encounter near the sea with the Hebrews."

Shani did the math in her head. She had arrived five years early. It would be another three and a half years before Mbizi, Micheal, and Julie would arrive. That thought was depressing.

"Leave me be," she said.

"You would rather be a slave than join me?"

"Either way, I'm a slave. At least this way, I won't be a party to murder."

Ra laughed. "As you wish. Perhaps a few years of use and abuse will change your mind. Enjoy your servitude."

There was a flash, and everything returned to normal. Ra had disappeared.

Her new owner took possession of her, and the caravan headed north into the Hittite Empire. It was a long month on the road. She was under constant guard and usually restrained. Her new owner promised she wouldn't be escaping as she had attempted to do before. She resigned herself to her fate, and now they were arriving at Hattusa, the capital of the empire.

CHAPTER 24: RAMESSES THE GREAT

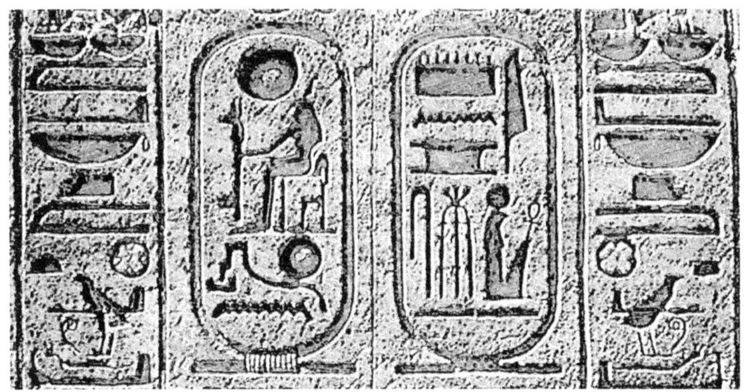

T HEY MADE A QUICK stop at Avalon to retrieve the Isis. Then, they had to elude many pirates en route to Egypt. Now, they were docking at River Palace. The water level was a bit low as the inundation was beginning.

Following the usual verification, they talked with the current palace manager, Raziya.

"My Lord, I must inform you that His Majesty is in residence here in the palace."

"We will show our respect."

Raziya led them to the Pharaoh's module. It was full of nobles as the Pharoah held court.

"Your Majesty, may I present Lord and Lady Avalon and Lord West," Raziya announced them.

Micheal was curious whether it would be Seti I or Ramesses II. 1279 BC was the transition year between them. If it were Seti, he would be in his 40s. If it were Ramesses, he would be in his 20s. Micheal could tell the Pharoah was young, so it must be Ramesses.

"My Lords and Lady, welcome back. I had hoped for your return during my reign. And you arrived just after I took the throne. Most fortunate." Ramesses rose from the throne.

"With your permission, we have a gift for you," Micheal said.

"How gracious of you."

Micheal stepped forward, presenting the offering. "This orb will show you the colors of the rainbow. Ramesses descended to accept the crystal prism orb.

He closely examined it.

"Give us privacy!" Ramesses indicated for the court to be cleared, then it was just the four of them. "I've been trying to reach out to the gods, but they are nowhere to be found."

"When was the last time you talked to one of them?" Micheal asked.

"Ten years ago. Ra, Set, and Anubis oversaw my divination at Karnak."

"What about Isis?" Julie enquired.

"She taught me from when I was four until just before my divination, but she hasn't contacted me since. Do any of you know how to contact them?"

"I don't know if that's a good idea. They're at war over Egypt. You can't trust any of them." Mbizi showed his newfound cynicism.

"I apologize, Your Majesty. Lady West has been missing for over a year," Julie explained.

"That being said, Ra no longer cares only for Egypt. He has designs on the entire world," Micheal said.

"Isn't that a good thing? To make Egypt even more powerful?" Ramesses looked at all of them.

"The problem is, the other gods stand in his way, and they aren't just going to let him claim their domains. There's going to be a war between them," Micheal said.

"And why should I care about a war of the gods? The gods of Egypt will surely win."

"Even if they do, there will likely be some collateral damage," Julie warned.

"When this happens, some other gods might attack Egypt to try and hurt Ra," Micheal added.

"Can any of you contact them?"

"We can try. Just give us a little time." Micheal led Julie and Mbizi out of the Pharoah's module.

"Mbizi, I wanted you to decide if Pharoah would know about your power, but see if you can contact any Egyptian gods except Ra, Set, and Anubis." Micheal requested.

Mbizi began the process. "No Isis, no Osiris… I think I got one…"

"Who?" Julie asked.

"Hathor."

At that moment, a green swirl appeared in the chamber, and the Mother Goddess emerged. Micheal had to look up. She was around seven feet tall. She had what looked like bull horns on her head with a light orb in the middle. She had a brown complexion with brown eyes and wore a turquoise sheath dress up to just below her breasts.

"Who has the Eye of Horace?" Hathor demanded.

"The new Pharoah desires divine counsel," Micheal explained.

She closely examined them.

"You must be the Lords of Avalon. Very well…"

There was a flash, and things shifted to a luminous purple, and they were in the Pharoah's module.

"How may I help you, Your Majesty?"

Ramesses appeared surprised.

"Since my father's death, the Near East has begun testing me, and the pirates have been controlling most of the sea passages. What would you have me do?"

"You don't require divine intervention. The Lords of Avalon have been able to thwart my husband Ra. They should be able to advise you on these issues."

"Are you helping Ra?" Julie asked.

"My husband and daughter have been fighting over power for millennia. I don't get involved."

"Then you're aware of what Ra is doing?" Micheal challenged.

"You mean upsetting the divine balance by targeting other gods? Of course."

"Then you're fine with that?" Mbizi chimed in out of nowhere.

"It would not be wise to oppose him. And it's not like the other gods are helpless. The likes of you have fought him many times and lived to tell the tale, and you're not quite gods yet."

"Do you know where Lady West is?" Mbizi suddenly asked.

Hathor stepped over to him and placed a hand on his head.

"You possess my grandson's gift."

Her hand began to glow.

"You will not find her… When the time is right, she may find you."

"What does that mean?" Mbizi seemed to be relaxing.

"I see the future of emotions, but they can be unpredictable. I see purple in your future, which means you will love again. But I can't say if it's with Lady West."

"How long does he have to wait?" Micheal wondered.

"Perhaps a year. Now, I have lingered too long."

A spiral of green consumed Hathor, and she disappeared.

"It appears the gods trust you to serve Egypt's interest. I would seek your advice." Ramesses headed for his private quarters, indicating them to follow.

"So what should I do about the problems I discussed before?"

"The princes in the Near East will only make noise for a couple years to come. So you don't need to focus on them just yet. But the pirates are another matter. Their harassment of the delta coast is a more present threat," Micheal advised.

"What else should I do? We're already trying to defend our transports at sea."

"Bait them into a trap. Over several seasons, slowly retreat toward the Delta. When they think Egypt is more vulnerable, they will become more bold. That's when you give them a valuable target. When they move their fleet in for the kill, you ambush them from the flanks," Micheal explained.

"You just passed through the sea. How strong did they look?"

"They control most of the Great Green Sea, at least the areas not dominated by the Myceneans or the Phoenicians," Julie said.

"Then we have a plan. Now I have something else I'd like to discuss. Follow me." Ramesses led them to the Lord's sanctuary.

They stopped in front of the Fall of Fenrir mural.

"When I was a boy, I would spend the inundation here at River Palace. It was my father's luxury pleasure palace. I was exploring with friends when we came in here. All these hieroglyphs are like nothing I'd ever seen before. This one quickly became my favorite. I eventually asked my father about it. He told me that 500 years ago this palace was built by some mysterious lords who were chosen by the gods. When I saw you, I knew you were the very same lords who built this palace because that's you." The Pharaoh pointed them out. "I know Avalon is some kind of magical realm where the gods reside, and clearly, you know the gods well. I've mostly dealt with the Sun God. I don't know about a battle between Isis and Ra, but Ra has been my principal sponsor. So, until I am convinced his actions are detrimental to Egypt, I will still work with him."

"Of course, Your Majesty," Julie agreed.

Ramesses ran his hand over the mural. "Whatever you are exactly, I'm glad you're here." The Pharaoh exited toward his module.

Julie stared at the mural for a moment, shaking her head. "We aren't going to oppose Ra anymore. Let's let the gods defend themselves." She walked off toward the Lord's module.

"Unless he's responsible for Shani." Mbizi left Micheal alone with the mural.

The Sherden Sea Pirates

The Delta flood came and went, but Mbizi barely noticed. Despite Julie's concern that he would lose his mind, he was determined to locate Shani. Even though the Mother Goddess said he wouldn't find her, Mbizi still spent most of his free time looking through the eyes of the world on the chance that someone somewhere was in the presence of her beauty.

There was a continual scan running on the sky-net. Most of the gods he knew were ignoring him or outright hostile.

He was on the Isis, out to sea with Ramesses as they were baiting the trap for the sea pirates. He was attempting another communication. He focused on the king and queen of the Anunnaki.

"My Lord of the West, why do you persist in this hopeless quest?" Inanna answered.

"As a goddess of love, I would have thought you would understand."

Inanna was quiet for a moment.

"Sometimes the love of nation should supersede the importance of personal love. And if the Lady of the West were in this time period, surely the Lords of Avalon would have found her." Inanna's voice sounded strange. "Now, if there's nothing else, I would like to get back to my work."

Mbizi felt there was more to learn from Inanna, "I think I'll stay," he said, refusing to sever the link.

Inanna apparently moved into the garden of whatever palace she was in; then, the view rapidly moved skyward. There was much confusion. Then he heard the Pharaoh shout. He looked up, and a large, winged figure descended toward the ship. Inanna hit the deck hard, causing the Isis to shake terribly, knocking Mbizi and the Pharaoh down. She towered over them with her wings spread. Then she spoke to them in Egyptian.

"Now, do I have your attention?"

Mbizi got to his feet.

"Who are you?" The Pharaoh looked captivated by the goddess.

"Inanna, Queen of the Anunnaki."

Ramesses glanced at Mbizi.

"Lord West, you will refrain from contacting us further about your wife, or next time, I won't be so forgiving."

"I just don't know what else to do."

"You told me Hathor said she might find you. Try patience. Now, once again, if you violate my edict, Egypt pays the price."

"You dare threaten my land?" Ramesses stood as tall as he could.

Inanna laughed. "Your Majesty, I could lay Egypt in ruin if I wished. Don't you have some pirates to deal with?" Inanna stared at Mbizi for a moment, then majestically took to the sky.

"What was that about?" the Pharaoh was squinting at him.

"I was looking for my wife again, and Inanna didn't take kindly to my use of her eyes."

"I feel for your situation, but you will never again draw another god to Egypt without my approval for any personal reason. Do I make myself clear?"

"Absolutely, Your Majesty."

"Now, let's draw our prey into the trap."

Mbizi slowed the Isis, and the growing fleet of triremes began to close the distance. The Valkyrie was being surrounded to the west. Both ships timed it perfectly to break through and make for the coast. The swarm of pirate ships formed a moving dragnet. The main bait fleet was sitting in an inlet on the Libyan coast. Once all the pirate ships had pushed into the inlet, Mbizi drew his bow, lit one of the special arrows on fire, and then let it fly into the eastern sky. As the arrow began to return from its maximum height, there was a thunderous boom, and streams of fire flew off in every direction. The Egyptian fleet emerged on the northern horizon. Within minutes, the escape to the sea was cut off, and a pitched battle began.

Mbizi turned the Isis on the pirate fleet using the prow-cutter on the front of the ship; he began crippling trireme after trireme by slicing their oars into splinters. Ramesses used his expert marksmanship to keep any enemies from boarding them. The Pharaoh appeared to be enjoying himself.

Before sunset, the pirate fleet had capitulated. Mbizi pulled the Isis up on the side of an unusual ship that was apparently run by the leader of the pirates. The Valkyrie was on the opposite side. Mbizi and Ramesses boarded the vessel. Micheal and Julie climbed on from the other side. They immediately went to search the ship.

"All of your ships and men now belong to me," the Pharaoh informed the captain.

"We will be honored to serve Your Majesty." The captain bowed, and all the crew followed.

As more Egyptian soldiers secured the pirate fleet, Ramesses pulled Mbizi aside.

"Our plan worked, and it was good to get into the action." The Pharaoh allowed a small smile.

"A great victory to honor you."

"Lord West, I would like to discuss what happened before."

"My apologies. Sometimes, I let my desire and familiarity with the gods to cause me to be reckless."

"How many gods are you familiar with?"

"Over the years, I've met dozens of them from different parts of the world. And I've communicated with more than that."

"And you do this through the Eye of Horace?"

"Yes."

"Why would you push this Inanna if she knows you to such a point?" Ramesses indicated the sky.

"I got the feeling she wasn't being honest with me about my wife."

"You think she knows where your wife is?"

"I don't know. It just felt like she was a bit too hostile against my intrusion."

"Well, while my edict still stands, meeting the Queen of the Anunnaki was amazing." Ramesses gave a slight smile.

"She is quite captivating." Mbizi laughed.

At that moment, Micheal and Julie approached.

"Mbizi, you need to see this." Micheal signaled to follow.

They made their way into the cabin of the ship.

"I think you'll find this of particular interest." Julie indicated a carving on the wall.

It was Egyptian hieroglyphics, and it said, "Shani loves Mbizi".

<u>Babylon</u>

The discovery of Shani's ship, along with Inanna's suspicious behavior put them on a revived quest to Babylon. Julie had been able to use the sky-net to track the ship back from the battle against the sea pirates to Shani's Atlantic crossing in the spring of 1283 BC.

"She's been on her own these past seven years?" Mbizi shook his head as he joined Julie on the bridge.

"I'm sure she's ok. Look at what she was able to do on her own."

"Why haven't I been able to connect with her these past few years?"

"The Anunnaki we've met clearly have temporal powers. What if they found a way to hide her temporal signature?"

"It certainly felt like Inanna was holding something back."

"Did you try going around her by looking through different eyes in Babylon?"

"That's what I spent most of my time doing since our encounter. I've seen nothing!" Mbizi slammed his fists on the railing.

"Well, it's three weeks to Babylon. You'll have plenty more opportunities." Julie steered the Valkyrie into the Mediterranean.

It was a relaxing voyage around Africa. Now, they were just entering the mouth of the Euphrates as the sun just cracked the eastern horizon. Julie slowed to 25 knots, but they were still too fast for the Babylonian patrol. A day of wide eyes and stares went by in a flash, and the outline of the famous city was impressive in the evening light. As they neared the main docks, a flotilla of ships was there to greet them. Julie followed the direction of a well-dressed man on the lead vessel. She thought he must be the harbor master. He guided her to the main peer. A large welcome party was waiting to escort them to the palace. They were each directed to a litter and carried through the streets with curious crowds gawking at them. Julie was confused. The atmosphere reminded her of London in 1696. It was like they were expected guests. An hour later, they were sitting before the king.

"His Majesty, Kadashman-Turgu bids the Lords of Avalon welcome to his kingdom," a herald spoke loudly in Babylonian. At least their ongoing language study had its uses. Since arriving in Egypt, they had made it a point to learn all the languages of the Near East.

"Your reputation precedes you. My ambassadors speak endless praise of River Palace. Surely the most spectacular in all the world," the King began. "I would also like to congratulate you and King Ramesses on defeating the pirate hoard."

"Your Majesty flatters us, but we would ask permission to enquire after our purpose," Micheal began.

"There's plenty of time for that, but first, allow me to honor you."

At that, many dancers emerged with rising music. The party ran into the night. They retired to a luxury suite that was prepared for them.

"They're just trying to stall us!" Mbizi walked to the balcony.

"Why would he do that?" Micheal followed.

"They're holding her hostage."

"No. Kadashman is just trying to impress us, to pull us away from Ramesses. Everything he said was aimed in that direction." Julie shook her head.

"Tomorrow, we go and demand to know about Shani."

"You might not have to wait." Micheal was looking up.

There was a glow descending from the starry sky. A rush of wind accompanied Inanna as she landed.

"So you've come to bother me here as well?" the goddess dropped her head.

"Where's Shani?" Mbizi glared.

"You're too late. She's gone."

"So you did have her?" Julie asked.

"I'm sorry. We needed her help."

"With what?" Micheal asked.

"It doesn't matter. Nothing matters anymore." Inanna's ruby eyes were watery.

"What happened?" Julie took a step toward her.

"You got what you came here for. Now leave me in peace." Inanna took flight and disappeared into the night sky.

Mbizi said, "Does she mean Shani's dead?"

"Not necessarily," Julie began.

"What else could she mean?" Mbizi snapped.

"All she said was that Shani was here, and now she's not," Micheal reasoned.

"So what do we do now?" Mbizi had new determination.

"We go back to Egypt and start the search from there. If she left Babylon on her own, she would make her way to River Palace. We will run scans on the sky-net as well," Julie decided.

"And I will reach out with my sight." Mbizi seemed to be less worried.

Following a week of extravagance at the host of Kadash-man-Turgu, they began the long voyage back.

CHAPTER 25: THE SLAVE

S HANI WAS IMPRESSED BY the great Hittite city. It was elevated above the surrounding area, and she thought it must be comparable to Memphis or Thebes. The wall seemed to span some 50 rods. The caravan climbed a ramp to the main gate. Two large Hittite sphynxes guarded it. They pushed through the crowded streets to the palace. As they entered the throne room, her new master addressed the king.

"Your Majesty, the great Muwatalli, I come bearing an exceptional gift—the beautiful exotic Shani. She's also fluent in multiple languages and highly intelligent."

Shani was brought forward. Muwatalli came to inspect her. He looked to be around 30 years old. He grabbed her chin and locked eyes. She closed her eyes, bracing for what would come next. His rough hands were like sand against her skin. Her eyes flashed open when he shifted her chin.

"So you can understand me?" The King asked in Hatti.

"Yes, Your Majesty."

"Serve with grace, and you'll be well-cared for." He nodded his head, and a woman came and took her arm. She was guided into a chamber with at least a dozen other women.

"Welcome. What is your name? The obvious matron of the harem approached.

"Shani."

"I'm Ania. And where are you from?"

"Egypt."

"All right, let's get you cleaned up."

Ania led her to a bath. She snapped, and two other women came and began scrubbing Shani. As they worked, Ania talked.

"It is such an honor to be chosen for His Majesty. You will do whatever the king needs. Outside of that, you will follow my commands. You must maintain your beauty, help prepare the chosen one for each night, and hope you give His Majesty an heir."

Apparently, Shani was the chosen one for tonight. Her chest started to feel tight. The last time she was a slave, the only one she had to serve in this manner was her master, and at least he waited until she was of age, so it was only a few times before Micheal set her free. That was over ten years ago. She couldn't think of any way out of this. She might be able to escape, but then what? She was in the middle of the Hittite empire. She wouldn't be able to make it far before they would catch her. It would just bring punishment.

After eating a small dinner, it was time for her to dress.

"His Majesty wants his Isis."

Ania brought her to a bench. Two women began straightening her curls while two others started her makeup. It took some time, but she was now fully decorated. They dressed her in a tight-fitting kalasiris. The red and green fabric stopped just below her breasts, with a strap running between them and over her shoulder. They showed her a mirror, and she saw that her eyes were lined and shaded. Her hair was smooth and straight, with a gold falcon crown.

Ania guided Shani to the King's private chamber. She swallowed as Muwatalli entered.

"My Egyptian Goddess of Beauty."

Shani felt his eyes crawl over her body. He came over and began the same process with his hands. He kissed her and brought her hands to his body. She began to get involved as he wanted. He threw off her crown and pushed her to the bed. He climbed on top, pressing her legs apart. She shuttered with her breath, trying not to repel his advance. Shani gripped the blanket tight, anticipating his thrust.

A bright flash brought a halt to his progress. The room was bathed in light. As Shani's eyes adjusted, she saw a woman who seemed to glow.

"Your Majesty will cease this action at once!" The woman was about as tall as Julie. She had stark pale skin. Her hair was golden like the sun, and her yellow eyes were illuminating. Muwatalli went to his knees, averting his eyes.

"My goddess, why do you interfere?"

"I claim the Lady of the West for my own service."

The king rose and asked, "The Lady of the West?" Muwatalli's eyes locked on Shani. "You failed to identify yourself?" he seemed to accuse.

Shani sat up. "The pirates enslaved me. I didn't realize my reputation traveled so far."

"Enough, Your Majesty. I've made my intention clear. My Lady..." the goddess extended her hand. Shani stood, taking it.

The king bowed to the goddess and then exited the chamber.

Shani turned to the goddess, "How do you know me?"

"I'm Arinna, Goddess of the Sun, and I sensed your aura. You come from time."

Arinna grabbed her other hand so they were looking face to face.

"So what happens now?" Shani's relief was becoming nerves.

"Now, we go to the heavens."

A spark ran through Shani's body. The room became enveloped in light, and her sight was washed out.

<u>Lady of the West</u>

Shani squeezed her eyes together several times, and her surroundings began to focus. Her eyes couldn't comprehend what they were seeing. The ground looked like the clouds in the sky, and it felt like walking on her soft bed back at Avalon. The sky was a soft purple shade. There were extraordinary plants of every possible color that looked like nothing she had ever seen.

"Where are we?" Shani finally asked when she could form a rational thought.

"My own personal heaven," Arinna's voice dropped.

"There's no one else here?"

"It's been years," her voice caught in her throat.

"What happened?"

"The other gods and I spent centuries enriching the Hittites, growing their glory, and in return, their devotion increased our power. Most of the others became too proud. They abandoned their duty to our people and became weak because of it. That vulnerability led to their downfall. In the end, it was just me and Ishara. For over a century, we blessed the Hittites and blessed each other's company. Then, a year ago, she vanished. When I found her, she was dead." Arinna broke down.

"How did she die?"

"She was strangled."

Shani had been worried it was from a temporal energy attack.

"Who could kill a goddess?"

"Another god."

"Do you think it was Ra?"

"I don't think he'd do that. He knew how much Ishara meant to me."

"How well do you know Ra?"

"We're both Sun Gods. It's not like there's that many of us."

"You've had sex with him?"

"When I first sponsored the Hittite people, Ra came and helped me. We've been friends for centuries."

"Do all the gods from all the lands know each other?"

"To varying degrees. There's not that many of us in the world, and when you live for centuries, you're bound to meet everyone."

Shani was trying to decide what to ask next when Arinna said, "Enough of this; let me show you around."

"What is there to see?"

"It's not just what to see; it's how to get there." Arinna floated up above her.

"But I can't fly."

"Yes, you can. In heaven, everyone can. You just have to have the will."

"I don't understand."

"All you have to do is decide to come to where I am." Shani focused, and suddenly, she was getting closer to Arinna.

"Got the hang of it?"

"I think so."

"Then follow me."

They soared through heaven. The rush of colors below was mesmerizing. The wind in her hair made her feel more free than she ever felt before. Finally, Arinna came to a stop.

"What is that?" Shani was studying the structure ahead.

"That's my home."

"It's all made of gold?"

"No, it's made of sunshine... Come on."

They landed next to the palace. It looked like a group of golden obelisks of varying heights. She'd never seen anything so tall before.

"I want to show you something."

Arinna flew up to the only flat top in the center of the obelisks. Shani followed, and as she was landing, there was some kind of animal she'd never seen before. It looked like a horse with wings.

"Come say hi." Arinna began stroking the animal's neck. "It's called a Pegasus."

"It's beautiful." Shani felt the smooth softness of the feathers. Then, the Pegasus took a few steps and dove off, spreading its majestic wings and flying out into the sky.

As it drifted into the distance, Arinna sat on a soft chair and signaled for Shani to do the same thing.

"This place is magical," Shani said.

"So, Lady West, how did you come to be a slave?"

"The most simple answer is that it's Ra's fault."

"He did this to you?"

"Perhaps not intentionally. I was passing through a time portal when he stalled me out. When I arrived at the end, it was five years too early. The Lords of Avalon and my husband still don't arrive for another few years."

"That still doesn't explain the bondage."

"I had no idea what year I was in. I just knew it was the wrong one. I built a ship to sail to Avalon, but before I could get there, I was attacked by pirates. They sold me to the merchant."

"You weren't able to escape?"

"I nearly did on several occasions."

"I thought the Lords of the West were more like me."

"We have time powers, but we're not invulnerable. I can still be killed."

"What are you capable of?"

"I have a temporal push power. That means I can resist temporal energy attacks. And if I push back hard enough, I can send someone through the timeline."

"And you can also time jump?"

"That's different."

"You said you were passing through a time portal when Ra stalled you out."

"The Lords of Avalon can predict where you need to be to open portals."

Arinna looked at her thoughtfully for a moment. "Why did Ra stall you out?"

"I don't think it was on purpose. His time-stopping power is like the opposite of my power. I think he was stopping time when I passed by, and our powers interacted."

"And he talked to you?"

"He tried to convince me to join him in his quest to take over the world."

"And you said no?"

"Of course. He's tried to kill me and my friends multiple times. He's only making this offer because I can interfere with his plans."

"You should join him. He always gets what he wants. It's better to be by his side than in his way."

Shani wasn't sure if her new friend was more likely to be an enemy. She was on Ra's side.

Over the next few years, Arinna taught Shani how to be a goddess. They would spend long stretches in heaven and shorter ones in Hattusa, then Tarhuntassa, after Muwatalli moved the capital. They would advise the king, and occasionally, Arinna would use her godpowers to fix something. It was mostly leisure time, and aside from random visits from other gods, they spent their time getting to know each other. They grew very close.

They were sitting on a cloud at on the rooftop terrace of the palace.

"Shani, I want to ask you something. Arinna was almost glowing."

"Okay..."

"Do you think I'm beautiful?"

"As the sun when it kisses the sea."

Arinna laughed. "And you're beautiful like the freshly fallen leaves of the autumn trees." She traced Shani's cheek.

Her luminous golden eyes enraptured Shani. The next thing she knew, Arinna's mouth was on hers. She felt the energy pulsing through her. The connection was intoxicating. She gave in to the feeling. Arinna started gently caressing her body. Arinna's skin felt like hot silk under her fingers. Her lips were sweet like cherries. Shani's dress fell away, and Arinna's hand found her breast. She breathed deeply, taking in the flowery essence of her friend. As Arinna's thumb circled her nipple, Shani kissed down Arinna's neck to her chest, pressing her to the bed of clouds and then licking her erect nipple. Arinna slid her hands lower, finding Shani's ass. In one motion, Arinna reversed positions, ending on top. For a moment, Arinna rose up and locked eyes with her. Arinna was glowing like the Sun Goddess she was. Arinna pushed between her legs, finding her lips with her mouth. Shani grabbed her golden locks, threading the tendrils through her fingers, then lost her mind to ecstasy. Her whole body shuttered with a pulse of energy between her legs. Every inch of her was tingling, and she wanted more. Shani laid Arinna down. She circled around so she was upside-down. Shani kissed her eyes, then her lips, continuing down her milky white skin to the pink between her thighs. Shani circled Arinna's clit with her tongue. As she picked up pace, she felt Arinna's tongue matching hers. Finally, Arinna quivered, and her thighs clenched Shani's head while her womanhood flooded. A moment later, a surge of pleasure from below washed over her body. She felt like she was floating..., and then she realized she was. Arinna came up and hovered next to her.

"What made you finally decide to do this with me?" Arinna asked.

"Through the years, I've come to love you. And while I am married, it didn't feel right to leave without showing you how much you mean to me."

"You helped heal my heart. After such a long time alone, your friendship was just what I needed."

"You have to promise to come and visit me."

"I will, but we still have one more week before your friends arrive?"

"Yes."

Arinna floated over so they were face-to-face.

"I shall cherish it. Wanna go again?" Arinna caressed her cheek.

"Okay."

This time, they stayed in the air for the duration.

The next morning, they were having breakfast in the garden with the pegasai when there was a flash of lightning. When the brightness dimmed, there were two people.

"Hello, Arinna. And it's nice to see you again, Shani," Thor said in Hittite with a wink.

There was a woman with him.

"Lady West, let me introduce Freyja, Goddess of Love, Sex and War."

"Nice to meet you." Shani bowed.

Freyja locked eyes for a moment, then locked gazes with Arinna. "It appears we just missed the fun." Frejya smiled.

Arinna laughed.

"Well, Lady West, you become more interesting all the time."

"I don't understand," Shani protested.

"I know the two of you had sky sex. I can smell it on you. They don't call me the Goddess of Sex for nothing."

"That's enough from the two of you. It's been decades since your last visit. I doubt this is just a social call."

"Some of us are trying to organize a council to address the situation with the Sun God of Egypt," Thor began seriously.

"Who is *us?*" Arinna asked.

"The Minoan sisters and Kiririsha from Elam," Thor responded.

"You haven't talked to Zeus?" Arinna asked.

"Olympus was empty. Marduk rejected us. And as usual, Shang and Xi were immediately hostile," Freyja volunteered.

"Have you talked to Isis? I'm sure she would support such a council," Shani suggested.

"Isis is in Egypt. He would know we came, and he would target us." Thor shook his head.

"The only chance we have is if Ra doesn't know about it and everyone joins forces. So, Arinna, are you going to help?" Freyja touched Arinna's hand.

"I can't. He and I have such a long history, and I won't betray that."

"He's already killed more than a dozen of us. He'll come for you eventually," Thor warned bitterly.

"What about you, Lady West?" Freyja locked eyes.

"I'm tired of the battles. It's amazing I've survived this long. Ra promised to leave me alone as long as I don't interfere with his plans."

"This is why he'll win." Freyja took Thor's arm and a bolt of lightning met the hammer he raised. The flash consumed them.

Shani and Arinna enjoyed each other for the next week, and now it was the night before she would meet her friends in America. Shani was laying her head on Arinna's chest. She felt Arinna's fingers in her hair.

"I promise I will visit from time to time," Arinna said.

"I will look forward to it."

"May I join in?" Ra's voice sent her heart racing.

"You never call, you never write," Arinna was casual.

"I'm sorry I've neglected you. I've been busy."

"For over a century?"

"You can thank Lady West for that."

"Now *I'm* responsible?"

"As I recall, you attacked us."

"We were defending the Israelites."

"They belonged to me. I couldn't just let them leave."

"You're going to rule the world soon enough. So why would it matter where they were?"

Ra laughed. "I love your spirit, Lady West. Now, let's let bygones be bygones."

"Fine."

"Now I need to talk to Arinna alone."

Shani went and started petting a pegasus. A few minutes later, she looked over and saw that Ra and Arinna were having sex, so she decided to go for a flight on a Pegasus. When she returned to the palace terrace, she saw ribbons of light beginning to form. Ra began to swing some kind of mace at Arinna's head. She tried to duck, but it was like she was moving in slow motion, and she took a glancing blow. As Arinna went down, Ra pounced on her. Shani dove feet first, kicking him off Arinna. Ra rolled to his feet. Arinna began to flicker, but Ra hit her with a temporal blast, and she staggered. Shani ran and kicked Ra in the side, but he caught her leg and slammed her to the ground, and everything went dark.

"Wake up, Lady West."

Ra came into focus.

"Now that you're both awake, I can explain why I'm really here."

"Why are you doing this to me?" Golden tears were on Arinna's cheeks.

"Why did you betray me? You were my Sun Goddess."

"I never betrayed you!"

"Are you going to deny Thor and Freyja visited here recently?"

"Is that why you finally decided to visit me? Everyone abandoned me."

"Don't try to turn this on me. I know you conspired with the others to kill me—"

"She rejected their request—" Shani cut in.

"You stay out of this. You pushing me centuries through the timeline caused this problem in the first place."

"Leave her alone!"

"Now, Arinna, what are they planning?"

"You know as much as I do."

"Don't lie to me!"

"You've changed. The Sun God I used to know had honor. You always wanted Egypt for yourself, but we agreed to respect each other's domains. Now that you can control time, you're breaking your promise. And for what? Control of the whole world?"

"The world belongs to me. I just never had the ability to seize it before."

"So now you're just a power-happy killer. Thor and Freyja were right to try and kill you."

"And there it is. You admit your betrayal. You could have been my queen. But now you must die."

Ra sent a blast of temporal energy into Arinna. She pulsed, and Ra stopped. He looked at Shani and said, "It looks like your power has transferred to Arinna. So there's only one thing I can do. Stabbing and beating won't work." Ra withdrew some kind of metal rope and began strangling Arinna.

"She's on your side! You don't have to do this!" Shani felt helpless.

"Shut up! I'll deal with you next."

Shani fought against her bindings with no effect, and the knot in her stomach was spreading into her arms and legs. The terrible situation dragged on for what felt like an eternity. The fight seemed to drain out of Arinna, and she locked eyes with Shani. Then, the light literally left Arinna's eyes. Suddenly, an explosion of light pulsed out of Arinna. As the wave washed over heaven, day turned to night. The sun in Hittite heaven had gone out, and Shani couldn't stop the tears. Another person who had meant so much to her was gone.

She didn't have much time to grieve as the blurry image of Ra filled her field of view.

"So, Lady West, I was content to leave you alone, but you have been a real obstacle to me, and I can't pass up the chance to remove that obstacle. It's nothing personal."

Ra wrapped another metal rope around his hands, then stepped behind her. The rope loop came down over her head, and her breath was cut off. She gripped the chair, but the pain only increased. The pressure in her chest overcame the sharp pain in her neck.

I don't want to die, she thought.

The flames spread from her chest through her whole body.

It's too much, make it stop!

There was no escape. The hopeless agony consumed her.

Just let it end!

The fire faded to a tingle that pulsed through her. As the numbness took her, the world became quiet. Arinna filled her narrow vision and and she wondered if the gods shared the same afterlife. And even if they did, Arinna was Hittite, not Egyptian... so would she see her in the Field of Reeds?

There was a flash in the mellow light, and the pressure was released. The heat drained from her head, and everything went dark.

The Shield

Shani woke up in a strange bed. The first thing she thought was odd was the size. It was twice the length of any bed she'd ever seen. The next thing was the room—everything was made of glass and metal. As she began to explore, the edges of the room illuminated like magic. The closest thing she'd ever seen before were the electric lights at Avalon. The walls had what looked like the image screens the Lords of Avalon used. The entire chamber was pristine. She couldn't find an ounce of dust. She approached a panel on the wall, and it slid open.

Shani entered a room with a bath. She turned and found her reflection in the mirror. There were dark shadows under her eyes and a bruise around her throat. As she examined her image, she wondered how she got here. And she didn't mean her strange location, which she decided must be some other god's heaven. She wondered how she had become a pawn in the games of the gods. She decided to try and find out where she was and who brought her here. She returned to the large chamber and approached another indented panel on the opposite wall. It opened to a grand hallway, at least ten cubits across and tall. But that wasn't the most amazing thing. Out the windows on the far side of the hall was a beautiful orb of white, blue, green, and brown. It was surrounded by total darkness. She realized it was Earth. She'd seen images of it from the sky-net. She must be in what the Lords of Avalon called space.

"Beautifully amazing, isn't it?"

Shani turned to find Inanna, who had addressed her in Babylonian.

"Where am I?"

"We call this place Nibiru."

"Why did you bring me here?"

"You needed medical attention."

"Did you try to help Arinna?"

"There was nothing we could do for her."

Shani's eyes welled at the thought of her friend. "How long was I out?"

"It's been a day."

"Then I'm late! ..."

Shani turned back to Inanna. "... I'm so grateful for your help, and I know I'm asking another favor, but can you take me to America? My husband will be worried sick."

"That won't be possible."

"Why not? I know you have the ability."

"Because we need you here." Marduk came up the hall.

"I'm confused."

"Let me make it clear, Lady West. We didn't interfere for your benefit. We need you to help us destroy Ra."

"I help you, and then you let me go?"

"Until then, you're our guest here," Inanna touched her shoulder.

"How long will it be?"

"It will take some time. We hadn't planned on taking you this early, but Ra forced our hand."

"How soon did you know?"

Inanna looked away.

"You let him kill Arinna?!"

"It was a risk to go there in the first place. And Ra and Arinna were together in the past," Marduk said.

"So that's why you let her die?"

"She wasn't our concern. You were," Inanna said.

"She could have helped you. Why didn't you join Thor and Freyja?"

"We work better on our own," Marduk said.

"This is why Ra will win—you divide, and he conquers."

"We will defeat him, and then you can go home," Inanna said.

"How long?"

"It will take some time to lay our trap," Marduk said.

"I will help you, but there's something I need to do. My husband and friends arrived in America yesterday. They will be worried sick. Take me to them and, when the time comes, come back to us and I will assist you."

"We can't take that chance. Ra might discover our plan, and you wouldn't be here to shield us," Marduk said.

"Fine, but at least let my husband know I'm alright."

"We can't do that either—" Inanna began, and Shani exploded. "Why not?!"

"—If they know, it increases the odds for Ra to find out. And I know your friends—they won't accept this arrangement. Then we would have another problem," Inanna said.

"You're cowards! You're just as bad as Ra! Maybe it would be better if he wins." Shani went back into the chamber and collapsed in tears on the bed. When she woke up, Inanna was on the bed.

"You're here to keep an eye on me?"

"Lady West, I'm sorry about all this."

"Go away. Let the pawn alone."

"You're not a pawn."

"I'm not? All of you gods seem to want to take advantage of my power. None of you care about me or my life. I'm just a shield against Ra."

"I don't think you understand the seriousness of the situation. For millennia, the gods have fostered civilization. We all respected each other's domains, but Ra has thrown the world into chaos. You're a young, potential goddess, so you don't know what it's like to live life as an immortal, and now death is a real possibility," Inanna's voice broke.

Shani touched her hand. "I think I can understand your fear. We mortals live with it our whole lives, so I will try to help you."

"Thank you," Inanna sniffled. "Now let me show you around... This will be your private chamber. Through here are the bathing facilities. And there's much more to show you and some people to meet."

Inanna guided her out and down the hall. Despite her prisoner status, Shani couldn't deny the beauty out the windows to her left. They turned into a large chamber—around 50 cubits in each direction. All the furnishings were massive—probably twice the size of regular furniture. It did match the new gods in the room, who were like Inanna and Marduk—twice the height of normal people. The men also shared the same glowing eyes as Inanna and Marduk.

"This room is the lounge. This is Enlil, God of Storms. And Enki, God of Water and Knowledge."

They had gray and white hair, respectively—and dark blue and light green eyes, respectively.

Shani followed Inanna back into the hall. As they were walking, another god approached. He had black hair and orange eyes.

"This is Nanna, God of Wisdom."

He looked at Shani but said nothing—just like the others.

They continued and entered an enormous room, at least 100 cubits in each direction. It reminded Shani of the recreation center in Avalon. There was a god lifting weights. He looked at her with his glowing yellow eyes. He had brown hair, and like all the others, he had a beard.

"This is the gymnasium, and this is Utu, the Sun God."

His title brought Arinna back to mind. It took a moment to steady herself. Then she had to catch up with Inanna, who had exited into the hallway.

As they made their way around, the moon replaced the earth out the windows. They finally turned into the chamber that had a dome of windows. Four goddesses were seated around a large table, speaking an unfamiliar language. Inanna introduced each of them:

"This is Ninlil, Goddess of the Air; Gula, Goddess of Healing; Kishar, Goddess of the Earth; and Mammetum, Goddess of Fate."

Shani was impressed by the color range of features the Anunnaki possessed. Ninlil had white hair and lavender eyes. Gula had yellow hair and turquoise eyes. Kishar's brown hair was normal, but her eyes glowed like emeralds. Mammetum was the most unusual, with hair the color of pomegranates and her eyes the color of a pink flamingo—a bird she saw in America before they jumped through time.

"And we have one final stop..."

Shani followed Inanna out the opposite side they had entered and entered an enormous, domed chamber. It was filled with strange plants and trees. The chamber was about the same size as the Hittite capital, Hattusa.

"This is the garden, my favorite place in Nibiru."

They walked through a mushroom patch as tall as Shani's knees, and there were flowers bigger than her head. They came to a clearing where two more gods were seated on a bench, kissing.

"My apologies. I'm just showing our guest around... Lady West, this is Anu, the Sky God and founder of the Anunnaki. And Ninhursag, the Mother Goddess."

Anu's hair was white like clouds, and his eyes matched the color of the sky. Ninhursag's hair was the color of oranges, and her eyes were purple like figs. They looked at her momentarily, then went back to kissing. Inanna led Shani down a path that led to a towering forest. Like everything else in Nibaru, these trees were twice as tall as anything she'd seen on Earth.

As the forest thinned to a grassy oasis, Inanna said, "I hope there's enough space that you don't feel trapped."

"So it's going to be a while?"

"It's not that bad here. Let me show you one more thing." Inanna guided her to the edge of the garden. "These stations..." she indicated an indent in the wall, "... will give you anything you need. Food, drinks, clothes, or things like writing materials... Let me demonstrate—Give me a glass of wine."

Like magic, a glass of wine formed from nothing. Inanna downed it quickly, then replaced the cup. "Return," Inanna said to the station, and the cup disappeared as it had appeared.

They left the garden and made their way back to Shani's chamber.

"I almost forgot—don't try to break the windows to escape. Out there is instant death... Don't forget it." Inanna left her standing there.

Shani got a glass of wine from the station in her room and then went and looked down at the Earth from above. She saw the American coast spinning into view. It seemed tiny. All she wanted was to be down there with Mbizi. But all she could do was pray she would get to see him again.

The Anunnaki

Shani sat in the observatory with a great view of Earth. It was her favorite place to write to help deal with the long wait for the Anunnaki's plan to come together. She decided to use Julie's example of writing a journal:

Another season comes to a close. This makes five since I was imprisoned here in Nibiru. Inanna has finally said that the trap is nearly set, so it won't be much longer. It has been almost eight years since I saw Mbizi. Thankfully, his image has yet to fade from my mind's view.

Shani paused, closed her eyes, and she could see him.

Ever since Inanna told me, the anticipation to touch him again has been building. Each day brings us closer to reunion. Life in Nibiru hasn't been so bad. I've had to stay active, training my martial skills to remain in peak physical shape. I may have spoiled my tongue because the god stations have allowed me to indulge in many exotic foods. I also like to spend time with what the Anunnaki call unicorns. They're beautiful multi-colored horses with a horn that extends from their heads. Another challenge I've taken on during my time here is learning the language of the Anunnaki. Their strange glyphs are all over Nibiru, and the gods usually only speak Babylonian when they address me. So I've had years to listen to their conversations with each other. It's come to the point where I'm almost fluent. Before I close this season-marking entry, I have to mention Arinna. Inanna has usually refused to discuss her, but recently, I discovered that they seem to have just left her the way she was, with no attention to honor or burial. I'm not sure what you do to honor the gods, but I need to return to Hittite heaven to show respect for my friend.

--Shani, Lady West, May 1, 1278 BC

She signed off using the Avalonian calendar as usual.

"Shani, I don't mean to disturb you, but there's something I feel I should tell you," Inanna said in Anunnaki, then led her into the gardens.

"What is it?" Shani replied in kind.

"Lord West and the Lords of Avalon discovered your ship. They will probably leave Egypt to look for you."

"How much longer will it be to take down Ra?"

"A few days more, and we'll be ready. And when we win, I will take you to your husband, no matter where he is."

"Thank you, Inanna. You've been good to me these past couple of years."

Inanna touched her shoulder, "I do value your friendship."
"As do I. Up for a game of Senet?"
They headed to the lounge.

A few days passed terribly slowly. Shani was trying to distract herself from the clock. She was sitting next to the large pond in the gardens, feeding the light fish. She always loved watching the fluid, luminous motion of their rainbow colors dancing below the surface of the water.

"Lady West."

Shani's trance was broken by spoken Egyptian. She stood, facing the Norse goddess Freyja.

"What are you doing here?" Shani asked.

"Ra knows! He's discovered the Anunnaki plot against him."

Suddenly, a loud noise pulsed through the air. In a matter of flashes, they were encircled by the Anunnaki.

"Freyja! You can't be here! You're risking our whole plan!" Inanna's eyes flared.

"I came to warn you! Ra knows your plan! You need to hide!" Freyja spun entirely around.

"Too late." Ra's unmistakable voice struck the air.

Anubis and Set flanked the Sun God. Then everything happened at once:

Freyja vanished in a flash. Then, the dozen gods of Babylon froze as the light ribbons filled the air. Shani felt the wave from Ra pass by, and she instinctively reacted. She forced the wave back, and the world sped up again. This sparked a melee clash. Anubis and Set were beaten to the ground in seconds, while Ra's temporal blast had a savage effect on the Anunnaki. But the numbers were showing their advantage. Ra was becoming overwhelmed. Just as it seemed the Anunnaki might claim victory, another pulse froze the battle.

Ra locked eyes with Shani, and he pushed back her counter-wave. The temporal state began fluctuating. Ra was clenching his fists, shaking his head. He broke eye contact, and his gaze shifted. He locked eyes again but opened his hand, reaching toward the ground. The Anunnaki were moving in, starts and stops all around him. A beam left his palm and began penetrating the grass. As time passed, Shani started to feel the strain in her bones. She was losing the battle of wills. The power from his hand was unrelenting. She tried to understand what he was doing. Finally, the wave pulsing from Ra became too much. She fell to the ground, and the light froze in the air. Shani had no strength to stand. Ra cut off the hand pulse and forced his way out of the grasp of the Anunnaki. He walked over to her, and her body wouldn't allow her to retreat. His massive hand took hold of her. The whole time, Shani was trying to restore the time flow. The streaks vanished, and things began a sluggish movement. Flame burst through the ground and spread toward her. She saw Inanna disappear in a flash. Then, as the flame expanded across the garden, ready to consume her and everything else, she was blinded, and a jolt struck her body.

Her sight cleared, and she was on the balcony in River Palace.

An explosion of light blared out the full moon in the starry sky. Once the flash faded, that terrifying voice sent chills down her back.

"Lady West, I've brought you home to Egypt."

Shani balled her fist, gritting her teeth to quell her stomach. She struggled to her feet and then asked, "What just happened?"

"I destroyed Nibiru, then brought you here so you would survive."

"And the Anunnaki?"

"I doubt they survived space without the protection of Nibiru."

Shani tried not to cry about the Babylonian gods. "I don't understand you. The last time we met, you tried to kill me. Now, you saved me when you could have let me die."

"I've decided to offer a truce to the Lords of Avalon. Allowing you to die would destroy any chance of that."

"A truce?"

"You and your friends have been a terrible problem for me. And the fact that it all began with mistaken identity, I feel we can come to an understanding if your side will let the past stay in the past."

"That's easy for you to say!"

"You think I haven't suffered at your hands?"

"No! You can't get hurt!"

"Do you realize every time you've pushed me through time, I've been trapped in a temporal suspension? The time still goes by like normal, but I can't move, I can't do anything. I'm trapped with nothing but my thoughts for centuries. Do you know what that's like?" Ra's stoic image faltered. His voice broke, and his eyes watered. He flinched his cheek, regaining his composure.

Despite everything, that realization turned her stomach. "I didn't know."

"That's in the past." Ra vanished in a blink.

Shani's new reality returned to her, and she ran to find the manager.

"Lady West, my name is Raziya. What can I do for you?"

"Are they here?"

"They left days ago. They went to Babylon to look for you."

The ground moved beneath her feet, her destination always out of reach. She would have to wait once more.

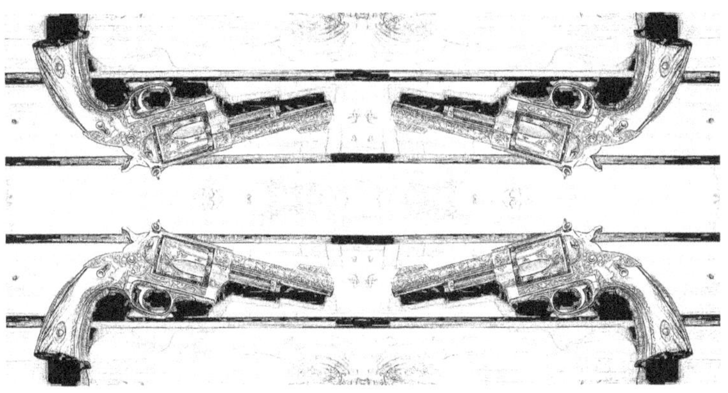

<u>Ancient Aliens</u>

T HREE WEEKS AT SEA had been busy. Micheal had discovered a large section of the sky-net had been knocked offline shortly after they had left Egypt.

"It's been a lot of work to restore the patch to operational status. But it looks like we'll finally get some clue about what happened."

Micheal had the feed come in on the ship's screen.

"What is that?" Julie touched a spot where light began to expand out of nothing.

"I'm zooming in. There!" Micheal could see a small object at the point of ignition of the flash.

"Data analysis indicates that the object is over a mile wide at a distance of approximately 12,000 miles." Julie was typing like a mad hacker. "The force measure of the energy wave just before blackout indicates an explosion of around 10,000 megatons."

"We would have seen that."

"I think we did. Remember when we were in that storm at night, and suddenly the night appeared as day?"

"That's right... What could cause such an explosion?"

"Based on these readings, it looks like it might have been a matter, anti-matter explosion."

"That amount of force would require about 500 pounds of antimatter, so it had to be artificial."

"I bet the gods are behind this."

"It could be an alien ship."

"Maybe the gods aren't from around here?"

"Ancient aliens?"

"The Anunnaki were supposed to be from Planet X, which was supposed to be called Nibiru."

"Maybe they were."

"And if that ship belonged to the Anunnaki, and Inanna said they're all gone, maybe that explosion killed the rest of them."

"You think Shani was on that ship?"

"I hope not."

"What ship?" They were interrupted by Mbizi.

"Don't worry about it." Micheal knew what Mbizi might do.

"You said Shani was on a ship."

Micheal looked to Julie, "He deserves to know."

"Okay, Mbizi, you might want to sit down."

"I'll stand."

Micheal took a deep breath. "Let me start by saying we don't know anything for certain..."

"But...?"

"...there's a chance Shani was on a ship that exploded last month."

"What ship?" Mbizi looked side-eye.

"This will be a little complicated. Remember how a large portion of the sky-net went dark last month, limiting our ability to scan?"

"Yes."

"We think that the electromagnetic pulse of an antimatter explosion knocked out part of the network."

"I don't understand."

"Ok, let me try this: we explained the concept of space, right?"

"Yes."

"We think the Anunnaki had a ship designed to sail through space, and based on what Inanna said, we think it's been destroyed."

"And you think Shani was on board?"

"It's possible."

"Could she survive?" Mbizi's eyes welled.

"That would be unlikely." Julie touched his shoulder.

Mbizi dropped his head as the tears streamed, then he staggered away.

"You're taking this better than I would have expected." Julie came over and took Micheal's hand.

"We don't know anything for sure." Micheal decided he would only accept hard proof.

"It's okay to mourn. You don't always have to be so strong."

"I'm a scientist. I need proof. And on that note, I want to discuss this discovery."

Julie studied him for a moment, then sighed. "Ok."

"Out of all the gods we've met, the Anunnaki are the most..."

"Alien?"

"For years, we've speculated about the nature of the gods, and the concept of ancient aliens has been a major possibility."

"Do you think all the gods are aliens?"

"That's hard to say. The gods we've met have covered a range of physical differences and superpowers."

"Because the Anunnaki and Egyptian gods are physical giants?"

"And the likes of David seem as normal as you and me."

"Do you think the gods created the human race?" asked Julie.

"Sounds like someone watched too much *Ancient Aliens*." Micheal laughed.

"They may have been on to something."

"The only ones we can say are likely aliens are the Anunnaki. That spaceship had to be from another world."

"We don't even know that for sure. The only thing all the gods have in common is their time powers. So how do we know they aren't humans from some distant future?"

"That's a good point."

"Well, I'm going to check on Mbizi." Julie kissed Micheal's cheek, then walked away.

Micheal brought the image of the ship up on the monitor and closely examined the object, then looked up at the stars with new interest. He wondered if there were other undetected spacecraft up there. He began a further analysis of the object as he turned the Valkyrie into the Delta.

<u>Truce</u>

The revelation of what likely happened to Shani had sent Mbizi into a rage. He had smashed everything available in his cabin, then broke down completely. When he finally reigned in the tears, he remembered there was a chance she wasn't there when it happened. And there was someone who should be able to give him a more accurate idea.

He sat amidst the destruction in his cabin and reached out to Inanna. Mbizi saw a view from a high location, looking down on a beach below with moonlight illuminating the sea beyond. He recognized it was Avalon.

"So now you want to take my home as well?" he spoke bitterly.

"Lord West, I'm not in the mood for this."

"I don't care. I know about the spaceship. You owe me an explanation."

Her eyes closed, and when they opened, the view was blurry. "What do you want to know?"

"Was Shani on your ship?"

"Yes."

"For how long?"

"Nearly two years."

"How could you keep her from me? You had to know the situation."

"Marduk needed her help to have a chance against Ra... but it wasn't enough. Ra found out our plan."

"Ra destroyed your ship?"

"Yes. All my family are dead." Inanna was clearly weeping.

"Is there any chance Shani escaped before it happened?"

"I don't know."

"Don't lie to me!"

"It's the truth. The time was dilating at different rates because of Ra's power fight against Shani. I saw an explosion beginning, so I teleported out of there. I don't know what happened after that."

"You left them all behind?"

"I just reacted. Thousands of years together, and now they're gone. I'm sorry, Lord West. I'm sorry for everything." She was beginning to sob.

"You have my sympathies." Mbizi cut the link.

He screamed his sorrow and punched the wall. He turned, and

Julie was standing there. He dropped his head; then he felt her embrace from behind. His bones ached, and his muscles failed, so he collapsed to his knees. Then, his mind went blank.

Mbizi must have slept because he woke up curled on the floor. He made his way to the bridge and found Micheal and Julie preparing for their arrival at River Palace. They docked at the Lord's elevator in the first light of dawn. As they reached the top, the doors opened. Raziya was waiting.

"Lord West, there's something I must tell you…"

At that moment, Shani ran through the door to the entry hall. Mbizi thought he must be seeing ghosts, but then she ran into his arms. Her pleasant perfume was intoxicating. Her skin was satin, and her lips were sugar. As each moment passed, he held her close, afraid the dream would end if he let go.

"Oh, Mbizi! I have so much to tell you—"

Before she could say another word, a flash lit the room. Set and Anubis appeared. A second later, Ra materialized in front of them. Micheal and Julie stepped up, prepared to fight.

"We didn't come for that." Ra opened his arms.

"Then why are you here?" Julie demanded.

"In a moment. First, Lady West, happy reunion. And allow me to apologize for my unintended interference that put you in this predicament."

"What game are you playing?" Micheal scowled.

"This isn't a game. I've come to offer the same truce I offered centuries ago—you stay out of my way, and I'll leave you be."

"Why would you make this offer?" Mbizi asked.

"We should never have been enemies. My mistake in attacking Lord and Lady Avalon centuries ago began this feud. It shouldn't have happened, and as I told Lady West, she pushed me through time and trapped me for centuries with nothing to do but think. And after I got over my anger, I decided this was the best course of action. The four of you have been a royal pain, and we could go back and forth with who did what to whom, but why don't we leave that in the past and agree to respect each other's space."

Everyone was quiet for a moment, then Julie stepped forward.

"You have a deal. Right?" Julie eyed each of them.

"Agreed," Micheal said.

"Deal," Shani said.

Everyone focused on Mbizi. "Okay," he decided.

He had to quell a storm of emotions that wanted to explode on the Sun God for the last two years of hell.

"Well then, I'll let you get back to it," Ra said. Then, the gods vanished.

"I'm so glad you're back!" Julie hugged Shani.

"We'll have to catch up," Micheal touched her shoulder. Then they exited to their quarters.

Shani pulled Mbizi into their private quarters and attacked him voraciously. Her mouth tried to consume him as their clothes scattered across the floor. His hands explored her like it was the first time. He needed a deeper connection, and she demanded the same.

"I need you inside me!"

He obeyed, and their bodies became one. His reckoning of time lost its meaning as his heart pounded a rhythm. His body released the pent-up years in a sensory explosion. Before he could catch his breath, Shani made a demand.

"I need more!" And they went for round two.

They exhausted each other.

The next morning, Mbizi's mind was calm for the first time in years.

"Mbizi?"

"Yes."

"I have so much to tell you."

"I want to know everything."

Shani explained her encounter with Ra in the time conduit, her time in America, being sold into slavery, and being rescued by the Sun Goddess of the Hittites.

"This is going to be the most difficult thing to share."

Mbizi became concerned, "What is it?"

Her head dropped. "I haven't been faithful."

Mbizi pulled back. "You cheated?"

"I was so lonely. All that time alone. In those three years with Arinna, I came to love her. And as it was time to say goodbye, I couldn't leave without a truer expression of my feelings." Shani shook her head, avoiding eye contact.

The confession sent a wave of emotions through his whole person: anger, relief, betrayal, compassion, and empathy all made an appearance. But mostly empathy. He understood the loneliness and knew it was far worse for her. He squeezed his fists and breathed deeply. Then he turned her to look at him.

"It's ok. I'm not happy about it, but I understand."

"I'm sorry, Mbizi."

"Shh..."

When she stopped crying, he broke their embrace and said, "I'm thankful she took care of you for me."

Her reaction to his statement was confusing as she began to weep.

"What is it?"

"Arinna's dead. Ra killed her."

His body pulsed with anger at Ra. "That bastard!"

"Forget about Ra. I need your help."

"My help?"

"The Anunnaki left Arinna alone in Hittite heaven. I need you to contact David so he can help us get there. Arinna deserves honor and respect."

"We should bring Micheal and Julie in on this."

They were on the balcony in Micheal and Julie's chambers. Mbizi thought about David.

"Lord West?"

"We need your help."

David materialized.

"You can access Hittite heaven, right?" Shani asked.

"Why do you want to go there? I doubt Arinna would welcome the intrusion."

"Arinna's dead. We want to lay her to rest."

David's typical stoicism momentarily faltered. "That's terrible. She was a good woman."

"So you'll help?" Shani stepped forward.

"Of course. Arinna deserves that."

"Thank you."

"Everyone gather around." There was a flash as they jumped out.

<u>Sun-Set</u>

They arrived at the front of the Golden Palace. Shani's bones began to throb as she looked up at the top.

"Arinna's up there."

"How do we get there?" Julie asked.

"We fly. Just think you want to move in that direction, and you will."

Shani levitated above them, along with David. In just a few moments, they were all approaching the roof. Arinna was in the same position she was when Shani was last here. She clearly had remained frozen in time.

Two years had done nothing to dim the radiant beauty of her friend. The metal rope was still tied around her neck, and Arinna seemed to be staring into the distance. Shani couldn't get any closer. She began to breathe rapidly. Then she felt a hand touch her.

"It's okay. I will take care of her for you." Micheal's eyes were kind.

He went and passed his hand over Arinna's face, and when it cleared, she seemed to be sleeping. Micheal worked on the rope around her neck while Julie and Mbizi untied her legs. Micheal picked Arinna up and carried her to the bed of clouds. Shani had an urge to cover her as she was completely exposed.

"Shani, is there anything to dress her with?" Julie was pulling her away.

"Oh. Yes. Follow me."

They returned with Arinna's favorite sundress and sandals. Her glowing crown completed the image of the Sun Goddess. Once Arinna was dressed, a new question arose.

"How do you lay a goddess to rest?" Micheal wondered.

"Allow me," David said. He'd been patiently monitoring the proceedings.

He stretched forth his hand, and the clouds above began to twist into a spiral. It reminded Shani of the tropical cyclones she'd seen from the sky-net.

"I made a bed for her up there," David explained.

Micheal took Arinna in his arms and flew up toward the spiral. Everyone followed, and as he placed her on the bed, they encircled Arinna, floating in the air.

Shani began to speak. "Arinna, Goddess of the Sun, when my night was at its darkest, you came and warmed me with your sunlight. You were my most true friend. You were the only god that wasn't trying to use me in some way. And your bright optimism made the years feel so much shorter. I still laugh at your instance of training me to be a goddess. I've missed you every day. The world lost some of its light when yours went out. So now I say farewell, and I will see you again someday. I love you, Arinna." Shani finished, then went and kissed her on the forehead.

"That was beautiful." Julie came and embraced her.

Micheal came and grabbed her hand, then touched Julie's shoulder.

Suddenly, a burst of light shone on Arinna, and the scene changed. Shani saw herself and Arinna flying with the Pegasus. She realized it was an actual moment from her past. She and Arinna had just returned from advising the king in Hattusa. As she and Arinna landed on the roof of the Golden Palace, the images faded, and her current moment was restored.

"Did you see that?" Shani asked.

"See what?" Micheal scanned the area.

"I don't know. It was like watching a memory."

"Your mind probably reacted to your emotional state," Julie suggested.

Shani wasn't knowledgeable enough about how the mind worked to disagree.

"You're probably right."

"Are we ready to return?" David hovered nearby.

"May I have a moment?" Shani asked.

Everyone descended to the palace. Shani ran her hand up Arinna's cheek.

"Don't worry. I can see you every day in the sky above. And here you remain a sun that never sets." Shani kissed Arinna and then slowly joined her friends. They jumped back to River Palace.

"If you want to visit in the future, I'm just a call away." David bowed, then vanished in a flash.

<u>The Battle of Kadesh</u>

May 28, 1274 B.C.

Today is the 4ᵗʰ anniversary of our truce with Ra. We've only had two respectful run-ins with the Sun God, and I feel we made the right decision. It has allowed us to live a more "normal" life. We've become close friends and advisors to Ramesses the Great. At the same time, Mbizi and Shani have moved into the Palace of the West, located near modern Alexandria on the Mediterranean coast. Ramesses had insisted on the project, and since the move, they had retired from court. Every so often, one of the other gods tries to rope us back into that mess of Ra's making, but we remain steadfast.

Micheal and I are like two parts of a whole. But I guess anyone would feel that way after 70 years together. I never thought I'd live to see 100 years, but here I am—a centenarian. Micheal still teases me about it. I wonder if any other triple-digit person would be preparing for battle. We are with Ramesses in Canaan, and Micheal says it will soon be known as the Battle of Kadesh. It will be my first combat in years. These situations always bring back terrible memories. I wish we would've told Ramesses no when he requested our help in the campaign. But here we are...

"Am I interrupting?" Isis appeared in the tent.

"Why are you here? We already told you of our deal with Ra."

"There's too few of us left to stop him."

"And why is that our problem? What have the gods ever done for anyone but themselves."

"We are more important than you know. We've propped up human civilization for a very long time. And I've helped you."

"Only in service of your own ends."

"That's not fair. I consider you a friend."

"A friend? You hardly ever visit. You are always so focused on this never-ending battle with Ra."

"You're right—I've been a poor friend. But I care about all of you. I'll do better in the future, but there might not be a future if you don't help."

"I'll assess our friendship going forward, based on your actions, but this fearmongering will not change our minds about this Ra situation. Just leave us out of this feud of the gods."

"I feel a disturbance in the future. This is about more than our conflict over Egypt."

"There's a saying where I come from: 'With great power comes great responsibility'. Unlike you, I hold no great power, so I have no great responsibility."

"You're wrong. You are one of us, and we all hold a responsibility. But have it your way. Stay here and watch the world fall." Isis spread her wings as she exited the tent, then took to the sky.

Julie picked up the quill and returned to the papyrus:

...are. And speaking of the gods trying to rope us in—my "friend" Isis just stopped by. Apparently, the world will end again, and the only people who can stop it are Micheal and me, as usual. I quote Riddick from Chronicles: "Had to end sometime." And with that happy thought, it's time for another battle.

Julie made her way to Ramesses' tent for the war council. She was dawning the new Isis-inspired battle suit they had crafted in Avalon. A tri-poly bodysuit covering from her knees to her wrist, patterned in red, white, and green. She wore matching knee-high boots and a golden head cover. Micheal was waiting outside the tent. He was sporting his Osiris-inspired battle suit. He was covered neck to knees in white, with green boots and gloves.

"You definitely look the goddess."

"I think I've had enough goddess for one day."

"What happened?"

"Never mind. I'll tell you later. I think we're expected."

They entered, and the council bowed.

"We have received information that Muwatalli is in the land of Aleppo, some twenty leagues away. What say you?" Ramesses inquired.

"What's the source of this information?" Micheal seemed to tense.

"Earlier, just after fording the river, two Shasu nomads said the Hittite king fears His Majesty," one of the generals said.

"They're a diversion sent by Muwatalli. He's already camped on the east of the Orontes."

"How do you know that?" Prince Amunherkhepeshef asked.

"Our unique connections are why we're here."

"So, did Osiris tell you?" another general mocked.

"If we don't prepare for battle immediately, the Hittite chariots will overrun this camp."

"If this is true, why didn't you alert us earlier?" Prince Ramesses asked.

"Our foresight is not perfect. Until I heard about the nomads, I didn't know the moment was here."

At that instant, a scout burst into the tent. He had two men with him.

"These are Hatti spies."

"Who are you?" the Pharaoh asked.

"The king of Hatti sent us to spy on you?"

"Where is King Muwatalli? I had heard he was in the land of Aleppo."

"The king has already arrived, along with many countries who support him. His armies are armed with chariots and weapons of war, more numerous than the sands on the beach. They are ready for battle. You cannot win this."

"Get them out of here... My governors failed me! ... send word: get Ptah and Set divisions here immediately!"

"What do we do?" Prince Khaemweset asked.

"You prepare the Amun division for the impending attack, Prince Pareherwenemef. Take the royal family to safety in the west. Princes Amunherkhepeshef and Ramesses with me," Ramesses directed.

"We will provide cover," Julie said.

She and Micheal ran to their chariot, sitting on a hill stocked with arrows. They'd had thousands made for this campaign. Julie drew her tri-poly recurve bow and sighted the Hittite chariots charging from the south. Once the enemy was at around 400 yards range, she unleashed a rain of bolts. She and Micheal let loose about ten arrows each before the chariots reached the shield wall of the Amun division. More than a dozen chariots had been taken down, slowing the charge. Julie continued the rain on the backside of the Hittite chariots. The shield wall failed, and the camp was overrun. The Amun division began to retreat.

"The Pharaoh is in trouble!" Micheal yelled.

Julie turned and joined Micheal in targeting the Hittites who'd surrounded Ramesses.

"Let's go!" Julie mounted up her horse and charged into the melee. She rapid-fired dozens of arrows before she was in the midst of it. Julie found herself being sucked into her battle zone. She became separated from herself. Her vision saw the stroke of her sword slicing through the enemy. Her ears heard the whoosh of arrows leaving her bow, even through the thunder of the battle. She felt the impact of spear thrusts and sword strikes deflecting off her body army. Her nostrils minimized the worst aspect of a battlefield—the combined smell of blood, shit, piss, vomit, and body odor. She tasted blood from a bitten tongue.

The ebbs and flows of the battle moved around her like she was on the sideline but also in the midst of it until she and Micheal were flanking Ramesses on a final pursuit of the Hittites fleeing the field. The Pharaoh called a halt to the attack on the banks of the Orontes. The remnants of Muwatalli's army were fleeing beyond Kadesh.

Julie closed her eyes, trying to reunite her battle zone and central aspects.

"Are you all right?"

Julie's eyes flashed open to find Micheal's hand on her shoulder. "I'm fine."

She shook her head and found herself whole again.

"The battle's over. Let's go."

They returned to the ruin of the camp.

"Do you ever feel like you have a dissociative aspect of yourself during battle?" Julie asked as she and Micheal began to wash the filth from each other in their private tent.

"I've always spoken of the zone I go into for battle, but my memory seems to prevent any chance of dissociation."

"You've also always said you never allow the battlefield to affect your everyday life."

"As you know, I compartmentalize my memory files. I have a deep recess where I keep those terrible things. Why are you asking now? In the last seventy years, you've rarely talked about any of this."

"I think my mindset changed over the past few years. We've fought so many battles together, and it's worn me down. I was relieved when Ra made his offer. I almost hoped the fight was over. But it won't ever end, will it?"

"We could move to Avalon. Then we'll have four years to decide if we continue this quest."

"Could you do that?"

"I could do anything for you."

"I doubt the gods would leave us alone, as today's visit from Isis portends."

Micheal wiped her face with a hot rag. "Tell me about this visit."

<u>Temporal Sync</u>

"Mbizi? Come here!"

He joined Shani in the bathroom of their private chambers in the Palace of the West.

"What is it?"

"Do you feel this?" She placed her hand on his stomach. She felt the movement again.

"What is that?"

"I think... I think I'm pregnant."

"Really? I didn't think that was possible."

"I have been in this time for 11 years. Maybe I've synced up."

"I'm going to be a father?"

Shani loved the smile on his face. She was equally excited to be a mother. Shani considered that though she was physically about 20, she was now 43 years old. After being out of sync for so long, she'd given up the idea of motherhood.

Mbizi wrapped her in his embrace.

She closed her eyes. When they opened, she saw something strange. A young boy, perhaps 3 years old, was running in the courtyard of River Palace. He was the very image of Mbizi. He ran into Julie's arms. She picked him up and spun around. As Shani looked into the boy's eyes, she saw her own, and the same feeling she experienced at Arinna's funeral passed over her. This wasn't the first time she felt she was seeing out of time. She realized the boy must be her son. It felt like he was looking back at her. Julie whispered in his ear, and Shani's son waved at her. Julie spun again, and their eyes met. After a moment, Julie gave her a sad smile and a small wave. Then the scene faded, and all she saw was her chamber.

"Do you think it will be a boy or a girl?" Mbizi asked.

"We're going to have a son."

"How do you know?"

"I don't know. Call Julie. She'll be able to know for sure."

While Mbizi used the sky-net communicator to notify Julie and Micheal, Shani considered the implications. They were little more than three years from the next time jump, but she wasn't sure she would want to continue once she became a mother.

Two hours later, Micheal and Julie arrived.

"Congratulations! How long have you known?" Julie gave her an enthusiastic hug.

"I just realized—I felt him kick."

Julie's eyes narrowed. "He kicked? If he's kicking, you've been pregnant for a while." Julie seemed to scan her. "May I?" she indicated Shani's stomach.

"Yes."

Julie felt her belly. "He's got quite a kick."

"You think it's a boy?"

"I don't know, but we can find out."

"You can do that?"

"I can use something called a magnetic resonance scan to image your baby inside you."

"This is why we question you being a goddess."

Julie laughed. "Come lay down."

Shani lay on her bed while Julie kneeled beside her. Mbizi and Micheal stood behind Julie. Julie placed something on her stomach, then a few minutes later...

"It's a boy! Would you like to see?"

"Please!"

Julie handed her the communicator. There was a moving image of what looked like a baby holding his hands to his face. She could see it was a boy, as his phallus was visible, and he kicked his right leg. It was incredible to see her son inside her. She felt an overwhelming feeling of love for him. Mbizi came and watched with her, holding her hand.

"Our son."

Shani kissed his hand.

"You've been pregnant for five months. You will give birth around the winter solstice.

As the shortest day of the year arrived, so did Shani's son. Julie had watched over her as she grew large with child, ensuring her son would be healthy. And now it was time.

"Ok, Shani—breathe and push. Breathe and push."

Mbizi was holding her hand throughout her labor.

"Breathe and push. I can see his head. Now push hard!"

"Aaah!"

"One more time!"

"Aaaaah..."

The pressure was released.

"Well done!"

Julie did something, and then Shani heard her son for the first time as he cried. A few minutes later, Julie lay him in her arms.

"What will you name him?" Julie asked.

"Merneptah. Which means: 'Loved of Ptah—joyous is truth'."

"It's beautiful."

The next day, Ramesses arrived to pay his respects. The Pharaoh was holding their son. "What's his name?"

"We named him in honor of Your Majesty and your great building prowess. His name is Merneptah." Mbizi nodded.

Ramesses smiled as Merne grabbed his finger.

"We have a special request," Shani asked.

"Of course."

"Would you honor us by accepting the title of Godfather?"

"I would love to, Lady West."

The scene transitioned. Shani saw herself in the Lord's Hall in the Palace of the West. Merneptah was several cubits away.

"Mama!" he said, then walked to her.

"Good job!" She picked up Merne and spun him around.

As she saw herself turn her back, Merneptah locked eyes with her. After a while, he laughed, maintaining eye contact. The same chill came over her. Then, the scene faded.

"Shani, are you all right?" Julie asked.

"I don't know."

"What's wrong?"

Shani hesitated.

"That's okay, you don't have to tell me," Julie began to walk away.

"Wait... I've been seeing things."

"Like visions?"

"Like events from different times."

"You see the future?"

"I've seen both past and future."

"How long?"

"The first time was at Arinna's funeral."

"That was four years ago."

"I just thought it was... in my head, as you say."

Julie examined her. "I think you're gaining a new time power. Or should I say *have* a new time power? It's similar to a friend I had ages ago. Melina had the ability to see across time and space. Past, present, and future."

"And you think that's what this is?"

"It's what makes sense to me."

"That sounds right."

At that moment, Mbizi, Micheal, and Ramesses approached.

"My godson is a strong young man." Ramesses handed Merne to her. "I must return to Pi-Ramesses. It was a pleasure to meet your son." Ramesses bowed, then left.

Shani thought about these windows in time she'd been seeing through and tried to believe it was another time power. The now familiar chill in her bones cast doubt on that idea. What if it was something else? Something much more sinister.

CHAPTER 27: RESPONSIBILITY

Thor and Freyja

A couple of weeks after the birth of Merneptah, Micheal, and Julie returned to River Palace to celebrate his 98th birthday and mark 71 years in the timeline. Then, they fell into a comfortable routine... until the deluge came.

Micheal had worn Julie out on the night of their 66th anniversary. He still had some energy, so he went to the balcony. The full moon blazed a silver path across the flooded Delta to the horizon. Peak deluge was always one of his favorite times of the year. Micheal looked up at the familiar patterns in the night sky. He focused on the precise positions of various stars and measured them against his memory of other points in time. This had become one of his favorite games. One only possible because of their time-trekking. Even then, he knew he was the only one who could tell the stars were moving through the sky. As he marveled at it, a bright flash blurred out his peripheral vision. Micheal turned to see Thor cradling a woman in his arms.

"Help! Lord Avalon, help!"

Micheal rushed over. "What happened?"

"Ra. He attacked Asgard. I barely got us out, but Freyja took a brutal hit!"

Micheal was momentarily curious about the Norse goddess. Then he remembered. "I don't know how we could possibly help her."

"He attacked her with a temporal energy blast, and you are the only ones who can help her."

"We're not gods. What can we do?"

"You're time rogues. We know you possess time powers. Frigg told all of us that if we were injured by time, the Lords of Avalon could fix it."

"I don't know how. We might have a time power, but it's latent." Micheal looked at Freyja—her eyes held a death stare.

"What's going on?" Julie entered the balcony.

"Help her! She's dying!" Thor was desperate.

"We can't get involved."

"Please!... I can't lose her..." Thor was in tears.

Micheal looked at the fluctuating hole in Freyja's chest. He closed his eyes and thought about the moments when their "power" seemed to emerge. Then he had an idea.

Micheal kneeled next to Freyja, "Julie, help me."

"Micheal, we can't."

"We can't just let her die."

"We made a deal."

"Fuck the deal! Now, are you going to help me or not?"

"You're going to get us killed." Julie kneeled next to him.

"Take my hand. Now put your other hand on her chest and focus on time." Micheal's mind became filled with events from their run through the timeline, and he saw a green river flowing through them. It all coalesced with energy surging through Julie. He opened his eyes, and a green glow illuminated their palms. The distortion in Freyja's chest began to shrink. Micheal remembered when he and Julie were on the table, and Ra was trying to kill them. He felt a connection in Julie's mind. The energy surged, and the aberration on Freyja's chest closed completely. A moment later, her eyes fluttered, and she took a sharp breath. A moment passed, and Julie broke the connection.

Micheal felt drained but relieved to have saved the goddess.

"Now you need to go," Julie commanded.

"I used the last of my energy to get us here. I can't teleport us out. And she's in no position to even walk out of here." Thor was struggling to stand.

"Micheal, they can't stay here."

"Okay. You make sure he doesn't fall on the way to the elevator." Micheal scooped up Freyja and carried her away.

"Where will you take us?" Freyja's voice quivered.

"To Avalon."

"You think that's safe?" Julie paused on the elevator.

"As far as I can tell, Ra doesn't know about Avalon. Now let's go."

An hour later, they were racing through the starlit sea.

"Thank you for everything." Freyja joined them on the bridge.

"How do you feel?" Micheal asked.

"Like a human."

"Now you know how we feel every day."

"You're not normal. I saw many of your feats 500 years ago. I can see your youthful aspect, but I know you're much older."

"I'm 98, how old are you?"

"Well, let's see, somewhere north of 3200 years. For one so young, you possess one of our common abilities. Your total recall?"

"I was born with it."

"Being born with the power of the gods isn't the only reason many of us would claim you as one of us. I possess the same total recall, and I remember vividly the Gods of Atlantis. Two thousand years ago, Aphrodite and Koios came to rule over the Atlantean Empire. Then 900 years later, you returned in disguise."

"We were misidentified and just went along with it."

Freyja laughed. "And you were able to pull it off."

"It was just technology."

"And where did that technology come from? You're beautiful mind. Perhaps there's more to you than you realize." Freyja leaned in and kissed his cheek. "Thank you for saving me." Then she walked away.

Micheal wondered at Freyja's logic. And as the lightening sky swallowed the last stars of night, a memory overtook him:

"Micheal?"

He closed his eyes, hoping his mom would leave.

"I knew I'd find you here. Ensign Peak is where you took Amanda on one of your magical adventures."

Micheal remained silent.

"Why don't you come join everyone else?"

When he held firm, his mom just continued.

"That's okay; I'll do all the talking. You did an incredible job working to save her. And more than that, you spent more time..." *His mom broke with tears in his eyes.*

"... You visited her more than anyone else. I'm her mother and I was too weak to visit like you did..."

When she broke off a second time, he had to go to her. "It's been a year, and I've barely visited her grave."

They held each other for a while.

"You had a courage and strength most people don't have. You left your feelings aside because it was what Amanda needed. There's an inherent strength inside you that you don't realize. It's been in our family for generations, but you are particularly strong. It was through your fight against cancer that I recognized this fact. I know you won't believe me right now, but I also know you'll remember. At some point, or in some time, you'll return to this moment and understand your special legacy. Time is the key."

Micheal came back to himself. He thought about some of the events of his past, like the situation at the Fountain of Youth in the Garden of Eden. When his family ring was the key to removing the flaming sword. He wondered if this was what his mom meant. Reliving the moment from 80 years in his past, his mother's statement was odd. It felt like she knew something, as if she knew the future.

Micheal was back on the bridge the next morning, guiding the Valkyrie to Avalon.

Thor came up from the lower deck. "I'm sorry we got you involved. It's just that I couldn't let her die."

"I know the feeling."

"I can't believe Asgard is gone. He's not going to stop, you know?"

"I don't think Julie will allow that to be our problem anymore. It's been rough for her over the years."

"But not for you?"

"It's different for me. I've had to carry all of the bad my entire life. And though that tends to constantly push me toward depression, it's also made me better at dealing with the bad things we've had to do over the last 70 years. But Julie had a pretty nice life before the fall."

"You mean a time fall?"

"Yes. We are from the distant future, and in most ways, the world is a much better place at that time. Most of the times we've lived in are far more dangerous, and that forces you to adapt or die."

"And that's been easier for you?"

"Because there's less civil control, there's far more situations where you have to make decisions about life and death. Neither of us had had to face that in our normal lives, but it's been a constant since the fall. Julie takes every kill hard, regardless of the necessity."

"Like the nuclear war we called Ragnarök?"

"We didn't know exactly what we had given them until it was too late. And our attempts to retrieve the information led to many more life-and-death situations. Then, to have it all end in failure... I know she still hasn't forgiven herself for that. I know that's why she doesn't want the responsibility of this war of the gods."

"With great power come great responsibility."

"We don't have great power."

"You used your superior intelligence to play gods. I would call that great power."

"That technology was lost many years ago."

"Why haven't you engineered it again?"

"It was a mistake to make it in the first place. Our first responsibility is to history, and we saw the consequences of that kind of power."

"Or it's an excuse not to do anything."

"Why should we *do* anything? This whole jumping through time is just an unfortunate accident. All we want is to make it back with ourselves and the timeline intact."

"Wouldn't it be easier to just go all in? Play the gods, and you'll be above all the common people and their common problems."

"Like you are?"

"That's fair. But nothing like what Ra is doing has happened before. If you help us defeat him, it will be another few millennia before anything like that happens again. And you would likely be back to your time by then."

"I don't think so. Now we're about to arrive."

Micheal sailed into the secret harbor and docked.

"Right through here are the living quarters. You can use most of the facility. Just stay out of the factory..." Julie trailed off her tour. "What the hell are you doing here?!" She demanded of Inanna in Babylonian.

"Lord West said I could stay here."

Five women came out of the shadows.

"Please don't be mad," one of them said.

"Who are you anyway?" Micheal scanned them.

The one who spoke had black curly hair and tan-colored eyes. The one to her right had dark blue hair and sun-yellow eyes. The one to her left had hair to match a fire truck with lavender eyes. They were all nearly as tall as he was.

The one in the middle introduced them. "I'm Potnia, Minoan Mother Goddess." She indicated right, "This is Therasia, Goddess of the Sun and Sky. And Ariadne, Goddess of Fertility." Potnia indicated the other side, "This is Diktynna, Goddess of Law. And Britomartis, Goddess of Mountains."

"Why are you here?" Micheal asked.

"Ra devastated Mount Dikti. We're all that's left to protect Minoa. Lord West gave us protection."

"Of course he did." Julie was livid beneath a calm exterior. "Can I speak with you?" Julie changed to English.

They moved out to the entry patio. "First, why is Mbizi turning Avalon into a sanctuary for gods without telling us? And with that in mind, I don't think we should allow them to remain here. When it was Thor and Freyja, it was questionable... Now this?"

"I don't know. We'll deal with Mbizi, but I'm not sure we can turn the gods out—"

"I'm tired of you giving allowance to everything. You consistently choose everyone else over me!"

"I'm not. This is about who I am. If I sit back and let someone like Freyja die, or I turn out people who are being hunted by a madman, who have no defense against him, giving them a death sentence, I lose who I am. And if I throw away what makes me who I am, then I am not someone you should be with..."

Julie's eyes broke into tears.

"... That *is* choosing you. I agreed to the deal with Ra because you wanted it. But I can't pretend I have no responsibility if these people die—"

"They're not people, they're gods."

"We don't know what their true nature is. All I know is they're sentient beings in need, asking for our help. Please don't ask me to betray who I am." Micheal stepped over to Julie and tucked her hair behind her ears. "I know you're scared. So am I. But can you allow them to die because of your fear? Please allow them to stay."

Julie's head dropped. He took her in his arms. After a moment, the gods approached.

"It's ok. We'll find somewhere else," Inanna said.

"No..." Julie pulled back and turned to them. "... You can stay as long as you need."

"Are you sure?" Freyja seemed skeptical.

"Yes. There's plenty of supplies—make yourselves at home."

"You have no idea how grateful we are," Potnia said.

Julie nodded.

"I hope this helps, but now we must go." Micheal led Julie to the Valkyrie.

Two days later, they reached the Palace of the West. Mbizi and Shani greeted them. Julie went with Shani to play with Merne.

"Mbizi, I'm going to make this short. You're my best friend, and I view you like a son. As such, I expect a certain amount of mutual respect. Don't you ever make decisions about Avalon or our deal with Ra without talking to us first."

"They needed help—"

"That's not the point. If you can't show me that you respect me, then there might be a problem with our friendship. Don't ever go behind my back again. Understand?"

"I'm sorry. It won't happen again."

"Ok. Now, let's go see your son."

They entered the chamber.

Mbizi went to one knee before Julie. "I beg your forgiveness. I'll never do it again."

"You're forgiven. We just need to be able to trust you."

"I promise."

Julie touched Mbizi's head.

Lords of the West

Several months passed, and Mbizi did everything he could to make up for his breach of trust. He was also occupied with lordly duties. By day, Mbizi was busy collecting the harvest of the West Delta. By night, he was putting his son to bed with stories of gods and kings. He was happy to distract himself with fatherly duties. Merneptah's first year of life passed with the winter solstice. He celebrated the Epagomenae Festival quietly with Shani and Merne.

"Shani, I have a day planned."

They sailed the Isis for about an hour west.

"Where are we going?"

"The coast of Libya. There's a beautiful beach next to some rolling dunes."

"And it's away from all the Lords of the West duties."

They climbed a tall dune, then, using what Micheal called a sled, Mbizi took Merne for a ride. His son's giggle was contagious, and he was laughing by the time they got to the bottom. The second time, Shani came for a ride. Mbizi watched Shani rolling in the sand with Merneptah. They were both giggling. He'd never seen Shani so happy. He ran over and began tumbling down the dune with Shani and Merneptah close behind. He picked up his son and ran across the beach and into the surf to cleanse them of the sand. Shani joined him, and they splashed in the waves.

"I think it's time for Merne's lunch," Shani said, carrying his son to the beach.

While Shani fed Merneptah, Mbizi laid out the picnic. After eating their fill, he decided to say what was on his mind.

"There's something I've been considering for a while now."

"This is about Merneptah, right?"

"It's about all of us. Micheal and Julie will leave in two years, but I think we should stay."

"I've been thinking the same thing. I mean, time is no place to raise a child."

"We can live at our palace, build a legacy. Micheal and Julie can visit our descendants."

"We've had incredible lives and so many blessings. More than two slaves could have hoped to receive.

"So it's settled. Our lives are in the here and now, the Lords of the West."

Micheal had laid out future events for them. They knew Ramesses would rule for 66 years until the age of 91. They would spend the majority of their lives in the stability of certainty, advising the Pharaoh, raising their children, and managing the West Delta.

They returned to Palace West. Shortly after that, a large procession of boats lined the river. Court was coming to the palace.

"His Majesty requests your hospitality," Vizier Paser said.

"With honor," replied Mbizi.

"I hope you don't mind my dropping in," Ramesses said with a bow. "Now, where's my godson?"

That evening, after dinner, Ramesses visited their chamber.

"When the flooding season comes, I will march back into Canaan to reestablish my authority. I will be bringing the Lords of Avalon, Vizier Paser, and my sons. I will need someone acting as regent in my absence. I want you to do it."

"It is a great honor... I'm just not sure I'm qualified."

"You're better educated than nearly anyone anywhere. You commune with the gods and command automatic respect from all the nomarchs and priests. I can't think of anyone more qualified than my friend Mbizi... Is there some other reason you're hesitating?" Ramesses furrowed his brow.

"It might garner unwanted attention from the Sun God."

"I fail to understand why Ra, Isis, the other gods, and the Lords of Avalon can't all just work together for the glory of Egypt."

"We all have a truce of sorts, but the domain of the gods is in turmoil because Ra is not satisfied with Egypt alone."

"Won't that be to Egypt's benefit?"

"The only one who gains from this is Ra. He wants every nation to worship him, not join Egypt. And worse still, there's a symbiotic relationship between the gods and those who worship them."

"What do you mean?" Ramesses sat on a bench on the balcony.

"The gods gain power when people worship them, and in turn, they work toward the interest of those people."

"So you mean what Ra is doing could cause nations to collapse?"

"Precisely."

Ramesses rose to his feet. "This has been very enlightening. That being said, I'm asking you to look out for my interests while I am on campaign."

"I will always help a friend in any way I can."

"Excellent. Now I think I've had enough for one night." Ramesses exited.

The palace was packed with court attendees and visitors from all over the land. After a month, the court moved on to River Palace.

Mbizi was grateful for the return of quiet. It was mostly just him, Shani, and Merneptah. They could put the Lords of the West on the shelf for a while.

<u>Death To Life</u>

April 12, 1272 B.C.

I feel the happiest I've been in decades. Nearly two years ago, Isis gave up her claim to Egypt, and Ra accepted her acquiescence. Since then, the tension has evaporated. Isis visits regularly and helps tend to Merne, which has been a joy. Even our occasional interactions with Ra have been mostly cordial. He may be working toward world domination, but that's not our problem. We have a little less than two years left before we jump out. I'm much more optimistic about our chances than I have been since we arrived in Egypt. Now, I must go as Isis is descending from the sky above.

Isis landed on the balcony of the Lord's module at River Palace.

"Am I interrupting?" They shared a laugh at the callback.

"How did it go in Ethiopia?"

"I was able to ignite the monsoon so drought will be averted."

"That's a relief. When I saw the flow coming into the highlands late, I worried for Egypt."

"Did you finish the tune?"

"I did." Julie retrieved her guitar. Isis danced while Julie played. She cycled through up-tempo and more melodic sounds. The music was cut short when a flash brought Hathor to the balcony.

"Don't stop playing on my account."

"What brings you here?" Julie asked.

"It's just been a while since I checked in to see how everything is going."

"Everything is going great. The normality of my daily routine has been good. Micheal and I just got back from touring the kingdom. That's the most exciting thing we've done this year."

"Sometimes I wish I could do the same. But we gods must maintain a certain mystique." Hathor sat up straight.

"Julie, what's something you wish you could do?" Isis asked.

"Go back to space."

"You've been to space?" Hathor raised her chin.

"A few times, actually. We even went to the moon."

"How long ago was this?" Isis smiled.

"Depending on how you measure it, the last time we went to space was nearly 700 linear years and about 30 lived years ago. Now the moon—that was more like 1100 years ago, about 50 lived years."

"In any of those visits to space, did you guys try to make love in zero gravity?" Isis raised a brow.

Julie laughed. "Of course we did."

"I'm curious—how long have you been together?" Hathor asked.

"72 years. And in our situation, we've become... I don't know... like a part of each other. I can't imagine what millennia would be like."

Hathor joined her on the edge of the balcony. "It's different for everyone. If you want, I can give you an idea about your future in this area."

Isis stepped up on the other side. "You may not want to know about your future. It wouldn't have been any better if I'd known what would happen to Osiris."

"I'm used to that responsibility."

"I can take a look for you as well."

"Ok."

Hathor and Isis placed their hands on her head. Julie felt warmth penetrate. She could feel emotions across time. She felt her mom and dad, and then Jessica came through. She felt Melina and her Delta friends. She felt all her family and friends from across time, then they broke the connection.

"This is odd. I've never seen anything like this before." Hathor said.

"What is it?" Julie asked.

"Your love line has no beginning or end."

"It's the same for your lifeline. It's like it's there, but it's endless."

"So I'm going to live forever?"

"I don't know. It's almost like I can't read you."

"I'm sorry we weren't able to give you more."

"It's ok. Let's go do something more relaxing."

Julie's goddess friends stayed late. As she watched Isis fly into the river of stars above, she thought about their readings. What did it mean? It couldn't mean she would live in love forever. Being a time traveler must have prevented a real reading.

Two days later, Julie was eating lunch with Micheal. In a jolt, Isis teleported onto the balcony.

"Julie, help me!" she collapsed.

Julie and Micheal ran to Isis. They rolled her to her back, and she could see Ra had attacked Isis.

"Micheal, help me!"

They duplicated the way they had healed Freyja.

"Thank you."

"Ra did this?" Julie asked.

"I was leaving Karnak, and he was waiting. His time-stopping is unstable. That's the only reason I escaped."

"We need to get you out of here."

There was a flash, and in a split second, Julie was sprayed with blood. She realized it came from Isis. Her throat had a gash across it.

"I knew she would come here." Ra stood with a bladed staff.

Julie sprang up and, in one motion, disarmed the Sun God and rotated the blade into his chest. Julie rushed back to Isis. The blood was pulsing out of her neck. She tried to put pressure.

"Micheal?!" He came with a towel.

A moment later, Julie was hit from the side and slid across the floor. She looked over, and Micheal had also been knocked down. Micheal hit Ra with a blast of electricity from his gauntlet. The Sun God stumbled back and collapsed. They hurried back to Isis.

"Stay with me. Don't die!" Julie tried to stem the bleeding while Micheal ran for the emergency medical kit. She watched helplessly as the life drained from her friend's eyes. Isis grabbed her arm, and Julie received a telepathic communication, saying goodbye. Isis's arm dropped limp. Micheal returned at that moment.

"It's too late," Julie broke down in tears.

In the midst of her grief, the shadow of Ra darkened the scene.

"We still have a deal."

"You had a deal with her too. You didn't have to kill her!"

"As long as she was alive, she was a threat."

"Get the hell out!"

Ra moved to grab Isis.

"Don't you touch her!"

"I'm not leaving without her."

"Get out! Leave now, or consider the truce over," Micheal stood, charging his gauntlets.

"You'll regret this."

"You have no honor. Your word is meaningless. Get out!"

Ra glared, then flashed out.

Julie cried for a while. Everything had been so good. Now, a battle loomed on the horizon.

"What do we do now?" Julie wiped the tears away.

"We lay her to rest."

"And where do we do that? Is the Field of Reeds real, like other mythical locations?"

"We could place her in Hittite Heaven with Arinna."

"I guess that'll work."

"Go get cleaned up. I will prep Isis."

Julie stood and looked down at another friend lost. The look in Isis's eyes felt like betrayal. She had only made a deal with Ra because Julie had chided her about friendship. That had left her vulnerable.

She came back refreshed. Micheal had closed Isis's eyes and washed the blood from her body. She was lying on a bed with a scarf around her neck. Julie began helping Micheal dress Isis.

"This is all my fault. Why does death love to haunt me?"

Micheal paused. "You always claim the blame for things you didn't do. I've watched you pile more and more death at your feet since the woods near Boston 70 years ago. I have the same blood on my hands."

"I'm sorry I couldn't get as comfortable as you with killing."

"How can you say that? You know I live with all of them every day. I have to convince myself they are all necessary, or it would eat me alive. You need to stop blaming yourself for the decisions of others."

"I know who's at fault."

"Things like the nuclear war and other major events you continue to blame yourself for belong on other people's ledgers."

"But they only happened because of us."

"Julie, there are evil people in this world who kill for selfish purposes. You're not God. You can't force Ra not to kill, just like you couldn't force George not to press the button. Please, Julie, this blame game is consuming you."

Julie closed her eyes, trying to remember what it felt like the last time she had total recall. She felt guilty for her harsh words to Micheal. She felt his arms take her from behind.

"I'm sorry, Micheal."

"Shh..."

He kissed her ear, then touched his cheek to hers.

When they finally finished dressing Isis, it was time to make a call.

"Mbizi, I need you to contact David, then come to our module at River Palace," Micheal said through the phone.

About 10 minutes later, a luminous spark signaled the arrival of their friends.

"What happened?" Shani asked.

"Ra happened."

"I never thought he'd actually do it." David seemed to be searching his thoughts.

"You know Ra could do this." Julie scowled.

"He was never like this for more than a thousand years. He's definitely changed, but I didn't think he could kill his own daughter. The look on his face said this was personal."

"You had a daughter, didn't you?"

"Two, actually, and a son, many millennia ago."

"I'm sorry."

"This isn't about me. Where do you want me to take her."

"Hittite Heaven. Arinna can have company."

Micheal picked up Isis, and David teleported everyone to the Golden Palace in heaven. David began building a cloud bed.

When he was done, Julie said, "I'll place her."

"Not yet."

"What are we waiting for?"

There was a flash, and Hathor appeared. She went to Isis and kneeled beside her. She wept for a while. Then, more bursts of light generated more gods—three men and three women. Based on their appearance, Julie deduced that the gods were Ptah, Thoth, and Sobek. The goddesses were Ma'at, Neith, and Bastet. The seven of them flew up to the cloud bed and began working the mist into a throne with cow horns supporting a glowing disc.

Before they finished, everyone halted when Ra, Set, and Anubis materialized.

"David the Elder, it has been too long." Ra and his lackeys bowed before him.

"You have a lot of nerve coming here!" Julie flew swiftly to confront them.

"I still hold to our agreement."

"How can there be an agreement with a dishonorable liar whose evil desecrates the resting place of his victims?"

Hathor hovered over to them, "I think you should go."

Before Ra could say anything, the other six gods lined up behind her. Ra scanned them, looked at Julie, and flashed out.

"That goes for the two of you, as well," Hathor directed at Anubis and Set.

They actually looked saddened by their exclusion, but they disappeared.

The Gods of Egypt finished the monument for Isis.

Everyone formed a semi-circle around it as Julie carried Isis to the throne. She turned to the group, and a portal opened behind them. All at once, the Avalon refugees appeared.

"We come to honor the Goddess of Light," Inanna bowed to Hathor.

"Welcome."

Over the next few minutes, more gods came. First was Kali, Shiva, Vishnu, and Brahma from India. Then Kiririsha from Elam. Even Shang and Xi came to pay tribute. While Hathor gave the eulogy, Julie couldn't help but marvel at the collection of gods assembled to honor Isis.

A strange thing happened when the ceremony ended, and all the gods but David had left. Shani seemed to focus on something. She flew into the distance for a little while. Finally, David gathered everyone and returned them to their palaces.

<u>Responsibility</u>

The funeral for Isis drew to a close, and most everyone had left. Shani had paid a visit to Arinna's monument. She was talking to Mbizi when a light caught her eye.

She turned, and heaven appeared as it had when she first saw it. Then, Arinna landed on the roof of the palace. Shani couldn't stop herself.

"Who died?"

That simple inquiry froze her.

"You saw that?"

"You're from the future."

Shani couldn't help herself; she went and embraced Arinna. "Is this real?"

"That's me, isn't it?"

Shani pulled back. Arinna caressed her face.

"That wasn't for you, but..." Tears began to stream. "...Ra is

going to..."

Arinna touched her lips.

"You're the Lady of the West?"

"How is this happening?"

"Time is fragmenting. I can read your aura, and you are from the counter to the cause of this distortion of the temporal flow."

"You mean Ra is causing this?"

"What is he doing?"

"He stops time, then he projects temporal energy to kill other gods."

"That must be it. I've been experiencing temporal distortions in the auras of people, and it's getting worse." Arinna stepped over and looked into the future. "You're the only one who can stop this."

"How?"

"I don't know, but you don't have long. The fabric of space-time is nearing critical mass. You must get Ra to stop."

"I don't know how."

Arinna studied her for a moment. "You will... Time is short—this crossing will soon dissipate."

"Arinna, if Ra comes, you need to flee."

"Lady West, I can't change the events to come."

"You're going to die!"

"If I alter events in this time, then no one can stop this collapse."

"There has to be a way."

Arinna traced her face. "It's okay. I understand why we must have become close, and I'll look forward to it. But it's my responsibility to protect my people and people everywhere. Even as a god, I am still just one person."

"Arinna..." Shani's protest was cut off by Arinna's lips. She felt the same surge of energy from years ago.

Arinna pulled back, looking into her eyes, then touched nose-to-nose. In a rush, the temporal link severed.

Now back at Palace West, Shani scooped up Merneptah. She spent the evening with her son and was lying him down to sleep.

"No matter what happens, remember me."

Mbizi kissed her neck from behind. He placed his palm on

Merneptah's forehead, then said to Shani, "Come to bed."

They entered their bed chamber, and Shani attacked Mbizi with her mouth. Their hands explored the contours of each other. Shani kissed down Mbizi's muscular torso til she was on her knees. She took him in her mouth, gripping his tight ass. A couple of minutes later, his legs buckled as he released. Shani rose to kiss him. He spun her to face the bed and pushed her down so she was on her stomach. Mbizi kissed the back of her neck, then worked his way down her back. Each movement of his mouth sent warm tingles through her skin. His mouth explored her ass, bringing the tension higher. Mbizi licked her upper thigh as he raised her leg until he found her lips with his. His hands were caressing her legs. His tongue worked its magic until she shuttered with pleasure. He slid her leg back to the floor. Mbizi lifted her torso, turning her head to meet her mouth with his. After a moment, he entered her from behind and began thrusting faster and faster. His hands traced up her side until he took her breasts in his hands. He kissed her ear and gripped her breasts hard as they climaxed. He collapsed on top of her.

"Do you think the deal with Ra is still valid?" Shani asked.

"I'm surprised it's lasted as long as it has."

"Do you think we have to worry about Ra?"

"He killed Isis because he viewed her as a threat, even with a deal in place."

"I just want to live a quiet life and raise our son."

"That sounds amazing, but I don't know if that's possible, and I've come to understand that Ra knows we're the only ones who can stop him."

"You think we can?"

"I don't know, but we need some sleep."

"Mbizi?"

"Yes?"

"I just wanted to tell you how much I love you."

"I love you too." He kissed her, and they drifted off to sleep.

Shani rose early and went to feed Merneptah. She felt the warmth of his love as his little fingers wrapped around hers. Then, she gently laid him back down. "Always remember how much I love you." She kissed his forehead. "Remember me."

Shani went to the balcony to write in her journal. As she finished the entry, she felt a strange feeling. It made her think of Ra. She closed her eyes, and she could see the Sun God. She could sense where he was. It was the necropolis at Giza. She opened her eyes, and she could see him in some kind of chamber. Shani stepped inside. Ra was manipulating a strange machine. She looked, and there were doorways all around. She could feel the temporal variations.

"How did you get here?" Ra stared down.

"You need to stop this."

"I've warned you to stay out of my way."

"All your manipulations of time are destroying the fabric of space and time. You need to stop!"

"I only have one left to do." Ra grabbed the handles of the machine. His hands began to glow.

Shani turned to one of the doors and saw a boy becoming a man. She knew it was Merneptah. She stepped through to the Palace West. The young Merneptah was about 14. He stepped over to her.

"Mom?" The tears came.

"You're such a man."

"I remember you, just like you wanted."

Shani took him in her arms. "I'm so proud of you."

"I love you, mom."

"I love you, Merneptah. The door is closing."

She stepped back, and the portal shifted.

Shani saw a large temple next to the river. There were four massive statues, perhaps 40 cubits high. A man approached. He was about 30 years old.

"Mother, is that you?"

She entered the door.

"How does this keep happening?"

"You come from time. The boundaries of the ages are splinter-ing."

"What happened to you and Dad?"

"I don't know. But know that even across time, we both love you very much, and I can see the great man you've become."

"Will I see you again?"

"I hope so."

The window closed, but another opened.

She saw the inner sanctum at Karnak. The only other time she'd seen it was at the divination of Amememhat. The man at the center of the ceremony turned, and it was Merneptah. He looked to be about 50. He locked eyes with her, and she moved to the inner sanctum.

"Mom, I'm now crown prince."

"And you will make a great Pharaoh."

"I've felt your presence my whole life, and I know you'll always stay in my heart."

"No matter what happens, keep my love and your father's with you, and I'll keep yours right here." Shani touched her chest.

Merneptah embraced her.

Then, the pull of time brought her back to the chamber. The doors were racing by now. The machine and Ra were both glowing. She had to do something. She grabbed Ra's forearms, and she could feel the energy. She focused on pulling the force toward her. The glow from the machine started to fade. Ra whipped his arms, and Shani hit the wall hard. Her tri-poly clothes absorbed the force. Ra had reignited the machine. She rushed over and grabbed his arms again. As she was sucking the power, Ra threw her off again, but she was determined. Ra threw her again, but this time, he came at her.

"You've interfered for the last time." He grabbed her by the throat, picking her up to his eye level and pinning her to the wall. "I'm going to enjoy this."

Shani grabbed his arms. She had to fight through the crushing pain. She focused on the power connection between them. The pressure in her chest was blinding, but she hoped she could drain him before he killed her. The longer this went on, the more she felt her own power weakening. Shani's whole body began to go numb, but she forced her hands to maintain grip. Her narrowed field of vision burst with light, and she dropped to the ground as Ra flew across the room.

Shani tried to suck air through her crushed neck.

Ra rose up, "What have you done?!"

He came and lifted her by the neck again. The little air she had taken was choked off again. She had no fight left; her arms had no strength to defend herself. Her world began to shrink, and she prayed the agony would end.

Shani felt Mbizi telepathically connect.
"Shani, what have you done?"
"I did what I had to."
Mbizi's presence brought her calm.
"Why is your vision blurry?"
"Ra is strangling me to death."
"Fight him!"
"It's too late."
"No! Shani, please, I can't lose you!"
"I wish there had been another way. I knew if you knew, you would stop me."
"Stay with me!"
"I love you, Mbizi. Give my love to Merneptah."
"Please fight!"
"I'm afraid. Please, I need to hear you say it."
"Shani!"
"The end is here. Please, Mbizi."
"I love you, Shani!"
The darkness closed in, and everything faded to black.

Vengeance

MBIZI WOKE WITH THE dawn and found Shani wasn't in bed. He sighed, and the scent of her lingered. He checked the bath, and she wasn't there. Merneptah began to cry, so he went to see if Shani might be there, but his son was alone in his cradle. Mbizi took Merneptah in his arms. He changed his diaper, burped him, and returned him to his cradle.

"I love you so much." He kissed Merneptah's cheek. "Where's your mother?"

He scanned the chambers...nothing. Mbizi went to the balcony and found Shani's journal. The feather sat in the inkwell. He had a bad feeling. He read the final entry, hoping there would be clues.

To my most loved husband, Mbizi.

There's so much to say. Our lives together have been so precious to me, and our world expanded with love when Merneptah came. I had planned out an amazing life. Raising our children, growing old together... but sometimes we don't get what we want. There has been a growing fear in my heart since Arinna's funeral. I didn't understand it for years, but I came to realize I was experiencing splinters in time. I thought there was a connection with Ra in one such temporal overlap; Arinna confirmed Ra was the cause. I think I'm the cure. That reality means I might have to sacrifice my life to protect the space-time continuum. That way, I can protect you and Merneptah. I wish there were another way. I wish I could see our son grow into a man. I wish we had our happy ending, but deep inside, I feel this is goodbye. In case it is, know that I've loved you since I first met you 30 years ago—the love of a lifetime. Take care of Merneptah. Give him my love every day. I will always be with you, and I will await you in the Field of Reeds. I love you, Mbizi, and I know that you love me.

Mbizi tried to see through Shani's eyes, and she was there. All his desperate pleas were in vain. He could only helplessly watch as Ra murdered his wife. He felt the connection die with her, which was a gut punch.

Mbizi's legs failed him, and his whole body ached. His grief morphed into rage. He blindly reached out to the gods, seeking their help. All of them groveled in fear. While running through the list in his head, he thought about dead gods as well and found a connection. To his surprise, the Anunnaki Mother Goddess, Ninhursag, appeared on the balcony.

"I can feel the vengeance in your heart. Ra must pay for the destruction of my family. Let's kill this bastard!"

Mbizi had suited up with his tri-poly armor and his kinetic weapons. Ninhursag teleported them outside the Great Pyramid in Giza. Ninhersag hid, and Mbizi connected to Ra.

"You vile wretch of a god! If only Apophis swallowed you in the night. You killed my wife! Come face judgment!"

Ra flashed in front of him.

"That whore attacked me—"

Mbizi hit Ra with the K-disc. He sailed into the pyramid. Mbizi fired his kinetic pellets, but they couldn't penetrate the armor. Ra fired a burst from his hand. Mbizi dodged and began striking the bastard with the K-staff, his rage fueling the fury. Ra hit him with force, sending him flying. Ra sent a burst from his hand, and Mbizi's chest felt like it was searing. The burst ceased with a flash as Nunhursag began her attack. Her size was proving the difference—she was over 6 cubits tall, nearly 2 cubits taller than Ra. She slammed him to the ground. Ra tried to blast Ninhersag, but Mbizi slashed his arm with his sword. The Mother Goddess began pounding Ra with fury. Mbizi combated any temporal blasts. Ninhurag stood and stomped on Ra. Mbizi kicked Ra in the head over and over again. Then, it was time to end it. While the Mother Goddess pinned the Sun God, Mbizi brought his sword down on Ra's neck. He decided he wouldn't survive a beheading. He had to hack repeatedly because Ra was trying to regenerate.

"Let me try!" Ninhursag raised the blade. Perhaps her awesome strength would work.

There was a flash, and then Ninhursage was skewered with a spear. Mbizi turned and Set was trying to draw the spear out. A burst of light from his periphery drew his eye to find Anubis. He failed to move fast enough, and Anubis's spear caught his shoulder. He tumbled away and back to his feet. Mbizi spun his staff, then struck Set before the Desert God could stab Ninhursag again. Mbizi became double-teamed by Ra's lackeys. He couldn't hold off for long. Set slammed him to the ground, and Anubis stomped him in the chest. Ninhursag took Anubis by the arm and stabbed him in the chest with Mbizi's sword. Set went on the attack against the Mother Goddess. Mbizi used the distraction to send his pellets, which went through Set's head. The Desert God dropped like a rock. Mbizi saw a streak of light hit Ninhursag. He turned to see Ra sending a burst at him. He fell to the ground, trying to take cover. The sustained blast brought Ninhursag to her knees. Then Anubis cut her throat with Mbizi's sword. Two more strokes removed her head.

Mbizi couldn't avoid Ra's blast. He felt his body trying to tear itself apart.

The force cut off, and then Ra said, "Anubis, Set, go guard against another attack." The lackeys vanished.

"I would have left you alone, and I understand your rage, but this only goes one way." Ra stood over him and hit him with a temporal shock. Mbizi was in searing pain. Then it all went numb. He went into his mind and found Micheal.

"Shani is dead; Ra killed her. I sought vengeance, but I failed. I'm sorry I didn't ask for help. I thought you would try to stop me."

"Where are you?"

"The Great Pyramid at Giza Necropolis. Ra has finished me. Please take care of Merneptah for us. I love you and Julie like family."

"We love you."

A white light flashed everything out, then it all went black.

<u>Shadow of Ra</u>

While eating breakfast with Julie, Micheal received a psychic connection from Mbizi. A brief communication ended slowly. He rose and leaned over the balcony, trying to catch his breath. He gripped the railing, tears coming to his eyes.

"Micheal! What happened?" Julie touched his arm.

"Shani and Mbizi are dead." He started shaking.

"How? How do you know?"

"Mbizi connected with me. He said Ra killed Shani, and he sought vengeance... I was with him when he died."

His stomach twisted, and he tasted the tears. Julie wrapped him in her arms. They wept together for a while.

"We need to get ready," Micheal said, reigning in his emotions.

"Not for vengeance."

"Ra will come for us. It's just a matter of time. Our best chance is to take the fight to him."

"What do we do? Call for help?"

"From who? We can't just connect to them. We'll have to do this ourselves."

"How do we even find Ra?"

"He's at the Great Pyramid."

Julie looked across the Delta, sighed heavily, then said in English, "Though I walk through the valley of the shadow of death, I fear no evil, for Thou art with me."

Micheal went and kissed the side of her neck. "Ok, let's suit up."

They dressed in their tri-poly battle suits and armed themselves with all their kinetic weapons.

"Should I bring this?" Julie held up Pandora's Box.

"There's no reason not to."

Micheal expertly guided the Valkyrie through the heavy morning traffic. He was able to maintain an average speed of 30 knots—they would reach Giza by noon. Julie joined him on the bridge.

"Why do you think Shani and Mbizi attacked Ra?"

"Mbizi was out to avenge Shani. He didn't say why she went, but she must have gone alone."

"There were a few odd moments over the last few years where Shani told me she was seeing things—like other points in time. I just assumed she had developed Melina's power. But what if it was something else?"

"Her original power was an inverse of Ra's time-stopping. The incident between them in the time stream may have intertwined them somehow.

"Shani said she had a battle of wills against Ra on Nibiru, trying to prevent his time-stopping. And Inanna said the dilation was varied. What if Shani's connection to Ra made her feel what he was doing... ?"

"... So she tried to stop him on her own? Maybe, but we must be missing something."

"What about Ra's trump card? We don't have Shani to unfreeze us."

Something occurred to him, and he desperately hoped he was right. "When I was connected with Mbizi, I knew time wasn't stopped. Maybe Ra can no longer stop time. Perhaps that's what Shani went to do."

Chills ran with the thought. Micheal was amazed that Shani would give up her happy life in the West and give up her life to stop Ra. The implication was—Ra must be stopped at all costs.

Two hours sail found them on the Giza shore.

"Look at that." Julie pointed to the pinnacle of the Great Pyramid, which was glowing purple.

"What is he doing?" Micheal asked.

"That must be why Shani came here. To try and stop whatever this is."

They began jogging the five-mile trek to the pyramid. The north end looked like bees fighting. Micheal could see half a dozen tiny figures flying or flashing from point to point. The ground also shook from impacts. They were less than a mile away, and a shadow spread from above the plateau in every direction, reminding Micheal of the totality of a solar eclipse. The sun was still visible above but appeared dark purple. They stopped to catch their breath.

"What's happening?"

"I'll check the sky-net." He tried to run a scan, but there was interference. "It's like something's hijacking our network."

"I think we know." Julie looked up at the sky.

Micheal turned, and people running the other way collapsed to the ground, their eyes glazed over with a purple sheen.

"What's Ra doing to them? And why aren't we affected?"

"I don't know, but we better stop it."

They began sprinting. Micheal wasn't sure how much time they had. He led the way to the north face of the pyramid. He saw that the bees from afar were gods in combat. Ra, Anubis, and Set were battling Shang and Xi. The scene brought a long past memory to the surface—the dream Joseph interpreted many years ago.

That dream said there was a threat to Egypt and the world—a threat he would have to stop. But the question was, how? Micheal scanned the sky, and the shadow shaded the land like in his dream. It was... the Shadow of Ra.

Temporal Force

They had finally arrived at the Great Pyramid. The battle between Ra, Set, and Anubis versus Shang and Xi from China migrated to the far corner. Ra hit them with a spray of temporal energy, and they dropped to the ground. Anubis and Set then skewered them with spears. A burst of light brought a new goddess to the fight, attacking Ra. Four more gods flashed in—three male, one female. The new goddess raised her arms, and a large bubble began to expand, encompassing most of the north-face region of the pyramid. Micheal and Julie reached the edge, and it was like a forcefield, except inside, the battle became distorted, with speeds accelerating and decelerating like a temporal pocket where she could control the flow of time to some degree. The barrier prevented Julie and Micheal from joining the melee. They could only watch and hope that the five attackers would defeat Ra. The three gods worked in harmonic sync. They devastated Anubis and Set. The sole goddess who had arrived first went to finish Ra's lackeys, while the trio of gods targeted Ra. As the battle ebbed and flowed, Julie kept trying to identify these new gods, but they were too small to see clearly.

"I can't figure out who they are."

"Based on their dress and how they work as a threesome, I would guess that they are the divine three from India: Shiva, Vishnu, and Brahma."

"And the bubble goddess?"

"The Indian Goddess of Time—Kali. She was at Isis's funeral."

"That's right. And now I'm pretty sure the other goddess is Kiririsha. Remember how it seemed she was friends with the gods of India?"

Julie reached out, and the forcefield was still as impenetrable as ever. "Do you think they can defeat Ra?"

"I certainly hope so. They seem evenly matched. If Kali would drop the forcefield so we could enter the fight, I think it's almost assured."

Julie and Micheal tried yelling and sending bolts of electricity, but Kali seemed to be in a trance and never acknowledged them. At first, the Indian gods appeared to have the upper hand, but Julie became more desperate as Kiririsha was overcome by Set and Anubis, who found gaps in her armor with their spears. She crumpled to the ground with blood pooling beneath her. With the lackeys coming to Ra's aid, the momentum shifted, and Ra began fighting his way to Kali. Two gods pounded down Anubis and Set, then made a last effort to stop Ra before he could reach Kali.

A beam of light came down from the heavens, pulsed through the pyramid, and connected with Ra. The Sun God illuminated until he created an explosion of energy that sent the Indian gods flying in different directions. Kali's bubble began to fluctuate. She focused her temporal force on countering Ra's. He pushed toward her, and the bubble started to fold. Ra was only a couple of feet from Kali when she lost the battle. The Sun God's burst of temporal energy knocked her flat. Then, before Micheal and Julie could come to her aid, Ra removed Kali's head with his bladed staff. Julie and Micheal sent lightning shocks at Ra, but they had no effect. The Sun God took a temporal shot at them. The energy felt hot but had less impact than the last time she'd experienced it. Julie looked to Micheal, and then Set and Anubis came to Ra's flanks, having punished the Indian Gods.

When she and Micheal hesitated, Ra spoke: "Lord and Lady Avalon, I wondered when you would come. I didn't want it to come to this."

"And yet, you murder our friends, bringing this very outcome."

"Lady West interfered with my plans."

"Shani would never leave her son unless there was an existential threat. So what are you doing that's so dangerous?" Julie demanded.

"There is no danger."

"Under these circumstances, why would you lie?" Micheal was getting angry.

"She claimed my temporal manipulations caused the time stream to fracture, but if that were true, I would have known!"

"Her power was the counter of yours. Maybe she could see something you couldn't. On several occasions, she told me she was seeing live moments from past and present. I thought she was just seeing it in her mind. Now it seems like they were windows in time." Julie wished she had been more curious about the matter.

"It doesn't matter now. She drained my time flow power."

"How do you know whatever this..." Micheal indicated the beam from the pyramid, "...is, isn't damaging the time stream?"

"This isn't the reason I wanted this parlay. I've indulged you for your friends' sake."

"Then why are we having this conversation?" Julie was actually glad for a moment before a fight to the death.

"I have always respected your ability to oppose me, and when I found out why you've been such a thorn in my side all these centuries, I decided to offer the truce."

"What you found out?" Micheal glanced at Julie.

"I discovered you were a relic from Atlantis. You are Aphrodite and Koios. Before I finished off the Norse Mother Goddess, Frigg, she swore you would defeat me. I demanded an explanation. Eventually, I forced your whole story out of her. More than 2,000 years ago, you ruled over an expansive empire. Then, in the millennia to come, you bore witness to the collapse of a highly advanced civilization. Not once, but twice. So I know you will understand what I'm trying to do here."

Julie couldn't believe that crazy "Gods of Atlantis" B.S. was still following her all these years later.

"And what is *that*?"

"I will unite the world, ushering in a new age of peace and prosperity."

"And I suppose this new age will increase your power?" Julie shook her head.

"Once the power is united in one place, I will be able to guide these barbaric humans toward the purpose of peace. And I know you may feel it harsh to use force to achieve this goal, but they are mere children, and a father must use strict discipline for the sake of his children's future."

"And I guess slaughtering all the other gods was necessary?"

"They're all inferior, self-aggrandizing wannabes. They selfishly split the power to rule their domains, making us too weak to really impose order on the humans. And worse, it inspired the infighting which causes endless war. Now, I'll be able to stop the cycle. I thought you, of all the gods, would understand."

Julie did recognize the "good" intentions, but we all know the saying.

"If you think we forced the Atlanteans to live in peace and prosperity, you've been misinformed." Micheal shook his head.

"That's not why I thought you'd understand. It's because you've experienced both sides of the issue—you were worshipped in Atlantis. Once it fell and you lost your power, you were forced to live amongst them. So you know better than anyone how primitive the humans are. And that brings me back to the respect that I hold for you. You are near-human physically, yet you can stand with the gods. True Gods of Atlantis. Which is why it saddens me that I must kill you."

"So, does that mean it's time to fight?" Julie took guard.

"Once last thing—I wanted to properly thank you, Aphrodite, for making this possible. Your time-gate altered my time powers so I could control the flow. Even now, my re-engineered version of your time gate feeds me my power from this world, making me a god amongst gods. So now, Aphrodite, Koios, it *is* time to fight."

Ra and his lackeys morphed their faces into their animal forms: Anubis, the jackal; Set, the set animal; and Ra, the falcon. Julie retreated, then sent a shock of lightning into Anubis. The God of Death stumbled back. Julie took a shot of energy from Ra. Then he jolted at her. The impact of his fist was devastating. She flew about 50 feet, tumbling across the sand. Julie rose, and Micheal unleashed all of his K-attacks in an onslaught. Ra abandoned his energy attack, as it was ineffective against them. He laid Micheal out, then pounced on top. Julie jumped on his back as he was trying to pound Micheal to a pulp and sent a full charge of electricity into the Sun God's eyes. He roared in pain, then got a hold of her. She gasped for air as it had been knocked out of her. Micheal tumbled to her side. The falcon-faced monster's shadow darkened the shaded view. She could barely move, and Micheal seemed helpless. To make it worse, the lackeys were back. A hint of fear emerged that this would be the end. Then a flash brought a wall of humanity... or was it gods?... between them and the Sun God.

Gods of Egypt

Micheal's vision shifted from blurry to clear. It was obvious Ra was more powerful than ever. The enhanced tri-poly suits they'd engineered specifically to stand against him were barely protecting them from total annihilation. A metallic taste was ever-present on his tongue. His body felt like one giant contusion. Through the ringing in his ears, he began to discern a discussion. He rolled over and saw six of the gods of Egypt standing between Ra and them.

"Get out of my way!" Ra demanded.

"We can't do that," Bastet replied.

"I don't want to hurt you, but I will."

"Listen to yourself. This mad quest for power is messing with your head. Father, this isn't you."

"Don't 'Father' me, Bastet; you abandoned me centuries ago."

"Why? Because I wouldn't turn on my sister? We all stayed out of yours and Isis's fight for power."

"Because you were all too cowardly to choose sides. So here we are—one big, unhappy family. Now move!"

"The Lords of Avalon have defended and served Egypt for centuries. They are now members of our big, dysfunctional family."

"This is your last warning. Don't think I won't go through all of you."

"Father? We all could understand what you did to Isis, with everything that happened between the two of you, but I can't believe you would so easily murder the rest of us," Anubis entered the fray.

"You and Set have proven yourselves for millennia, but they've betrayed me by their acquiescence to Isis's treachery. And now they commit treason again."

Micheal got to his feet, and Julie was standing beside him. He wanted to tell the other gods to leave—he didn't want them to die defending them.

"We don't want to fight you," Bastet said.

"It won't be a fight."

Ra blasted a spray of temporal energy that blew across half the area, all in front of him. The sustained a wave forced Micheal and Julie back against the pyramid. The gods of Egypt tried to avoid it, but it was too late. One by one, they collapsed. The moment Ra ceased the attack, Micheal and Julie attacked. In tandem, they released a barrage of kinetic shots. Ra tripped and fell. Julie jumped and came knee-down on his chest. She blazed his eyes with lightning. Ra released a terrible roar. Julie flipped off before Ra could get his hands on her.

Micheal conceived of a way to finish the fight. He did a cartwheel, wrenching the bladed staff from the Sun God's hand, and as he came upright, he whipped the blade into Ra's neck. The decapitation attempt came up just short as the blade became stuck in Ra's spine. Micheal tried to wrest the weapon free, but Ra grabbed the staff and removed it, sending Micheal to his ass. He thought that would at least temporarily cripple the Sun god, but he watched in horror as Ra reached toward the ever-expanding beam above the pyramid. His neck closed in seconds, and he rose to his feet.

Micheal and Julie both sent shocks of electricity, but Ra's only apparent vulnerability was his eyes, and he shielded them while he closed the gap to Julie. The strike with his blade opened up a gash in her armor, and she tumbled across the ground. Micheal rushed to her defense, grabbing Ra's staff as he was going for a finishing blow. Micheal wrapped his legs around Ra's right leg and used the force of the Sun God's swing to trip him down. Micheal rolled to his feet, but Ra was just as nimble and caught him in the chest with the blade in a similar motion. The stroke penetrated his armor, and he could feel the edge on his skin. Micheal was on his back, next to Julie, looking at the Sun God above.

Then a flash split the air, and Hathor was behind Ra. She plowed into him, and they rolled together. Then Anubis and Set, who'd been spectators, came to Hathor's aid. Ra was knocked into the wall of the pyramid. His face shifted to its human form.

"And now the treachery is complete."

"You've lost your mind. You casually killed most of the family who've been with you for thousands of years. We haven't betrayed *you*. You betrayed *us*. Can't you see that if you've lost Anubis and me, the problem is you?" Set charged.

"Please, Ra, end this now." Hathor extended a hand.

"You're all just as pathetic as these pretender gods who litter the sand around us. It's time you join them."

Ra sent a shot of temporal energy at the three of them. Anubis and Set shielded Hathor. She vanished in a flash, and then Anubis and Set dropped hard. The Sun God turned a fierce gaze on Micheal and Julie.

Eclipse

Julie took a strike from Ra's bladed staff, and his ever-increasing strength showed through. The blade cut into her inch-thick chest plate; it even sliced past her soft tri-poly undershirt. She knew she was bleeding beneath her armor but didn't know how bad it really was. Her head was aching from the impact against the pyramid. The tender pain of bruising bit to the bone every time she moved. That lethargic reaction was about to prove fatal as the shadow of Ra darkened her view.

The Sun God raised his staff, about to strike a killer blow. In that instant, Micheal tackled Ra to the ground. They came to their feet together, and Ra connected a vicious strike against Micheal's chest. He tumbled to the ground, landing next to her. Julie never thought it would end this way—at the hands of the Sun God of Egypt, but at least Micheal was with her at the end.

Julie had to laugh when another stay of execution arrived in the form of Hathor. Even though the last three gods of Egypt fell before the power of Ra, it allowed enough time for her and Micheal to rise for one last round in the pyramid ring.

Julie quieted her mind, narrowing her focus to one end—the fight to live. She went into the battle zone in her mind. She and Micheal became a single battle force. Julie rushed in, jamming her K-staff into Ra's neck, then dropped to the ground, avoiding his counterstrike. Micheal's baseball swing connected to the side of the Sun God's head. Julie used his imbalance to bring him down. She drew her sword and dove on top of him, plunging the blade into his eye. Micheal arrived on cue, driving his blade into Ra's other eye. The Sun God blindly swept them off his chest. Julie scooped up Ra's abandoned staff—it was her turn to deliver the final blow.

Ra ripped their swords out of his eyes, and Julie hacked down on his throat. The gash cut deep, Ra backhanded her, and she lost the staff. Micheal was Johnny on the spot and delivered another blow. Ra began to glow. Before they could continue the assault, the Sun God exploded, sending a temporal pulse across the field, knocking her to the ground. By the time the searing faded, Ra had regained his composure. The damage they had inflicted healed away. They were so close to victory, but that window was now closed. The zone adrenaline evaporated away like a short rain in a hot desert. How could they possibly win this?

Micheal came to her side. He charged his gauntlets. She did as well. They fired electricity at Ra, countering his next attack. They flanked in opposite directions, maintaining their bolts. Ra jumped, tackling Micheal, then initiated a ground and pound. Julie sprinted to the fight, kicking the Sun God's head. He caught her next kick, then lifted her above his head and whipped her brutally to the ground. Ra stepped on her stomach, then flipped her sword like a dagger. He was targeting the gash in her armor.

A flash interceded as he brought the death jab down, and the newcomer carried Ra away. The raven wings had to be Inanna. A flurry of attacks on the Sun God signaled that the Avalonian refugees had arrived. Hathor was with them. She must have called in the cavalry. Julie knew this was only a temporary reprieve. They had to try something different, but what else was there? She remembered an item in the pack she'd left at the edge of the battle zone.

"I'm going to open Pandora's Box!" Julie yelled to Micheal.

He crawled over. "What do you think it will do?"

"The scans indicated it was some sort of temporal transmitter. It seemed Ra is using my time gate for a similar purpose. Maybe it will do something."

"It can't hurt."

They staggered to their feet. Her bag was a football field away. They began sprinting, the battle raging around them. Ra pounded Inanna into the ground, then blasted her with temporal energy. Thor was buzzing around like a wasp, dodging Ra's blasts. Freyja was backhanded across the ground. Hathor took a full shot of temporal force. Ra moved to intercept Julie and Micheal, but the Minoan goddesses swarmed him. Ra sprayed temporal energy, blowing them down. He whipped his staff like a propeller, severing two of their heads. Julie reached her pack and furiously fought to find the item. Ra charged at her, but Micheal unleashed lightning, stalling him. Julie ripped the box out and flipped the lid open. A force knocked her on her back, and Pandora's Box landed on its feet.

A light shot into the heavens and began expanding. The bigger it got, the smaller the pyramid beam became. Ra's essence began to glow and seemed to be attracted to the box. The Sun God roared like he was being torn apart, the pyramid beam sputtered out, and Ra's brilliance intensified until he was brighter than a noonday sun. A moment later, Ra was like a star going supernova. A wave of light shot past Julie then contracted to Pandora's Box. The beam ceased, and the lid slammed shut. The shadow of Ra contracted to nothing, and the eclipse stars were swallowed by the return of the sun. Ra struggled to his feet.

"You stole my power! Give it back!" He tried to grab the box, and a discharge blew him back.

Julie rose up and examined Pandora's Box. Ra came back, but they all surrounded him.

"It's over," Hathor said.

"This will never be over."

"You're power-mad; just let it go," Julie said.

"You, Aphrodite, will pay for this. I promise I will not stop until you are dead."

This threat prompted an attack by Micheal. He hit Ra with a relentless shock of lightning that finally got him to collapse, but it was just momentary. Micheal tried to finish Ra with the bladed staff, aiming at his neck. Ra blocked the stroke with Julie's sword, then wrestled the staff away. Thor brought the hammer down, but Ra dodged it and batted Thor away with his staff. Then he whipped it around in time to skewer Hathor, stopping her attack cold.

"I'll be back!" Ra vanished in a flash.

"Where did he go?" Freyja quickly scanned the field.

"Look at that!" Micheal pointed at the pinnacle of the pyramid—it was pulsating.

"He's inside the pyramid. Freyja, can you get us in there?" Julie recognized that with just the three of them left, and she and Micheal walking wounded, the odds favored Ra.

Freyja teleported them into a chamber that was about 20 feet in all directions. Ra was gripping her re-engineered time gate by some handles. Julie ripped his left arm off the handle and received a punishing blow for her trouble. Ra slammed Micheal to the ground and slashed a gash in Freyja's neck. She collapsed to the ground, and Ra rotated the blade around to finish the job, but Julie kicked the staff out of his hand. The Sun God spun on her and, in one motion, drew her sword from his belt and plunged it through the gash in her armor. Julie felt the tip pierce her stomach, the terrible pain in her gut magnified with the extra thrust Ra punched into her.

"I always keep my promises, Aphrodite, but this one brings great satisfaction." A grin formed on his face.

She felt the shock setting in. At that moment, blood sprayed her face. Ra's head tumbled off, and his body crumpled on the ground to reveal Micheal standing there. Julie looked down and found only the hilt of her sword visible.

"Micheal..." She slid down the wall.

"No, no, no!"

"I'm sorry, I can feel I'm slipping."

"No! Stay with me! Help!" Micheal's face was streaming.

Each breath brought a shock of pain. A chill spread through her, and then the pain dissipated. Julie came out of her body. This time, there was no confusion like back in Salem. Julie gazed down at herself; her lifeless eyes stared back. Freyja came to her side.

Micheal looked inconsolable.

"Micheal, help me." Freyja laid her body flat, then withdrew the sword. "Get this armor off."

Micheal helped Freyja strip the chest plate and undershirt. Her body was covered in blood. The earlier gash from Ra's blade angled across her stomach.

"This just might work." Freyja opened up her wrist and forearm and pressed her wrist to the stab wound.

"It's too late." Micheal shook his head.

"Patience. It might take a moment."

"I was waiting for you." Julie turned, and Shani was there.

"But you're dead."

"So are you, technically. But we have little time."

"You knew this would happen?"

"I saw it just before I died, and they've allowed me to remain just for this purpose. I want you to take care of Merneptah for me until your departure."

"You don't want us to take him with us?"

"Time is no place for a child. Before you leave, give him to Ramesses. He will adopt him as his own son. I got to meet my son at several points in time. He will be the next Pharaoh, and that's a much better future than living in time."

"I promise... Is Mbizi here?"

"He is. He was ashamed to talk to you because he allowed his want for vengeance to get him and Ninhursag killed in the process."

Mbizi floated out of the shadows. "Now I won't get to raise my son into a man."

Julie hugged him. "We'll make sure he's cared for."

Shani broke them up. "We're almost out of time. So Ra has been defeated?"

"You sacrificed yourself to protect time?"

"My power allowed me to see the fracturing. I could interact with different times. In one such moment, Arinna told me Ra's distortions would destroy the time stream. I came to understand that my power could cancel his. I didn't come here intent to die, but when Ra refused to stop, there was no other option."

"You are such a hero." Julie embraced Shani.

"I'm so glad I got to say goodbye. You are my hero. Your bravery and goodness inspired me to put others before myself."

"I love you both. I can feel the pull of my body, so I will say farewell."

They all embraced.

"We will be waiting for you in the Field of Reeds."

And with that, Julie felt the aches and pains of her body.

"Thank goodness!" Micheal fell on top of her.

"Help me up."

Micheal and Freyja brought her upright. Julie examined her bare chest and stomach. All of her wounds were rapidly healing. She could feel the bruises seeping out of her.

"You gave me some of your special blood?"

"I did owe you." Freyja bowed.

"Give some to Micheal. Then we can see if we can help any of the other gods."

With his armor removed Micheal revealed a deep laceration in his chest. Freyja's blood worked its magic. Now, they had a somber task ahead.

CHAPTER 29: INTO THE WEST

F REYJA'S BLOOD WAS TRULY magic. Micheal felt nearly normal in minutes, and now they had a battlefield to tend to. Micheal kneeled next to Shani, and his vision blurred. She was like a daughter to him. He gently closed her eyes and kissed her forehead. He took a quiet moment, and then Freyja teleported them all out.

The first gods they came across were Shiva and Vishnu. They were both barely alive. Micheal and Julie used their power to heal the temporal wounds.

"Where's Ra?" Shiva asked.

"His body's inside the pyramid."

"He's dead?" Vishnu asked.

"He's dead." Julie nodded.

"What about Brahma and Kali?" Shiva looked around.

"I'm sorry." Micheal indicated their bodies.

"We're grateful for your help," Vishnu said.

They each took up one of their friend's bodies and vanished in a flash. Shangti and Xi-Wang-Mu didn't survive. They placed their bodies against the pyramid. Kiririsha had a faint pulse.

"She's still alive. Quickly!"

Julie joined Micheal, and they gave their healing power.

"Her wounds aren't healing. Freyja!"

The Norse goddess donated some blood, and the puncture began to close.

"Oh, that hurts," Kiririsha said through a cough.

"Do you need more?" Freyja asked.

"I'll manage. Thank you all."

Micheal helped her up. She scanned the field littered with bodies.

"Ra has destroyed everything." She began to cry.

"Come on. We need to keep moving."

Micheal moved to the next, and it was Mbizi. "Julie! Help me!" She came. They tried, but it was in vain.

Julie touched his arm. "There was no chance. I didn't want to bring it up until we were done, but I saw Shani and Mbizi as ghosts."

"What do you mean?"

"Before Freyja's blood worked its magic, I died. I was a ghost in the chamber. I could see and hear everything you were doing. Then Shani and Mbizi were there. They both explained their actions, then asked that we take care of Merneptah." A tear came to her eye. "I got to say goodbye for both of us." Julie wept on his shoulder. "We really should get back to it," she sniffled.

Micheal placed Mbizi next to Shani. They cared for the Gods of Egypt, but only one survived.

"Micheal, Hathor is alive."

They worked their magic, and she sat up.

"Did anyone else survive? ... Wait, did Ra ever come back?"

"Ra is dead. And, I'm sorry, Hathor, none of the other Gods of Egypt survived." Julie comforted Hathor while they gathered the other Egyptian Gods.

Freyja had gone to check the rest of the gods. They each laid a goddess against the pyramid.

Then Freyja yelled, "Come quick, it's Thor!"

They ran over, and Thor's body was shimmering in temporal energy. They countered the effect. A minute later, the Thor of old was back.

"My most special friends!" He slapped Micheal on the shoulder, then planted a kiss on Julie.

She shoved him down and slapped him. "You're welcome."

Everyone laughed.

"Thor, what am I going to do with you?" Freyja shook her head.

While Thor and Freyja had a moment, Hathor checked the Minoan goddesses. All three that weren't beheaded were alive. When they were on their feet, only one goddess was left to check. They found Inanna fluctuating and beaten to a pulp.

"Freyja, we're going to need your help here. Her pulse is extremely faint."

Micheal connected with Julie, and as they worked to fix the distortions, Freyja rained blood over Inanna's face and then her body. All the energy dispersion was taking its toll. Micheal had to fight to stay awake. Finally, he and Julie collapsed. He hoped it was enough.

"Are you all right?" Therasia was kneeling over him.

"Just give us a minute."

A few minutes passed, and he felt the life energy return to the point he could stand. Micheal struggled to help Julie to her feet. The survivors surrounded them.

"So what do we do now?" Kiririsha asked.

Micheal noticed they were all looking at him and Julie. "You're asking us?"

"It's a show of respect to the senior gods here." Potnia bowed slightly.

"We're not gods." Julie protested.

"You don't need to keep up the pretense just because your civilization ended, Aphrodite. We all know about Atlantis." Freyja touched Julie's shoulder.

"We all understand how it must be to lose your powers. There's no shame in failing to control human civilization. They do stupid things," Britomartis added.

"If anything, we all have even more respect for you because you defeated Ra without god powers. Which is truly divine." Thor chuckled.

"So, Koios, what do we do with all of them?" Inanna asked.

"Hittite heaven is already a memorial to Arinna and Isis. Why not make it the Heaven of the Gods?"

"A beautiful idea," Hathor agreed.

The survivors prepared the fallen for the jump. Micheal cataloged the living and the dead. The first group was the Indus gods because they already left. Brahma and Kali died, and Shiva and Vishnu survived. Next, both Shangti and Xi-Wang-Mu were dead. Hathor was the lone Egyptian left, so Anubis, Set, Ma'at, Ptah, Bastet, Thoth, Neith, and Sobek died. From Minoa, Diktynna, and Ariadne were dead. Potnia, Britomartis, and Therasia survived. Of the Annunaki, Ninhursag died, Inanna lived. The rest of the survivors were Thor, Freyja and Kiririsha. The most devastating of the fallen were Shani and Mbizi. The final tally was 17 dead, and ten survived.

"What about this box?" Kiririsha was knocked 100 feet by a surge from Pandora's Box. She sat up.

Micheal cautiously approached the box, running a scan on his phone. The tachyon readings followed a path to Kiririsha. The closer he came, the lower the reading was. He extended his hand. There was a tingle in his finger but no shock. Micheal held the box out toward the gods. They all seemed intimidated, except Thor.

"It's just a box." His laugh was cut off by a power surge.

All but Julie took a step back.

"It'll be okay," Micheal assured her.

She stepped forward, took a deep breath, and made contact. Julie let the air go and accepted Pandora's Box, placing it in her bag.

"Let's go to heaven." Julie scanned the group.

"Everyone join hands," Inanna instructed.

The fallen were all touching. Julie reached for Shani and took her hand. Micheal accepted Freyja's in his. The circle was encompassed in a green glow. The scene shifted, and they were on the roof of the Golden Palace. The gods divided by region and began crafting the monuments. The exception was Kiririsha, who was preparing a place for the Chinese. Thor and Freyja were standing with Micheal and Julie.

"Aren't you going to build?" Freyja asked.

"We don't have that power," Julie protested.

"You do. It's similar to the flying, just a little more concentration.

This entire place is a temporal construct. Allow your time essence to connect to it."

Micheal closed his eyes. After a minute, he could feel it. There was a learning curve, but the connection created a link with Julie. It felt strange but comfortable. They coordinated their efforts, and the clouds slowly became like a giant snow globe—20 feet across. Eight small obelisks bordered an octagonal platform. A pedestal bed was in the middle. They used hieroglyphs to engrave the story of Shani and Mbizi on the obelisk. Glowing embers began falling slowly from the dome. With the monuments complete, all the fallen were ceremoniously laid to rest. One by one, everyone gathered together to hear each eulogy. They started at the pyramid monument featuring Hathor, given in Egyptian. Then they transitioned to a ziggurat monument to the Anunnaki, not just Ninhursag. Inanna spoke in Babylonian. Next was a labyrinth. Potnia honored the Minoa in Greek Linear B. The one that followed was the most unusual: a pagoda monument crafted by Kiririsha honored Shang and Xi, and in the one language Micheal didn't understand, Kiririsha spoke in Ancient Chinese. Micheal and Julie were last. He stepped up to give the eulogy. He chose Atlantean, as they all understood it, and it differentiated it from Hathor's speech.

"What to say about Lord and Lady West? It's amazing that such great acts came from such humble origins. Five hundred years ago, when I was at my lowest, in captured servitude, I met Shani and Mbizi. They were slaves since childhood, but their goodness was clear. Once I freed them from bondage, they blossomed into an honored Lord and Lady. As their power grew, so did their sense of responsibility. They sacrificed their lives to protect the world, not only from tyranny but from time itself. They gave up a life with their son to protect us all. In my many years, few have I chosen to call my friend, but they were both worthy. Though I will miss them eternally, they will always remain in my heart. We would like to dedicate this monument with a fitting song."

Micheal picked up the guitar they had found in the palace. He played the melody, and Julie sang *Into the West* from the Lord of the Rings movie.

With the memorial finished, most of the gods went on their way. Hathor jumped Micheal and Julie back to Giza, inside the Great Pyramid.

"What should we do with this time machine?" Hathor asked.

"If you could place it in the main lab at Avalon, we will study it," Julie said.

"What about Ra?" Micheal indicated the body.

"I will deal with that. Before he went mad, he was part of my life for thousands of years. I owe him a measure of respect." Hathor kneeled next to Ra's body. "Now, where should I take you?"

"We should see to little Merneptah, so Palace West, please." Julie bowed.

"Of course."

They were on the balcony in Shani and Mbizi's chamber a moment later. They found Merneptah with the nurse. As Micheal took him in his arms, he thought it would be nice to play dad for a while.

Legacy of the West

The next day, Julie was taking Merneptah for a walk on the east beach at Palace West. When Ramesses's ship, the Sun Chaser, came sailing into the Lord's docks, Pharaoh came down the plank.

"Majesty." She bowed.

"How is my godson?"

"Doing well, all things considered."

"So something did happen?" Ramesses took Merneptah.

"You could say that. Ra attempted to enslave everyone in the world. In the process, he was destroying time itself. Lord and Lady West were killed trying to stop him…"

She had to take a second to maintain composure.

"What happened to Ra?"

"The Sun God is dead. So are most of the other Gods of Egypt."

"Who will protect Egypt?"

"The Mother Goddess, Hathor, is the lone survivor."

"Are you going to help her?"

"For another five seasons, then we move on to another time."

"Are you allowed to tell me all this?"

"Hathor is devastated by what happened. I'm not sure if she'd be up to managing Egypt alone. You have gone through the divination ceremony?"

"I have."

"You may need to prepare for a time when the Gods' assistance is no more."

"What if I can't?"

Julie stepped over to face him directly. He was looking up at her.

"You possess all you need to bring Egypt to greatness. And I'm not saying Hathor will stop, but she's just one goddess. Hope for the best, but prepare for the worst."

Ramesses handed Merneptah back. "I'm assuming you're no longer advising me on my latest campaign?"

"Our place is here. If you return before 70 days, we will celebrate Shani and Mbizi's transition at that time. Good luck on the campaign."

"I shall return victorious, in time for the Lords of the West."

Julie bowed, and Ramesses sailed down the river.

Over the next two months, thousands of temporary workers came to Palace West to help construct Shani and Mbizi's tomb. The location was 20 miles southwest of Palace West, where the Sahara meets the West Delta. The project was finished just in time for Ramesses' glorious return from Canaan. All the dignitaries gathered at West Gate Memorial. A 100-foot pyramid sat on the coastline. In the surf, immediately next to the pyramid were five circular stone gateways, partially buried in the sea. The middle circle was 200 feet in diameter. The flanking gateways descended in size before and after the main gate. On the seaside of the gateways stood obelisks rising from the water, mirroring the gateways in height. Many of the aspects of the Egyptian memorial rites were performed, but the last element was unique. With the help of Hathor, they used Julie's time gate to make the West Gate Memorial a permanent link to the Heaven of the Gods. If you were temporally distorted, the gateway would transport you to the Golden Palace.

So, the empty sarcophaguses of Shani and Mbizi were placed

on the Isis, and they prepared to autopilot the ship to heaven. Julie stepped up to dedicate the memorial.

"I understand that Avalon may appear mysterious to many of you. People often question our connections to gods and kings. I want you to know that we care greatly for this land and its people. To fulfill this purpose, Lord and Lady West devoted themselves to safeguarding this great kingdom from complete destruction. They have earned their place among the gods. We now send them on their final journey to transition to their divine phase of life."

Julie gave a signal, and Micheal activated the Isis with his phone. They had retrofitted the ship with generators used in Philadelphia jumps. It would help facilitate the transfer. Silence greeted the Isis as it glided toward the gates. Julie wondered if the gate would work. They had never tested it. The familiar green glow slowly appeared as the Isis progressed through the gates. It rapidly increased luminosity. The light bubble contracted to nothing, taking the Isis with it. There were audible gasps at the display.

The transition festival began in the desert south of the pyramid. Everything was set up for the guests to celebrate into the night. Micheal and Julie weren't staying.

"You're leaving?" Ramesses asked.

"We have to get back to the palace," Micheal said.

"To care for Merneptah?"

"He will be our focus for the rest of our time here. I promised Shani after she died."

"While I may seek advice occasionally, I won't expect to see you at court. I do intend to see my godson regularly."

"We look forward to it." Micheal nodded, and Ramesses returned to the festival.

Half an hour later, they were back at Palace West. Micheal received Merneptah, who ran to greet them. Julie took in the scene, feeling that fatherhood became him. Micheal carried Merneptah to the balcony's edge, silhouetted in twilight. Julie slowly approached.

"My son, today is a bittersweet day. It will be many years until you reunite with your father and mother, but they have taken their place in heaven. And that is worth celebrating. I promise to tell you about their great deeds daily. We'll make sure you don't forget them." Julie put her arm around Micheal and palmed Merne's smooth head.

The seasons passed, and Merneptah grew in stature, as well as in their hearts. River Palace was preparing a special celebration.

December 21, 1271 B.C.

Little Merne turns three today! And I love him like he was my own son. I'm struggling with my emotions. We will leave Egypt in two weeks, but I don't want to. If it were up to me, we would stay. But I made a promise to Shani....

Tears smeared the ink, so Julie had to take a break. She steadied herself, then continued.

...This experience of motherhood only emphasized what I'm missing in my life, but I wouldn't give up my time with Merne for anything. The fact that he may not remember me when I'm gone makes it hurt that much more. I know he'll be the next Pharaoh. I can only hope the lessons I've tried to instill in him will help him rule justly. But about today, happy birthday, my beautiful boy!

Julie went and joined the party in the main module. The scene was a madhouse of children running around. Laughs and cries filled the air. Toy boats and chariots littered the courtyard. Merne spotted her.

"Mama!" He ran into her arms, and she spun him around.

"Always remember your mother and I love you very much," Julie whispered in his ear.

"Mom," Merneptah replied in her ear, but it sounded different. Then she thought...

Julie spun around, and Shani was visible through some kind of doorway. Her expression showed they could see each other. Julie smiled and waved her fingers. Shani faded back into the mists of time. Julie was happy to see her again, and it solidified the promise she'd made.

The Great Ancestor

Micheal found Julie in the bath and joined her. She moved so she was in his lap.

"So another major chapter comes to an end," Micheal said.

"What do you mean?"

"I don't know when we might return to River Palace. The great Bronze Age collapse will sink Egypt into turmoil and permanent decline." Micheal ran his hand down her arm.

"The age of the gods has ended, and the Bronze Age is next? Do you think there's a connection?"

"Supposedly, there was a power dynamic between the gods and their worshippers, and I don't believe in coincidences."

"So you don't want to visit here amidst the chaos."

"If we come during that time, we'll get pulled into the civil wars, and River Palace's neutrality could be threatened."

"At least we were able to coat it for protection."

Micheal slid his fingers between Julie's. "I'm going to miss this place. It's been our primary home for more than 20 years."

"One thing I won't miss is representing the gods."

Micheal laughed. "Oh, Aphrodite, you don't have to keep up the pretenses."

Julie shook her head and laughed, then she sobered up. "But I will miss this place... There is one last thing we have to do before we leave. Julie rolled over and prepared him for action.

They emerged to the central courtyard and found all the service staff waiting for them.

"I'm going to miss this little guy." Raziya set Merne down.

"Bye-bye, auntie." Merneptah waved.

"It's been an honor to serve you and the little Lord." Raziya bowed.

All the servants did the same as they went to the exit.

"Alright, Merne, we're going down the stairs."

"Yay!"

By evening, they reached Pi-Ramesses. The Pharaoh had a welcome/farewell party prepared that ran into the night. The next day would be their last. They spent it with Ramesses, and there was a special visitor.

"I've come to say farewell," Hathor directed to Ramesses.

He looked at them, then back at her. "You mean to me?"

"I've tried to manage over the last couple of years, but it's become clear that it's too much. I return to the heavens tonight."

"What do I do if I need divine assistance?" Ramesses sat down with a scowl.

Hathor sat next to Micheal.

"Your Majesty is our official representative of the divine on earth. You have all you need inside to manage any crisis. I've seen your future. Your glorious reign will last for longer than any who came before you. It will be marked by untold numbers of grand achievements. Your divine aspect is the Great Ancestor. Your legacy will echo across time. You don't require my assistance."

"If you abandon Egypt, who will protect us against nations whose gods still protect them?"

Hathor rose up. "Fear not, Your Majesty, the age of the gods is at its end. We shall see if the human race will rise or fall, standing on their own two feet. Be the man you were born to be. Be the king you were raised to be. Be the god you were blessed to be. Now I say goodbye, but I must talk to them for a moment."

Ramesses exited with Merneptah.

"What will you do next?" Micheal asked.

"I don't know. The other gods are discussing where we should go from here. We want you to join us."

Micheal chuckled. "Our path lies before us."

"Do you really want to live amongst these simple people?"

"Simple sounds great after everything that's happened." Julie grinned.

"Oh, Aphrodite, just accept that in a life this long, you can't dwell on every tragedy. Even gods can't control everything."

"Send everyone our regards." Micheal stood.

Hathor stepped over to him. "Okay, Koios. Just know the invitation stands." She stepped over to him and kissed his cheek. She moved on to Julie.

"Aphrodite, I will miss you." Hathor closed her eyes, pressing her cheek to Julie's.

The intimacy took down Julie's resistance. Her shoulders dropped. Then a grin came as her eyes met Micheal's. The Mother Goddess stepped back into a bow, then flashed out.

"So she's gone?" Ramesses came hand-in-hand with Merne.

"She is," Micheal said.

Julie went to a knee. "Come here, Merne."

"Mama."

She touched cheek to cheek, whispering in his ear. After a little while, Merneptah ran to Micheal.

"Dada!"

He picked him up. "We have to go away now. Always remember you are loved."

"Dada and Mama are going to live with Mom and Dad?"

"You're such a smart young man. Mind your studies, practice with your bow daily, and never forget you were born to privilege, which comes with a responsibility to use that privilege in service to others. Understand?"

"Yes, Dad."

"Good boy." He kissed Merne's cheek. "I love you, son."

"I love you, Dada."

Micheal held Merne tight for a moment, then set him down. "Go to your mother and father."

Merne went to Ramesses, who was joined by his second royal wife, Isetnofret, who had promised to raise Merneptah as her own son. The three saw them to the Valkyrie. Micheal and Julie departed, leaving love, legacy, and Egypt in the hands of Ramesses, the Great Ancestor.

<u>Centenarians</u>

A month passed, and the triangle beckoned once again. They'd spent the week since arrival in preparations for the jump. But Julie had to stop and take in the natural beauty of their departure location. In modern times, it would be known as Mosquito Bay on the Caribbean Island of Vieques. Micheal was playing in the surf, and the dinoflagellates' bioluminescence was lighting up in blues and greens. Before she could join him, she had to finish her journal.

February 8, 1270 B.C.

Our time in Egypt was far stranger than I ever imagined it could be. 23 years ago, as we sailed up the Nile toward Memphis, I was excited to see the ancient world's most storied civilization firsthand. Knowing how strange we would appear, I anticipated meeting a Pharaoh or two, but in the process, we discovered an entire world of mystery, power, and mythology behind the world we thought we knew. The gods are real. Famous names of mythological origin, including Isis, Thor, and Shiva, belonged to actual beings. But what is their true nature? Where do they come from? It appears some hail from across the stars.

The Anunnaki, for example. From the first time we met Marduk and Inanna, they were very "alien". Their massive size and unusual features were not of this Earth. However, the strong evidence of an extraterrestrial origin came from Nibiru. An antimatter-powered spacecraft, cloaked in orbit. It was invisible to our sky-net. Had it not exploded, we wouldn't have even known it was there. And what about the other gods? Some, like Thor and Freyja, seem just as human as Micheal and I do, except for elements like Freyja's magical healing blood.

Regardless of their level of strangeness, one commonality between all the gods was powers based in time—the manipulation of the space-time continuum. The most common temporal powers were seeing across time spectrums and moving instantly between time and place, more specifically, teleportation. But there were less common powers, like Ra's time-stopping and temporal projection, or the power Isis transferred to Mbizi—the Eye of Horace. Allowing a temporally static telepathic connection, anywhere in the world. I still wonder how Isis knew how to do that.

The gods also shared non-temporal powers, such as super healing and enhanced strength and durability. And while less common, many could fly. Despite years of interactions, I never could figure out what all of this meant. Several times they used the word "time rogue" to describe the gods. And this brings me to us and our friends.

Shani developed a time power we call temporal pushing because she could push back against Ra's time manipulation and send him sliding through the timeline. Then there's me and Micheal. What is our power exactly? We were immune when Ra tried to hurt us with his temporal manipulation. We could also heal temporal damage, although it required us to work together. I still don't know what any of this means. The final note on the gods I'll mention here is about Ra. The terrible damage he inflicted on our relationship nearly destroyed us. I wanted to hate him, but all the times we crossed paths, in war and peace, gave me a more nuanced image of the Sun God. His intentions seemed pure, but you know what they say about intentions. He nearly cast a permanent shadow across the entire world. He was only stopped by Pandora's Box. That brings the next question about biblical people and events.

Pandora is the wife of Noah's son, Shem. I met Abraham and Isaac. Micheal met Joseph with his coat. Then, of course, Moses and the exodus. Does the reality of this evidence confirm that an Abrahamic faith is the one true faith? Because much evidence also backs the mythological religions. All of this confuses what I believe. These questions about faith and belief, mixed with the documented historical people and events, to give us a unique Egyptian experience.

Now, I must talk about the most unexpected and rewarding experience. We had our first-time companions and friends in Shani and Mbizi—two beautiful people who became family to us. Their legacy—Merneptah—brought pure joy to all of our lives. Through tragedy, I received the gift of becoming a mother. I survive our necessary parting through knowing that Merne will live a full and rewarding life. Most mothers don't have such luxuries. I do miss all three of them every day.

This final entry has become excessively long, so I will go to *the final topic: Micheal and I are officially centenarians. He just turned 101; I am a few months into my 104th year. Every time I close a chapter in our run through the timeline, I take stock of my life...*

Julie picked up a mirror...

...My eternal youth prevents a true reflection of the passage of time. I'm forever young but perpetually aging in time. I never thought I'd live to see 100 years; now I wonder what 200 would be like. When I think of the gods speaking in terms of millennia, these long timeframes feel like true milestones. So, in honor of our first century, here's to the next. In final reflection, our time in Egypt taught me about the ancient world, about faith, about what's possible, but most importantly, it taught me about myself. Whether I belong to Club Divine, as the gods seem to believe, if I'm the Lady of Avalon or just Julie Hall. The choice to accept the responsibility of my circumstances is entirely up to me. While we were able to bring some light to the shade, the shadow of Ra might be a turning point in history. If Micheal's new theory is correct, the end of the age of the gods will bring on the late bronze age collapse, ushering in history's first "dark age", which will bring much suffering and death.

A part of me agrees with Ra's desire to end all the struggles of humankind. But the cost—freedom—is too high a price. What does the future hold for us? Hathor and the gods invited us to attend their meeting. Even if Aphrodite follows me throughout our journey, as it seems she will, I absolutely need a break from that aspect of my life.

To that end, I look forward to my and Micheal's next major milestone together. Our 70th anniversary is rapidly approaching. To my dearest Micheal, I continue to love you now, and 'till the end of time.

I am Julie Hall, Lady Avalon, and this is my continuing chronicle:

The Book of Avalon, Volume 10

Julie closed the book and then noticed Micheal emerging from the bay and the luminous water streaming down his naked body.

"Wanna join me?"

"I'd love to."

She dropped her clothes to the sand and waded into the water. The glow traced her movement. Micheal took her hand, pulling her deeper.

"You look magically beautiful."

"It is certainly magical."

They swirled together.

"We've experienced so many amazing things together, but sometimes Mother Nature still impresses."

They swam around, laughing and playing.

"I know I don't say this enough, but, hell of a life."

"Hell of a life." Micheal met his lips to hers.

"You know... we have a couple of hours before we have to leave." Julie grabbed Micheal's ass.

"I can think of a way to pass the time."

She kissed him. They enjoyed each other in the bioluminescence for a couple of hours; then, they continued on their journey.

ELYSIUM

Z EUS PERCHED ON HIS Elysium balcony, surveying the world below. Something big had gone down. The world had been shrouded in a dark shadow that had just lifted. None of his god powers could inform the situation, so he dispatched an agent to investigate.

"Your Majesty, Ra has been defeated," Iris said.

"Call the council to order."

"Yes, Majesty."

Zeus entered the Chamber of the Twelve.

"Thank you all for coming. I called this council to discuss our next move."

"What has happened?" Hestia asked.

"Ra has been defeated."

A murmur rose amongst the gods.

"Are you sure? From everything we knew of his powers, the chances were so unlikely," Apollo challenged.

"Iris has seen it with her own eyes. She reports that the old gods of Atlantis, with help from Hathor and Freyja, managed to survive a battle in Giza. The *how* is still a question."

"So what do we do now?" Dionysus asked.

"We could try and help the surviving gods?" Athena suggested.

"Why would we do that?" Aries scowled.

"Why wouldn't we? We've known most of them since the beginning." Demeter opened her arms.

"You think they would do the same for us?" Aries laughed.

"Clearly, they helped each other—Norse, Egyptian, Atlantean, and who knows how many others." Demeter shook her head.

"All the arrangements between the different gods were out of convenience and fear, not friendship," Hephaestus said.

"So what's the current dynamic of the divine order?" Hermes asked.

"Domains left in ruin include Asgard in the North, the Shang in the East, Mount Dikti, and Hatti next door to us. And, of course, the destruction of Nibiru," Zeus said.

"What of the Indus?" Artemis asked.

"They're mostly intact, but they're also isolationists. So, in conclusion, there are less than a dozen surviving gods from all the rivaling pantheons."

"Does that include Aphrodite and Koios of Atlantis?" Artemis inquired.

"Atlantis fell a thousand years ago. They're a powerless relic from a bygone era," Poseidon scoffed.

"Perhaps you should take them more seriously. They were the primary ones to stop Ra." Hera had heard Iris's report to him.

"Enough. Any suggestions for our next move?" Zeus focused the council.

"I think we have an opportunity to extend our influence," Poseidon offered.

"Now you sound like Ra." Demeter scowled.

"We could invite the refugees to join us," Artemis added.

"And dilute our power? No." Aries shook his head.

"Silence! I have decided to fill this power vacuum for the benefit of all. We can decide on the other gods later. The fall of the divine order will bring major turmoil to human civilization. It will take centuries to recover the belief in our power. The long game begins now. It's time to leave Elysium behind and return to Olympus. We have work to do." Zeus dismissed the council.

Back on his balcony, he gazed at the world below. It appeared tiny. He extended his arm, and it looked as if the colorful orb could fit in his mighty hand... and it was there for the taking.

<<<<>>>

LATE BRONZE AGE

NEAR EAST

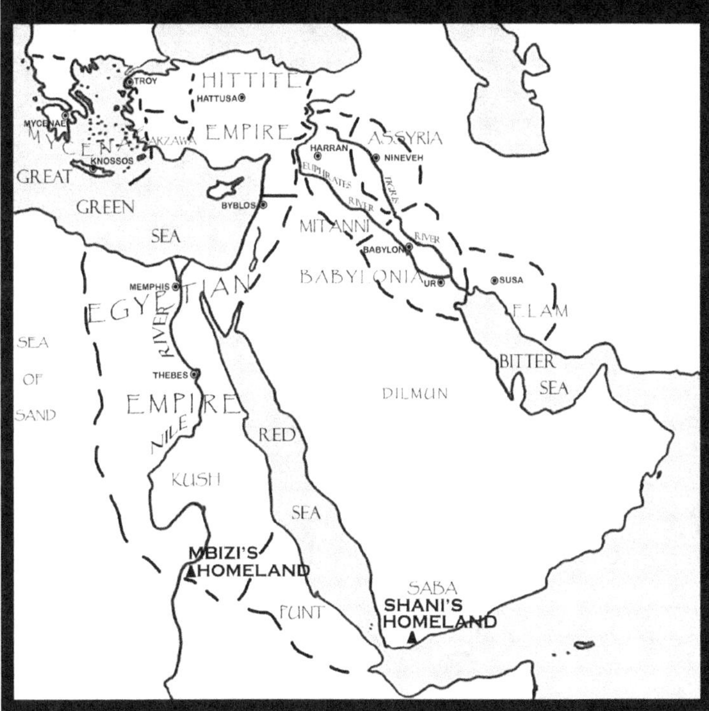

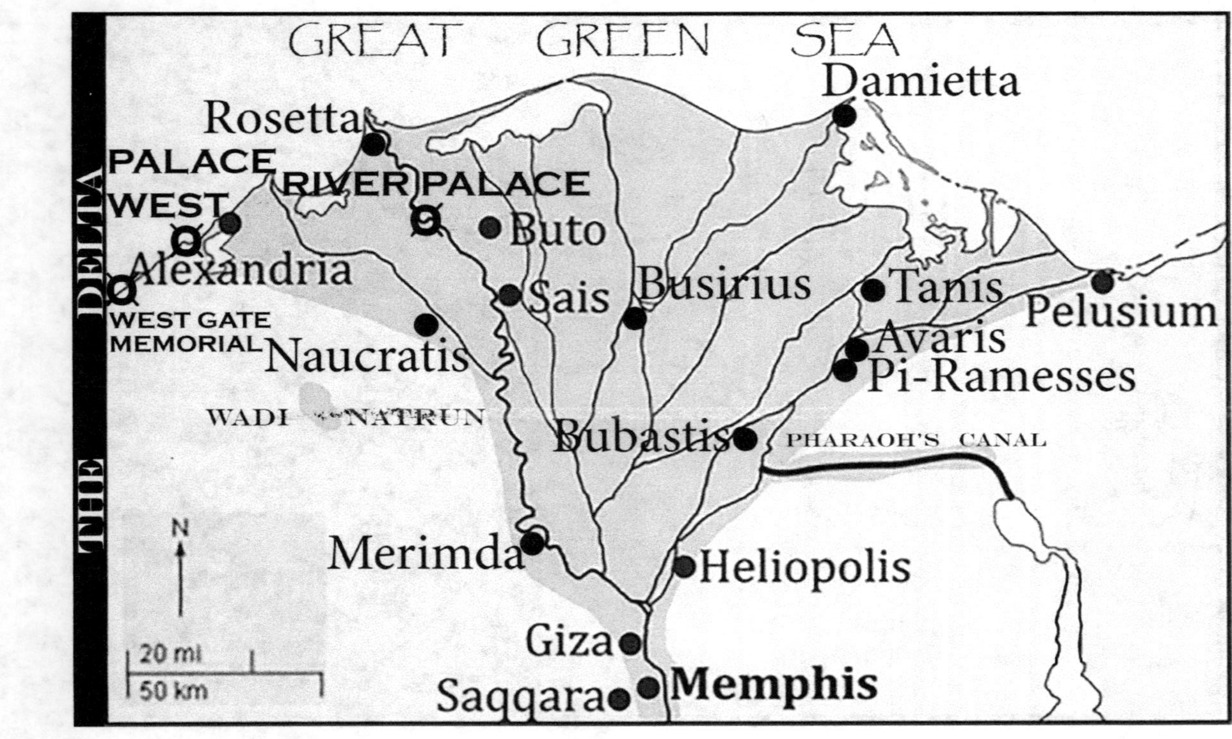

THE DELTA
GREAT GREEN SEA
Damietta
Rosetta
PALACE
WEST
RIVER PALACE
Buto
Alexandria
Sais
Busirius
Tanis
Pelusium
WEST GATE
MEMORIAL
Avaris
Naucratis
Pi-Ramesses
WADI NATRUN
Bubastis
PHARAOH'S CANAL
Merimda
Heliopolis
N
Giza
20 mi
50 km
Saqqara
Memphis

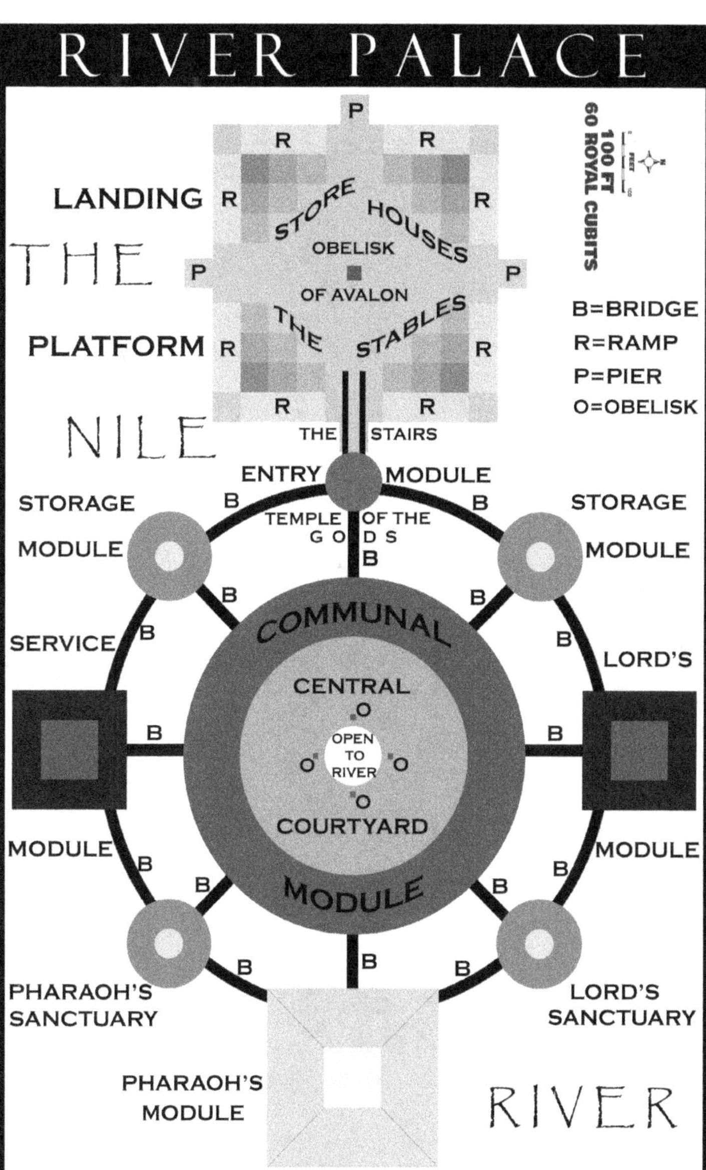
RIVER PALACE
LANDING
THE
PLATFORM
NILE
STORE HOUSES
OBELISK
OF AVALON
THE STABLES
P
R R
R R
P P
R R
R R
THE STAIRS
ENTRY MODULE
TEMPLE OF THE GODS
B=BRIDGE
R=RAMP
P=PIER
O=OBELISK
STORAGE MODULE
STORAGE MODULE
SERVICE
LORD'S
COMMUNAL
CENTRAL
O
OPEN TO RIVER
O O
O
COURTYARD
MODULE
MODULE
MODULE
PHARAOH'S SANCTUARY
LORD'S SANCTUARY
PHARAOH'S MODULE
RIVER
B B B B B B B B B B B B B B
100 FT
60 ROYAL CUBITS
N

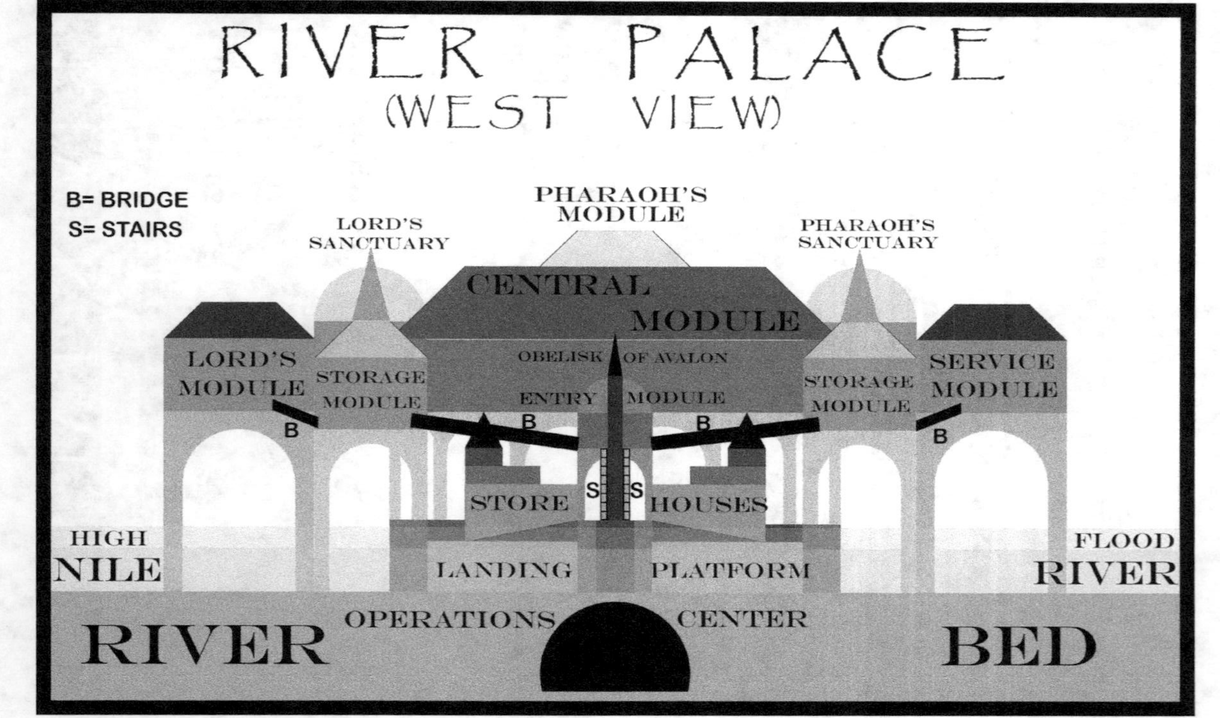

RIVER PALACE
(WEST VIEW)
B= BRIDGE
S= STAIRS
LORD'S SANCTUARY
PHARAOH'S MODULE
PHARAOH'S SANCTUARY
CENTRAL MODULE
LORD'S MODULE
STORAGE MODULE
OBELISK OF AVALON
ENTRY MODULE
STORAGE MODULE
SERVICE MODULE
B
B
B
B
STORE HOUSES
S S
HIGH NILE
LANDING
PLATFORM
FLOOD RIVER
RIVER
OPERATIONS CENTER
BED

THE PHARAOHS

SOBEKNEFERU
12TH DYNASTY, 8TH PHARAOH
4 YEARS(1777-1773BC)(43 YEARS OLD)
1ST FEMALE PHARAOH

SESOSTRIS II
12TH DYNASTY, 4TH PHARAOH
19 YEARS(1877-1858BC)(50 YEARS OLD)

NEBSENRE
14TH DYNASTY, 14TH PHARAOH
2 YEARS(1677-1675BC)(30 YEARS OLD)

THUTMOSE III
18TH DYNASTY, 6TH PHARAOH
54 YEARS(1479-1425BC)(56 YEARS OLD)
PHARAOH OF THE EXODUS

RAMESSES II (THE GREAT)
19TH DYNASTY, 3RD PHARAOH
66 YEARS(1279-1213BC)(91 YEARS OLD)
LONGEST REIGNING PHARAOH

THE ANCIENT EGYPTIAN CALENDER

The ancient Egyptians used a 365 day calendar. It was divided into 3 seasons of 4 months. Each month was 30 days in three 10-day weeks. And there was a 5-day festival to the gods at the end of the year.

<u>Season I: Akhet(The Flood)</u>
1: Thoth(September)
2: Phaophi(October)
3 : Athyr(November)
4: Choiak(December)
<u>Season II: Peret(Growth)</u>
5: Tybi(January)
6: Mechir(February)
7: Phamenoth(March)
8: Pharmuthi(April)
<u>Season III: Shemu(Low Water)(Harvest/Planting)</u>
9: Pachons(May)
10: Payni(June)
11: Epiphi(July)
12: Mesore(August)
Inercalary: 5-day festival to the gods

ANCIENT EGYPTIAN MEASUREMENTS

<u>Length</u>
Digit: Finger Width (1 Inch)
Palm: (4 Inch)
Handbreadth: Open Hand, Fingers Stretched, From Pinky to Thumb (9 Inch)
Cubit: Elbow to Finger Tips (20 Inch)
Rod: 100 Cubits (167 FT)
Schoenus: 20,000 Cubits (6.3 Miles)

<u>Area</u>
Sa: 12.5 SQ Cubits (37 SQ FT)
Heseb: 25 SQ Cubits (74 SQ FT)
Remen: 50 SQ Cubits (148 SQ FT)
Ta: 100 SQ Cubit (297 SQ FT)
Kha: 1000 SQ Cubits (2967 SQ FT)
Setat: 10,000 SQ Cubits (0.68 Acres)

<u>Volume</u>
Ro: 1/320 Heqat (0.5 OZ)
Dja: 1/16 Heqat (10 OZ)
Jar: 1/10 Heqat (1 Pint)
Barrel(Heqat): Base Unit (1.28 Gallons)
Double Heqat: 2.55 Gallons
Quadruple Heqat: 5.1 Gallons
Sack: 20 Heqat (25.5 Gallons)
Deny: 30 Heqat (38 Gallons)

<u>Weight</u>
Deben is Base Unit, 5 Deben = 1 LB
Deben: (3.2 OZ (91g))
Qedet: 1/10 Deben (0.32 OZ (9.1g))
Shematy: 1/12 Deben (0.27 OZ (7.6g))

ACKNOWLEDGEMENTS

MAREN JENSEN
THE LINCOLN WRITES TEAM
KJYRSTEN ASHDOWN
RALPH & CHARLOTTE JENSEN
CAROL JENSEN

ABOUT THE AUTHOR

STEPHEN JENSEN grew up fascinated by the world around him. He spent his childhood studying science and history. In his youth he became interested in the stories and worlds of Sci-Fi and Fantasy. As an adult he's spent the last couple of decades traveling the world to see the history and cultures firsthand.

ALL OF THIS fostered his imagination to create his own fantasies and worlds in his head. The last few years he's put pen to page to bring some of those stories to life.

The AVALON SERIES is the culmination of this life journey. He lives in Salt Lake City, Utah.

www.ingramcontent.com/pod-product-compliance
Lightning Source LLC
Chambersburg PA
CBHW060602300726
48975CB00005B/1419